INHERITANCE OF SECRETS

ROBIN PATCHEN

JDO PUBLISHING

To Misty.
I couldn't do this without you.
Your friendship means the world to me.

CHAPTER ONE

Her throat swelling, her eyes burning with tears she wouldn't release, Aspen Kincaid held her father's hand.

At the restaurant the night before, he'd been perfectly fine in his serious, tender way.

That morning, she'd been awakened by a call from a police officer. Dad had been riding his bicycle, something he did along the narrow roads near their apartment every single day.

A teenage driver, not paying attention, had swerved into him.

Aspen had made it to the hospital just moments after he did and had been waiting in the ER when a nurse called her back, telling her to *hurry, hurry.*

Aspen had run, skidding past doors and machines and doctors until she reached the room.

Now she stood at Dad's bedside and took his hand, trying not to react to the scrapes and cuts on his face and neck, to the way his breath wheezed. This was the man who'd raised her and loved her so well. His kind brown eyes were rimmed with red. His tan face was pale. She brushed his hair back, feeling soft strands and gritty sand left from the fall.

She lifted a prayer and tried to smile. "How you feeling?"

Before he could gather enough breath to respond, a white-coated doctor and four other people crowded in, one pushing a machine.

"You've got five minutes," the doctor said. "Then we need to do this."

"Do what?"

"Intubate. One of his lungs collapsed, and the other—"

"What are you waiting for? Do it." Panic rising in her chest, she stepped back. "Why did you wait?"

The doctor only nodded toward her father, who said, "I have to talk"—he took a wheezing breath—"to you first." He gasped, and she felt the pain of it, inhaling and exhaling with him as if she could infuse him with her strength.

"We can talk after, Dad," she said.

He shook his head.

The doctor squeezed her arm. "He insisted." A flicker of sadness filled his eyes, but he masked it quickly. "We'll be back in five minutes." He followed the others from the room, leaving the machine that would keep Dad alive until he recovered.

"Dad, that was foolish." Aspen tried to keep her tone kind, despite her frustration. "You should have let them do what they do. What could be so important—?"

"I need to tell you…" Another wheezing breath, then another.

The tears she'd barely held back slipped down her cheeks. "There's nothing that can't wait—"

"…about what happened…to your mother."

Her mother?

Aspen's heart pounded.

Because those words told her two things in an instant. First, that Dad didn't believe he'd have another opportunity to talk to her.

And second, that he'd been lying to her all her life.

Aspen had heard a lot of words to describe her mother over the years, certainly more than her father had ever intended for her to hear. Unkind words from extended family who visited on occasion.

Cracked.

Deranged.

Psychotic.

But when Daddy talked about Mom, it was always with a kind, gentle tone. *Your mother was unwell, Aspen.*

Funny how, in all those words, what she remembered wasn't the adjectives used to describe the woman who'd given birth to her, the woman she had no memory of.

It was the verb.

Was.

Your. Mother. Was.

Past tense.

Daddy had told her that, though no body had been found, she'd been presumed dead for years. He'd claimed not to know what happened to her.

Aspen leaned closer to him, squeezing his hand, refusing to be angry in what could be their last moments together. "What about her, Dad?"

"The house," he said. "You'll get the house."

In all their years in Kona, despite his restaurants' successes, they'd never lived in a house.

"The apartment? What about it?"

He shook his head. "I'm sorry." He took a shallow breath. "I didn't do right...by her. Or you. Don't..." He gasped for breath.

"I'm sure you did your best." Her voice squeaked. She leaned down and kissed his cheek. "You're a good, good man. I'm sure whatever you did, you felt you had to."

Tears dripped from his eyes and soaked into the pillow beneath his head.

He licked chapped lips and tightened his hold on her hand until her fingers ached. "Wanted to..." His words were interrupted by raspy breaths.

"What do you want me to do?"

He shook his head and pressed his hand to his chest. "Me." He shook his head, tapped his chest. "Find her. Do what I never...had the courage...to do."

"What do you mean? Is she alive?"

He opened his mouth to speak, but a cough choked out the words, the sound tearing through her soul like a dull knife against tough meat.

The nurses hurried back in. One propped him higher, speaking words Aspen couldn't make out over his coughing and the dull roar whooshing through her brain.

Another nurse gripped her shoulder. "You need to step out."

"No." Her father's eyes filled with terror. "You don't... I have to—"

"Ma'am." The doctor's voice drew Aspen's attention. "We've got to do this now. I'm sorry."

She tugged her hand, but Daddy held on and tried to speak. He didn't have the breath.

"You're going to be all right." Somehow, she didn't think it was fear of death that put that panic on his face.

"Now, please." Someone tugged on her arm.

"I love you, Daddy." She pulled her hand from his and moved into the hallway. She watched the scene through the open door, barely glimpsing her father beyond all the medical personnel trying so hard to save his life.

It was too late.

Three days later, after he'd been airlifted to the trauma center in Honolulu, her father slipped into eternity. In his last moments, unconscious, the tube no longer down his throat, a smile graced his lips. She imagined him in that thin space between this life and the next, getting his first glimpse of the Savior he'd loved and trusted as long as she could remember.

As awful as her grief was, Aspen knew her daddy was at rest.

She feared she never would be again.

CHAPTER TWO

ONE YEAR LATER.

Aspen's phone rang, and she hit the button on her steering wheel to answer it.

"I meant to call earlier." Jaslynn Matsomuto's voice was the only thing that felt familiar in this unfamiliar landscape, and Aspen's eyes stung at the sound of it. "I take it you got there all right?"

"I'm about an hour from Coventry now," Aspen said.

"Are you going to the house tonight?"

"It'll be dark by the time I get there, so I got a room in town. I may end up staying there, depending on what I find when I see the place. I'm meeting the contractor tomorrow morning."

"How was the flight?"

Aspen had kept her best friend informed about her plans in the months since she'd made the decision. It didn't matter that Jaslynn and her husband had moved to Kathmandu, where they served as missionaries. Now that Dad was gone, her best friend was the only person who cared enough about her to check in. She had other friends, of course, but over the years, most of them had married and had families. A few had moved away.

Aspen had socialized with people she worked with, but since she'd left her job, she hadn't kept up with them.

She wasn't sure how, but despite being surrounded by friendly faces all her life, she'd somehow become incredibly alone.

"The flight was long," she said. "I don't know how you manage that all the time."

"You get used to it. You know me—I love traveling."

"You know me. I love staying home."

Jaslynn laughed. "The car's all right?"

Aspen had bought a used four-wheel drive SUV online a couple of days before. "Just as advertised. I didn't even have to stay in Boston, thanks to the overnight flight."

"But are you awake enough for the drive? What is it, two hours?"

"Close to three, but I'm fine. I slept a little on the plane." Very little, but she'd be in town by dinnertime. Between her anxiety about what she was going to find and the multitude of caffeinated drinks, she wouldn't fall asleep behind the wheel.

"What's it like in New Hampshire?"

"Cold."

"That, I guessed already. It's January. What else?"

Aspen gazed around at the tall pines and naked trees, at the snow-topped mountains reaching to gray skies. "You know Mud Lane up in Waimea? All those tall trees? It's sort of like that, times a million and with snow."

"I bet it's pretty."

Aspen shrugged. "I'm just glad the roads are clear. It's getting dark already, even though it's only"—she glanced at the clock on the dash—"three fifteen. If there's a sunset somewhere, I can't see it, and the skies are cloudy and..." Her voice hitched. She stopped talking before she revealed too much of what was swirling in her thoughts.

"Oh, honey." Jaslynn always saw through her. "How are you? Really?"

She swallowed a sob. "I can't believe he's been gone a year. It feels like a blink. And it feels like a lifetime since I talked to him. I miss him so much."

"I wish I could be there with you."

"Fly over. How far could it be?"

"Don't think I didn't consider it. It's only about a twenty-four-hour flight."

Aspen groaned at the thought. "And probably a million dollars."

"Not quite that bad. If you stay there, Danny and I will come visit for sure."

"That would be…" The very thought of her best friend making a trip to see her choked her up again. But she wouldn't be staying. She didn't know a soul within a thousand miles of New Hampshire.

"Once you get a good night's sleep, everything will seem brighter. You have a plan, of course."

Aspen always had a plan. She had a notebook, where she'd lined out exactly what she'd be doing when she got to New Hampshire, beginning with meeting the contractor and getting the renovations going. Then she'd search the house and figure out why her dad had bought it. Then she'd…

Well, it got a little murky after that. Somehow, she'd find her mother and do right by her. Whatever that meant. If only Dad had given her a few more details.

It didn't matter. The to-dos would fill themselves in.

"This is going to be good for you." Jaslynn's voice took on the confident tone she used whenever she talked about the Savior she trusted so well. "God loves you, and He has good plans for you. I have a strong feeling that this trip is a big part of those plans."

"I hope you're right." Her life couldn't go forward until she unlocked the secret her father had tried to share.

"I'll be praying for you, my friend. Keep in touch."

Aspen ended the call and swiped at her tears. Thoughts of her father gave way to thoughts of his final words, and then to the reading of the will in Kona.

Her father *had* owned a house, one he'd purchased a couple of years before his death. He hadn't traveled to New Hampshire in that time, which meant he must've bought the place sight unseen.

In Coventry, New Hampshire, the town he had grown up in. The town where Aspen had spent the first year of her life.

The last place Aspen's mother had been seen alive.

Dad must have known something about her mother's disappearance, but he'd kept that information from Aspen.

As hard as this was going to be, she was going to figure out why.

CHAPTER THREE

GARRETT MCCARTHY GLANCED BACK at the big old house. This was his opportunity to establish himself as a general contractor. He'd taken small jobs here and there—a kitchen remodel, an addition over a garage—but he'd never been hired to manage the renovation of an entire house. When he completed this job well, new opportunities should open up.

He'd arrived at the two-story home early that morning, plowed the drive, and had almost finished shoveling the walkway when the growl of an engine interrupted the silence. As remote as this house was, he assumed his client was arriving. With the shovel propped beneath his hand, he faced the road. A small red SUV turned down the long driveway and parked beside his pickup. A woman in a puffy parka, the hood pulled up over her head, stepped out of the vehicle and approached him.

When she reached the shade of the house, she took off her sunglasses and pushed back her hood.

His heart did a weird little hitch.

He didn't know what he'd expected, but not this.

She was beautiful with dark blond hair and pale green eyes.

Despite her puffy blue jacket, it was clear that she was trim and fit and...

"Aspen Kincaid." She held out her hand, covered in what looked like expensive leather, and he yanked off his dirty work glove to shake it.

"Garrett McCarthy. Welcome to your house."

She looked up at it, and so did he, feeling protective of the old place that had been so poorly used in recent months. The cedar siding was faded, splintered in places. The concrete steps behind him, though clear of snow, were cracked, and the iron railings listed to one side. From the front, it didn't look like much, especially with the rise that blocked most of the structure from the road. But, despite all that, the fresh snow enshrouding it made it look...well, if not new, then at least bright and clean.

He couldn't read the look on her face. She seemed shocked.

"It's not as bad as it seems," he said. "We can freshen up the siding, or even paint it." Though the thought of painting it did not set well. "Either way, it'll look great when we're done. A few of the rooms have been updated already. Not the kitchen or... most of the baths." He'd have to explain about the creepy rooms in the basement, but not yet. "It's functional. You should be able to live here while we do the renovations." He wasn't sure why he felt the need to defend the property. It was what it was. Maybe it wasn't her dream home, but his understanding was that she'd inherited the place free and clear. Whatever she could sell it for would be money in her pocket.

And the renovation price would be money in Garrett's, as long as she didn't choose a different contractor. Her attorney— an old friend of his uncle's—had recommended she hire him, though there were plenty of other guys who were looking for work in the winter.

"You'll see the potential," he said, "once we go—"

"It's not that." Her voice had taken on a breathy quality. She backed up a few steps into the snowy yard. She wore waterproof boots that looked brand new, so she'd probably barely realized she was standing in six inches of snow as she gazed toward the second floor. "It's so big." She looked up the hill that rose in front and to the side of the property, then to the trees on the other side. "And all this land. So much land."

He wasn't sure what to say to that. She'd seen photos, hadn't she? She'd understood what she'd inherited. They'd talked about it on the phone.

She looked at him, her smile shy, maybe embarrassed. "It's just... I can't believe my dad owned this."

"You didn't know?"

She shook her head. "We never owned a house. The biggest place I've ever lived was a three-bed, two-bath apartment. It had a small office and a large living room, and it felt like the lap of luxury."

Garrett waited until she seemed to shake off the confusion and awe. "You ready to see the inside?"

"I am." She tucked her gloved hands under her arms. "It's cold out here." Then she squinted at him. "Aren't you freezing?"

He'd worn a jacket that morning, but after working in the sun for an hour, he'd tossed it in the cab of his truck. Besides, it was almost thirty degrees, not so much cold as slightly chilly. The temperature would be practically balmy that afternoon, over forty degrees. Almost unheard of at this time of the year this high in the mountains.

He probably looked like an idiot wearing a T-shirt and winter gloves. "Shoveling is hard work."

"Thanks for doing that."

"Wouldn't want you to drive through all that snow to get into your driveway and then walk through it to get to your door. Fortunately, I have a plow."

Her brow furrowed, and she glanced at the shovel in his hand.

He couldn't help it. He laughed. "This is a snow shovel."

She didn't seem offended by his amusement. "That makes sense. I've heard of plows, but I thought they were giant things used on highways and stuff."

"There are giant ones for highways, and there are little ones for driveways and parking lots." He pointed to the front of his truck and the plow attached there.

"Ah. Must be convenient."

"Incredibly." He didn't add that plowing was one of his sources of income in the winter months when most construction jobs were put on hold. After remodeling Aspen Kincaid's house, new opportunities would open up for him as long as he earned a good review.

He climbed the steps and pushed open the front door. "Well, let's check it out."

CHAPTER FOUR

SHE GAZED at the living room with its vaulted ceilings. A gorgeous gray stone fireplace took up one entire wall. On the other side, a staircase led to the second floor, where a walkway lined with doors was open to the living area below.

Aspen had known the house was almost three thousand square feet. She'd known it sat on five acres. She'd been told all that when Dad's lawyer had read the will. She'd even seen a few photos.

She was still stunned.

Maybe because, deep down, she'd hoped to walk in the door and find her mother. Dad had given Aspen the impression she was here. Or maybe Aspen had filtered his words through a heavy dose of wishful thinking.

Still, she couldn't help but wonder if her mother was still alive.

The thought thrummed in Aspen's chest, beating a rhythm of hope.

When Aspen turned thirteen, she'd demanded to know what had happened to the woman who'd given birth to her. Dad had seemed reluctant, but she'd argued she was old enough to understand. Finally, he'd conceded. She could still see the kindness in his face when he sat her down that day.

"Your mother suffered from a mental illness. When you were a baby, she got into some trouble, and then she disappeared. Though we've never found her, she is presumed dead."

Aspen had wanted to hope Dad was wrong, but he'd been so confident, adding, "If she were alive, sweetheart, she would have come home."

Daddy had always been honest with her, and she'd accepted his words as truth. But ever since he'd told her about the house, about how he hadn't done right by her mother, Aspen's hope that she'd find her alive had grown. And hope didn't disappoint, right? Wasn't that what the Scriptures said?

She had a feeling she was interpreting that wrong.

Truth was, when she was thinking clearly, she couldn't imagine a scenario in which she wasn't disappointed by what she discovered. Nevertheless, she would stay on this journey until she learned the truth, however painful.

Her focus shifted from her missing mother to the house. Had her mother ever been there? She must have. Why else would Dad have bought the place? Mom hadn't lived here, though, nor had her parents or Dad's. Aspen had done the research and discovered where both her mother and father had lived in high school and the first couple of years of college, and it wasn't here. After they married, they'd rented a house in town, but they hadn't had much money. Dad had told her that much. Surely they couldn't have afforded this.

What was their connection to the house?

It felt surreal being here. In a house she *owned*. An actual house on actual snow-covered land. She'd figured the place would be falling down. Wouldn't it have to be if her father'd had the money to purchase it—in cash?

It wasn't, though, not even close.

Garrett crossed the scuffed and scratched hardwood floors and stopped beside an open door beneath the staircase. There was another door beside him, probably a coat closet.

"Needs some work." Garrett said. "But the fireplace is in great shape. We need new paint on the walls, and I'd recommend painting that dark woodwork white or cream to brighten the place up. Obviously, the floors need to be refinished. You don't want to replace them. They're in great shape, and it's hard to find genuine hardwood these days. Everybody's putting in vinyl or laminate. These"—he tapped his booted foot on the floor—"are unique. Other than that, this room doesn't need much."

She pulled a notebook and pen from her purse and started jotting down everything he said. It felt so foreign, this contractor talking to her as if she had the right to be there, to make decisions about a house she'd never even seen before. Everything felt so... bizarre and out of control.

She just needed to make a list. Stay organized. She could do this as long as she didn't let any detail slip away.

After she wrote down what he'd said, she looked at him, really looked at him, for the first time. She'd been so overwhelmed outside, she'd barely noticed the man who'd greeted her. Now she wasn't sure how she'd managed that. He had short light brown hair that somehow was both messy and perfect, and he sported a neatly trimmed beard. His eyes were blue, his lips lifted in a slight smile. He wore jeans and a thin T-shirt as if it weren't freezing outside—and inside, come to think of it.

She rubbed her upper arms with hands still in rather useless leather gloves. She needed to get a pair like he'd been wearing.

"You're not cold, are you?" He sounded amused.

"It's no better than outside."

"Only about forty degrees warmer. I turned on the heat yesterday. It's sixty-nine in here. Plenty warm."

"Maybe if you're an Eskimo. It's a wonder we can't see our breath."

He chuckled, the sound deep and inviting. "Does it ever get cold in Hawaii?"

"Sure, in some places. It snows at the top of Mauna Kea. But I've only been up there once."

"Too far away?"

"Too cold. Nothing's too far on the Big Island."

Another low chuckle. As if Aspen hadn't been overwhelmed enough, now she had to deal with a gorgeous contractor with a voice that soothed and a smile that drew her in.

"You'll get used to it," he said. "Truth be told, I set the thermostat for seventy-two, figuring you'd prefer it warmer, but the furnace is having trouble keeping up. We'll need to talk about having it serviced. Meanwhile"—he nodded to the fireplace—"I took the liberty of bringing you some firewood. I recommend you buy a cord or at least a rick."

"Cord? Rick? I assume these aren't people?"

"Uh, no." His expressive eyebrows lowered. She doubted if he had any idea how obvious his thoughts were. Right now she'd guess he was thinking, *How dumb is this lady?*

Might as well confirm his guess. "I've never started a fire in a fireplace."

His eyes narrowed, almost as if he were suspicious. "Where do you usually start fires?"

"You know, on the beach or at campsites. Outdoors."

"You like to camp?"

"Not in New Hampshire. You'd have to be out of your mind."

"Stick around. It's not always winter."

She didn't think she'd be staying long enough to experience the other seasons. She just wanted to find her mother. But, as long as she had to be there to do that, she might as well renovate the house before she put it on the market. It would give her an excuse to get to know the town where she'd spent the first year of her life. The town where Dad had grown up and Mom had lived.

She'd sold Dad's restaurants to the manager of his first one. Gene had worked for Dad as long as Aspen could remember. Though she'd hated to part with the places that meant so much to her father, she wouldn't be going back to Hawaii anytime soon. Truth be told, even though she'd worked for Dad since she was old enough to wipe tables, she didn't love the restaurant business. The problem was, she didn't know what else she could do.

Now, with no job, Dad gone, Jaslynn in Nepal, and the rest of her friends marrying or moving away, Kona held no appeal. When she finished up here, she was going to college in Florida to study hospitality and tourism. She'd probably be one of the oldest full-time students, but what did that matter? Though the school she'd chosen had a great reputation, she'd chosen it more because it was near her dad's parents. She hadn't seen them much as she'd grown up, but they were the only family she had any contact with anymore.

There was no chance she'd be staying in the great white north.

"Should we continue?" Garrett pushed open the door he stood beside.

She stepped through. Same floors, bare walls, small windows that looked out at a snow-covered hill.

"No closet," Garrett said, "and there's no shower or bath on this floor, so it wouldn't work as a bedroom. Could be a second living area or an office, or even a formal dining room." He knocked on the wall behind him. "Kitchen's right here, so we could open it up."

No chance she was getting that deep into renovations.

She jotted down what he'd said. When she was finished, he stepped out, and she followed him through the living area to a door beneath the open walkway above.

"This is the current dining room," he said.

The space was barely large enough for a table for four. She crossed to the window on the back wall beside a narrow doorway.

Beyond a snow-covered yard, the naked branches of a thousand trees were covered with a thin layer of snow. Dark green pines rose higher than the rest, reaching toward the bright blue sky.

It was gorgeous.

"I guess you don't see a lot of scenes like that in Hawaii," Garrett said.

"When I drove up yesterday, the world seemed gray and dingy, but this is... Wow."

She was still staring at the scene when he cleared his throat.

"Like the living room, this room doesn't need much."

The yellowing paint needed to be covered, as did the brass light fixture on the ceiling. It was dark even on the sunny day, the one small window not nearly large enough to take advantage of the view.

"I don't know your budget," Garrett said, "but I have some recommendations for this room and the kitchen. If it were up to me, we'd tear this down"—he knocked on the wall separating them from the living room, then pointed to another wall with a door—"and that one, open this up and make it a great room."

"That's an idea." One she wouldn't be implementing.

Garrett pushed open the door and waited until she walked through.

The kitchen. It was as dark as the dining area, and everything was brown, from the cabinets to the wooden backsplash, from the butcher-block countertop to the vinyl floor. Even the walls, which might've once been white, were so dirty they were practically brown.

She groaned, and Garrett said, "Yeah. I know. It's outdated in every way."

There was an almond-colored refrigerator and a green built-in oven that must have come straight out of the seventies. The dishwasher matched it in color and age.

She couldn't help a laugh. "It's dreadful."

Garrett smiled wide. "But imagine how beautiful it can be. Once we tear down these walls, it'll be open and spacious. You'll be able to see the fireplace from back here. We can put a bar where I'm standing, or maybe a peninsula that connects by the window, or maybe not. We could leave it open to the dining area. It would make the room so much more spacious."

She could picture his vision. "It would be lovely, but—"

"The cabinets are in great shape. I don't know how you feel about a white kitchen, but we could paint them white or even light gray. Replace the backsplash, add granite or quartz countertops."

Catching his vision, she swiveled and pointed to a tiny window beside a door. "Any chance we could enlarge that?"

"Absolutely. Maybe even replace both the window and the door with glass French doors to let in more light."

"I love that idea." They could make this place beautiful.

But...but that wasn't why she was there.

She had to remember her purpose, and it wasn't to create her dream home in a place she had no desire to live. Whatever she sold this house for would be gravy to her.

And how would renovating this place help her find her mother?

She forced a smile. "Those are all great ideas, but I'm not that ambitious. I just want to do what we have to do to honestly be able to call it updated. So I'm on board with paint, new appliances, new countertops and backsplash. We can have the floors refinished, replace this." She scuffed her boot on the vinyl beneath her. "But beyond that—"

"This place is a world of potential. Don't you want to see what it can become?"

She shrugged. "I'm not going to live here, so I honestly don't care that much."

He sighed. It was clear that he wanted to say something more. Instead, he gestured back through the door. "Let's keep going."

After peeking into a downstairs half-bath off the kitchen, which looked like an explosion of seventies orange, they headed upstairs.

"I think you'll be pleasantly surprised by the second floor."

Garrett wasn't wrong. Dad's renter had painted the master bedroom and replaced the carpet. It was large enough for a king-sized bed and furniture. Like the ones downstairs, the windows were too small, especially considering the view. From this vantage point, she could see beyond the treetops to an expanse of white far below and a mountain rising in the distance.

"It's gorgeous."

Reluctantly, she moved on to the bath which, though outdated, was clean and functional.

Back in the walkway overlooking the living area, Garrett said, "With new paint and refinished floors, the bedrooms will be fine. I mean, you could replace that tiny window in the master with a bay, but..." He glanced at her, his expression one of dismay. "Anyway, up here, just the bathrooms need a lot of work." He stopped by a door. "This one is the worst."

Worse than what they'd found downstairs?

She pushed through and got her answer. The peach-colored tub was cracked. The vanity's drawers were crooked. There was no mirror, just bare drywall where one should have been and, above that, an opening for a light fixture. Wires poked out of it. A tiny window high on the wall over the tub enabled them to see the space without flashlights.

"Obviously, everything needs to be replaced in here."

He was standing behind her and, when she turned to respond, found he was very close.

He backed away. "Sorry. I was looking over your shoulder."

"I'm glad the other bathroom is in decent shape, or living here would be very hard."

"You got lucky there." He showed her two empty bedrooms in decent shape. "Keep the doors to the rooms you aren't using shut, and the other rooms will stay warmer."

After she peeked into a linen closet, he stopped at the final door on the second floor. "This is where I put the things that were left. The house was filled with furniture and... Well, you'll see."

He opened the door, and she gasped at the sight. It was a bedroom, but filled with furniture, boxes, fabric. Stuff, everywhere.

"I got rid of some of it, but—"

"Where did it all come from?"

"Most of it was left by the renter. Some of it, I think, was left by the previous owners. Everything belongs to you, so I didn't feel right going through it or making decisions about it."

"Why did the renter leave so much?"

Garrett's eye contact slipped. "That's sort of a long story. I'll tell you later."

An odd answer, but it didn't matter.

She didn't care about the renter's stuff. She *did* care about anything left by the previous owners. Maybe the clues she needed to find her mother were in that room somewhere.

She couldn't wait to start digging through it.

Aspen thought their tour was over, but when they got back to the first floor, Garrett stopped beside the second door beneath the stairs. He looked...nervous.

"Uh-oh," she said. "What's behind door number two?" She meant it as a joke, but when he took a deep breath as if gathering courage, her heart rate sped up. "What? Damage or something? Are you storing a crazy relative down there?"

"Crazy relatives are kept in the attic," he said, his lips twitching in an almost-smile. "Everybody knows that."

Bodies were buried in basements.

Surely, her mother wasn't—

She cut off the thought with a shake of her head. Obviously, her mother's body wasn't lying in the basement in plain sight. She needed to get a grip. "Just tell me what's in the basement. You're freaking me out."

"Sorry. Sorry. I'm just not sure how to... It turns out, your renter was sort of a... Well, he was a..."

When he didn't continue, she said, "How bad can it be?"

"A child pornographer, and a kidnapper, and, it turns out, a murderer."

She stepped back, horrified. "Oh. Oh. I had no idea. Surely my father didn't..."

"Your dad died a year ago, right?" At her nod, he said, "The guy rented after that. It's a really long story, and thank God it had a happy ending. But he did some renovations down here. I just wanted to warn you."

"There's nothing gruesome or—"

"No, no, nothing like that. It's just... Come on. It's easier just to show you."

He opened the door, pulled a chain to turn on the light, and stepped aside for her.

Thanks to the anxiety bubbling in her stomach, she wanted to ask him to go first, but she wasn't a child. She could do this.

She took the rickety wooden staircase to the bottom and found a normal cement basement with a washer and dryer and one small window just below the ceiling, through which she could see nothing but snow. Shelves holding a few tools covered the wall straight ahead. Otherwise, the room looked perfectly normal.

Except...

She looked up at the ceiling, tried to imagine the floor plan upstairs. "I'm probably just being paranoid, but it feels too small."

"I'm impressed you noticed."

"You alerted me to look for something, and there's nothing to see here."

If she were staying, she'd definitely install better lighting to dispel the spooky factor. She stepped further into the room and saw a giant metal... something under the stairs.

"The furnace," Garrett said.

"Ah. That explains why it's warm down here."

"Come on." He crossed to the bookshelves, reached behind one, did something she couldn't see, and then pulled the shelf inward.

Not just the shelf, though. It was a hidden door.

Garrett stepped in and flipped a switch.

As the light flickered on, she followed. There was one door on the far wall. Otherwise, the space was empty, but something creepy and terrifying slid down her spine. Despite the warmth, she suddenly felt cold and afraid. "What is it?"

"It's an empty room," he said, his voice soothing. "Just an empty room."

"Why does it feel so...?" She didn't know how to finish her sentence without seeming like a crazy person.

She wasn't crazy, was she?

Familiar doubts crept in. Was she more like her mother than she'd known? Was she losing her mind? "Do you feel it too?"

"I know what you mean," he said. "It's the hidden doorway and"—he gently shifted to the side so she could see it better—"the locks. I took the liberty of removing them. I hope you don't mind. They only opened from the other room, and it seemed like a hazard. If someone were to get trapped in here, there's no way out."

She saw the holes in the door and tried not to think about what he'd said.

"They were electronic locks, and they're still wired. We could turn this into a panic room, if you wanted. Or just remove the false wall entirely."

"So did he... the pornographer—?"

"This was his photography studio, but from what I understand, he was never able to use it." Garrett's gaze flicked to the empty space beside them, and she got the feeling there was something he wasn't telling her.

She was too creeped out to ask. She focused on the door across from them. It, too, sported holes where locks must've been. "Where does that lead?"

He pushed it open and turned on a light.

It was a small bedroom with two twin beds, a nightstand, and a bureau. She opened a door and found a closet, where sheets and blankets and towels were stored. Another door led to a bathroom. Everything in both rooms looked brand new.

"I can move the beds to the master, if you'd like. I got rid of the renter's mattress, the one he had there. I didn't figure you would want it. It was old, and also, you know... He was a—"

"Good choice. Yes. Thank you."

"But these are brand new," Garrett said, "never used."

"You know this how?"

"I was here when..." He blew out a long breath. "Let's go back upstairs."

She wasn't sorry to leave that horrible place.

Back in the living room, he said, "Are you hungry?"

"After that? Not particularly."

"Well, I'm starving. Let's go to town and grab some lunch. I'll tell you the story on the way, and then we can talk about what you want to do with this place."

Despite what she'd just said, it'd been hours since the lemon scone and coffee she'd bought at a charming bakery not far from her hotel. She needed to get out of the house, into the bright sunshine and fresh air—frigid as it was. She needed to shake off the fear that clung to her and think.

"I'll probably be hungry by the time we get there. I'll follow you."

At the front door, he dug into his pocket and held out two keys. "These are yours. I took the liberty of making a second. Maybe if I need to work and you're not home..." He let the unspoken question hang there.

She wasn't quite ready to let him keep a key to her place. "I'll leave it somewhere for you."

He dropped both keys in her palm. "Fair enough." He opened the door. "I'll drive."

"But you don't need to come back today."

"I gotta move that furniture and get a fire going for you. Until we get the furnace looked at, you'll want to be able to keep the place warm, right?"

"I can stay in the hotel again tonight."

"You can do that if you want, but I figured you'd prefer to save the money. Or..." He stepped away. "Or maybe you're nervous to be in the car with me, which I could understand. I mean, you barely know me."

She laughed, the sound echoing off the tall ceiling. She

stifled it quickly. "We went down to a creepy basement with hidden doors and a prison cell, and I survived. I think we're beyond all that."

He smiled. "Then I'll drive and come back with you and get that furniture moved today, whether you want to stay here or not. That way, you'll have the option. Tomorrow, I can focus on putting together a plan. Fair enough?"

WHEN ASPEN STEPPED into The Patriot, a homey restaurant in downtown Coventry, she could swear the room quieted, and every eye turned to her.

Of course she was being paranoid. Garrett didn't seem to notice anything amiss as he lifted his hand to wave at a man behind the lunch counter before he led her that direction.

She was still feeling spooked after the tour, and Garrett's explanation in the car had only heightened the feeling. He'd told her about her renter and the woman and girl he'd planned to imprison in the house.

Aspen's house. The thought was horrifying.

As Garrett had promised, the story'd had a happy ending. She'd focus on that and not the rest.

They reached the bar, and Garrett said, "Aspen Kincaid, meet James Sullivan."

The man reached across the bar. "Nice to meet you."

She yanked off her leather gloves and shook his hand.

"James owns this restaurant," Garrett said, "and another business in town."

"Just the one now," James said.

"That's right. You no longer give backpacking tours." Garrett faced Aspen. "Their new baby is crimping his style."

She could swear James's chest expanded two sizes.

"You're just jealous, man." He yanked out his phone, tapped the screen, and tilted it toward Aspen. "Would you want to leave them at home to take a bunch of strangers backpacking?"

She studied the photo of the woman and child, a bald little blue-eyed infant girl. "They're both gorgeous," Aspen said.

The man beamed. "I know. Hallie is perfect. Gets her looks from her mom."

"Anyway." Garrett's voice was tinged with irritation and humor. "If you're done bragging about your family—"

"Envy doesn't look good on you." He turned to Aspen. "I'm guessing you lost a bet if you're having lunch with this guy."

She laughed while Garrett growled beside her, which only made James's smile spread.

Garrett said, "She inherited that old house up on Rattlesnake Road."

James's eyebrows hiked. "Does she know about—?"

"Just told her. She's new in town."

"Oh. Well, it's a great house. Beautiful views."

"I'm excited about it," Aspen said, almost meaning it.

"Do you care where we sit?" Garrett asked James.

"Nope. You beat the lunch crowd. Grab a table, and I'll send a server over." To Aspen, he said, "Nice to meet you."

"You too." She followed Garrett to a table by the window, but he changed his mind and led her closer to the back.

"Don't want to be seen with me?"

He turned, grinning, and waited until she slid into the booth before sitting across from her. "It's chilly by the windows. I figured you'd be warmer back here."

"How thoughtful."

A woman set two menus on the table and took their drink orders.

After she walked away, Aspen said, "Your friend seems nice."

"He's a good guy. We met at church." He watched her as if gauging her reaction. "Maybe you'd like to come sometime?"

Aspen hadn't missed a Sunday at her church in Kona since Dad's death. Some people let tragedy separate them from God. Not Aspen. She'd leaned into Him in the last year, more desperate for her heavenly Father now that her earthly one was gone. "Which church?"

"Coventry Bible Fellowship. Modern worship, great pastor, in a hundred-year-old building."

"I would love that," she said. "I'll be there Sunday."

He smiled, seeming genuinely pleased. "Great. I'll save you a seat, introduce you to some friends."

Even though she wouldn't be staying, the thought of meeting people in town, of having friends here—even temporarily—appealed to her.

The server returned to take their orders. Aspen hadn't looked at the menu and scanned it quickly before ordering soup and salad.

"Seafood platter and onion rings." Garrett handed over their menus. When she was gone, he said, "Now that you've seen the house, what do you think?"

She was formulating an answer when an old man stopped beside their table and greeted Garrett with a handshake. His hair, what was left of it, was dark gray, his eyes brown and clear when he turned to her.

"Bart Bradley." He held out his age-spotted hand, and she shook it. It was cold, but his grip was strong.

She said, "Nice to meet you. I'm Aspen Kincaid."

Without letting up his grip, the man studied her like one might a science experiment involving mold or bat feces. "You're Jane's daughter."

Shock silenced her, but she managed a quick nod.

"You look just like her." Bart's eyes narrowed. "She ever turn up?"

It wasn't the words so much as the tone, not to mention the way he was glaring at her, that had Aspen's heartbeat racing.

Before she could respond, Garrett said, "Not sure her life or her mother's are any of your business, Mr. Bradley."

The old man finally let go of Aspen's hand. He turned to Garrett. "What do you know about it?"

"I know you're not being very friendly to someone new to town," he said. "Either be polite or move along."

This man had information about her mother, information she wanted, but she didn't have the courage to ask questions, not seeing the sheer hatred in his eyes.

"Pardon my rudeness." He looked anything but sorry. "Your mother caused a lot of heartache. I just wondered—"

"She disappeared when I was a baby," Aspen said.

He glared, and she held his eye contact, refusing to back down as if they were in some sort of battle of wills. Then he huffed and spun and stalked across the room.

This wasn't about Aspen, it was about Jane. What had her mother done to garner such hatred?

And why did Aspen suddenly think she'd prefer even the creepy basement to this public restaurant?

In that low, soothing voice, Garrett said, "Sorry about that. He's a crusty old man. I don't know what it is that makes some old people shed their manners, not that Mr. Bradley ever had many to begin with."

"He's lived in town a long time, I guess."

"All his life, I think." Garrett seemed to be studying her now, and why not? He must not have known her connection to this town. He must be curious, but unlike Bart Bradley, he was too polite to ask.

"I was born here, but I haven't lived here since I was a baby."

"It's none of my business."

"I guess Bart Bradley thinks it's his." The old man knew more about her mother than Aspen did.

"You know what that was about?" Garrett asked.

"Not really." She swallowed the grief and fear that rose in her throat. "But I need to find out."

CHAPTER FIVE

GARRETT HAD WITNESSED Bart Bradley grousing and grumbling his way through life, but he'd never seen the man be outright rude.

What in the world could Aspen's mother have done to elicit that much animosity? And so many years after the fact? He'd ask Uncle Dean. He and Aunt Deborah had been in town all their lives. Surely, if there was some scandal involving Aspen's family, they'd know about it.

Except... he'd been right when he'd told Aspen it wasn't his business. He had no right to go behind her back or to encourage people to gossip about her family just to satisfy his own curiosity.

He wouldn't. He'd do his job and make no effort to learn her secrets. If she wanted to tell him anything, he'd be a willing listener. And an ally that, based on the confrontation with Bradley, she might need.

He'd excused himself to use the restroom and was on his way back to the table when he caught sight of more than one person sneaking glances at Aspen. He could only see the back of her head, but she seemed to be looking down. Maybe oblivious.

Maybe avoiding their eyes.

He glared at an older guy who attended his church and kept glaring until the man turned his way. He seemed embarrassed to have been caught staring.

Aspen was beautiful, but he didn't see admiration in the guy's eyes. Curiosity, maybe. But also animosity.

Why?

Did she feel it in the room? Did she know?

He slid into the booth across from her, and she glanced up from her phone. Her skin was pale, her countenance almost... sad. "Everything okay?"

She seemed to force a smile. "Sure. Why wouldn't it be?"

Should he mention what he'd seen? Or let it go.

The server delivered their meals, asked if they needed anything else, and then walked away.

"Want me to say grace?" he asked.

Her eyes brightened considerably. "That'd be nice."

He squelched the desire to reach across the table and take her hand and bowed his head. He prayed not just for God to bless their food, but for Him to lead both of them as they planned the renovations. And then, thinking of the people who were likely watching them, he prayed for Aspen's peace and protection. Though he had no idea what was going on, he figured she'd appreciate the first and feared she'd need the second.

After his amen, she looked up with a shy smile. "Thank you."

"Of course." He grabbed a fried scallop, dipped it in tartar sauce, and popped it in his mouth.

After she tasted her meal, he said, "How is it?"

"Delicious. Yours?"

"Great. Do you want to try something?"

"Oh, that's okay."

He scooted his plate closer to her and pointed at the items. "Shrimp, scallops, cod, and onion rings. Help yourself."

"I'm guessing you could eat all that by yourself, especially after all the shoveling this morning."

"I don't mind sharing."

She chose a scallop. "That's really good."

"Anything else you want to try?"

"That's all right. I'll know what to order next time." And then her expression dimmed. "Maybe I'll get takeout."

So she *had* noticed the people staring.

He usually loved this little town, but at that moment, he felt like giving the whole room a piece of his mind.

Rather than asking the questions hovering between them, he said, "You've seen the house. What do you think?"

"It's in better shape than I thought it would be."

Better shape? What had she expected? "What's your goal for the property?"

She shrugged. "Fix it up and sell it."

"Do you have a deadline?"

She swallowed her spoonful of soup. "Not a specific date. And I assume that, if I decide to leave town, you could continue the renovations without me."

"Of course. The time difference will make it harder, but we can figure it out. How many hours behind is Hawaii?"

"I'm not going back to Hawaii, not right away."

"Oh. Where are you going?"

She shrugged. "I have grandparents in Florida, so I'm planning to go there."

"I'm sure they'd like that."

"I don't know them very well. We never visited them, and they only came to Hawaii a few times when I was growing up. But since they're the only family I keep in touch with..."

"You could stay here."

She laughed, the sound musical. The flash of amusement transformed her face. Wow, she was a looker. Not that he was interested. No sense getting involved with somebody who clearly had no desire to stick around.

"I don't think I could get used to the weather," she said. "I'm a beach girl. A surfer and swimmer. What would I do here?"

"I'm guessing that, if you can surf, you can ski. And the lakes are beautiful in the summer."

"And cold."

True. Why would she choose to live in the mountains in New Hampshire when she could go anywhere in the country? The world, really.

He tamped down a surge of disappointment. He barely knew this woman. Why did he care where she lived? "What would you do in Florida?"

"I've always wanted to get a college degree."

"In what?"

"Probably hospitality. I always thought I'd work for Dad, so I never really let myself think about what else I want to do."

"That's a good job, though."

"Working with my father was great. But dealing with tourists and servers and cooks and suppliers... It has its challenges."

"What *do* you love?"

She seemed to consider the question for a few moments. He ate a few bites of his lunch while she thought.

"I've been volunteering at my church since I was in high school," she said, "and I love that. Working with the kids and mentoring teenagers. I used to help run an internship for teens and young adults—sixteen to twenty-two. It was an amazing program that pulled them into the church, made them feel a part of it. I'd love to do something like that for a job, but I wouldn't even know how to get started."

"That sounds like a great dream," he said. "I used to think that God's will for me was probably something I'd hate. I've since learned that God gave me gifts and talents and dreams not to torture me or discourage me but to use in His kingdom. Not that remodeling people's houses is akin to mentoring young people in their faith, but—"

"But it's important. You can serve God in whatever you do by glorifying Him and doing your best."

He admired her faith, especially considering her situation. Most of the trials Garrett had faced had been the result of his own stupid choices. But hers—her mother missing almost all her life, losing her father. Even now, being judged by a bunch of strangers because of who her parents were. None of that was her fault, yet she seemed to face it all with faith and dignity.

Impressive.

He might have looked at her too long because she lowered her head and lifted her spoon.

He wanted to ask her questions, to learn more about her. But when she said nothing else, he shifted back to the reason for their lunch. "I assume you want to get as much money as you can out of the house."

"I guess."

"Do you need the cash from the sale right away?"

"I have enough to live on for a while, and I can support myself. I'll use the money for college, but I'm not starting until fall. I need to be there by May."

"Why, if school doesn't start until August?"

"That gives me three full months to get a job, find a place to live, and buy everything I'll need to live there. I'll also need to find a church and hopefully get involved. I assume it's harder to judge churches in the summer, with so many people gone, so I'll need time to evaluate the different options. Three months should do it."

She'd put a lot of thought into that answer. He glanced at the notebook she'd barely looked up from since she'd first stepped into the house. What other plans had she laid out in that thing?

"If the renovation takes longer, though," he said, "will it be a big deal? What would happen if you didn't make it to Florida until June?"

"The plan is May," she said, as if that settled it.

Why did it matter so much that she stick to her plan?

More importantly, what difference did it make to him? "What's your budget?"

"I took out a home equity loan on the house. The lawyer here, Mr. Christiansen, suggested I get the loan for a hundred and fifty thousand, so that's what I did. Not that I want to spend that much, but I know renovations can be expensive. Do you think we can do it for that price?"

"Depends on what you want to do, of course."

"I figure that, without more money, I won't be able to do more than just the cosmetic stuff we talked about today, especially if we have to replace the furnace." She flipped the notebook to a different page. "I did some research before I left Hawaii. Based on that and what we saw today, I figure we can get by with the basics." She read off a list—floors, walls, countertops. "And then there's the furnace. What will that cost? I'm guessing ten to twenty thousand, right?"

"Uh, ten at the most, and that's assuming it can't be repaired."

"Oh." Her eyes brightened. "Really?"

He allowed a little chuckle. "I have a feeling Hawaii is more expensive than New Hampshire."

"So this stuff on my list, what will that cost, and how long will it take? I have some things I need to do while I'm in Coventry, things related to my parents. Hopefully, you can get it finished up while I'm here."

"What kinds of things? I mean..." He shook his head quickly. "I've been told I ask too many personal questions."

She glanced past him toward the other diners. The place had filled for lunch, and he wondered if anybody else had noticed her. She pushed the notebook aside. "As you already know, my parents have history here. My dad would never talk about what happened before my mother disappeared or why he left New Hampshire. But before he died, he said some things that made me think I might be able to get answers here—at the house, actually. I want to learn what I can, and once I do, I imagine I'll be ready to leave." She lowered her voice and leaned toward him. "Considering the reception I'm getting, I don't feel exactly welcome."

He hated that he couldn't disagree. "You must look a lot like your mom."

"Yeah." The admission seemed troubling to her. "I just hope looks are the only thing we have in common."

He didn't ask the obvious question and was thankful when Aspen continued.

"Mom had some mental health problems. Significant problems."

"That doesn't explain why people would treat *you* with animosity."

"There's a lot I don't understand. I hope to, and when I learn what I came to learn, I want to leave, move on with my life without all the unanswered questions—and the glares from strangers."

While he'd dreamed of creating a beautiful mountain retreat, all she wanted was to get answers about her parents and get out of town.

But he didn't want her to miss out on what her house could be.

And, selfishly, he wanted to transform it, make it something he'd be proud to show off, something that would help him grow his business.

He sent up a quick prayer for wisdom while he ate a few bites of his lunch.

After a sip of water, he said, "How about I draw up two plans, one with the bare bones updates, the things on your list"— he nodded to the notebook as if paying it respect—"and one that incorporates the ideas I mentioned this morning. Tomorrow, we can get together, and you can decide what you want to do."

"I don't want you to waste your time. I'm really not open to doing anything too aggressive or time-consuming."

"I'm just getting started in this business. It'll be good practice for me." And maybe, if he did his job well, he'd be able to convince her to do it his way.

BACK AT THE HOUSE, Garrett crouched beside Aspen in front of the fireplace. The temperature had dropped outside, and the living room was chilly even to him. Hopefully, this would keep it warm until he could get the furnace serviced.

"It's not that different from starting a fire outside." He'd stopped on the way to buy a couple of newspapers and now ripped one section into long strips. "You need something that will light easily. I've always used newspaper. Some people buy kindling, but there are enough twigs and brush in the woods that I've never seen the need." He covered the rack with paper, then added some kindling he'd brought in when he'd delivered the wood. He added the smallest split logs from the pile.

She turned to him, a slight smile on her face. "This part I get," she said. "I have made my share of fires."

"Sorry. I don't mean to...what do they call it? 'Mansplain?'"

She chuckled. "I get the feeling you're going to be explaining a lot of things to me before our work together is finished, considering I know nothing about living in a place like this, or about renovations, for that matter. I'll try hard not to be offended if you'll try hard not to laugh at my ignorance."

"I'm not making that promise." He turned her way and winked. "Laughing is good for the soul."

"In that case, I'll do my best to amuse you."

"I don't think you'll have to try that hard." He nudged her shoulder with his, immediately regretting the familiar gesture. She was his client. He needed to keep that in mind.

But he felt a weird kinship with her, as if they'd known each other for years, not hours. She was beautiful, but it wasn't that. There was a connection there. And after Bradley's attack, Garrett had wanted to protect her. Still did, now that he thought about it.

Which maybe explained why he was crouched on the floor building her a fire. Definitely not a normal part of his general contracting duties.

He showed her how to open the flue, then heat up the chimney so the cold air wouldn't sink. Then he lit the paper.

The fire blazed to life.

They watched it for a few minutes. He grabbed the poker from the fireplace tools left by some past occupant and adjusted the logs to help them burn. When they'd caught and he was certain they weren't about to go out, he put the fireplace screen back where it belonged.

He stood and brushed off his hands. "The wood here"—he nodded to the pile he'd left on the hearth—"ought to last you all night. Do you want me to bring you a rick of split wood tomorrow?" Another one of his winter income sources.

"Is that a lot?"

"More than enough to last you a month or so."

"If you could, that'd be great."

He told her how much it would cost, and she laughed. "A small price to pay to not freeze to death."

How could she seem so happy? She should be jet-lagged, grieving, and frustrated at the rude customers at The Patriot. Not to mention creeped out by the history of her house. Instead, she was smiling and laughing as if all were well in the world.

Her smile faded. "So, anyway..."

He'd been staring. "Yeah... My friends should be here any minute." He'd called Reid, Thomas, and Fitz from the car while Aspen was in the hotel, gathering her things and checking out. Fitz, a police detective in Plymouth, was on duty, but Reid worked from home and Thomas was off. They both said they'd be happy to help. "I'm glad you decided to stay here. No sense staying in town when you have this big place all to yourself."

She shuddered. "I'd be more comfortable in town than in this big secluded place, but I'd rather not spend the money on the hotel if I can help it. Since there's furniture and something that sort of passes for heat..."

He chuckled. "You'll be warm enough. I'll take your suitcase upstairs."

"Thanks. I'll put away the groceries."

When they'd left the hotel, she'd said she'd go back to town later to buy what she needed, but he swung by the little store so she wouldn't have to. It was supposed to snow that evening, and he didn't want her driving in it just to pick up dinner.

Come to think of it... "I bet I can find you a kitchen table. Nothing fancy, but at least you could sit to eat."

"Don't go to any trouble."

"Are you planning to buy furniture?"

She gazed around the empty space. "I'll need to."

"I'll see what I can do."

By the time he'd carried her suitcases upstairs, his friends were at the door. He let them in and introduced them to Aspen.

Reid was tall and fit and some might say handsome, but he was happily married.

Thomas, on the other hand, was a bachelor. Successful and confident and charming, not to mention good looking, the guy volunteered for the fire department and search-and-rescue. He kept himself physically fit as if those were his day jobs. Everybody in town liked Thomas. He eyed Aspen a little too closely and with a little too much admiration.

The feeling that rose in Garrett was so unfamiliar, he almost didn't recognize what it was—possessiveness. Idiotic, considering he had no claim on her at all.

Still, as Aspen chatted with Thomas, Garrett barely resisted the urge to tell his friend that she was off limits.

When Garrett forced himself to quit staring at the two of them, he saw that Reid was watching him, a little too much amusement in his eyes.

He ignored his friend. "Let's get to work so we can get out of Aspen's hair."

"Right behind you," Thomas said. To Aspen, he added, "Be right back."

Before she responded, Garrett snapped, "Let's go," and stalked to the basement door.

Together, the three of them carried one of the twin beds and mattress—she insisted she didn't need both—to the master bedroom. They also took up the nightstand and the bureau. She'd put the bedding in the wash, and Garrett almost asked her if she'd like him to stay until it was finished. Knowing what had happened in the basement, he hated to think of her down there by herself.

But this was her house, and she was an adult. She didn't seem like the type of woman to run scared from a creepy basement.

In the junk room on the second floor—that was what he'd been calling the bedroom where he'd stored everything he'd found—he and his buddies located some pots and pans and plates, utensils and glasses and cups, and brought them to the kitchen.

"That ought to tide you over," Garrett said, setting the items on the counter.

She looked up from where she was scouring the kitchen sink. "Those are perfect. Thank you." Her gaze moved to Reid and Thomas. "I can't thank you enough for helping me out."

"A friend of Garrett's is a friend of ours," Thomas said.

Garrett managed to not glare at him.

Reid said, "I hope you'll join us at church Sunday. I'm sure my wife would like to meet you."

"I'll be there. I'm looking forward to it."

"You need anything else?" Garrett asked.

She scanned the kitchen. "Nope. Thanks to you, I'm good for now."

"If you think of anything, don't hesitate to call. Otherwise, I'll get back to you when I have those plans drawn up. Probably tomorrow morning."

She walked them to the door, they said their goodbyes, and Garrett reluctantly followed his friends out.

In the driveway, Garrett said, "Thanks for your help. Now she'll be able to stay here instead of the hotel."

"It's nice to get out of the house." Reid glanced at his watch. "But I need to get back to town. It's almost time to pick up Ella from dance."

As Reid opened the door of his SUV, Thomas glanced at the house. "So you two, uh...?"

"We just met." Garrett hoped his words sounded casual, even if he felt something completely different.

Thomas turned to him. "I get it, man. I'll keep my distance."

"What? I didn't say—"

"Your feelings are so obvious, they might as well be tattooed on your face."

"I have no *feelings* for her." None that made sense, anyway. "And besides, she's only staying temporarily."

Thomas glanced at Reid, who tapped his watch. "So was Jacqui. Oh, and Carly." Thomas referred to Reid's and Braden's wives. "And even Grace—"

"You'd better go," Garrett said. "Reid'll kill you if he's late picking up his daughter."

Thomas chuckled. "Just saying..." He rounded Reid's car and climbed in.

When Garrett was alone in the driveway, he glanced at Aspen's front door. She'd be fine by herself. She had food, she had heat. Still, as he walked to his pickup, thinking of the looks from the customers—and Bart Bradley's comments at lunch—he lifted a prayer for her safety and protection.

CHAPTER SIX

It was dark by the time Garrett turned down the long tree-lined driveway to his aunt and uncle's house, the place where Garrett lived from when he was fourteen through college. His uncle had texted while Garrett was at Aspen's, but he hadn't gotten the notification until he was a few miles down the mountain.

Aspen didn't have cell phone service at the house. He'd forgotten that. That was a problem that needed to be solved soon.

Garrett's uncle had asked him to stop by on his way home. Even though Garrett had bought a condo years back, when he thought of home, he thought of this little split-level in the woods.

As he parked his truck, Aunt Deborah pushed open the front door. She was still dressed for work in slacks, a purple blouse, and a black jacket. She'd put on weight over the years and was constantly talking about going on a diet. Not doing it, but talking about it. As far as he was concerned, she didn't need to. She was as healthy and pretty as ever. She dyed her hair a tad lighter every year, and now what used to be dark brown was fully blond. She looked younger than her fifty-something age.

He'd just reached the walk when she said, "Hurry up before you let all the cold air in."

He bounded up the concrete steps to the door, stepped inside, and kissed her cheek. "You could just leave the door shut until I get here."

She squeezed his cold fingers. "Too eager to see you, kid."

Thirty-five years old, and she still called him kid.

From the top of the half flight of stairs, Uncle Dean said, "What do you want to drink with dinner?"

"You don't need to feed me." But Garrett picked up the scents of ground beef and onions. "On the other hand...Salisbury steak?"

"With mashed potatoes and gravy." Uncle Dean was the cook in the family, always had been. Aunt Deborah rarely got out of work before six, while Dean was a carpenter and worked from home. The bottom floor had been his workshop as long as Garrett could remember.

"You know that's my favorite," Garrett said.

Uncle Dean's smile softened the hard lines of his face. Unlike his wife, he wasn't wearing his work clothes. He ended most days covered in sawdust and sweat, so his first task after he closed up shop was to shower. Now he wore a pair of gray jogging pants and a black sweatshirt. He'd lost much of his hair and what was left was starting to turn gray. He peered through his wire-rimmed bifocals. "If I remember correctly, anything with beef is your favorite."

"Good point." Garrett gestured for Aunt Deborah to precede him, then followed her up the six steps to the main floor. There used to be three small rooms at the top of the stairs —living, dining, and kitchen. But years before, Dean and Garrett had remodeled it, making it one great room. They'd even removed the low ceiling and covered the rafters above with drywall to create a vaulted ceiling. The skylight was Garrett's favorite part of the new space.

It'd been a huge undertaking, and he'd loved every minute of it. That was when he'd decided he wanted to be a general contractor, to restore dingy, ugly, and aged spaces and make them beautiful again. Sort of like what God had done in his heart when he'd trusted in Christ.

And like Dean and Deborah had done when they'd taken him in.

Dean patted him on the back. "Coke? Or we got some of those fruity, bubbly things you like. Some weird flavor."

"Tangerine," Deborah supplied. "I'll get it. You have a seat."

They were always like this, treating him like an honored guest, as if he'd done them a favor by coming by. As if he didn't owe them everything.

Over dinner, they chatted and caught up. Deborah usually had an anecdote about the patrons and fellow employees at the library where she worked. The stories were amusing at the least, often downright hilarious. As usual, the three of them laughed their way through the meal.

When Garrett had eaten more than he should have, he started clearing the dishes. "The least I can do."

Deborah settled back in her chair. "Not that I did anything but comment on the gravy, but I'll let you."

"You bought the groceries," Dean said to her. "And worked all day."

She shrugged. "Not as hard as Garrett, I'm sure. But he's young and strong."

"My day was easy," Garrett said. "Met my new client and got her settled at the house."

"How is the place?" Deborah asked.

"Could be worse. Furnace is barely keeping up, but the fireplace'll keep it warm. Do you two still have that old kitchen table in the garage? The little one with the sides that fold down?"

"I think so." Deborah turned to Dean.

"It's behind a bunch of stuff, but it's there."

"Would you mind letting her borrow it? Except in the bedroom, she has no furniture."

"Sure," Dean said. "She can keep it."

"And don't we still have those old chairs?" Deborah asked. "You were going to refinish them."

"Right. They're ugly as sin, but she can have 'em. We'll load them up before you leave."

"You two are so generous. I'm sure she'll appreciate it."

AFTER GARRETT FINISHED THE DISHES, he and his uncle loaded the furniture in his truck, and Deborah excused herself to her room. Dean seemed ready to tell Garrett why he'd asked him to stop by.

He cleared his throat and nodded to the living area. "I heard you had lunch with your client today. The Kincaid girl, right?"

"Girl?" Garrett slid onto the soft cushions that'd been his spot since he was a teen. "She's in her twenties."

Dean set his glass of water on the table beside his recliner, sat, and lifted the footrest. "She's thirty-one."

Surprised by the detail, Garrett let his expression ask the question.

"I knew her mom pretty well."

Garrett had decided he wasn't going to drill his uncle for details about Aspen, but it seemed he was going to get some anyway.

"It's a long story," Dean said, "and not a particularly pretty one. Her mother... She was a little"—he tapped the side of his head—"mentally ill. Probably more than a little. Not that we realized that. She seemed perfectly normal when we first met her. But the older she got..."

When he didn't finish the thought, Garrett asked, "How did you meet her?"

"Their family moved here Jane's senior year. She graduated and went to Plymouth State, where your aunt and I went. I got to know her through Deborah, and even more when Jane started dating a friend of mine."

"You were friends with Aspen's father?"

"Uh. No. It was someone else."

"So this was before Aspen was born."

Though Garrett's statement had seemed both obvious and innocuous, Dean didn't confirm it. "Jane was passionate and charismatic. She had some pretty strong beliefs."

"About?"

"The environment. Loved the forest, loved trees. I mean, she named her kid Aspen, for crying out loud. That's how much she loved trees."

"Nothing wrong with that," Garrett said. "In New Hampshire, trees are the canvas of our lives."

Dean's eyebrows lifted. "Thank you, Robert Frost."

"I'm just saying, you'd be pretty miserable if you lived in this state and didn't like trees. I mean, except when the leaves fall. Only an idiot likes that."

"Gosh, how you used to complain when I made you rake."

Garrett gestured to the picture window. "Do you know how many trees you have out there?"

"Why do you think we took you in? I haven't raked since."

Garrett chuckled. He used to hate the annual project, but as he got older and grew more and more to appreciate his aunt and uncle, he went out of his way to get the leaves taken care of for them—and manage a lot of the other more difficult chores around the house. It was the least he could do. "I was a pain in the rear."

"You were a kid," Dean said. "A normal kid."

Far from normal, considering the trouble he'd gotten into before he'd moved in with Dean and Deborah.

Dean continued. "Aspen's mother was obsessed with saving the trees. All the trees."

"Ah." Lumber was one of the biggest industries in New Hampshire. He imagined a lone woman carrying a sign and protesting the billion-dollar industry.

"If she'd become a lawyer or gone into politics, perhaps she could have gotten legislation that changed the way the industry worked, but she didn't want to change it. She wanted to do away with it. She had a following, a bunch of fellow college students who practically worshipped her. Obviously, they had no real impact."

"More Don Quixote versus windmills than David versus Goliath."

"Exactly. But Jane was determined, and like I said"—again, he tapped his head—"not entirely sane. She'd discovered one company that she was convinced was destroying the earth, and when they refused to bow to her demands—"

"She had demands?"

"That they stop murdering the trees."

"Very rational."

"In her defense, there are rules to protect the forest, and this company was not following them—and covering it up. But Jane was fierce. She did her homework. She became obsessed with proving their neglect."

"Did she?"

"Yup. And they received a slap on the wrist and a fine and kept on going, business as usual. Though by all accounts, they started obeying the rules, so she did have an impact, albeit a small one. But it wasn't what she wanted. She'd hoped they'd be put out of business, and when they weren't, it pushed her over the edge."

Dean lowered the footrest on his recliner, leaned forward, and propped his elbows on his knees. In that moment, he looked older than his years. His wrinkles more pronounced, his skin nearly gray.

Was his uncle healthy? Surely if he wasn't, he or Deborah would tell Garrett.

He couldn't imagine losing this man, who was more of a father than his own had ever been.

"Uncle, are you okay?"

"Yeah, yeah. I'm fine. Just..." He blew out a long breath and sat back. "Look, I don't want to get into everything that happened back then."

"You don't have to."

Dean obviously needed to rest, and the last thing Garrett wanted was to add stress to his uncle's life. He'd done enough of that as a kid.

Dean rested his head against the headrest. "Like I said, it was an ugly story, and it brings back a lot of painful memories."

Garrett didn't understand, but as he'd reminded himself earlier, Aspen's family history was none of his business. "We don't have to talk about it."

"Your client's mother disappeared under a cloud of suspicion."

"What was she suspected of?"

He shook his head at the question. "The point is, people got hurt."

"Aspen isn't her mother."

"True. But a lot of people want to know what happened to Jane Kincaid."

"You think she's dead, right?"

Dean's eyebrows lifted. "Why do you say that?"

"You've only referred to her in the past tense."

"Yeah. I think she's dead."

"Why?"

"I can't imagine a woman like her staying hidden for long."

"What do you mean, 'like her'?"

"Beautiful, charismatic, radical, and insane. Those characteristics don't exactly fly under the radar. If she were still alive, she'd have turned up by now."

Garrett lowered his head. Poor Aspen. No wonder her father had taken her away from New Hampshire.

Except he'd bought a house here. Why? What good could possibly come of Aspen learning this ugly story about her mother? Though how could her dad have known he'd die so young? Maybe he'd never thought Aspen would find out about the house.

But why buy it in the first place?

"Unless someone's been keeping her hidden."

Dean's words had Garrett's gaze snapping up. "What do you mean? Who—?"

"I need you to do something."

Aside from household chores, Dean never asked Garrett for favors. The thought of being able to repay, even in some small measure, what Dean and Deborah had done for him... "Anything. You know that."

"I need you to keep an eye on Jane's daughter. I need to know if she says anything about her mother or what happened back then. Let me know where she goes and who she talks to. Maybe ask some questions, see if you can get her to talk about what she's doing."

Garrett sat back, stunned. "You want me to *spy* on Aspen? On my client?"

"Not spy, son. Just… just listen and watch and let me know what you learn, that's all. If she has any idea where her mother is or what happened to her, there are people in this town who need to know."

"Why? What is it to any of them?"

"It's possible Jane Kincaid was responsible for a woman's death. If she's still alive—"

"Wait. You think she killed someone?"

"Not…exactly." Dean heaved a deep breath and blew it out. When he lifted his glass of water, his hand was shaking.

Worry almost had Garrett asking again about Dean's health, but he stopped himself. He would honor his uncle's privacy.

"It's okay," Garrett said. "We can talk—"

"If her husband's been protecting Jane all these years… Maybe he hid her somewhere. Maybe he had her committed."

Garrett was shaking his head before his uncle stopped talking. "Aspen has no idea where her mother is. She said as much to Bart Bradley—"

"If she knows anything about what happened back then, she wouldn't tell Bart." Dean set the glass back on the table, nearly tipping it in the process. "It's not like I'm asking you to betray a friend. You just met her. She's only a client. You're her contractor, not her attorney."

Garrett swallowed hard. Aspen was only a client, despite how attracted he was to her. "That doesn't change anything. I'm the only person she knows in town." And she trusted him. How could he do what Dean was asking?

But how could he not?

"If you're right and the girl knows nothing about her mother's whereabouts," Dean said, "then you'll have nothing to report to me. But if you're wrong…"

"You can't be serious. I mean, how old was Aspen when this happened?"

"She's an adult now."

"Even if she knows what happened back then—and how would she unless someone told her—we're talking about her *mother*."

"I know where her loyalties lie. And I get that she might not know anything. The thing is, son, there are people in town who need to know what she knows. It'll be much easier if you find out on the sly than if somebody else, somebody less patient and more invested than you, confronts her directly."

"Who?"

"People. People whose lives were destroyed because of Jane."

Destroyed?

What happened back then? Everything in him wanted to press his uncle for answers.

Deborah stepped into the room. "Sorry to interrupt." She smiled at Garrett, then glanced at Dean. When she did, her eyes popped wide, and she hurried to him. "Are you all right? Do you need anything?"

He shook his head but didn't speak.

"What is happening?" Garrett stood and looked from his aunt to his uncle. "What's going on?"

Dean waved off the question. "It's fine. I just get..." But he huffed as if he'd just run a race.

"That's it," Deborah said. "I'm making you an appointment tomorrow." To Garrett, she said, "He's been having these episodes where he can't seem to catch his breath."

Suddenly, Garrett felt the same way. "What is it?"

Dean sat back in his recliner and inhaled deeply, then blew the air out.

"We'll figure it out," Deborah said. "As soon as we know, we'll tell you."

Garrett gripped her forearm. "Is that a promise?"

She glanced at Dean, who said nothing, and turned back to him. "It's a promise."

Dean took Deborah's other hand. "We're almost done."

Her lips were pressed closed, but she kissed his cheek and hugged Garrett. "Come back soon." She lowered her voice to a whisper. "Two more minutes, okay?"

He nodded, and she grabbed a bottle of water from the fridge and returned to her bedroom.

Garrett sat on the edge of the sofa. "How long has this been going on?"

Dean's color was returning. He glanced at the hallway entrance. "She's overreacting. I'm sure it's nothing."

"You're going to the doctor. You're not going to get all stubborn and stupid on me, right?"

The older man smiled. "When have I ever—?"

"I can make a list."

Dean chuckled, but the sound died fast. "What I need is for you to do this for me. And don't tell her we had this conversation or anything about me."

How could Garrett do this to her?

"If she knows what her mother did or where she is," Dean said, "just let me know. If she doesn't know anything, then there'll be nothing to report."

Dean was right. If Aspen knew nothing—and he suspected that was the case—then what would it hurt to report that to Dean? Garrett could put his mind at ease. In fact, he could be doing Aspen a favor by convincing Dean, who could convince others in town, she knew nothing about her mother's whereabouts or complicated history. He could be protecting her.

And anyway, how could he refuse his uncle?

This could be good for Aspen. As long as she never found out what he was up to, everything would be fine.

CHAPTER SEVEN

THIRTY YEARS AGO.

The Planner was the first to enter the seedy bar off the interstate. Early, of course. He ordered a beer and found a table in the back corner, where he sipped and studied his notes while he waited.

After a few minutes, two more people stepped into the dark interior. They paused to let their eyes adjust to the light and then made their way to where he sat at a round table in the far back corner.

All three were students, which anybody who cared to look would guess. He himself had a notebook. The second wore a sweatshirt emblazoned with the college's logo—which earned a glare from him. Everything about the third—from the glasses to the leather messenger bag—screamed *intellectual*. But the bar was mostly empty, and the bartender was too busy flirting with her customers to pay any attention to them.

Once they were all seated at the table, the Planner started the meeting. He directed the conversation, never using the others' names. He called them the Crusader and the Builder. They were all integral to the operation, of course, but it was the

Planner who would make it happen. And keep them all out of prison.

He focused on the Builder. "You're sure you can do it?"

"No question."

"And the supplies?"

"It'll take time. I'll need to go on a few day trips, make sure I buy everything out of state."

He turned to the Crusader. "And the target?"

"You know who it has to be." As usual, her voice was too loud, earning a vehement *shush* from the Builder. The Crusader lowered her volume and leaned in. "They got a slap on the wrist, barely a hiccup in their operation. We have to make them pay."

The Planner didn't know if that was true, but the idea of what they were going to do filled him with a heady sense of power. He'd gotten away with everything he'd ever done. Thanks to his parents' positions and money, nobody'd ever looked twice at him for the petty crimes he'd committed. He'd been labeled a good kid early on, and everybody believed it.

He was good, still. This plan wouldn't benefit those doing it, but it would benefit the world. It was worth the risk.

Not that he planned for any of them to go to prison. He'd mitigate all the risks. The lumber company would pay, and the three of them would walk away without so much as a blemish on their records.

It would just take very careful planning.

CHAPTER EIGHT

As soon as the sheets were clean that evening, Aspen lay down for a short nap and ended up sleeping for almost three hours.

She woke up starving. She stoked the fire, fixed herself dinner, which she ate on the floor in front of the hearth, and then settled onto her bed to read a few chapters of her novel. But the chill in the air and the strange creaks and groans of the old house kept pulling her focus from the book.

She'd never lived so far from civilization. Except for the last year, she'd never lived alone. At various times over the years, she'd thought about getting her own place, but she and her father had gotten along so well. And with the rent prices in Hawaii, it was either live with him or live with roommates.

Even after Dad's death, surrounded by neighbors she'd known for years, she'd hardly felt abandoned. Back in Kona, all she had to do was step out her front door, and she'd almost always see a friendly face.

The novel failed to hold her attention, so she thought she'd watch an old sitcom on the tiny screen of her phone, hoping the familiar voices might lull her to sleep, but she had no service.

When she couldn't sleep in Hawaii, she went for a walk. The evening air, scented by the sea and the flowers that bloomed everywhere, never ceased to relax her.

But she wasn't in Hawaii anymore.

She was creeped out. Being in this strange wintery world, so far from everything, had her nerves on edge. She needed to find a way to feel comfortable in this place if she was ever going to sleep.

She wished she could settle in front of the fire downstairs where it was warm. But the hardwood floor wasn't exactly cozy.

Tomorrow, she was going to get furniture. And deal with the internet and phone issues.

And she'd buy a TV, if for nothing other than noise. Could she get cable up here? Wi-Fi?

Why hadn't she managed any of that rather than taking a three-hour nap?

Stupid jet lag had her system all out of whack.

She added those tasks to her to-do list, then closed her eyes.

But lying on the bed was doing her no good. After dressing quickly, she moved into the walkway, thankful for the overhead lights, which she flipped on along the way. Downstairs, she stoked the fire and added another log. She figured she'd want it roaring when she got back. Then she put on her new boots and coat, slipped on the nearly useless leather gloves, and trudged to the back of the house.

She could do this. She could face this scary, secluded world. She could survive here.

When she opened the door, a blast of cold air almost had her changing her mind. But...

Wow.

She stepped onto the deck and closed the door behind herself. The clouds had moved out and the moon was full, its light bouncing off the fresh snow that had fallen that evening, which covered the ground and the trees, making the world much brighter than it ought to be at nearly midnight.

Millions of stars twinkled overhead. She picked out a few constellations, and the familiarity was comforting.

The world seemed so different, but the moon had come with her. The stars had come with her.

The Lord had come with her.

She wasn't alone.

The scent of wood smoke filled the air, comforting.

And then the silence hit her.

Had she ever experienced such silence?

There was always noise in Kona. The whir of traffic, the conversations of locals and tourists, the chirps and calls of birds.

At night, when everything else was quiet, she could pick up the sound of the surf against the rocks not far from her apartment.

But here, she heard nothing.

She couldn't decide if it was peaceful or terrifying. Maybe both.

After carefully maneuvering down the snow-covered steps, she wandered across the backyard—*her* backyard—and stepped into the woods. She couldn't go far, though. The trees and brush were thick, and she feared falling and breaking an ankle. She'd freeze to death before anybody found her. She turned back to the yard and walked the perimeter, spying a narrow path that led into the woods near the detached garage.

She took a few steps down it, then thought better of venturing into the unknown in the middle of the night.

On the other hand, this wasn't going to be much of a walk if she was afraid to leave her yard.

Why did she feel so nervous? After Garrett and his friends left, she hadn't heard a single car drive by. She was safe and, though she might have felt differently, she reminded herself that she wasn't alone. God was at her side.

That thought gave her courage to venture around the house. Halfway there, she heard something and paused to listen.

It was the sound of a car engine, coming closer.

She was nearly to the corner of the house when she saw headlight beams shine on the narrow road coming from town. She'd thought the car had been coming quickly, but it seemed to slow.

Before the vehicle came into view, its headlights quit bouncing. Then they went off entirely.

She could hear the vehicle idling on the far side of the thick forest, but all she could see was moonlight glinting off metal. Sedan, SUV, pickup—she couldn't tell.

Somebody was watching the house, and the last thing she wanted was to alert that person that she was all alone outside, completely vulnerable.

She dared not move.

She had no way to call for help.

Two minutes passed. Three.

Though her hands were shoved deep in the pockets of her jacket, her fingers ached with cold. Her teeth chattered. Her heart raced.

When the car made no move, she inched away slowly. So slowly. Finally, she reached the back corner of her house and bolted across the yard, up the back steps, and inside. She locked the door behind her.

After she shed her coat and boots, she crossed into the living room and peeked through the blinds and out the front window.

The watcher was gone.

~

Aspen was still in bed the next morning, barely awake, when the doorbell rang. She checked the time on her phone—nearly ten o'clock.

She never slept that late in Kona. Of course, in Kona, she didn't have creepy people stalking her in the middle of the night.

She threw on a pair of jeans, an old sweatshirt, and some socks, then hurried down the stairs, where she opened the blinds. She couldn't see the front step, but Garrett's truck was parked in the driveway.

When she opened the door, she barely caught his smile before it morphed into a frown.

"Did I *wake* you?" He shook his head. "I mean, not that you should have been awake already. You can sleep as long as you want." He pressed his lips closed and quelled the babbling.

She caught sight of two steaming cups in his hands and prayed they held coffee. She'd brought her grinder and French press from home, not to mention a bag of beans, but she didn't want to wait for the kettle to boil.

Come to think of it, she didn't have a kettle.

Considering the look Garrett was giving her, she should've spent a little more time getting ready before rushing downstairs. She stepped back and held the door open. "Just give me five minutes."

Leaving him in the living room, she washed her face and brushed her teeth and hair, then found her fluffy slippers.

Downstairs, Garrett was trying to maneuver an old wooden ladder-back chair into her house.

"Here, let me help." She held open the storm door, and he carried the chair through to the dining area. She followed and discovered he'd brought another chair and a small table. "Where'd these come from?"

"My aunt and uncle." He arranged the three pieces in front

of the tiny window. "My uncle's always collecting furniture to refinish, but he never gets to it. They said you could have these. They're not much, but at least you can sit to eat."

"How kind of them. Tell them I said thank-you."

He nodded and handed her the cup. "I thought maybe it'd be too late for coffee, but I guess..."

She took a long, grateful sip. It wasn't Kona coffee, but it was good. "This is exactly what I needed. Thank you."

"Did you sleep all right?"

"Not exactly. Any chance you drove up here last night to check on me?"

He squinted, and his head tilted to the side. "Uh... no. Should I have?"

She sat in one of the chairs. It felt solid, but the once-white paint was peeling off the seat. The table was a dull brown, but it seemed sturdy and solid. She took another sip, wishing she didn't have to burden her contractor with this. But who else did she have?

He sat in the other chair. "Did something happen?"

"I couldn't sleep." She told him about her walk and the vehicle she'd seen.

By the time she was finished with the story, his lips were pressed together. "Somebody was watching the house?"

"I thought so at the time, but maybe...I don't know. Maybe people come up here to look at the stars or something? Or maybe... Are there any other houses on this road?"

"Summer homes for tourists farther up." There was something in the set of his mouth, the lowered eyebrows, that made her think he was angry.

"I'm probably just being paranoid."

"There are miles of road between here and town. Whoever was driving that car, if they wanted to look at stars or peer into the woods or...make out, if it was a couple of kids, they could've done it anywhere along the road. They stopped here for a reason."

"So you think—?"

"Exactly what you think." He stood and ran a hand over his head, then swiveled to face her. "First, Bart Bradley and all those glares at the restaurant."

He'd seen that? She hadn't thought—

"And then..." He swallowed hard, shaking his head. "Now your house is being watched. What's going on here, Aspen?"

"I don't know." Had her voice shaken? She'd lain awake for hours, terrified, not falling asleep until the world outside her window started to brighten. At some point, she'd convinced herself that she'd overreacted.

It seemed Garrett disagreed. "You have no idea?"

"I've never been here before. This is your town. I don't know these people."

"They seem to think they know you, though." He sat and studied her. He wore a dark gray chamois button-down that looked warm and soft, so unlike the glare he was giving her.

"Are you angry about something?"

"You came to fix up this house and sell it," he said. "And what else did you say? Do something that has to do with your parents? What exactly?"

"How is this your business?"

"It's not." He dropped his head back and stared at the ceiling, taking a deep breath. "I'm not angry with you." He pushed back the chair and stepped through the door into the kitchen. He returned a moment later and set a backpack on the table. "I drew up the plans we talked about. Do you want to look at them now?"

"Uh..." The change of subject had her reeling. It was too early in the morning for this.

Well, not early, exactly.

"I guess," she said.

After another long moment of him watching her, he said, "Why don't you get something to eat, try to wake up a little."

He was right. Food would help. "You want anything?"

"I'm good."

In the kitchen, she put an English muffin in the broiler. While it cooked, she scrambled herself an egg, then buttered the muffin, put the egg on top, and added a slice of cheese.

She returned to the dining room with her breakfast sandwich to find Garrett had opened a laptop.

While she ate her breakfast, he focused on the screen. Neither of them spoke.

She missed the easy camaraderie they'd shared the previous day. For reasons she didn't understand, someone had driven halfway up the mountain in the middle of the night to watch her house.

And Garrett seemed to blame her for that.

It didn't make sense. None of it made sense.

She barely tasted the breakfast, but the calories kicked her brain into gear. Who cared what Garrett thought of her? He needed to get her house prepared to sell, and he didn't have to like her to do that. She'd worked in restaurant management long enough to learn that people didn't have to like her to work for her. In fact, sometimes it was easier when they didn't.

She finished the sandwich, carried the plate into the kitchen, and returned to the table. "Look—"

"—I'm sorry."

They'd spoken at the same time. She sat and nodded for him to continue.

He blew out a long breath. "I'm not being very nice."

She knocked on the table. "You brought me furniture."

The tiny smile transformed his face from good looking to gorgeous. She was sorry when it faded. "I'm just worried, that's all. Trying to figure out what's going on. But seeing as how I know absolutely nothing... It's frustrating."

"I'm as much in the dark as you are."

"Are you?" When she didn't respond, he said, "I think you'd be safer back at the hotel."

Maybe.

But Dad had bought this house for a reason. She assumed that reason had something to do with the reception she'd gotten in town the day before—and her middle-of-the-night visitor. She also assumed this house was the key to finding her mother. If she left it empty, would its secrets be safe?

Or was somebody else also looking to uncover those secrets? Maybe Aspen's presence had opened the proverbial can of worms, and now everybody in town knew that the worms were hidden somewhere on this property.

If that even made sense.

"I'm sorry I encouraged you to stay here last night," Garrett said. "You need to go back to the hotel. I'll wait while you gather your things and—"

"No." Terrified as she was to stay... "I'm not leaving."

His smile seemed forced. "It's not going to be a problem. Even if we were to do all the renovations I want, it won't cost you a hundred and fifty grand, and you'll get plenty of money out of this house. You can afford to stay in the hotel, or... Why don't you find a rental property? I have a friend who owns condos in the community where I live. I could ask him—"

"It's not about the money. I need to stay here."

"That's insane. Why would you—?"

"I am not insane." Her heart raced at the word, and she pushed to her feet. "Look, I don't know who you think you are to come in here and tell me what I should do. Just because you don't understand my reasons doesn't mean I don't have good ones."

His hands went up, palms out. "I didn't mean—"

"My life is none of your business."

Both his arms dropped, his shoulders along with them. "You're right." Silence settled between them, but she wasn't about to break it. The nerve.

After a staring contest—his pale blue eyes were enchanting, so it really was no chore—he blinked. "Are those reasons really worth the risk, if somebody's stalking you?"

It was a fair question, and she considered it as she took her seat again. Was it worth the risk?

To do what her father had asked?

To find her mother?

To find the answers to questions she'd been asking all her life?

She closed her eyes and prayed. Most of her days began with prayer and Bible reading. Not that she hadn't done a lot of both the night before when she'd feared the stranger outside, but having missed her time with God that morning, she felt off her game. *I need You, Lord. Give me wisdom.*

Am I being foolish?

Am I like my mother? Am I crazy?

She'd spent years praying she wasn't like her mother, watching for signs of her own insanity. Was this one?

But God's peace settled into her heart. God had been with her throughout this journey, and He was with her now.

She opened her eyes to find Garrett watching her closely.

"It is worth the risk. I know that doesn't make sense to you, and I can't explain it."

She expected him to ask her what she was up to, what she hoped to gain by staying there. Maybe she should tell him, but she wasn't ready to share her plans. Fortunately, he only nodded.

Aspen liked that he didn't pry. "I'm not crazy," she reiterated. "I don't want to stay here without some protection. Will you help me?"

For the first time since he'd stood on her front porch with two cups of coffee, he gave her a genuine smile. "What'd you have in mind?"

"An alarm system, for one. But without a landline—"

"As it happens," Garrett said, "I remembered last night that you don't have cell service. You can cancel the appointment, but—"

"Wait...appointment?"

"They're going to install phones. I made some assumptions about what you'd want." He shifted in his chair, seeming nervous. "I should've asked you, but I didn't want to come back that late, and if we hadn't called until today, they probably wouldn't get out here until tomorrow—or even Monday. I know a guy at the phone company, old friend from school. I did a little cajoling, and he's gonna come out around four. Along with the landline, I got you their best internet service—the price difference between that and the next one down is negligible. And TV service. You won't get any reception up here without it. You can change or eliminate anything, but my friend told me to order everything so the tech would have the equipment in his truck, whatever you decide." Garrett took a piece of paper from his breast pocket and slid it across the table. "You can call from town if you want to change the appointment."

A phone, internet, and cable? Garrett had taken care of that for her? "That was..." Her eyes stung. She blamed fatigue, and maybe relief. "Thank you so much."

He shrugged it off and glanced at his watch. "If we head to town soon, I can get an alarm system installed before they arrive, and then we can hook it up so the police will be alerted if anyone tries to break in."

"I have my own errands to run—and my own car. I don't need to go with you."

"I'm not leaving you alone here, if that's what you're thinking. Do you own a gun?"

"Uh...no." She wasn't sure what to respond to first—his thinking he could tell her what to do, or that crazy question about the gun. She decided to ignore the first and deal with the second. "Do you?"

"Several handguns, a few hunting rifles, and a shotgun. I'll bring you one. Handgun, that is." His lips twitched as if the idea of her having a shotgun were humorous.

As if the rest weren't.

She was still processing. "You own *several* guns?"

"I'll teach you how to use it. You need to be able to defend yourself."

"It's not that I'm against guns, but—"

"Let's hope not, all things considered. The locks on this place have all been updated, and the windows are nailed shut. But there's no—"

"Nailed shut? Why?"

"The guy who lived here before..."

"Oh. Right." He'd made the house into a prison. This was getting weirder all the time.

Garrett kept right on talking as if she were keeping up. "So if somebody were to come in through a window, they'd have to break the glass. You'd hear that. I'll grab a couple of motion-sensor floodlights for outside in case somebody decides to approach the house at night. Maybe a video camera. We'll have to price them. Anything else?"

"Seems you've thought of everything." She was glad of it, too, since she wouldn't have known where to begin.

"You could always get a satellite phone in case you're in the woods and need to make a call."

She couldn't help the laugh. "That feels a little extreme."

He studied her a long moment but said nothing.

Before he could convince her that she needed a phone that would enable her to order pizza from space, she glanced at his laptop. "Did you have something you wanted to show me?"

"Right. Yeah. Let's make a plan."

ASPEN SCROLLED through the images on Garrett's laptop. Awed.

He could make this old place look like *that*?

In the first picture, the old brown siding seemed fresh and new. He'd leveled out the front yard and added a walkway to the door. A few bushes and flowers made it look pretty and inviting.

But it was his vision for the inside that had her jaw dropping.

In the rendering, he'd removed the walls to open up almost the entire downstairs and added a semi-circular island—barstools and all—between the kitchen and living room. He'd rearranged the large appliances and sink so the layout made sense for both cooking and entertaining. In the dining area, he'd removed the small, solid door leading to the backyard and the window beside it and added glass French doors in their place. The adjacent wall held a bay window. The two walls now offered an expansive view of the forest, practically bringing the outside in.

He'd even added furniture to show how it would look when it was finished.

Garrett scooted his chair closer. "I didn't open up the other space down here. I think the great room is large enough already, and that'd be a nice office. Do you mind?" He inched his fingers toward the trackpad, and she moved to give him access.

As lovely as the house on the screen was, his scent—some delicious combination of cedar and man—was just as attractive.

Maybe more so.

She leaned away and tried to focus on the images as he scrolled. "We'd have to rebuild the stairs to the basement, move the opening closer to the front door. That sounds like a bigger undertaking than it is. But then we could..." Finally, he stopped scrolling, and she saw what he meant.

"If we added French doors here, between the office and the hallway—"

"I love that." The office doors would be just around a short hall to the great room, so it would be both private and accessible.

"Or we could build a closet in there and close it off, but since there's no full bath on this floor—"

"Yeah, it doesn't make sense as a bedroom. And there are four upstairs."

"Exactly."

She glanced his way in time to catch a little smile.

He scrolled to the next picture, this one of the interior of the office. "Obviously, we have to replace all the old windows."

"Why is that obvious?"

"Those old wooden windows might as well be sieves. What you'll spend on the windows, you'll save in your heating bill."

"*I* won't."

He nodded. "Your buyer will thank you. If you don't replace them, any buyer with half a brain—and every real estate agent— will know it needs to be done. It just makes sense for you to do it. So, since we have to do that anyway, why not put another bay here? It'd bring in so much natural light, which this place desperately needs."

She could think of a few good reasons *why not*, the first being the expense. But it could look amazing.

He'd already shown her what the place would look like with the changes she'd asked for, and she'd been happy with that plan. New countertops, new appliances, refinished flooring, fresh paint. It would be fine.

But this was...

"It's wonderful." She turned his way as she said it. He'd inched closer and was so near that she caught the scent of mint on his breath.

He cleared his throat and leaned back. "Thanks. I've been putting these plans together for weeks, ever since Christiansen..." His Adam's apple bobbed, and he scooted his chair away. "Obviously, the budget's much bigger on the second option. But I talked to a friend in real estate last week, and she seems to think you'll get back twice what you put into it, if you're willing to spend the money and spend it well. She was throwing out numbers in the seven-hundred range. I know it's not Hawaii prices, but—"

"But aside from what I spend to do the work, it'll be all profit."

"Exactly."

"Did you show her these plans?"

He nodded. "Some of the ideas were hers—to level out the yard, for instance. She said it would improve curb appeal, which will add a lot to the value of the house without spending much money."

"I can see that." Aspen looked around, surprised to see the dingy space after looking at what it could be. She'd love to see that transformation. And she wouldn't mind the return, either.

"How long will it take?"

He scooted his chair a little farther away, blowing out a breath as he did. "That's the issue, of course. If we were to go with your plan, it'd take a month, maybe six weeks, depending on how quickly we can get the supplies. My plan will take twice that long, at least."

"So, three months?"

"Maybe longer. I'm not one of those contractors who'll tell you four weeks when I know it'll be closer to eight. I'm trying to be as honest as I can here. Truth is, everything's in short supply these days. And if it's coming from overseas—"

"I get it."

"I hope it takes less than that but"—his shoulders lifted and fell—"it might take four months, worst case scenario, six. There are things out of my control. I can tell you that I'll do everything in my power to get it done as quickly as possible. And once we get going, if we're organized and have all the decisions made up front, you don't have to be here. You can do what you have to do and then go on to Florida."

"Where strangers don't glare at me? And stalk me?"

"Not that I'm in a hurry to get rid of you, but yeah."

She scrolled the rest of the images to see updated bathrooms, clean and bright bedrooms, pretty light fixtures, new windows everywhere.

It was gorgeous. If he could make this place look like that, she might want to stay.

Well, if the town didn't hate her, that was. And it weren't so cold.

She shivered at the thought and pushed the laptop back to him.

"The furnace guy is coming tomorrow, by the way."

"Thank God."

He laughed and closed the lid. "I'll let you think about it. Meanwhile"—he stood and pushed in his chair—"we should get going so we're not late to meet the phone installer. What do you need to do today?"

What she wanted to do was curl up in bed and spend some time with God. But she doubted Garrett would be willing to hang around while she did that, and he'd already said he wasn't leaving her alone at the house until he knew she was safe. Which was sort of overbearing and sort of sweet. Considering she didn't exactly want to be there alone—even in the light of this sunny day—she wasn't going to argue.

"I need to hit a Target or Walmart or something, a place where there's food and other household goods. And I need furniture."

"Okay. We should be able to get everything in Plymouth. If not, we can pop down to Tilton, but it's another half hour, so we should get going."

"I can go by myself. My errands will take a lot longer than yours. We can just meet back here later."

His smile was disarming. Maybe he knew that. Maybe that was why he'd donned it. "You tired of me already?"

"You must have better things to do."

"Nope. Yours is my only job right now. Besides, I doubt you're going to fit everything you need, plus living room furniture, in the back of that SUV."

He made a point.

"Come on. It'll be my pleasure."

CHAPTER NINE

RATHER THAN TURN toward the interstate, Garrett detoured into the center of Coventry and parked downtown.

"I know I'm new to the area," Aspen said, "but this isn't Plymouth."

He gestured toward a thrift store. "You've got money to play with, but why waste it on brand-new furniture if you can find some used. This place usually has a decent selection."

"Great idea." Before she opened the passenger door, she flashed him a smile that had his heart doing a weird little flip.

He met her on the sidewalk. Though there wasn't a cloud in the sky, the sun hadn't warmed the air much, Aspen pulled up her hood for the thirty-second walk between his truck and the entrance. He could picture that wavy blond hair blowing in the wind as she surfed, but all bundled up like that, she was adorable.

She glanced his way. "What are you smiling about?"

"Nothing, nothing."

He needed to remember that she was a client. And that he was spying on her. Which meant he could not get emotionally involved.

But he wasn't truly spying. He was being a friend. If she decided to tell him something about her mother, he'd listen. And then he'd pray about what to do with the information.

If God told him not to tell his uncle, then he wouldn't.

Even if the thought of denying the uncle who'd saved his life sent acid to his stomach.

He scooted ahead and held the door open for Aspen. Bells overhead announced their arrival as they stepped in. He pulled the door shut behind him. It was notorious for flying open at a gust of wind.

"Come on in. And make sure you got that door..." The woman's voice faded as she looked up from behind a cash register. "Oh, hey, Garrett."

"Hey, Trudy. This is Aspen. She's looking for some furniture." To Aspen he said, "Trudy goes to my church."

"Nice to meet you."

"Same," The older woman said. "You two on a date?"

Did Aspen's cheeks turn a little pink? Probably just a remnant of the cold.

"She's a client," Garrett said. "I'm helping her out."

Trudy nodded, but she didn't seem convinced. "What do you need?"

"Pretty much everything." Aspen looked around, and he followed her gaze.

The place was nicer than other thrift stores he'd seen, with all the items neatly merchandised. Trudy not only employed people who were down on their luck, she also donated a portion of her profits—and a good deal of clothing and other items—to the local food bank. She'd opened the store to serve the poor, especially those who were too proud to take charity.

Racks of clothes filled the front half of the store. Household and decorative items were behind that, and way in the back, furniture. He'd bought a sofa and recliner here when he'd first moved into his condo.

"You know where to go." Trudy turned back to her work. "Yell if you need help."

Aspen grabbed a shopping cart and headed down an aisle.

"Not sure furniture will fit in that."

But she beelined toward kitchen items. "It's amazing the things you don't think about."

She wasn't wrong. When he'd moved, Aunt Deborah had brought over everything she'd thought he might need and a whole bunch of stuff he'd still never used.

Aspen filled the basket with utensils and gadgets and dish-cloths and plates and silverware and bowls...it went on and on.

While she shopped, she checked items off in an ever-present notebook. He'd thought she was finished when she said, "Oh!" and headed in another direction.

He took the first basket, which she'd already filled, to leave by the register and grabbed a second.

After she loaded it up, she looked up at him with a wide smile. "That's almost everything I need besides furniture, food, and a few small appliances."

He checked his watch. "Record time."

"Ha. You wanna talk records, wait until you see the tally."

A woman who could get that much shopping done in a half hour—and save money to boot.

She was getting more attractive by the minute.

"I'm gonna take this up front." He wiggled the basket handle. "The furniture's right..." But she'd already started heading that way.

When he returned, he found Aspen in front of a dingy brown sofa. An ugly, dingy brown sofa.

She glanced at him. "Is this too big?"

"Do you like it?" He hadn't meant his incredulous tone.

"It's dreadful, which probably accounts for the price."

The giant yellow sticker—almost covering a pink sticker, and a blue sticker beneath—indicated it had been marked down more than once. He could see why. Not only was the color awful, but it was stained and... He bent toward it. "It smells."

"But the price."

He took her elbow and guided her toward a gently used off-white sectional. "What about this one?"

"It's twice as much."

Only because Trudy was practically paying someone to take the other off her hands. "I thought *I* was cheap."

"I'm not cheap. I'm just trying to be wise, you know. I don't want to make any crazy decisions."

He studied the better sofa. No stains that he could see on the fabric. No tears. He turned over the dangling price tag. "This is an excellent brand. It'll last for years, and it'll look great in the space."

"I'm not going to live here for years. I need to be rational."

"Okay." Hands on her shoulders, he shifted her back to the brown sofa. "Go lie down on that thing, rest your pretty hair against the fabric, take a deep breath—in through your nose—and then decide."

She took a few steps toward it and stopped, giving him a sheepish look. "I see what you mean."

He chuckled and yelled, "She's taking the white sectional."

Trudy called back, "Got it."

He looked down at Aspen. "What else?"

"You're satisfied with yourself, aren't you?"

He wasn't lying when he said, "This is the first time I've ever enjoyed shopping."

She smiled and moved along.

It took a little time, but Aspen picked out a coffee table, an end table, an old entertainment center, and a couple of lamps.

She also found two throw blankets for the sofa—light gray and dark blue—and some pillows to match.

"Because, you know, it's cold, and I might want to snuggle up in front of the fire." She said the words as if she had to justify her purchases.

"Good thinking."

They were on their way to the front when he spied a display of winter gloves. He aimed her that direction. "The ones you have are as impractical as they are pretty."

"I discovered that last night when my fingers nearly froze off."

While he took her things to Trudy, who started ringing everything up, Aspen looked at her glove choices. When he returned, she lifted a pair. "These'll work."

He checked the tag. They were cheap for a reason. "You should get a better brand."

"Is it that big of a deal?"

"Said the woman who wore a hood to walk from the car to the door."

"It's freezing out there."

"Uh-huh."

"Okay. I see your point." She turned back to the display but seemed flummoxed.

He snatched a pair, checked the brand—Hamilton Clothiers—and held them out. "These."

She slid them on, aiming a smile his way. "They're really comfortable. And warm."

"Which would be the point."

"Wise guy." She punched his shoulder, but between the puffy gloves and his flannel shirt, he barely felt it.

"Ow," he deadpanned. "That's *not* gonna leave a mark."

Laughing, she headed toward Trudy, who he guessed had

kept one eye on the whole exchange, definitely getting the wrong idea about him and Aspen.

Except it didn't feel all that wrong. It felt right.

Which was, all things considered, very, very wrong.

GARRETT GLANCED toward his passenger seat, where Aspen's fingers were flying over her cell phone screen. He didn't mind. She had no service at her house, and she had things to manage.

After hearing about her middle-of-the-night visitor, he'd wanted to stay by her side. Dumb, but the thought of somebody outside her house, watching... It raised a level of protectiveness in Garrett he hadn't known he had.

Much as he wanted to ensure her safety, he hadn't looked forward to spending an entire day with her, not because he didn't enjoy her company—he did, too much. It was shopping itself he hated.

But shopping with Aspen had turned out to be a breeze. After he bought the alarm and floodlights at the hardware store, he took her to a discount super store, dreading it. He should have known better. She'd picked out a thousand dollars' worth of furniture and household goods in less than an hour at Trudy's. She proved just as fast, efficient, and cost-conscious at grocery shopping. She chose the few household items still on her list—including a small microwave, a toaster, and two cord-less phones—in record time, then headed to the food, where she led him down the aisles, snatching this and that along the way, all the while laughing, smiling, sharing stories about her life in Kona—not to mention rejoicing at the prices as if it were unimaginable to be able to buy a pineapple for two dollars, less than half what she usually spent.

"Don't they grow pineapples in Hawaii?"

She shrugged. "Don't ask me to explain it. Just trust me."

That he did. Despite Uncle Dean's suspicions, he found Aspen open and honest.

They'd turned onto the highway back to Coventry by the time she set her phone down.

"Get everything taken care of?"

"There wasn't much. My best friend lives in Nepal. She wanted to know how I was doing. We don't get to talk much with the time difference, so I caught her up on what's going on."

"Nepal?"

"She and her husband are missionaries."

"How'd you become friends with her?"

"They were in Kona for years. There's a big missionary organization not far from where I lived, and Dad and I were involved a lot when I was in high school and college. Jaslynn and I have been friends since I was nineteen. They moved a few months before Dad died."

"Must have been hard not having your best friend around."

When Aspen didn't say anything, he glanced her way to find her nodding. She looked out the opposite window into the dense snow-covered woods.

"What was he like, your dad? Or is it too hard to talk about him?"

"No, I like talking about him." She faced Garrett again. "He was generous and funny and sweet. He worked a lot of hours, but when I was a kid, he always managed to be there for me. He owned a restaurant that was within walking distance of our apartment. Every day after school, he'd meet the bus and walk back to the restaurant with me. It was my favorite part of the day, just Dad and me catching up. While he worked, I'd do my homework, talk to the customers, clean off the tables. Even when I was old enough to stay home by myself, he preferred for me to be with him. And I did too."

Garrett couldn't imagine. His own father had commuted from their house just north of the Massachusetts border to Boston every day, leaving before Garrett woke up and returning after dinner. The little time they had together, Dad had spent lecturing Garrett about his grades or berating him about how he dressed or how he should choose better quality friends, as if the kids at his expensive private school weren't good enough for him.

Garrett said, "Your dad sounds like a good man."

"He was the best."

Garrett detected emotion in her voice. He gave her a moment before asking, "How long ago did he die?"

"It was a year on Tuesday. I thought it would be symbolic or something, starting this journey to fulfill his final wish exactly a year after his death. It was stupid. I cried all day long and then had to get on a plane and travel. It's no wonder I'm still so tired."

"And it hasn't exactly gotten easier this week."

She sniffed beside him, blew out a breath, and said, "I'm fine. It's fine." Her voice was forced-cheerful.

"It's okay to not be fine, you know." He looked her way and caught her eyes. "It's okay to grieve, and to be angry at your stupid nosy stalker guy. And Bart Bradley and all the rude people at The Patriot yesterday."

"You remind me a little of him." She let out a short laugh. "Not Bart."

"Your dad? I'm flattered."

"It's just... you're kind, and you anticipate people's needs, like the way you got the house ready for me. And managed the phone and internet installation and brought over the furniture this morning."

"The furniture was just taking up space in my aunt and uncle's garage."

"But you asked them for it and brought it. And most people

don't ask about my dad. I guess they think maybe it'll be painful to talk about, or maybe they don't want to deal with my emotions. Dad would have asked too. He had a way of drawing people out, getting them to share. Like you, he genuinely cared about people."

Garrett caught her shrug and looked her way to find her cheeks were a little pink, and this definitely wasn't the cold. She was blushing.

He might've been too.

"Would it be pushing my luck to ask what your father's dying wish was?"

After he asked, he drove a good mile before she spoke.

"You heard me tell that guy at the restaurant yesterday that my mom's been missing most of my life."

Garrett hadn't been trying to pry. He'd promised himself he wouldn't do that, but maybe he'd asked the right question to get the information his uncle wanted.

He half wanted to change the subject before she could share, not wanting to be in the position of having to decide what to do with what she told him.

But the other half of him was too curious to interrupt.

"Dad told me that she was missing and probably dead. He always referred to her in the past tense. My mom had some mental problems, and because of that, he didn't think she'd be able to disappear and never be found."

Exactly what Uncle Dean had said.

"All my life, I've believed she was gone. But right before he died...he was having trouble breathing, and he didn't have enough time to say everything he wanted to say before they put him on the vent. He said he wanted me to find her and do right by her. Whatever that means."

"And you think she's here, in Coventry?"

A moment or two passed before Aspen spoke, but she didn't answer his question. "Dad was always frugal."

How that was related, Garrett had no idea. "You get that from him, I guess." He looked at her and caught her smile before returning his attention to the road.

"Even though, by the time he died, he owned five restaurants that were all doing really well, he and I always lived in apartments. We had everything we needed, don't get me wrong. When I started managing the Kona restaurant, I saw how much money he was making in profit. It was significant. And the other restaurants did just as well. But I never questioned how we lived. I figured there were expenses I didn't know about, maybe debt or something. And then I found out about the house here. Which he owns... owned outright."

"But he didn't own it for long," Garrett said. "Didn't he buy it a couple of years ago?"

She turned his way. "How did you—?"

"When it came on the market, I tried to buy it. I thought it would make a good house to fix up and sell for profit. But your dad got it first. I mean, he bought it under the name of his company, so I didn't know it was your dad. Not that I would have recognized his name."

"So you've been thinking about redoing that place for a long time."

He lifted a shoulder and let it drop. "I hadn't seen the inside until Christiansen talked to me about working for you. Did your dad tell you why he bought it?"

"Nope."

"Do you think it has something to do with your mother's whereabouts?"

"It must, right? Why else would he buy a house in New Hampshire? In fact, a part of me..." Her voice trailed.

He waited a few beats before prompting her. "Part of you...?"

"I sort of hoped I'd get to the house and she'd be there. My mom. Cooking dinner or something. In my head, I knew that wasn't going to happen. All my life, even though I knew she was dead, because there's no proof, deep down, I guess I hoped... It's stupid."

He recalled Aspen's reaction to the house when she first arrived. He'd thought her overwhelmed by how much work it would take to make it decent. Turned out, she'd been dealing with so much more.

Before he realized what he was doing, he reached across the console and laid his palm over her hand resting on her knee. "I'm sorry." He squeezed and then brought his own back to the steering wheel. He shouldn't have done that.

She said nothing for a long moment.

And then, as if nothing strange had happened, she continued. "I'm thinking maybe there's something in that extra bedroom that'll give me a clue about where she is."

He'd seen everything in that room. "I don't think so. The stuff from the attic is older. The rest of it is pretty new."

"I'll look through it anyway. I have to start somewhere."

True, though he dreaded the disappointment when she discovered nothing helpful.

A few minutes later, he turned onto the mountain road that led back to her place.

"Would I be insane to go with your design for the house?" she asked. "Wouldn't a wise person just do the bare bones and sell it?"

"Just the opposite. If you do that, you're going to have to sell it for cheap. It's a really nice house with a lot of potential. Why wouldn't you want to profit on that?"

"What if the market shifts?"

"What if it does? It's not going to be worth less than what you put into it. The economy would have to completely collapse for you to lose money. Even during the real estate downturn a decade ago, our housing prices held steady. There's no bubble up here."

"But it's a risk."

"A slight risk." He needed to stop trying to convince her. It wasn't his place to tell her what to do, and he had a vested interest in her choosing his design. "You should do what makes you comfortable."

A moment passed before she said, "My father took risks. Every restaurant was a risk. He opened a second location in Kona, and it failed. But that didn't stop him from trying again."

Garrett nodded, though he was praying she'd choose his design over hers, for both their sakes.

"Okay. Okay, we'll do your design."

"You're sure?" His heart pounded. "I really don't mean to pressure you."

"It'll be beautiful, and if your real estate agent is right, I'll make back every penny and more. It's not like I need the proceeds immediately. I have the luxury of time. The more I think about it, the more I'm convinced that your plan seems like the best course of action."

He barely resisted pumping a fist in victory. "I think that's the right choice."

"Good." She lifted her phone. "I made a list of the rooms that need to be dealt with as soon as possible. At this point, the kitchen is the most pressing. If you could start there, I'd really appreciate it."

"Uh... It doesn't work that way. We'll just have to—"

"No, no. It needs to work that way. The kitchen is dingy and gross, and I really need it to be cleaned up if I'm going to live there. So start there, and then move on to…" She rattled off the list of the rooms in the order that she wanted him to do them.

"There are supplies that need to be purchased," he said carefully. "And subcontractors to hire. Those things might not fit into your plan."

"You'll figure it out. I mean, there's some wiggle room. If you'd rather do the office before the living room, that's fine. And the bedrooms upstairs can be done in any order you want, as long as they're done one at a time. And I'm going to help with the painting, so that'll make it easier."

Cheaper for her, but not easier for him. He'd planned to hire a professional to paint.

"If you want it done quickly—"

"Speed isn't the most important thing," she said. "I have time."

"My time matters too."

"It won't make *that* big of a difference."

He loved the confidence in her voice, especially coupled with the fact that she had no idea what she was talking about.

Her plan wasn't going to work, but he didn't want her to change her mind about his design. Rather than argue further, he simply nodded, turning into the entrance to his condo complex.

"Where are we going?"

If he picked up a hint of nervousness in her voice, he figured it was about to get worse.

Remembering her reaction when he'd suggested it earlier, he sent a smile her way to soften the blow. "We're here to get you a handgun."

CHAPTER TEN

By the time Aspen's phone, internet, Wi-Fi, and alarm system had been installed on Friday night, it was well past dinnertime. Trudy's nephew had helped Garrett deliver Aspen's furniture from the thrift store while the phone installers were still there. When everyone else was gone, Garrett had stood in her living room looking as nervous to leave her alone as she'd felt. But with her new phones, not to mention the security system and motion-sensor lights he'd installed all around her house and even along the driveway, she'd be safe. She'd shooed him out and promised to see him Sunday.

She wasn't going to think about the handgun she had stowed in her nightstand drawer, nor the holster he'd convinced her to order online. She'd argued that she couldn't carry a concealed weapon without a permit, but apparently, New Hampshire didn't require a permit. Quite a change from Hawaii, where one couldn't carry a concealed weapon at all.

Did Garrett really think she was going to walk around packing heat like Annie Oakley?

On Saturday, although she'd wanted to start digging through the stuff in the junk room, instead she spent the day cleaning.

The kitchen was the worst, grimy in spots that required lots of elbow grease, and the bathrooms had needed a good scrubbing as well. She'd thought she'd spend a couple of hours at that task and was shocked when it was four o'clock by the time she finished and plopped down on her new sectional.

She'd never been more thankful for a couch in her life.

The furnace man had come by that afternoon, tinkered in the basement, and then spent ten minutes explaining what he'd done, none of which she understood. He'd told her the furnace was in perfect working order and the bigger problems were the insulation and windows. Until she took care of those, the temperature might go a few degrees higher, but that was as good as it was going to get. When he mentioned that her oil tank was full, she'd worked hard to pretend she'd known she *had* an oil tank.

These were the kinds of conversations she'd never needed to have in Hawaii.

As promised, the temperature in her house rose about two degrees.

She was thankful for the stack of firewood Garrett had delivered. She was clearly going to need it.

Sunday morning, she felt like a new person. Her house was clean, she had everything she needed to survive, all neatly organized in scrubbed and lined cabinets. She'd had two good nights of sleep in a row and no sign of the stalker.

She dabbed the last of her makeup on, then checked her reflection in the mirror over the sink, half wishing she'd bought a full-length one so she could see how she looked in her slacks and boots.

She'd gone to the same church for as long as she could remember. The thought of trying a new one sent not butterflies to her stomach but killer bees in a turf war.

In the bedroom, her phone rang, the old-fashioned sound

loud and jarring. Pressing a hand to her pounding heart, she hurried that way and snatched the cordless handset, pressing the button before she brought the giant thing to her ear.

So weird.

"I thought I'd pick you up for church," Garrett said after her hello. "Are you almost ready?"

"I can drive myself."

"You saw where I live. It's not like it's that far out of my way."

True. He was about ten minutes down the mountain. She hadn't gone into his condo the other night when he'd grabbed the handguns—he'd brought out three so she could decide which felt the best in her hand—and the complex seemed new and well-kept.

"Besides," Garrett added, "we got a little snow last night. I thought you might chicken out on driving."

She stepped to the window and looked outside. Sure enough, her driveway was white. "You're sure it's safe?"

He laughed. "I'm almost there."

Five minutes later, she climbed into Garrett's pickup, where tall coffee cups steamed in cupholders. She'd made her own that morning, but the temperature hovered somewhere in the *what kind of idiot would live here* range, so a second cup of something warm was perfect.

"On your website, it says you're a full-service general contractor, but this still seems outside your sphere of responsibility."

He let out a low chuckle that had her insides thrumming with a reaction she wasn't ready to name.

"I do like to please my clients."

She clicked on her seatbelt, then reached for the cup nearer her, looking at him for permission.

He nodded, and she grabbed it.

"You'll have to tell me your preference," he said. "Personally, I love Josie's lattes, but she makes everything."

That must be the owner of Cuppa Josie's, where Aspen had gotten coffee her first morning in Coventry. Which meant he'd driven to town, gotten the coffees, and then headed back up the mountain. In other words, he'd gone *way* out of his way.

"Caramel macchiato. What's yours?"

"Vanilla latte."

"I'll buy next time."

"Deal." He backed onto the road and headed toward town.

As Garrett had said, his was an old-fashioned white church, steeple and all, that looked like it'd been there for a hundred years or more. There were many such churches in Hawaii. The first white settlers to the islands had been missionaries from New England, so the building weirdly reminded her of home.

Rather than enter at the front, they walked into a lobby area beside the church—an addition, Garrett explained, that connected the sanctuary with the building next door, which housed classrooms. Garrett's friends made a beeline their way. James introduced his wife, Cassidy, who was cradling their newborn, Hallie. Reid introduced Jacqui and his daughter, Ella, who Aspen would guess was about six. Thomas was there too. She also met Andrew and Grace, who were engaged, and Fitz and Tabby, who'd just moved back to town. And Dylan and Chelsea. Apparently, Chelsea owned Hamilton, a big clothing manufacturer located in Coventry.

The company that made the gloves Garrett had insisted Aspen buy. She might suspect he'd steered her that direction out of loyalty, but the gloves really were very warm.

Tabby, the curly-haired brunette, said, "Hey, we're having a girls' night tomorrow at my house. Do you want to come?"

"Oh, uh..." Did she?

"That's a great idea," Grace added. "I live in the condos

down the street from you. Why don't I pick you up? About six twenty?"

She looked at the faces of all the women waiting to see what she'd say. Did she want to get to know them better? She wouldn't mind having a friend in town besides Garrett, even if she would only be there a short time.

Beyond all the smiling faces of Garrett's friends, Aspen had caught more than one stranger looking her way, people her father's age or older. They definitely weren't wearing the welcoming expressions she'd expect to see at church.

Were they like that with all the guests?

Somehow, she doubted it.

Yes, she definitely needed friends on her side. "I'd love to come. What can I bring?"

Tabby said, "Whatever you want—or nothing. We always have way more than we can eat."

Buoyed by the invitation, Aspen followed Garrett further through the addition and up a short flight of stairs. They'd almost reached the sanctuary when she felt a touch to her shoulder.

"Are you Aspen?"

She turned to a tall man—six-two at least—with salt-and-pepper hair and warm brown eyes. By the wrinkles, she'd guess he was her father's age, early fifties. But, unlike her father, who'd developed a paunch, this man was trim and fit.

She'd heard the expression about people's eyes lighting up, but she'd never really understood it until that moment. When he looked at her, it was as if his whole expression brightened.

"You look just like your mother."

People were streaming around them toward the double doors just ahead. Music filtered out.

Garrett nudged the small of her back. "Maybe we should get out of the way."

The man shook his head quickly. "Sorry. Sorry. Can we just...?" He backed out of the crowd and into a corner.

She followed, feeling both nervous and excited. Here was somebody who looked at her, saw her mother, and didn't despise her for the resemblance.

She liked this guy already.

When they were out of the stream of parishioners, he held out his hand, which she shook. "I'm Brent Salcito." Before she could introduce herself, he said, "And you're Aspen. I'd heard you were in town, but even if I hadn't, I'd recognize you anywhere."

"Nice to meet you."

Behind her, Garrett said, "I can wait for you inside, if you two need to—"

"It's all right," Brent said, then focused on her again. "I just wanted to introduce myself and welcome you to Coventry. What brings you here?"

"My father passed away a year ago."

"I'm sorry. I hadn't heard. That must have been very difficult."

"Yes, thank you. Anyway..." She'd been about to tell this man about the house, but at the last second, she shifted. Maybe this person truly was a friend, but she felt like she had enough foes in Coventry that she needed to be cautious. "He used to talk about Coventry all the time. I wanted to see it for myself, get a sense of where he and my mother lived."

"You picked an interesting time to come. Unless you're a skier, you might prefer to visit in the summer."

"I wanted to experience a winter here." She exaggerated a shiver. "I had no idea that air could be so cold."

When Brent smiled, his whole face got involved, lifting his cheeks and crinkling the skin around his eyes. "Where did you grow up?"

"On the Big Island of Hawaii."

"Wow. This is different, then." He slipped his hand into his jacket—he wore a suit, though most people dressed more casually—and came out with a business card, which he held out to her. "If you need anything, anything at all, don't hesitate. My wife and I are at your service." He lowered his voice and leaned closer. "Your mother and I were good friends."

She thanked him, pocketing the card, and he slipped into the crowd entering the sanctuary.

To Garrett, she said, "Do you know him?"

"Everybody knows him. He's the mayor. Should we?" He nodded toward the double doors. The crowd had dwindled, and the volume of the music was steadily building.

Fortunately, Andrew and Grace had saved them seats, and they were able to slip in just as the worship team started singing.

Aspen recognized all the worship songs, and their familiarity made her feel comfortable. The pastor was apparently in the middle of a sermon series on the book of Ephesians, one of her favorites because it had taught her who she was in Christ. The reminder that, though her earthly father was gone, her heavenly Father was right by her side, brought fresh peace. As much as she'd pressed into Him in the year since Dad's death, she feared she'd need God's guidance now more than ever.

AFTER THE SERVICE, Aspen and Garrett were following the crowd toward the lobby when a man approached. "Aspen Kincaid?"

He stood out of the way of the church members streaming into the cold morning as if he'd been waiting for her.

She moved toward him, feeling Garrett at her side. "Have we met?"

He held out his hand. "Only on the phone. Jeff Christiansen."

Over her shoulder, Garrett said, "Hey, Jeff. Aspen, I'll see you outside."

Garrett walked out, and she and her father's local attorney moved farther from the crowd into the corner.

"I just wanted to introduce myself," he said. "Have you gotten settled?"

"I have. Garrett's been a great help. Thank you for recommending him."

The man nodded. Barely taller than Aspen's five-six, he was older than her dad would have been, probably in his mid to late sixties, with a ring of gray hair around a shiny bald head.

"Have you made a plan?" he asked.

Jeff had encouraged her to sell the house immediately, but she'd wanted to come here and fix it up first. When she'd told him that, he'd suggested she do so from Hawaii. *"No sense traveling all the way to New Hampshire,"* he'd said. *"I can manage the details on this end."*

He'd been surprised when she'd called in November to say she was coming.

More than surprised. He'd tried to talk her out of it.

She'd detected a hint of... she wasn't sure what it was. Not displeasure so much as concern when she'd told him her plans. She'd forgotten about that until this moment, maybe because she detected the same thing on his face now.

"Garrett has some great ideas," she said. Come to think of it, it wouldn't be a bad idea to get Jeff's feedback. "He thinks that if we redo the entire house, I'll get a lot more money out of it than if I just do the bare bones. What do you think?"

"Define *redo*," he said.

She gave him a quick rundown on what they planned.

His bushy gray eyebrows lowered over light brown eyes. "That's a huge undertaking."

"He can do it, though, right? You said Garrett—"

"He's more than capable. And the numbers sound right. But you're not going to stay the whole time, are you?"

The way he asked the question had her defenses rising. She crossed her arms. "Why shouldn't I?"

"I just thought... Don't you have a business to run back in Hawaii?"

"I sold it."

The attorney's gaze darted behind her, and she was tempted to turn and see why. She could tell by the lack of noise that most of the church had already filed out.

This conversation—and the lawyer's concern over her staying in town—seemed very important.

"Is there something I should know, Mr. Christiansen?"

"Please, call me Jeff. What do you mean?"

"I've been getting a lot of strange looks since I got to town, and some older guy questioned me the other day about my mother's whereabouts."

"Lots of people are curious about what happened to your mother," he said. "It was a scandal back then."

"What kind of scandal?"

"Look, your father moved to Hawaii to protect you."

"Wait..." She processed his words, then asked, "Did you know my dad before?"

He bobbed his head once. "Your dad and I go way back."

She hadn't told Jeff about Dad's last words, figuring he'd handled the purchase of the house and nothing else. But, now that she thought about it, why had her dad needed a lawyer in New Hampshire? He had one in Hawaii who'd managed his business and his will and trust. A person didn't need to hire a lawyer to buy a house, right?

To clarify, she asked, "So you knew him when...when my mother disappeared, when he moved away?"

"Knew you too." He offered a grandfatherly smile. "You were the prettiest baby I'd ever seen."

She wasn't going to get sidetracked. "Did you know my mother?"

He shifted on his feet and cleared his throat. "We met, of course, but I didn't know her well."

"What can you tell me about what happened back then?"

"Young lady—"

"I'm thirty-one." She didn't mean the words to come out curt, but she wasn't a child. He needed to see her as a capable adult, not the baby he'd known before. For good measure, she added, "And I deserve to know."

"Your father left for a reason. He didn't want you involved."

"There's nothing to be *involved* in now. It's been three decades. I just want to know—"

"I'm sorry, but it's not my place."

"Dad sent me here. Did he tell you that?"

The old man's eyes snapped wide. "What do you mean?"

"Before he died, he told me to come here and..." Now she did turn to see who might be listening. Because it seemed there were people in this town who weren't on her side, and her business was not theirs. But the lobby was empty. Still, she lowered her voice. "Can I trust you to keep this to yourself?"

"I've been acting as your attorney since your father died, so attorney-client privilege applies."

"On his deathbed, my father asked me to find my mother and do right by her. I have no idea what he was talking about, but he mentioned the house. Do you have any idea what he wants me to look for?"

Before she stopped talking, Jeff's head was shaking. He took a step back. "Your father must've been delirious. Was he on painkillers or something? Your mom's been missing a long time, and nobody knows what happened to her."

The confident words coming out of his mouth did not match the fearful expression on his face.

"Why are you lying to me?"

He rubbed his lips together, and his gaze darted all around the lobby. "Your mother is gone, Aspen. There's nothing you can do to change that. Coming here and stirring up the past is only going to cause trouble."

"For who? You?"

"I had nothing to do with it."

"With what? What is 'it'?"

"Whatever happened to your mother, it had nothing to do with me. I just know that there are people in Coventry who won't take kindly to you digging up things that should remain buried."

Before she could argue, he slid an age-spotted hand over her forearm. His grip was strong. "Go back to Hawaii and your life there. Let Garrett fix up your house, and I'll handle the sale. You don't need to be here."

"My father—"

"Forget what your father said. He shouldn't have put this on you. It's not your responsibility."

"She was my mother."

"She was..." He pressed his lips together.

"I know she was suffering from a mental illness. My father told me that much."

He relaxed the tiniest bit. "She did a lot of damage and left nothing but destruction in her wake. That's not your fault, but people around here have a long memory. The fact that you look just like—"

"There you are."

Aspen turned as a woman walked toward them from

outside. She was heavyset with pretty silver hair and giant round sunglasses, which she pushed up on the top of her head.

As she approached, Jeff cleared his throat. "Maury, this is Michael Kincaid's girl, Aspen."

The older woman smiled at Aspen. "I'm Jeff's wife, by the way. You're gorgeous, just like your mother." She held out her hand, and Aspen shook it.

"You knew my mom?"

"Oh, not well." She waved the words off, so casual, especially compared to her husband. "We met a few times. She was a fiery one, your mother. I've never met anybody with so much passion."

Passionate. Fiery. Aspen had rarely heard a positive adjective used to describe Jane Kincaid. She gripped the words like a lifesaving drug. "About what?"

"Oh, everything she cared about. She was in college, and there was something..." She turned to Jeff. "Was it nuclear power plants?"

He shrugged. "Something about the environment." He sounded too casual. He knew more than he was saying.

Maury didn't seem to notice. "And she was charismatic. Everybody loved her. I once saw her stir up a group of mommies into demanding a nursing room downtown."

Aspen smiled, trying to imagine such a thing. "Did they add it?"

"Nobody defied Jane Kincaid." Maury said the words with a little laugh before turning to Jeff. "The kids are holding a table for us. We'd better hurry."

Jeff said goodbye, and Aspen watched as the older couple walked out the door, reeling from all the information she'd gotten.

Her mother'd been passionate and charismatic, and everybody had *loved* her.

This was the first she'd heard anything like that.

Aspen wished the facts had stopped there. But Jeff's words were the ones that resonated.

Your mother did a lot of damage and left destruction in her wake.

And there were people who didn't want Aspen digging into what that meant.

But who? And why?

CHAPTER ELEVEN

The last thing Aspen had wanted to do on Monday was shop, but Garrett had insisted they couldn't get started remodeling until they picked out and ordered everything they'd need.

Which made sense, of course. He couldn't exactly install tile —or anything else—if she never ordered it.

It didn't make her dread the day any less, though.

She and Garrett spent the bulk of the day at a builder's warehouse in Manchester, where he made suggestions about the types of products she should buy, and she took almost all of them. She chose lots of creamy whites and pale grays, which would contrast nicely with the finish she'd chosen for the hardwood floors. When the house was completed, it would look bright and fresh and new. Some buyer was going to pay a premium for it.

"You're really good at this remodeling thing." They'd just left Manchester and were on the interstate that would take them north into the mountains. To her surprise, Aspen had enjoyed every minute of the day. "How'd you learn it?"

"My uncle. He and my Aunt Deborah took me in when I was fourteen."

"What happened to your parents?"

Garrett didn't glance her way. "They still live in the house I grew up in, happier now that I'm gone."

She detected only the slightest bitterness in his tone. "I assume there's a story there."

"There is." A moment passed, and he said, "Are you sure you want to hear it?"

"If you don't mind sharing, I'd love to."

"My father never liked me," Garrett said. "When I was a kid, I thought there was something wrong with me. I could never do anything right. He hated the way I dressed. He hated my friends. If I made straight A's, he criticized me for not being involved in more activities. He ridiculed me for not being a starting player on my Pee Wee football team like he was."

"Oh, Garrett, that's awful." Aspen couldn't imagine growing up in a household like that.

"When I was young, my entire life was consumed with trying to make him proud. I asked for a BMX bike for my twelfth birthday. My father thought it was stupid, but Mom bought it for me anyway. I spent the first week I had it learning to do tricks on that thing. I was pretty good at it, too. I mastered the bunny hop—which is basically just like it sounds. You just yank back on the handles while you lift the bike and get it in the air."

"Sounds scary."

"Nah. It's pretty easy. Anyway, I mastered that, and then I used the trick to ride over a picnic table we had in the backyard. It was a pretty cool stunt, and I couldn't wait to show my father. Deep down, I thought I'd finally found something that would make him proud."

She had a bad feeling about where this story was going.

"He got home from work, and I pestered him until he went

outside with me. Then I got on my bike, and I hopped up on the picnic table and rode across it and then landed back on the ground. It was flawless."

"There's not going to be a happy ending to this story, is there?"

He glanced her direction and smiled. "Very insightful." The smile shifted into a grimace. "He said, 'That's it? All those hours you've been on that stupid bike, and that's all you can do?' He decided the BMX was a waste of time, that *someone like me* ought to spend all his time improving himself."

"What was that supposed to mean?"

"Dad thought I was fundamentally flawed."

"Based on what?"

Garrett shrugged. "I never knew, but that was the day I realized I would never be able to make my father happy. So I quit trying. I started getting into trouble, and by the time I was fourteen, I'd traveled pretty far down a dark road. I ended up getting arrested for breaking and entering, and only because the judge had pity on me, did I escape going to juvie. Dad was done with me by then. He enrolled me in a boarding school."

"What did your mom think about that?"

One side of Garrett's mouth tipped up. "Mom could never stand up to him. She never defended me or protected me, but not because she didn't love me. Dad's got a stubborn streak, and Mom's never been strong enough to fight him. That time she did the best thing she could have done. She called her brother."

"Your uncle Dean?"

"He and Aunt Deborah took me in. Uncle Dean taught me what a father's love should look like. They changed my life."

"So your mother came through in the end."

"She did. I have a decent relationship with her. Dad and I are civil to each other, but I doubt it'll ever be more than that.

"As I've gotten older, I've realized that Dad's issues were never about me. He hates himself. I have no idea what happened to make him that way. But he hates himself, and he thinks I'm like him, so he hates me. It's that simple."

"And it's that awful," Aspen said. "Would that he knew who he was in Christ. Would that he knew how God sees him."

Garrett glanced her way, a small smile on his lips. "That's a very good point. Dad's an atheist. All my efforts to tell him about Christ have been met with scorn."

"Your mom?"

"She listens, but she believes like Dad does."

"Are Dean and Deborah believers?"

"Yeah. Dean told me that he'd once done something much worse than breaking and entering, and he'd been given a second chance, and it was his pleasure to offer that same grace to me."

Aspen reached across the console and laid her hand on Garrett's forearm. "Thank you for trusting me with that story."

"I find you very easy to talk to."

To prove it, Garrett shared stories about life with his aunt and uncle, about all the remodeling projects they'd done together over the years, about his uncle teaching him to cook—which he hated—and to build furniture, which wasn't his forte. "I mean, I can measure and cut and build things, no problem. But my uncle makes these ornate and beautiful pieces." He lifted his large hands on the steering wheel. "These things don't do ornate."

"But you have an eye for beauty. That's clear in the designs you did of the house."

He shrugged. "I guess. Just don't ask me to carve a table leg into the shape of a lion's paw and we should be fine."

She giggled. "I think I can live without that."

They'd made almost the entire drive, and Garrett's truck

was rolling up the mountain road to her house. Through the trees to her right, she watched the world fall away and caught sight of what looked like a white field below. "What's with that big valley?"

He glanced that way. "I think you're looking at Lake Ayasha. Coventry is right on the edge of it. Three seasons a year, it's beautiful."

"But it's white."

He cast her an amused look. "It's frozen."

"Oh." She felt foolish, but in her defense, she'd never seen a frozen lake. "Ayasha. What a funny name."

"It means *little one*. You can see it from your house, you know."

"I can? I thought..." Right. The snow-covered valley she had peeked at through the trees. "That's the lake?"

"You ought to hang around and see it in the spring. It's beautiful." Garrett made the turn into her driveway when he said, "So I guess I'll start in about three weeks."

"What?" She studied his profile and caught the hint of humor in the twitching of his lips. "Why three weeks?"

"You want me to start in the kitchen. You were very clear about that."

"It is the most logical place."

"If you say so."

When he added nothing, she asked again. "Why exactly are we waiting three weeks?"

"Well, we don't want to start tearing out your current kitchen until we get the new cabinets and island, and they won't arrive for—"

"Three weeks."

"Of course, I have almost all I need for the bathrooms already, and they promised to deliver the new tub on Thursday, but you want me to start in the kitchen." He shrugged, and she didn't miss the smug look on his face.

"Why don't you start wherever you want?"

"Well, there's an idea." He shot her a smile. "I wish I'd thought of that."

∽

WHEN THE DOORBELL rang that evening, Aspen pulled it open to find Grace on the front step. Though the woman smiled, her mouth apparently hadn't told the rest of her face the plan. Her eyes were wide, her skin a little pale.

Maybe she'd had second thoughts about picking Aspen up. Aspen could offer to drive herself, but at this point, that would make it seem as if Aspen didn't want to ride with her, which wasn't the case at all and would only make what was suddenly an awkward situation even worse.

Instead, she did her best to keep her own smile in place. "Come on in. I just need to grab the cookies, and—"

"I'm going to wait in the car."

Before Aspen could respond, Grace fled to a waiting SUV.

Okay then.

Aspen donned her coat and grabbed the plate of snickerdoodles she'd baked that afternoon. After setting her alarm and locking up, she approached the car, praying all the way. The last thing she wanted was to spend time with people who didn't want her around. She'd agreed to this evening because these ladies were among the few people in Coventry who didn't shoot her dirty looks or warn her away. Maybe they'd heard rumors about her mother since church that made them want to avoid her.

Well, if they had, then Aspen would figure out what they'd heard. If she could learn something, then it would be worth it.

Besides, she was in it now.

They'd been driving in silence for five minutes before Grace spoke. "I'm so sorry about that. I thought I could do this without…" Her voice trailed, and she sent Aspen an apologetic look. "I was at your house before. I was caring for a little girl, and there was this man who—"

"Wait. That was you? With the renter, who was…?"

Grace nodded.

"Oh, Grace. I had no idea. Garrett told me what happened when he showed me the rooms in the basement, but he didn't mention any names."

Grace blew out a long breath. "I'm glad you know the story. I really don't feel like telling it tonight."

"No, no. Of course not. If I'd known… I should have met you at your condo. I could've driven." The roads were clear again. Weirdly, Aspen hadn't driven herself anywhere since she'd arrived at the house the previous week. The afternoon before, she'd cleaned snow off her car and parked it in the detached garage. It was a pain that she'd have to trek outside to get to it, but at least it would be protected if it snowed again.

"If you come to the next girls' night," Grace said, "you can drive."

"That's a deal."

Tabby and Fitz lived in a newer neighborhood close to town. There were two cars in the driveway and another two on the road. Grace chose a spot on the road.

Tabby greeted them at the door, took the plate of cookies, and led them into a kitchen-dining combo, which opened to the living area. Aspen greeted the women she'd met the day before. Cassidy was the one with the unusual blue eyes and the newborn. Aspen didn't see the baby, but she'd spied a car seat inside the door and figured the baby was asleep somewhere in the house. Jacqui had red hair—she was the one married to Reid, who'd helped move her furniture. She wasn't very talkative but paid close attention to their conversation, as if there might be a test later. Carly had dark brown hair and brown eyes—she might have been at least part Hispanic, but Aspen couldn't be sure. Apparently, she had a baby she'd left at home with Braden.

It seemed all the boyfriends and husbands went to Carly and Braden's house every Monday, which was what had prompted the girls' night.

They were seated at a huge round table, enjoying soup, salad, and sliders, when Carly asked how Aspen's previous afternoon had gone. Carly had invited her and Garrett to lunch after the service, but thanks to the conversation with Jeff, Aspen had only wanted to get home.

"Did you find anything interesting?"

Aspen had spent the afternoon searching the junk room.

She'd dug through every drawer, glanced at every slip of paper, studied every photograph, and flipped through every book.

Garrett had told her that much of the stuff had come from the attic. One box she unpacked held old dishes wrapped in yellowing newspaper dating back to the sixties.

Long, long before her mother's disappearance.

She'd found a few envelopes of snapshots all showing the same family. Based on the clothes and hair, they were taken in the late seventies or early eighties.

The boxes held nothing that could help her.

Garrett had piled newer items in one corner, but they must have belonged to the renter. Men's clothes, razors, some books, and a couple of cheap watches. A lot of his things had been confiscated by the police, Garrett had explained. All the camera equipment and photographs. Thank God those things were gone.

There were more pots and pans and silverware, some plastic containers. Just everyday stuff.

Aspen had found nothing that led to her mother's whereabouts.

Why had her father bought the place?

What was she doing there?

But she didn't explain any of that to the ladies at the table. "Nothing noteworthy, unfortunately. I'm planning to take everything to the thrift store."

Aspen enjoyed the meal and the company more than she'd anticipated. Grace filled them in on her wedding plans. She and Andrew would marry in the spring.

Cassidy shared a few funny stories about James and the newborn.

Tabby told them about a new client she'd just started working for. Apparently, she was a decorator, and considering what she'd done with her own place, a very good one. If Aspen were staying, she might hire her to decorate the house.

Carly asked the ladies about something she'd read in the Bible, which set off a conversation about faith and the armor of God, and even Jacqui, though generally quiet, contributed to that conversation.

This group of friends seemed knitted together as if they'd known each other for years, but Aspen learned that Carly, Grace, and Jacqui were new to town. Cassidy had been gone since high school, only returning a couple of years prior. Only Tabby was local—and Chelsea, but she hadn't made it that night.

Apparently running a multi-million-dollar company demanded a person's time.

Aspen loved their friendship and easy conversation. Unexpectedly, the thought of leaving Coventry brought a twinge of regret. Maybe more than a twinge. This camaraderie was exactly what she needed. Friends, a community.

They were enjoying dessert when a sound had her head turning toward the living area. An older woman emerged from the hallway carrying an infant.

"Mom." Tabby stood and went to her. "Cassidy said the baby needs to sleep."

The woman patted the child's tiny back as she settled in a rocking chair by the fireplace. "She was fussing. I don't mind holding her."

Tabby shot Cassidy an apologetic look, but the pretty brunette only laughed. "You rock her as long as you want, Mrs. Eaton. If she starts fussing again, bring her to me."

"Can I get you something?" Tabby asked her mother. "You know you're welcome to join us."

"You don't need an old lady ruining your night. Besides, I'm content to hold this little one." The woman sent her daughter a look. "If I had my own grandbaby to rock—"

"Have you met Aspen?"

Aspen held in a laugh as she stood and stepped into the living area, happy to help her friend avoid that conversation. "Nice to meet you."

The woman looked her way, then blinked. "Oh. Oh. You must be Jane Kincaid's daughter. I heard you were back."

Amusement fading, Aspen worked to keep her smile in place.

"Mom." Tabby's sharp tone did nothing to divert her mother's staring. Tabby turned to Aspen, eyes wide, embarrassment clear in her expression. "My dad's out of town, so Mom is staying with me for a few days."

The woman kept rocking, but she was focused on Aspen as she shook her head. "How rude of me. I'm Marion Eaton. I'd get up but—"

"It's fine." Aspen could see the resemblance between Tabby and her mother, though the older woman's wrinkles indicated more frowning in life than smiling. "You knew my mother?"

"Everybody knew Jane," Marion said. "She was a force."

Fiery. Passionate. Charismatic. A new description...a *force*.

Aspen could feel Tabby's shock beside her and turned to face her. "I'm going to talk to your mom for a second."

After a squeeze to Aspen's forearm, Tabby returned to the kitchen, and the women resumed their chatting. The water came on and dishes clanged against one another as they cleared the table and tidied up.

Aspen slid onto the sofa closest to Marion's rocking chair. "Were you friends with her?"

"I hardly knew her. My husband and I were married with kids when all that stuff happened."

"All what stuff?"

Marion turned her attention back to the child, but not before Aspen caught the surprise in her expression.

"I'm sorry to pry." Not that it wasn't Aspen's business, whatever Marion had to say. "I've heard that my mother got into some trouble"—her father's words—"and caused heartache"—Bart Bradley's—"and left destruction in her wake." The last from Jeff Christiansen. "But nobody will tell me what happened."

When Marion looked up from the baby, she gave Aspen a sad smile. "This must be really hard for you. Do you remember her at all?" Before Aspen could respond, Marion continued. "What am I saying? You were a baby. Of course you don't. Well, I can tell you, she was beautiful, and I think, deep down, truly wanted to do good in the world. It didn't work out the way she planned."

"Please tell me what you know."

Marion glanced past Aspen to the ladies in the kitchen. It

was one big room, but they were far enough away and their conversation and the sounds of cleaning were loud enough that the women wouldn't overhear.

Marion leaned closer to Aspen, keeping her voice low. "There was a lumber company in town. Your mother thought they were breaking some laws or something. I don't know the details. But..." She paused and studied Aspen a long time. "Somebody set off a bomb that destroyed that company's head-quarters."

"Oh my gosh. A *bomb?*" Aspen's stomach dropped. She hadn't known what to expect, but she'd never conceived of that.

"It went off in the middle of the night. The place should have been deserted."

Should have been.

"What happened?"

"There was a woman there."

For a split second, Aspen thought Marion was going to say Jane had been in the building, that they thought she'd died in the bombing, but Marion continued.

"A secretary or something. She and her husband had fought that night, and she'd gone there to get away. I guess he got violent when he drank."

Definitely not Aspen's mother.

"The woman was killed," Marion said. "The thing was, her car was in the parking lot. Whoever set off the bomb had to have seen it."

"That's awful." Aspen couldn't figure out what this had to do with her mother. Hoping Marion would explain soon, she asked, "Did you know the lady?"

"It was a much smaller town back then. Everybody knew everybody."

"I'm sorry. That must've been awful. Was she friends with my mother or something? Or did Mom try to find out who did it? I'm just trying to figure out..." Her words trailed as Marion shifted the baby to one arm and reached toward Aspen with the other. Not knowing what else to do, Aspen took her hand.

"Your mother didn't try to solve the crime." A long moment passed before Marion spoke again. "Your mother set off the bomb."

CHAPTER TWELVE

THIRTY YEARS AGO.

The students met in the same bar and sat at the same table. As before, the Planner arrived first. As before, he was in charge. "How's the hunting and gathering going?"

"I've got almost everything I need," the Builder said. "One more trip to the city should do it. I'll go next month."

"And our friend?"

"Knows nothing."

He turned to the Crusader. "What have you learned?"

She was both the best and the worst person to do the recon on the target. The best because her presence was never surprising. She'd shown up there at least once a month for over a year, demanding they make changes, sometimes picketing all by herself. They saw her as a nuisance and mostly ignored her.

Which made it easy for her to watch the comings and goings at the place without arousing suspicion.

She was the worst person for the job because, when it was done, she would be the most logical suspect.

But the Planner had a plan.

The Crusader gave her report regarding the lumber company's business hours, the employees' schedules, the security personnel, and what she'd observed of the alarm systems. The Planner wrote everything down in his notebook, carefully vague in case anybody got ahold of it.

When she was finished, he said, "We need to talk alibis. Mine is in place."

"You really think your father will lie for you?" the Builder asked.

"No question."

His father would believe him. Even if he didn't, he'd protect him. He always had.

To the Builder, the Planner said, "You'll be at work, right? How about our friend?"

"I'll figure something out. I'll make sure of it."

Then the Planner took the Crusader's hand.

He loved holding her hand. Never mind that she was married. Never mind that she had a kid. She'd give up on that life soon enough, and then they'd be together.

Doing this with her...doing this *for* her...would prove his devotion. His mother would be horrified. His father might disown him. He didn't care. He'd do anything for her.

"Your alibi is the problem," he said.

"I don't care!" Her voice was loud enough that people at the bar turned to stare.

"Please lower your voice." He kept his low and steady.

She did, marginally. "I don't care who knows. I'll take the blame for it."

"But your little girl," the Planner said. "You don't want to leave her, do you?"

The Crusader blinked a couple of times. Sometimes her dreams were so lofty, so strongly felt, that she forgot she had to live in the real world. That was why they were perfect together. His feet were always planted firmly in reality.

Reminding her of her baby usually pulled her back in.

"Okay, you're right." She nodded a few times. "What's your idea?"

"Like me, you won't have a true alibi. You'll need to fabricate one. You'll need somebody to lie for you."

She seemed to realize who he meant. "He won't do it."

"He will."

"He'll use it to take her away from me."

"That's why we have to be strategic." The Planner told her exactly what to do. Carefully, slowly, repeating the ideas over and over. Because when the Crusader got like this, sometimes she couldn't focus. Sometimes she couldn't comprehend.

It was a long time before she nodded her understanding. "His clothes."

"Which the Builder will wear to assemble the bomb."

"His tools," she said.

The Builder spoke. "I'll get you a list of what I need."

The Planner said, "A few strands of his hair."

It wasn't very long, but it was long enough.

"And you'll plant a couple of books in your house," the Planner said. "To prove to anybody looking that he could have done it himself."

"He would never, though. Nobody would believe—"

"To make it look like you did it? To get custody of his daughter? To prove you were unfit? It's not about what he would do. It's about the story we can spin. It's about what we can get people to believe."

Hurt filled her eyes. "He would never betray me like that."

The Planner tamped down a surge of irritation. "You and I know that, but the authorities don't."

The Crusader agreed, but he could see the reluctance in her expression. "I don't want him to go to prison. The baby needs him."

The baby.

It always came back to the baby.

Other words hovered between them, but the Crusader wouldn't admit them. That *she* needed her husband, or thought she did. That she'd chosen him for a reason.

The Planner leaned closer and lowered his voice so that only she could hear. "We're not trying to frame him. We just need him to believe we will. He won't risk going to prison, being separated from his daughter. He'll cover for you to protect himself."

The truth dawned, and the Crusader smiled. "I see. I'll do it."

CHAPTER THIRTEEN

GARRETT TOOK a big bite of his cheesesteak slider, hoping the guys would get distracted while he chewed and swallowed.

But they were watching him, waiting for him to respond to Braden's question about Aspen. Garrett and his friends got together every Monday night at Braden and Carly's place to watch whatever sporting event was on. It had started with Monday Night Football the year before, but when the regular season ended, they'd kept meeting. Tonight, they were watching a hockey game, not that Garrett was paying much attention.

After he sipped his soda, he took his time setting it down and wiping his mouth before saying, for at least the third time, "She's just a client."

"Awfully pretty client." Braden was seated in one of the club chairs, his baby girl tucked against his chest.

Andrew, who'd been the focus of similar teasing just a few months before, showed about as much mercy as Garrett had shown him when Grace first came into the picture. "Makes sense. I always take my clients to church with me." He turned to Fitz, seated in one of the chairs behind the sofa. "Don't you?"

"In my case," Fitz said, "my 'clients'"—he actually made air quotes around the word—"are criminals who mostly end up in jail, but otherwise—"

"I'm choosing to believe him." Thomas had pulled his chair to the end of the couch, so Garrett had a good view of his face when he added, "Aspen's hot. I think I'll ask her out."

Garrett wasn't sure exactly what his face did, but his thoughts on that remark must've shown.

His friends laughed.

Thomas gestured toward Garrett. "And we have our answer."

"You have nothing," Garrett snapped, trying hard not to give in. It was a matter of principle. "I can be friends with a woman without it turning romantic, even if the rest of you idiots can't. I mean, she's smart and funny and I enjoy her company. What's wrong with that?"

"Sure," Reid said. "Why would you want to date a woman like her? She sounds awful."

James added, "And let's not forget Thomas's observation, not that I noticed, but I hear she's attractive."

"The word was 'hot.'" Braden snuggled little Desiree in his arms. "Not anywhere near as pretty as your mommy, sweet girl. I'm just quoting Tommy over there." He looked up from the wide-eyed baby to Thomas. "I say go for it, man."

Garrett did his best to keep his expression neutral this time, but the thought of Thomas asking Aspen out...

It grated. More than that. It filled him with equal parts dread and fury. Maybe he and Aspen were just friends at the moment, but Garrett wouldn't mind if it were something more.

If she were going to date any of them, it should be him.

He would ask her out, too, if she weren't moving to Florida.

If he weren't supposed to be spying on her.

Thomas was watching him. For everybody else, this was all

a big joke, but Thomas was serious. He'd pursue Aspen unless Garrett asked him not to.

So fine. He leveled his gaze at his friend. "I'd rather you didn't."

Thomas nodded once. "Fair enough." He turned his attention to the game.

The rest of the guys chuckled, and the conversation resumed, though Garrett didn't take part. Now that he'd admitted it, he couldn't stop thinking about Aspen. He was attracted to her. She was beautiful, but it wasn't just that. He liked her. He went out of his way to spend time with her not because he wanted to be a good neighbor but because he wanted to be with her.

All things considered, he needed to get over it, or it was going to be much harder when she moved away.

Or, God forbid, if she found out he was spying on her.

Which he wasn't. And wouldn't, even if Dean thought he would.

Fitz's phone rang, and he snatched it from the coffee table. He listened, then met Garrett's eyes. "What time?" He waited through the answer, then said, "Tell her to wait until one of us comes to get her. Nobody should enter until the police do a thorough search."

Considering Fitz's gaze hadn't wavered, Garrett had a very strong suspicion that the *her* in question must be Aspen.

He got that acid-drop feeling in his stomach. "What happened?"

But Fitz spoke into the phone. It must be Tabby. "No. You stay there. In your—" His eyes widened, and he averted his gaze. "With all that company, you need to stay home. I'll be there soon." He hung up the phone.

"What happened?" Garrett said.

"Aspen's alarm is going off. She's at our house, so—"

He lurched to his feet. "She's waiting for me?"

"She doesn't have a car. She was trying to get one of the women to drive her home, but Tabby thought—"

"I'll get her." Garrett dug his keys from his pocket on his way out the door.

Six minutes later, Garrett pulled up outside Fitz and Tabby's house. Before he shifted into park, Aspen stepped outside and hurried to the passenger side. He pushed open the door, and she climbed in. "Thanks for—"

"Do you know what happened?"

"The alarm company called and asked if I was at home. They said my alarm was going off. This happened about twenty minutes ago. They sent the police."

Thank heavens he'd gotten the alarm installed.

A cruiser idled in her driveway. Aspen's SUV wasn't there. "Where's your car?"

"I moved it to the garage."

Her front door was wide open, and a cop stepped onto the stoop as Garrett parked.

Aspen hurried up the walk, Garrett right behind her.

The uniformed officer asked, "Do you live here?"

"I'm Aspen Kincaid. I own the house."

He stepped aside for her to enter, and Garrett followed, pulling the door closed. No fire smoldered in the fireplace. She'd need one, considering how cold it was in the house.

"I'm Officer Tyler. The front door was wide open when we arrived, so we went ahead and searched. Nobody's here."

Aspen nodded but said nothing.

Garrett asked, "Any chance you didn't get the door closed when you left? Maybe the wind blew it open." His hopes that this was all a mistake fled when Aspen shook her head.

"I closed the door and locked it behind me. I remember because it was no easy feat with a plate of cookies in my hands."

Tyler added, "It looks like the lock was picked." He opened the door again and lit the area around the keyhole with his flashlight. Garrett saw what he was looking at and stepped away so Aspen could see as well. "Unless those scrapes were there already," the cop said.

Before Aspen could answer, Garrett said, "I replaced that lock myself a few weeks ago. There were no markings on it."

Aspen's eyebrows lifted, giving him an *I can speak for myself* look.

"Sorry." He breathed deeply and stepped into the living room, telling himself to shut up.

She turned back to the cop. "What else did you find?"

"We think whoever did it came inside, despite the blaring alarm."

The alarm was off now. The alarm company must have done that. Or maybe the cops had some magic way of getting it done.

Aspen looked around, but the living area looked untouched. "What makes you think he came in?"

"Upstairs."

As the cop said the word, a second uniformed officer jogged down the stairs. "Master bedroom's the worst." When he reached the bottom, he stuck out his hand. "Officer Fontier. Sorry about this. Far as I can tell, the burglar spent most of his time in the master."

Aspen said, "Can I—?"

"Go ahead."

She was halfway up before she turned to Garrett. "Will you come with me?"

He jogged up to join her, thankful she'd asked. He hadn't wanted to intrude, but everything in his being ached to know what had happened.

All the doors were open, but the extra bedrooms seemed untouched.

The junk room was almost completely empty. He'd known she'd gone through the things in there but was still surprised to see it, considering what a mess it'd been.

They continued to the master.

She froze in the doorway, but he could see over her head.

The room was wrecked. Her clothes were strewn all over the floor. The bedding had been ripped off the bed.

The bureau drawers were open. One lay face down on the carpet.

The bathroom looked about the same.

He swallowed a rise of nausea at the sight and followed Aspen inside the smaller space. He wanted nothing more than to pull her into his arms and comfort her.

But she was focused on a box on the bathroom counter. It was brown leather, about the size of a bag of hot dog buns, and wide open, its contents spilling out.

Jewelry.

"Is something missing?"

She picked through the pieces, then shook her head. "Not even the necklace Dad gave me for graduation..." She lifted the chain, and he saw a sizable diamond surrounded by other diamonds dangling from her hand.

Finding the treasure didn't seem to comfort Aspen. Her skin turned ashen. "What did they want?" She glanced around, then moved past him back into the bedroom. "As far as I can tell, nothing is missing." Again, she turned to him. "Are they trying to scare me? To..." She shook her head.

Officer Tyler stood in the doorway.

"How long did it take you to get here?" Garrett couldn't help the irritation in his voice as he gestured to the space. "He wasn't in any hurry."

"We were in town," Tyler said, voice level. "It's about a fifteen minute—"

"I know where town is," Garrett snapped.

The officer didn't react to his tone, focusing on Aspen. "Let's go back downstairs."

She led the group to the living room, where she sat on the sectional.

Garrett sat beside her and took her hand.

Officer Tyler stood nearby. "You didn't see anything missing?"

She shook her head. "Nothing. He didn't even take the jewelry."

The two police officers looked at each other. Tyler said, "We noticed that. We've had some trouble at this house in the past."

Garrett said, "I told her the story about the previous occupant."

"After that," Tyler said. "Kids, I think, wanting to check out the basement. Since the place was unoccupied…"

A voice came through one of the walkie-talkies, and a moment later, Fontier pulled open the front door.

Cote, the chief of police, stepped in. He was an older, heavyset man who'd been on the force since Garrett had moved to Coventry. Considering all the trouble he'd gotten into when he lived with his parents, it was rather astounding that he hadn't had a run-in with Cote. In fact, they hadn't met until Garrett had helped Andrew find Grace and Lily that fall.

Cote greeted Garrett with a nod and then introduced himself to Aspen, who explained what she'd found.

"You're sure there's nothing missing?"

She sighed, then pushed off the sofa. "I haven't checked the kitchen. Let me just…" She disappeared through the door. When she came back, her skin looked even paler than it had before.

He wouldn't have thought it possible.

"My laptop's missing."

Cote made a note while Garrett kicked himself. At the hardware store on Friday, he'd suggested she buy a video doorbell, but she'd balked at the idea, arguing that it wasn't as if her middle-of-the-night visitor was going to knock.

If they'd gotten it, they'd have a recording of whoever'd broken into her place.

He should have insisted. Or bought it himself.

"Your car wasn't here?" Cote asked. He'd settled on the other side of the L-shaped sectional.

"It should be in the garage."

Tyler said, "It is. We checked."

Aspen continued. "I moved it today, but it's been in the driveway since I got here the other day."

"So, presumably, the burglar didn't believe you were home." He peered at her over reading glasses. "That's good news."

None of this was good news.

But he saw what Cote was getting at.

Though she was putting up a good front, Aspen looked shaken, almost on the verge of falling apart.

Garrett slid his arm around her shoulders and pulled her in for a slight hug, just enough to remind her that she wasn't alone. She gave him a grateful look before focusing on Cote again.

Cote asked a few more questions, told her to be sure and change any passwords at sites that might be vulnerable with her laptop in a burglar's hands, and promised to keep in touch.

Just like that, he and the uniformed officers were finished asking questions as if they'd done all they could.

Maybe they had, but Garrett wasn't sure he'd ever feel comfortable leaving her alone again.

~

GARRETT WATCHED as Aspen saw them out and closed the door. She locked it, then double-checked, before she returned to the sofa and collapsed beside him. "I can't believe this."

"I'm sorry. My laptop is in the truck. You can use it to log on to your accounts and change your passwords."

"My dad always harped on me about security. None of my passwords are saved on my hard drive. Even if they manage to break into it, they won't get anything out of it. It's just...it was mine. Why would somebody do this?"

He pulled her close, tucking her against his side, wanting to comfort her, to protect her. "I don't know."

"Do you think it was my stalker guy?"

He shrugged, wanting to give her answers he didn't have.

And then her shoulders heaved. She turned her face against his flannel shirt and sobbed.

"Hey, hey." He tightened his hold, wishing he knew how to comfort her. Wishing he understood what she was feeling.

She'd had so many things to deal with in such a short time— the break-in, the stalker, the rude people in town, not to mention the anniversary of her father's death. No wonder her emotions overflowed.

"It's okay," he said, patting her back, feeling useless. "It's going to be okay."

She backed up and wiped her tears with the sleeves of her sweater. "You don't know what I..." She shook her head, sniffed, and looked away.

"What don't I know?"

"Tabby's mother was at her house tonight," Aspen said. "She knew my mom. She knew the"—her voice hitched—"the story." Aspen swallowed hard, eyes filling again. "She said my mother blew up a building." The pitch of her voice rose. "She killed a woman."

"Oh. Oh, I'm sorry." He pulled her against his chest.

Dean had implied that Jane Kincaid had killed someone, but Garrett had guessed there'd been a car accident or something. He'd never imagined... "Was she sure it was your mother?"

Aspen nodded against his chest. "She seemed sure. But before I could question her further, I got the call about the alarm."

"Okay." He held her close, not knowing what to say. Not knowing how to react to such news. No wonder this town hated Jane Kincaid. No wonder they wanted to know where she was.

"And now..." Aspen pushed back and gestured to the house. "There's nothing here, Garrett. There's nothing here to tell me where my mother is or what happened to her. Why did Dad buy this place? Why send me here to learn all this awful stuff?"

"I don't know."

"It doesn't make sense. There has to be something." She leaned back and took a deep breath. "I don't understand what he was thinking. Why wait until he was on his deathbed to tell me what he knew? Why not write me a letter explaining? Better yet, why not be honest with me all my life?"

"What do you mean? Did your father—?"

"He told me my mother got into trouble and then disappeared. But when I asked for details, he acted as if he knew nothing more, nothing of consequence, anyway. But buying this place, asking me from his deathbed to do right by her... He knew more than he ever let on. Why lie to me?"

Aspen hadn't told Garrett that whole story, but now didn't seem to be the time to ask for details. "Your father didn't expect to get hit by a car. He thought he had time. This wasn't his plan. Maybe he never planned to tell you anything."

"Is that supposed to make me feel better?"

He heard the frustration in her voice and made sure his

response was gentle despite it. "Are you glad you know what you know? I mean, is this better for you?"

"She was my mother!"

He nodded, unsure exactly what she meant by the statement.

"I have a right to know."

"Maybe," he said slowly. "Maybe you could have lived your entire life never knowing, and maybe you'd have been happier if you had."

She dropped her head into her hands, hiding her face from him.

She didn't speak again for a long time.

While she processed what she'd learned, or grieved, or whatever it was she was doing, he lit a fire in the fireplace, then checked all the doors to make sure they were secure. They were. If her alarm sounded while she was home, she'd know it. She had the gun to protect herself. The cops hadn't asked about it, which led him to believe she had it on her. That was something. He'd taught her how to use it Friday night, even having her fire a couple of shots at a tree in the backyard. She'd hit it—albeit from ten feet away, but an intruder in the house wouldn't be farther than that.

Whether or not she *would* shoot in self-defense—that he couldn't know, which made him never want to leave her side.

In the kitchen, he found an herbal tea bag and heated a mug of water for her. Deborah had told him once that tea warmed a person better than coffee, and herbal wouldn't have caffeine. He settled in beside her again. "I thought you might want something."

She dropped her hands from her face and took the mug. "Thank you."

He nodded, and she sipped, then set it on the table.

"Is it okay?" he asked. "I wasn't sure if you took sugar or milk or—"

"It's fine. Thank you."

"The gun wasn't stolen, was it? Did you leave it in your room?"

"You told me to keep it with me. It's in my purse."

"Did you get the holster?"

Her lips hinted at the slightest smile. "It came today, but... I feel like an idiot with that thing on. And it's not exactly comfortable."

He didn't want to make her nervous, but on the other hand, all things considered... "Neither are intruders."

She conceded the point with a nod. "The thing is, I can't quite figure out how it works. It doesn't feel right."

"Go get it, and we'll figure it out together."

She disappeared into the kitchen and returned with the neoprene strap, which she held out to him.

It couldn't have been more obvious how it worked, but he didn't say that. He laid it flat on the coffee table. "Where's the gun?"

She dug it out of the bottom of her purse. Fat lot of good it would do there. *Hold on a second, Mr. Murderer, while I find my weapon.*

Wisely, he held his tongue, checked that the safety was engaged, and slid the gun into position. "It goes here."

"Yeah, I get that, but... It's going to stick out. I thought the holster would hide the fact that I was carrying it."

"If it were tucked away too much, then how would you get to it?"

Her mouth opened, then closed, and she shrugged.

He lifted the strap off the table. "Arms up."

She complied, and he positioned it around her middle just

above the waist of her slacks. He perched on the sofa and secured it, trying not to pay too much attention to her trim waist and the faint scent of vanilla wafting off her. "Is that comfortable?"

When she said nothing, he looked up to find her cheeks were pink.

"Is that where I'm supposed to wear it?"

"It's pretty flexible." He turned it so the gun was on her right side. "There, you can grab it quickly. Or you could put it"—he slid the weapon toward the front—"here, if that feels more natural."

"None of this feels natural. I really don't think—"

"You could slide it around to the small of your back, though that wouldn't exactly be comfortable in a chair." He wasn't going to argue with her. She could wear it or not. She didn't have to do what he said, so there was no sense in them discussing it further. He backed away and indicated the area around his chest. "I know some women like to wear it higher, under, uh... You know, you have some space there beneath, uh..."

She giggled. "I see what you're saying." She scooted the holster up beneath her breasts, then shook her head. "Yeah, how stupid do I look trying to get it from there?" Her right elbow jutted up as she pulled the gun from the holster.

"I take it your goal is to defend yourself and look good doing it?"

That made her smile. "But wait. I wouldn't wear it over my clothes, so first I'd have to lift my shirt, flash the guy."

He looked away, realizing what she was saying and trying not to picture it. "It would be a heckuva distraction."

That elicited another laugh.

When he glanced back, she'd pushed the strap down and below her pants' waistline. "I guess that's okay. I could tighten it, and it could double as a girdle."

As if she needed that. As if she wasn't enticing enough already.

"I feel like a crazy person," she said.

Her words brought Garrett's thoughts and eyes back where they belonged. "If you were crazy, you would make no effort to protect yourself, despite the stalker and the burglar. This doesn't make you crazy, it makes you sane."

She held his eye contact for a long moment, then nodded. "Okay. Okay, you're right. I'll try to get used to it." But she moved to take it off.

He laid his hand over hers on her hip. "What are you doing?"

"I don't need to wear it here."

"First, you want to get used to it. You just said that. Second, if someone were to break in, don't you want it with you?"

"But..."

He heaved a sigh. "Do what you want, but if I were you, I'd wear it around the house. Not when you're sleeping, but have it close by. Otherwise, what's the point?"

She studied him for a long moment, then collapsed on the sofa. "Fine. I'll keep it on. For now."

Until you leave. She didn't need to say the words out loud.

"Maybe we should revisit the idea of you moving back to the hotel."

He thought she'd shoot that down immediately, but she seemed to consider it. "He or she or...they were looking for something. I don't know what, but if there's some clue about my mother's whereabouts—"

"Is that what you think they're after?"

"What else could it be? If Marion Eaton was right, my mother killed a woman. Dad told me she got into some trouble and then disappeared, so I'm thinking she must have gone missing right after that happened. I mean, that day, that week? I don't know. Maybe they think I know where she is."

Her words tracked very closely with what Uncle Dean had said.

"Or maybe they think the answer is here at the house. If that's the case, then I need to be the person to find it, to do right by her as Dad asked. If they think *I* know, then moving to town won't do me any good. They'll find me there, whoever *they* are." She shook her head. "No. No, unless I leave town entirely, I don't see how moving to a hotel will do me any good. I might be safer—maybe—but I'd be exposing the house. I need to stay here and finish what Dad started."

Garrett regarded her a long moment. Her cheeks had more color than they'd had before, but her eye makeup was smudged, thanks to her tears. She looked somehow both exhausted and determined. "Would your father really want you to put yourself in danger?"

Aspen's eye contact faltered. "He's not here." She met his gaze again, shoulders squared. "I'm going to figure out what happened back then—and find my mother—and no intruder or stalker is going to stop me."

He wouldn't be able to talk Aspen out of her chosen course, which meant he would need to stick very, very close.

But first, he was going to find out exactly what his uncle knew.

CHAPTER FOURTEEN

Aspen's first thought as she came to awareness was that something was wrong.

But wrong wasn't the right word because she was warm and cozy and perfectly comfortable—except for her irritating need to visit the bathroom.

She opened her eyes to find she'd fallen asleep on the sofa.

In Garrett's arms.

No light came through the windows, and a glance at her watch told her it was just after four a.m.

She hadn't wanted to tackle the mess of her bedroom the night before, nor had she been eager to be alone. And maybe Garrett hadn't been eager to leave because he'd suggested they find a movie.

They'd grabbed the throw blankets and snuggled up together in front of the fire and the TV, where they started a nineties romantic comedy she'd watched a thousand times but he'd never seen.

She wasn't sure how long she'd been awake after that. Not long.

Shifting, she angled to look at Garrett. He was leaning

against the corner of the sectional, head resting against the cushions, breathing softly.

She wanted to go back to sleep beside him, where it was warm and comfortable and safe.

If he woke, he'd leave, and then she'd probably stay awake the rest of the night, however long that might be.

She closed her eyes and tried to drift off, but it wasn't happening, not now that she knew he was there.

He'd been so kind since he'd picked her up. Even his protectiveness, though it bordered on demanding, stemmed from his concern for her. And the way he'd held her when she cried. Laughed with her about the holster. Stoked the fire to make sure she was warm.

He'd started as her contractor and quickly morphed into a friend. Now, even that line was blurring.

She liked this man. She really liked him. Her feelings were far stronger than they should be for a guy who would only be in her life for a short time. Because she wasn't staying in Coventry, and he seemed as much a part of this town as the mountains and forests and lake.

With that thought, she shimmied out of his arms and headed for the downstairs bathroom.

She did her business, then wiped the smudged makeup from her face to remove the raccoon eyes. She still wore the holster, though it no longer felt as foreign as it had at first. She could get used to it. And having it with her did make her feel safer.

When she returned to the living room, Garrett was standing by the door.

"Did you like the movie?"

He laughed, the sound low and alluring, and she told herself not to step closer.

Her feet moved that direction anyway.

"I do love Billy Crystal," he said. "We'll have to try it again when we're more awake."

"It's a date."

Ugh. Why had she said that?

But he smiled and held his hand out.

She took it, and he pulled her in and wrapped his arms around her.

When she looked into his eyes, they were smoldering like the coals in the dying fire.

"Hey, you." His voice was low and rumbly. "Is this the part where we're supposed to toss out our see-you-laters and pretend like nothing's changed?"

"I didn't read the script."

"If there is one, we should use it for kindling."

Before she could come up with a witty response, he lowered his head and brushed a kiss across her lips.

An entirely different fire blazed to life.

She opened her lips to him, and he dove in, pulling her closer.

In all her life, she'd never experienced anything like it. It was the kind of kiss they wrote about in romance novels. The kind of kiss that shifted hearts and changed lives.

He was the one to end it, wrapping her more tightly in his arms.

She pressed her face against his soft shirt, and he rested his cheek on her head.

"Wow."

He'd said what she was thinking, so she added, "Yeah."

He backed away to look at her. His expression was open but shifted as his eyebrows drew together. "I probably should've asked already. Is there a boyfriend? You haven't said anything about—"

"No boyfriend."

"How can that be?" He looked equally pleased and confused. "Are the guys in Hawaii all idiots?"

Her laugh was short and loud in the quiet room. "I have some rules. I don't date tourists, and I don't date people I work with. Those two groups made up a large proportion of the men I met. There've been some casual dates, but nobody who..." *Who made my heart sing.*

That was what she'd always craved, but nobody'd ever come close.

Garrett definitely had her heart warming up its vocal cords.

"I still don't get it," Garrett said. "How does someone like you make it to thirty-one without finding a guy? I'm not complaining. I'm just saying—"

"Wait." She played back over what he'd said, then over all the conversations they'd had since they'd met. "How do you know how old I am?"

"Oh." His face, that expressive face, showed guilt as plainly as if it were tattooed on his forehead.

She backed out of his arms and waited.

"I don't know. You must've said it at some point."

"I didn't."

"Well, I mean... Somebody did."

"You were talking about me to somebody?"

"It's not like that. Your being in town is a topic of conversation, and—"

"And you've been involved in those conversations?"

He ran a hand over his short hair, messing it up and somehow making it look better. "It's not like that."

"What is it like, exactly?" Maybe the frustration rising inside her was irrational, but he was her only true friend in town. She'd trusted him. Had he been talking about her behind her back?

She was a novelty, and he had the best vantage point. Had

people been questioning him about her? What had he told them? She swallowed all those questions and went with, "Have you really had so many conversations about me with so many different people that you can't remember who told you my age?"

His Adam's apple bobbed. "It was my uncle, the day I asked for the furniture. He remembers your mother and when she disappeared."

"All this time, I've been trying to figure out what happened back then, and we could have asked your uncle? Or..." Something else, something horrible, occurred to her. "You knew, didn't you? About the bombing, and my—"

"No." He stepped toward her and took her hand. "I didn't know about any of that. My uncle told me there was a story, an ugly story. I tried to get more information out of him, but he had some sort of... He was short of breath and shaky. My aunt says it's been happening, these episodes. I didn't want to press him when he was in that condition, and I haven't seen him since."

It made sense. Except there was something in Garrett's face, something guarded, that made her nervous. Perhaps he felt guilty that he'd gossiped about her. Perhaps he felt guilty he hadn't told her about his uncle's connection to her mother already.

He ducked his head until she was looking in his eyes. "My uncle's going to the doctor tomorrow. Later today, I guess. I'm telling you the truth. It just threw me off guard when you asked me about it, and it took me a minute to remember where I'd heard your age." He rested his forehead against hers. "I'm sorry I didn't tell you Dean and I talked about you. I know you want to find out what happened to your mother, but my uncle means the world to me. I can't... I'm worried about his health." Garrett backed away to meet her eyes again. "I'm on your side, Aspen. You can trust me."

She wanted to, more than anything. Because if she didn't

have Garrett, she wouldn't have his friends either. She wouldn't have anybody.

More than that, she wanted to trust him because...because he was more than a friend. As crazy and impossible as it seemed, she could see herself falling for this man.

She stepped into his arms, choosing to believe him. After all, what did he have to gain by lying to her?

CHAPTER FIFTEEN

THE SUN WAS BARELY BRIGHTENING the winter sky when
Garrett parked, but a light was shining through the bottom floor
window of his uncle's house. As long as Garrett could remember, Uncle Dean had gotten up between five and five thirty and
started work. Today, it seemed, was no exception.

Rather than ring the bell and wake Deborah, Garrett used
his key to let himself in, went down the half flight of stairs, and
knocked on the wall leading to the shop.

Dean was leaning over his workbench sanding a table leg.
He looked up, his eyes widening when he saw Garrett. "What
are you doing here so early?"

Garrett stepped inside. The space looked just as it always
had. The pieces off to the side had changed over the years—
tables, chairs, cabinets, rocking horses, chests. His uncle was a
talented carpenter, well-known all over the state for his work-
manship. But though the pieces were always changing, the shop
looked just as it had when Garrett was a teen. A couple of work-
benches, shelves holding the tools of his trade. Though it was
quiet now, often the sound of one of his power tools would carry
up through the floorboards, weirdly comforting. A fine layer of

sawdust covered everything and filled the air with the scents of cedar and pine and oak.

His uncle gave him an appraising look, and his eyebrows lifted. "Did something happen? You look like you just rolled out of bed."

Garrett stepped closer, thankful for the gum he'd found in his truck. He winced at the thought that he'd kissed Aspen with morning breath.

She hadn't seemed to mind.

"Coffee?" Dean nodded to the one-cup maker on the small counter beside the sink, and Garrett started it brewing.

Dean went back to his task.

It'd always been this way with them. How many hours had Garrett sat in this workshop, watching his uncle work? It made it easier, somehow, to open up when Dean wasn't watching, just listening silently, bent over some project.

This man meant everything to him. Everything.

Which made this so much harder.

"Somebody was watching Aspen's house the other night."

Dean's hand stilled, but only for a moment before he resumed the tedious task of rubbing sandpaper against the wood, the sound rhythmic and familiar.

"It freaked her out enough that she bought an alarm system. I installed it for her last weekend."

"Good idea," Dean said.

"It went off last night."

Dean looked up at that. Waiting. The room, usually so peaceful, suddenly filled with tension. There was nothing Garrett could do about that.

"She wasn't home," he said. "Somebody broke in. Went through her stuff. Stole her laptop. I'm guessing it's somebody who wants to know what she knows about her mother."

Dean's eyebrows lowered.

"Do you know anything about that?"

Carefully, Dean set the sandpaper on his table and straightened. "Are you asking me if I broke into her house?"

"I'm asking you—"

"Are you really standing in my workshop at the crack of dawn to accuse me of going through that girl's things and stealing her laptop?"

Suddenly, Garrett was a fourteen-year-old kid again, desperate to stay on his uncle's good side, knowing that if Uncle Dean didn't want him, nobody would. Garrett's father would send him off to a faraway boarding school. He'd be all alone in the world.

Later, he'd tried to stay on Dean's good side because he craved his love so badly. Because he'd never had his father's, and he'd needed to know he mattered. That he was worth the trouble.

Garrett's hands got clammy, and more than anything, he wanted to laugh the whole thing off. Because Dean had given him...everything.

But Garrett had Aspen to consider.

"I'm not accusing you of anything." He kept his voice level. "I'm asking if you know something about it."

"I know I'm not the only person who wants to figure out what happened to Jane Kincaid."

"Okay." Garrett hoped Dean would say more. His coffee had finished brewing, and he added a little creamer and took a sip.

Dean asked, "Did you hear the story yet?"

"Aspen heard it last night from Marion Eaton. A total stranger. If I'd known it was so... If you'd told me, I could have told her myself. It would have been easier for her."

"And you're sure she didn't already know?"

The image of Aspen weeping on her couch, overwhelmed

and distraught at what she'd learned... "She had no idea. She was shocked. And when she told me, so was I."

Dean nodded but didn't seem convinced. Then his eyes narrowed. "What were you doing over...?" His voice trailed, and he gave Garrett another long look. "Is that why you look like you just woke up? Is that where you spent the night?"

"Not like that. She was nervous after the break-in. I slept on her couch." He didn't add that she'd been on the couch with him, that she'd slept in his arms. That would only muddy the already mucked-up waters.

"Why you? I mean... Good grief. Don't tell me you're falling for that girl."

"First, stop calling her *that girl*. She's a grown woman, and she has a name."

Dean flicked off the words, but Garrett wasn't finished.

"And second, so what if I am? She's beautiful and kind and—"

"All alone and wounded, and you're just the person to save her. Except she's not that bird you hit with the truck when you were learning to drive. You can't stick her in a box and nurse her back to health."

Garrett set his cup down hard, sloshing some coffee over the side. "It's not like that."

But Dean continued as if he hadn't spoken. "I get that there's something attractive about a woman who needs help, but people like Jane Kincaid—"

"Aspen is not Jane."

"—crush people. They draw them in and squeeze the life out of them and use them up. I know you think she's different, but what if she's not? What if she's just like her mother?"

"She's nothing like her mother."

"How would you know?" Dean tossed the words out. "You didn't know Jane, and you barely know her daughter."

"Jane Kincaid was mentally ill, and Aspen is perfectly sane."

"We thought that about Jane, and we knew her a lot longer than you've known Aspen."

Garrett glared at his uncle. Dean didn't understand.

He rounded the bench to where Garrett had perched on a stool and sat on the one beside him. He took a long, deep breath and blew it out.

"You're still going to the doctor today, right?" Garrett asked.

"Been trying to come up with a way to get out of it, but short of death, I think your aunt's determined."

"Those episodes you're having aren't normal. Better to figure out what's going on and deal with it than let it fester and get worse."

Dean grabbed his insulated mug and took a swig. "You and Deb are working from the same playbook."

Garrett sipped his coffee and swallowed. "Just to be clear, it never crossed my mind that you'd broken into her house. I know you wouldn't do something like that."

Dean nodded slowly. "Just to be clear, I know she's not her mother. Her father was a decent guy, and I have no doubt he raised her right."

Garrett was thankful for the words, but Dean wasn't finished.

"Problem is, mental illness runs in families. Maybe she's fine, but it's possible her kid could end up like her mother."

"You can't say that. You don't know—"

"That's not a risk I'd be willing to take. That's not the kind of life we want for you."

"Who's having children? I like her, yeah, but we're not—"

"Don't go there with Aspen Kincaid. You have to trust me on this, son. Even if she's sane... The world doesn't need any more people like her mother."

Garrett stood and dumped the contents of his coffee into the sink.

He wasn't going to discuss his love life—it was barely that—with his uncle. That wasn't what he came here for.

"Somebody broke into her house. I need to know who these people are who want to know what happened to Jane Kincaid."

Dean studied him a long moment.

Then he returned to his table, picked up the sandpaper, and resumed his work.

"That's it? You have nothing to say?"

"There's the family of the woman who died."

"Who?"

Dean glanced up. "The victim was Rachel Bradley. She was married to Norm Bradley, Bart's son."

Oh. That explained Bart's vitriol the other day at the restaurant.

"Her parents moved away a long time ago, but her sister is still in town. Rhonda. It's Patterson now, but the maiden name is Foley."

There were a lot of Foleys in town. They were almost as common as Cotes.

"If Rachel was a Foley," Garrett said, "then there'd be a lot of people in town who cared."

Uncle Dean shrugged. "I think most of 'em have let it go. But Rhonda and Rachel were twins. I'm guessing Rhonda would be pretty motivated to find out what happened to the woman who killed her sister."

Garrett had no siblings and couldn't imagine how difficult it would be to lose a twin—and in such a horrible way.

Dean continued. "After Rachel died, Norm lost custody of the kids to her parents. He was a drunk, used to beat up on Rachel pretty bad. Story was after she died, he started knocking around his son. So it was no tragedy that he lost custody.

Tragedy was when he drank himself to death after that. Rachel's folks took the kids out of state. Word is that Bart and Rhonda never saw them again."

Garrett plopped back in a chair, the heaviness of the story weighing him down. "Anybody else?"

"I imagine the people who owned the lumber company wouldn't mind seeing Jane Kincaid punished. Some of the stockholders are still in town. Her little stunt didn't just knock down their building, it set a blaze that took out an acre or more. Cost them a pretty penny."

"Anybody I know?"

"There were a few. The Sullivans."

"James's parents?" Surely James had nothing to do with any of this. He'd have been very young when all that happened. Did he even know about his connection?

"'Course they're dead 'n gone," Dean said. "There's the Christiansens."

"Seriously? Jeff's her lawyer." It was like a giant web that Garrett had known nothing about. "He was her father's attorney."

"Huh. Interesting. The major stockholders were out-of-towners. Don't know their names, but they're not around anymore."

"They could be interested."

Dean shrugged. "Point is, there're people who care."

That all made sense, but Garrett still didn't understand something. "Why do *you*, though? Why do *you* care what happened to Jane Kincaid?"

Dean turned the table leg over and rubbed the sandpaper along the opposite side.

A minute passed, two, and still he said nothing.

"Uncle?"

Dean looked up and met his eyes. "We were friends. What

Jane Kincaid did, it hurt all of us, your aunt most of all. Jane blew up more than just that building. She destroyed a lot of lives, and then she vanished. So yeah, I want to know what happened to her. Your aunt wants to know."

"Don't put this on Deborah. You're the one—"

"For her sake, son. I want to know what happened to Jane for Deborah's sake."

The look in Dean's eyes, the way he lowered his gaze back to his work, sent a jolt of suspicion through Garrett. For the first time in his life, he had the strong feeling his uncle wasn't telling him the truth.

CHAPTER SIXTEEN

A TERRORIST.

Aspen had hoped that Marion Eaton's wild claims about a bombing and a murder were exaggerated, or perhaps an outright lie.

She hadn't realized that she'd been harboring that hope until she sat in front of the computer monitor at the library the next morning. Thanks to her missing laptop, it was either the library or her phone, and she hated trying to read on her phone's tiny screen.

She'd searched for all the information she could find about the lumber company bombing thirty years before. Her fear that she'd have trouble digging up old articles turned out to be in vain. Not only had the story been covered in the local newspaper, it'd been picked up in news outlets all over the state and in both major Boston papers.

The articles claimed the bombing was the work of environmental terrorists.

And more than one reporter attached Aspen's mother's name to that label.

A terrorist.

Aspen's mother was a terrorist.

And a murderer.

Aspen felt sick to her stomach.

Everything Marion Eaton had told Aspen had just been confirmed, via multiple sources.

What occurred to her as she walked out of the library late Tuesday morning was that, if at any time during her childhood she'd typed her mother's name into a search engine, she'd have discovered this information.

It had never crossed her mind that her mother's disappearance had been part of a larger news story.

She was thankful, so thankful she hadn't learned this when she was in her teens or even her twenties. She wished she didn't know it now.

On the sidewalk in front of the library, she paused and looked up and down the street, trying to remember where she'd parked. It hadn't been that long since she'd arrived, but she felt off, confused, as if her body had been transported to a different time, maybe a different universe. How could the world outside the library still be the same as when Aspen walked in? Everything in Aspen's universe had shifted, and yet the world appeared exactly as it had before.

A hand slid around her upper arm, and she glanced up to see a man's face. Tall and handsome with salt-and-pepper hair and a strong chin. He seemed familiar, but she couldn't wrap her mind around him being there, or how she knew him, or why he was giving her that quizzical look.

"You seem a bit flummoxed."

She blinked a couple of times. How long had she been standing there?

"Brent Salcito. We met at church Sunday."

Right. The mayor. He'd been kind, even said something nice about Aspen's mother.

Concern was etched in the lines around his eyes. "What do you need? Water? Maybe something to eat? We could go to The Patriot."

But she'd see James there, and maybe others she knew. Worse, she might see people who'd known her mother.

Perhaps sensing her hesitation, Brent nodded toward the corner. "Let's walk." He led her around a corner and up a short street to the next block. There, she recognized the old house with the round sign hanging over the door.

"How about Cuppa Josie's?" Brent said. "This time of day, it's probably pretty empty."

The thought of having a conversation with somebody who knew her mother as something other than a domestic terrorist sounded good to Aspen, so she nodded.

Brent kept his hand on her arm, a gentle touch she appreciated, for the two blocks to the coffee shop. Was he worried she'd collapse? She wasn't usually so fragile.

As he'd guessed, the place wasn't crowded. A clock in the shape of a teapot behind the counter told her it was not quite eleven o'clock. The woman there, a slender brunette with big brown eyes and long hair pulled back into a ponytail, nodded at Brent, then smiled at Aspen. "Good to see you again."

Aspen had only been in the shop once, her first morning in town after she'd stayed in the hotel. The barista—or maybe she was the proprietor—had a good memory for faces. Aspen attempted a friendly expression despite the emotions roiling in her belly.

"Where is she?"

The words came from behind. Aspen spun to see an older woman. Based on the light gray hair and wrinkles, she was probably in her sixties, maybe older. Her arms were crossed over a dark gray velour tracksuit, her coal-dark eyes glaring.

"Nobody wants you here," the woman said.

Aspen blinked. Everything in her wanted to shrink and disappear. But she hadn't done anything wrong. Instead, she pushed her shoulders back. "I don't believe we've met. You must have me confused with somebody else."

"I know exactly who you are. Where's your mother?"

Brent Salcito shifted beside her. "Now Rhonda, there's no need to make a scene."

The woman's gaze barely flicked to the mayor. "Tell that to my nieces and nephew, who grew up without a mother because of her."

Brent said, "Not because of—"

"Who are you?" Aspen probably shouldn't have cut him off, but after everything she'd just read, she understood this woman's anger, even if it was misplaced.

"I'm one of her many victims. The day your mother blew up that building, I lost my sister. My twin. I want to know where she is. Now."

"Truly, I have no idea. I have no memory of her."

"Your father knows where she is. I don't believe for one second that she didn't go straight home that night. He hid her somewhere, and then, when the dust settled, he left town."

"He didn't know where she—"

"That's a lie. That's why he's been hiding out all this time. Disappeared, just like her. He probably stuck her in some mental institution. She might be crazy, but she needs to face her crimes."

"My father didn't hide out." Aspen worked to keep her voice level, thanking God the coffee shop was nearly empty. The few patrons who were there had turned to watch the scene. "He simply moved away."

"Where to, then? Where is he now? Why hasn't he ever had the nerve to show his face here?"

"That's quite enough," Brent said. "Rhonda, you need to—"

"She can answer the question." Rhonda glared at Aspen. "Unless she has something to hide. Unless she knows exactly where her mother is."

Aspen laid a hand on the mayor's arm to keep him from interrupting. The sooner she responded, the sooner they'd be finished here. "My father wasn't in hiding. He never changed his name." Though, to be fair, they'd always had unlisted phone numbers. Now she knew why. "We moved to Hawaii when I was a little girl. He was a business owner and an upstanding member of the community."

"Give me his number, then. I wanna have a chat with him."

"Unfortunately, he passed away a year ago." Considering all she'd learned and dealt with that day, Aspen was proud of herself for not shedding tears with the words. "He always said he believed my mother was dead, and there was no indication in his will or any of his papers that he knew where she was. I'm sorry, but I can't help you."

"You can help. Get out of this town."

"That's enough." The pretty barista had come around the counter. She held out a cup of coffee. "Mocha cappuccino, just like you like it. It's on the house today."

Rhonda's gaze flicked around the room. She accepted the offering.

"I'll look forward to seeing you tomorrow," the barista said, an implicit suggestion that she'd seen enough of her today.

After one final glare sent Aspen's way, Rhonda spun and left.

The rest of the customers averted their glances, but Aspen knew what they were thinking. The same thing she was—that she never should have come to Coventry.

~

THIS COFFEE SHOP had once been a home, and the owner clearly hadn't done much remodeling aside from adding the counter and glass case filled with pastries. The room where Aspen waited had a small fire flickering in a fireplace. Brent led her past a couple of empty café tables to an upholstered chair near the hearth. Only when she felt the heat did she realize how cold she was.

While he ordered, Aspen took a few deep breaths, trying to come to terms with everything she'd learned and heard that day. The fact that people actually suspected her father of having hidden her mother for all those years...

If only that were the case. Surely Aspen would have learned the truth at his death. If her mother were in a mental institution somewhere, somebody would have had to be responsible for her.

No, Dad wouldn't have done that. He wouldn't have protected her from facing the charges. He'd have trusted the justice system.

"Here we go." Brent set two steaming mugs on the small table between the chairs and walked away again.

She lifted hers and sipped, then relaxed into the well-worn fabric. She'd asked for a caramel macchiato, and this one was good. With the coffee and the flickering fire, despite everything, she started to feel like herself again.

Brent returned with two plates, which he set on the table between them before taking the adjacent seat. "You looked a little green. I thought food might help."

She would have refused if he'd asked, but as the scent of the warm cinnamon roll and—was that a blueberry muffin?—reached her, she realized she was hungry. "Which one's mine?"

"Whichever you want."

Too difficult to choose. She cut each in half, shifted them so each plate had a portion, and lifted one of the plates for herself. She cut off a bite of the cinnamon roll and ate it.

It was delicious.

Brent hadn't taken his pastries or sipped his coffee. Instead, he watched her, a small smile on his face.

"Thank you," she said. "You know that woman?"

"She hates me, too, if that helps. Apparently, the traffic is my fault. And also, she's against taxes of all kinds. I'm not sure how she thinks wider roads can be built without tax money."

"I guess you deal with that kind of thing all the time."

"Not exactly *that* kind of thing, no. Nobody's ever demanded I leave town, though I wouldn't put it past some people if they thought I'd do it. But yeah, I'm used to some people not liking me."

"I can handle being disliked, but having the whole town hate me—"

"Not the whole town," he said. "People who hold grudges tend to do so loudly." He sipped from his mug. "Josie's good at coffee."

"The barista?" At his nod, Aspen said, "It is good. Maybe not as good as Kona coffee—"

"Ah. You're one of those." His eyes twinkled. "A coffee snob."

She let out a short laugh. "Probably. But this really is good." She sipped again to prove her point.

He was fatherly, seeming almost indulgent as he sat beside her, tender and kind. When he set down his half of the muffin and reached for his drink, she caught sight of a scar across the bottom of his palm.

"That looks like it hurt," she said, nodding to it.

He regarded it a moment. "That's what I get for trying to slice a tomato without a cutting board."

"Ouch." She didn't know his politics, but she could see why people voted for him. He felt trustworthy and gentle.

When she'd eaten as much as she wanted, she set the plate down.

"What had you so discombobulated when I ran into you outside?"

"I was looking at old articles about...what happened. With my mom. And that lumber company."

Brent looked pained as he leaned forward. "I'm sorry. That must have been very difficult."

"Surreal. Dad told me she got into some trouble and disappeared. He never said anything about..."

"Your mother was an amazing woman. She was passionate and beautiful, and she loved the forest. She loved the earth." He smiled at Aspen. "And she loved you, very much."

She was thirty-one years old, and nobody had ever said that to her. Not even her father, though until that moment it had never occurred to Aspen that he should have.

"You were the driving force of her decisions," Brent said. "To be fair, her decisions weren't the best. What she did..." He blew out a long breath. "I wish I'd been there. I wish... I had no idea what she was planning. If I had, I could have talked her out of it. What she did was wrong. So wrong. But her heart was pure. She only wanted to save the forest from a company she felt wasn't treating it well."

"Was she right?" Aspen asked.

He shrugged. "At the time, a lot of people thought so. They'd been fined and claimed to have cleaned up their act, but I believed, like Jane, that they would slip back into their old ways when nobody was looking. In retrospect... You know how it is when you're young. We were barely twenty years old, and so confident. Cocky. And stupid. That lumber company is still in business today, and as far as I know, they follow all the rules. So maybe we were wrong." He shrugged. "But your mother was sure, and she was going to save the forest for her daughter, no matter what it took."

Aspen wondered if Brent's words were supposed to make her feel better. But how could knowing she'd been the motivation for a bombing that had led to a woman's death be any kind of comfort?

"What you read about your mother this morning," he said, "That's true. I wish I could tell you it was all a big mistake, a misunderstanding. But Jane did what the papers say she did. She got it in her head something needed to be done, and she did it. I'm sure your father told you—and the articles, probably—that she suffered from mental illness. As far as I know, she never sought help, though we all tried to convince her to. It got to where she simply couldn't think rationally."

He paused as if waiting for Aspen to contribute something to the conversation, but what was there to say?

Brent continued. "So what she did, she did. That's true. But there were other things about your mother that were also true. Equally true."

"Like?"

"She was charismatic. People who met her remembered her, and people who remembered her liked her. She could stir up a crowd and get them laughing or crying or...or whatever she was feeling. It was amazing to watch. She loved people. She never forgot anybody. I remember once we were at school, and she saw this little slip of a girl. Mousy hair, glasses. The kind of person nobody noticed. I certainly hadn't. But your mother had been in a class with her. She walked right up to her, called her by name, and gave her a hug. She asked her about a research project and then listened as if it were the most interesting thing she'd ever heard. I swear, when that girl walked away, she looked like she'd grown a foot taller. That's how your mother was. That's the kind of impact your mother had on people."

How could the person he described also have killed a woman?

Where had it all gone wrong?

"If things had been different," Brent said, "she could have run for president."

Aspen's disbelief must've shown in her expression because he added, "I'm serious. We used to joke that she was the female version of Bill Clinton. Attractive and charismatic and smart. She was amazing."

Aspen worked to fit Brent's description of Jane Kincaid in with everything else she'd heard. She was getting a picture of the woman who'd birthed her.

"It seems like you and my mother were very close."

He leaned back in his chair, nodding once.

"How long did you know her?"

"I met her when she and her family moved here. We all went to Plymouth State together."

"Who is *we all*?"

"Oh, just some old friends."

Aspen wanted to ask for names, but something else occurred to her. "Mom was in college, but she and my dad were married, right?"

He nodded, but she saw tightness around his lips.

She'd hit on something, something important.

"Dad never talked much about their relationship, so I don't know their story. Were you and my dad friends too?"

Brent's focus had hardly moved from her face, as if talking to Aspen were the only thing that mattered. Now he shifted his attention to the fire and didn't look at her for a long time.

"I take it by your silence the answer is no. So you and my mother were...?"

When he looked at Aspen again, she saw pleading in his eyes. He leaned close and lowered his voice. "First, this has to stay between you and me. Talking to you about this... I'm the mayor. I'm not sure if you knew—"

"I heard."

"I have a reputation. A business and a family. People know I knew your mother, but most don't know the extent of our relationship, and I'd like to keep it that way."

He seemed to be waiting for her to say something, so she nodded. "I'm not here to ruin your life. I just want to find out what happened. I need to know."

"Why? Why does it matter now?"

It was a good question. The obvious answer—that her father had sent her there—wasn't the real one, not anymore. Yes, Aspen had come to Coventry because of Dad's last words. But it was more than that now. Now that her father was gone, Aspen had nobody in the world. She felt...adrift. Like she no longer had anything solid to hang onto.

Without her father... Without her dad's restaurants and her job, without her home back in Kona, Aspen didn't know who she was. She'd always been a daddy's girl, but she'd had a mother too. She didn't feel like she could ever truly know herself until she knew where she'd come from.

She didn't say any of that to this virtual stranger. Instead, she said simply, "She was my mother."

He studied her another few moments before he seemed to make a decision. "I knew your father, of course. Coventry is a small town, and we were in the same grade. You know how they call people 'old souls'?" At her nod, he said, "Your dad was an old soul. Always so mature and grown-up compared to the rest of us. He was a great kid. But there were goofballs, and there were normal kids, and then there were people like your father. Smart and mature, even from a young age.

"Your mother had a thing for him. I don't know why. Your mom was so vibrant, and your dad... Don't get me wrong, he was a great guy. He worked full time in the summers and put away all his money to cover his tuition. But his family barely got by. I think your grandfather worked at the factory."

He seemed to be waiting for her to confirm or deny that, but she had no idea. Nobody'd ever talked with Aspen about their time in Coventry.

"He made great grades. He took life seriously. He was just a nice, normal, sort of boring guy."

"Not good enough for my mom." Aspen heard the irritation in her voice but didn't temper it. "Is that what you're saying?"

"Just...different. That's all."

Aspen sat back and waited for him to continue.

Brent gave her an apologetic look. "I'm not doing a very good job of this. Everybody liked your mother. I'm pretty sure most of the guys at Coventry High were half in love with her. For whatever reason, your mother liked your dad. She dated lots of guys, but your dad never asked her out. I always figured he knew she was out of his league. And then something happened in the summer between our freshman and sophomore years in college. I'd been gone for an internship, and when I came home, she was pregnant with his kid. By Christmas, they were married. You were born a few months later."

Dad had married Mom because she was pregnant? Had they loved each other at all?

Today was a day for revelations, but with every one, Aspen felt she had more questions, many of which would never be answered.

"Your mom didn't want to give up school," Brent said, "so your father quit and got on full time with the construction company. His parents kept you while he worked. That fall, your mom went back to class as if nothing had changed."

Aspen tried to fathom what that must have felt like for her father, to give up college when he'd worked so hard to go. To suddenly be saddled with an infant when his wife didn't seem to care.

Meanwhile, Mom was off at college. And so was Brent.

"I take it you continued to be friends with my mother after they got married."

He was looking at the flames when he nodded. "We were more than friends. She loved you, but she didn't like being married. She didn't want to be tied down. Truth is... Maybe the other guys we graduated with were *half* in love with her. I was completely in love with her."

"You were having an affair."

He met her eyes again. "It's not something I'm proud of. Certainly not something I run around telling people."

"Of course not. Your girlfriend murdered a woman. I'm sure you did your best to keep that on the down low."

He winced, but Aspen wasn't sorry.

Brent's shoulders drooped. "I have nothing to gain by telling you any of this, Aspen. This story only makes me look bad." He exhaled a long breath. "Your mother loved you, and I loved her. I'm trying to be honest with you. I wanted your mother to divorce your father. He was a nice guy, but he wanted her to fit into a box. To stay home and take care of the baby."

As if that was too much to ask of a new mom.

"Your dad couldn't give her the life I could. The life I wanted to give both of you. My parents had money. My dad built a business for me to take over when I graduated. I could offer her much more than your father could. Meanwhile, your dad wanted her to give up on her dreams and forget her passions. He wanted her to be somebody she could never be."

That didn't sound like the father Aspen had known her whole life. Maybe Brent was trying to justify his own behavior. Or maybe Dad had changed over the years. Aspen guessed that the truth was much more complex than Brent was making it out to be.

"Jane could never have been happy in that role. Your dad didn't understand her."

"But you did."

"God help me, I did. I understood her, and I loved her for who she was, and I would have married her in a heartbeat if he hadn't beaten me to it. It was just a matter of time before she left him, and then the two of us"—he nodded to Aspen—"the *three* of us would have been together. It was selfish. I realize that now. But we were young and in love, and the fact that she had a husband...?" He shook his head. "I'm married. I have a wife I love and three kids of my own, and I realize how stupid I was. How incredibly self-absorbed your mom and I both were. But at the time..."

At the time, Aspen hadn't mattered to this man or her own mother. At least Mom had the mental illness to blame.

"I thought you'd want to hear a different viewpoint," he said. "I can see I've only upset you more, and I'm truly sorry for that. I think that, if she'd seen a psychiatrist, if she'd gotten on medication, maybe she would have left your father. Maybe she and I would have..."

He must've read the horror on her face. He shifted gears.

"Or maybe she would have stayed with your father, and they'd have made it work. I know he was trying very hard. I can tell you one thing. Your mother would never have set off that bomb if she'd thought there was somebody in that building. And now I've taken up enough of your time. I didn't mean to upset you more." He started to push to his feet.

"Wait."

Seeming wary, he settled in the chair again.

"From the articles I read, after the bomb went off, the authorities immediately started looking for her."

"She'd made so many threats—"

"But nobody ever saw her again. She just vanished. What do you think happened to her?"

He took a long time answering. Finally, he said, "If your mother were still alive, I'd have heard from her. Again, I'm not proud of this, but if she'd contacted me, I'd have done everything in my power to protect her. She never contacted me." Brent hung his head so long that Aspen feared he wouldn't continue. But then he looked up and met her eyes. "I looked for her. I looked everywhere I could think of, everywhere we'd ever been together, everywhere we'd ever talked about going. I searched for her for months."

Aspen didn't speak, just waited for Brent to answer the question she'd asked.

"I think she heard about the woman in the building, and it destroyed her. I think she went somewhere remote, somewhere nobody would ever find her, and committed suicide. Either that or..." He pressed his lips and swallowed hard. "There's only one other option I can think of, and I hesitate to say it."

She couldn't imagine what he could add that would be worse than what he'd already told her.

But then he said it, and it was so much worse.

"Or your father found out what she did, and he killed her."

CHAPTER SEVENTEEN

THIRTY YEARS AGO.

They were six weeks out from the incident the next time they met. The Crusader was empty-handed when she followed the Builder across the dark bar to their table.

The Planner wasn't happy. He glared at the Crusader. "You said you would bring the things."

"She did," the Builder said. "They're in my car already."

He relaxed as another piece of his plan clicked into place. "You have everything you need then?"

The Builder nodded, plopping into the chair.

The Crusader sat but fidgeted, eyes bright, smile fixed in place. She'd been like this for weeks. Ideas flying, not that they made much sense. Her grasp on reality seemed to be slipping.

He worried.

When this was all over, he'd insist she see a psychiatrist. He wasn't sure what was going on with her, though he had his suspicions. She wasn't crazy, just...unstable. But they had medication. She could get on something. Then she'd be fine.

He'd help her. He'd stay with her and protect her. He understood her far better than her husband ever would.

"The wrench even has a little bit of his blood on it from when he was fixing the car last weekend." The Crusader practically bounced in her chair. "No question they'd be able to trace it to him."

"That's not the goal," the Builder said. "We just want to convince him to establish your alibi."

"I know, I know. I'm just saying..." Gone was her reluctance to drag her husband into it.

It would be back, though. Her mood would swing in the other direction. Sometimes it swung too far. The Planner had seen that side of her too. Dark days when she refused to leave her house.

The medication would help that too.

After they did this, her husband wouldn't want anything to do with her. He'd quit pretending their marriage could work. He'd take the kid and leave.

And the Planner would have her all to himself. He would take care of her without putting all the demands of motherhood on her. He would protect her—from others and from herself. He was exactly what she needed.

"There's one more thing you need to do," he said. "You need to establish a place. Someplace where, if you ask him to meet you there, he'll know exactly where to go, and he wouldn't question you too much. Someplace out of the way, remote."

"Like Ayasha Point?"

"No." He took a deep breath for patience. "It has to be someplace you can drive to. You can only hike to Ayasha Point."

"Right. Right. I see, I see."

The Planner and the Builder shared a look. Could she hold it together for six more weeks?

He would hold her together if he had to.

"I was thinking maybe up past where they're building those new condos," he suggested.

The Crusader's eyes brightened. "Yeah, yeah, yeah. There's a view."

"Exactly."

"Okay, okay." Her head bobbed. "We'll have a picnic. I'll pack sandwiches and wine and something for the baby. I have the perfect plaid blanket we can sit on. It'll be nice. We'll call it our place. We'll kiss."

The Planner forced a smile. "Whatever you think will work."

"I'll do it. It'll be fun."

He kept his face neutral, even if the thought of her creating a romantic spot for herself and her husband sent red hot jealousy through his veins. He'd imagined them going there to discuss their failing marriage.

Her way would work too. The Planner could be flexible.

She had to do this to keep herself out of prison.

Whatever it took. When it was done, her husband would drop her, and she'd realize she'd never needed him to begin with.

It would all work out. They just had to stick to the plan.

CHAPTER EIGHTEEN

ASPEN'S CAR was in the driveway when Garrett arrived at her house that afternoon. Since she'd finally trusted him with her key, he'd already been by once to unload the things they'd purchased the day before. Then he'd returned to his condo to get the tools he'd need that hadn't fit in the truck the first time around.

He jogged up the walk, and, after knocking to announce himself, propped open the glass storm door and pushed open the other door into the room. It was a mess, from two-by-fours to sheets of drywall, from new toilets to floor tile. He was about to announce his presence when he caught sight of Aspen bent over a five-gallon bucket of paint. She seemed to be trying to lift it. "Hey, don't—"

"I can't live like this." She let the paint bucket tip back to the floor with a thud.

"No, I know. I was—"

"You can't just leave all your crap in the middle of the living room." She stood to her full height—which still left her about six inches shorter than he—and glared. "This is unacceptable. I come home to find my house in total disarray, you nowhere in sight, probably off to get lunch. You seem to have zero regard for my property. You need to get this taken care of and taken care of right now."

Hot rage rose from the very center of his being.

He would not have orders barked at him as if he were a naughty child. Her words, her attitude, brought back too many memories of his father's demands. The more Dad had asked of Garrett, the less he'd done.

When his dad demanded that Garrett shovel the driveway by hand—despite the snow-blower in the garage—he'd piled all the snow right behind his father's sedan and then took off for a friend's house.

When his dad demanded that Garrett make better grades, he'd quit studying altogether.

When his dad demanded that Garrett stop hanging out with losers, he'd befriended the neighborhood troublemaker. They'd broken into houses, cars, and eventually a video game store.

He'd nearly gone to juvenile detention for that.

Which was how he'd ended up in Coventry.

Uncle Dean and Aunt Deborah never demanded anything of Garrett. When they wanted something done, they asked. They'd always been kind and respectful, and he'd always been willing to do whatever they needed.

Aspen had been respectful, too, until that moment.

A very small, very petty part of him wanted to leave everything exactly where it was and leave to make her accusations true. An hour or so at The Patriot would calm him down. And teach her a lesson in respect.

But even from where he stood on the opposite side of the large space, he could see tear tracks on her face.

"Having a rough day?"

"That has nothing to do with this." She bent again and tried to heave the bucket by her feet.

He slammed the door with his foot and rushed across the room. Gently, he slid his hand around her arm. "You can't move that."

"Why is it so...?" She looked up at him, and he could almost see the curse word forming on her lips. She managed to finish with "...ridiculously heavy? Who buys paint in five-gallon buckets, anyway?"

"General contractors," he said. "Painters. Handymen. It's significantly cheaper."

"It's impossible to move."

"Five gallons of paint weighs almost sixty pounds, Aspen. You can't possibly—"

"At my church there was an eight-year-old who weighed more than that." She propped her hands on her hips. "I used to lift him every Sunday."

The more irrational she sounded, the less angry Garrett felt. Something was very wrong, and it had nothing to do with the mess in her living room.

"Paint is dense, denser than water by about twenty percent." Maybe random facts and numbers would shift her focus. "I can see you lifting a sixty-pound child, but children are easier to maneuver. They have armpits, for one thing—convenient little handles. They're taller, so they don't have to be lifted as far. You can toss them over your shoulder or prop them on a hip, and they'll wrap their legs around your waist and their arms around your neck. They'll hold on. Their weight is distributed on your body. But you can't prop a paint bucket on your hip like a child. A paint bucket isn't going to hang onto your neck. Obviously, a can of paint is much less pliable—and helpful—than an eight-year-old. And of course there's the density issue."

Her lips twitched as if a tiny smile were trying to break through. "You sound like a physics teacher."

He shrugged. "I always liked science. Got it from my uncle. He was a chemistry major in college."

"Your uncle the carpenter?"

"I know. Go figure."

He held her eye contact, and she didn't look away. Seemed like a good sign. "Just so you know, I didn't go to lunch. I went back to my condo to pick up the rest of the supplies I'd need."

"I see. If you'd warned me or something..."

"I texted you. You said you were going to town, so I figured you'd get it."

"Oh." She swiveled and headed for the breakfast room. When she stepped back in a second later, her focus was on her phone. "It was on silent." She shoved it in her pocket and looked up at him. "I'm sorry."

"It's fine." He smiled to show he meant it. "We all have triggers that make us crazy."

"I am not crazy." All amusement drained from her face. She shoved her hands on her hips and scowled at him. "I am not crazy just because I like things to be in order. I'm not—"

"I didn't mean anything by it."

She blinked, then turned and marched into the other room.

He needed a redo. Would that he could delete the last five minutes and start over.

Instead, he set to unloading his pickup and moving everything to where it needed to be. Aspen had already given him the go-ahead to set up shop in the basement, so he hauled many of the items downstairs. The other things he moved into the office. He was coming down the hall, maneuvering the empty hand truck he'd used to move the paint, when Aspen stepped through the door and saw him.

"So that's the trick."

"If I want to not end up in traction, yeah."

"Smart."

Rather than risk another spat, he rolled it into the living room and then carried it down to the basement. Heaven forbid he should leave anything in her way.

He stopped in the center of the dark space and inhaled a deep breath. He blew it out with a prayer.

Whatever was going on with Aspen, it had little to do with her house being in disarray. He wanted to be a friend to her, but he also had a job to do, and he needed to do it well. He needed wisdom. He needed to concentrate on the work and not be distracted by the woman upstairs.

He'd brought a sandwich in his backpack, so he dug it out and munched it while he decided on a plan. He had everything he needed for the downstairs bathroom, so he was going to start there. She'd told him she'd prefer he only work in one space at a time, and he wanted to honor that request as best he could.

Lunch wolfed down, he headed upstairs to the bathroom and got started.

He'd removed the old toilet and ripped up the cracked linoleum floor when Aspen knocked on the open door. "Hey."

He looked up from where he was measuring to find she'd washed off the streaked makeup. She looked younger, more vulnerable somehow. "You okay?"

She leaned on the doorjamb. "I don't deal well with chaos."

"I'll keep that in mind, but home improvement projects are chaotic," he said. "They're messy and unpredictable. There's no way to avoid that."

"I know."

"I understand why you want to stay here, that you want to find out what happened to your mother, but if the work is going to be a problem—"

"I don't think I do."

He wasn't sure exactly what she meant, so he brushed off his hands and stood, waiting for her to continue.

"Want to find out what happened to my mother, that is. Maybe everybody's right. Maybe I should just let it go."

Maybe she should. Would that get people off her back? Would the burglar leave her be? Would his uncle no longer be curious about her activities?

Not that anybody else knew that was why she was there. So...no. As long as she was in town, people would be curious about her. Some more than just *curious*.

He lifted his water bottle and shook it. "I could use a refill."

She turned and headed for the kitchen.

He followed and was filling his bottle when he asked, "What happened when you were in town?"

"I spent about an hour reading articles about the bombing." Standing by the door of the dingy space, she related some of the facts and the evidence against her mother.

"The world seems convinced she did it." He tried to infuse gentleness in his voice. "Are you?"

She shrugged. "Either she set off that bomb or somebody else did an excellent job of making it look like she did."

But based on the defeat he saw in Aspen's eyes, he guessed she wasn't holding out hope for the second.

And then she told him about a woman who'd accosted her at Cuppa Josie's, a woman who accused her of knowing where her mother was.

"Who was it?" he asked.

"Rhonda something. The sister of the woman who was killed."

Dean had mentioned her that morning. "That must have been upsetting."

"Yeah. I was there to talk to Brent Salcito. He tried to intervene, but she was pretty determined to have her say."

And then after securing his promise to keep it confidential, she told him about her conversation with Salcito, who'd been having an affair with Jane Kincaid after Aspen's birth.

As if that hadn't been distressing enough news, he'd gone on to share his theories about what happened to Jane.

Either the woman had committed suicide, or...

"He actually said that to you?" Garrett didn't try to temper the anger in his voice. "That he thinks your father *murdered* your mother?"

Aspen nodded, face ashen.

Garrett tamped down a wave of fierce protectiveness, which had him wanting to hunt down the mayor and give him a piece of his mind, or maybe his fist. Instead, he opened his arms.

She stepped into them, pressing her cheek against his T-shirt.

He held her tight. "Considering Salcito's relationship with your mother, he's probably not the best judge of your father or your parents' marriage."

She tipped her head back to face him. "That's true."

"What did your dad say about your mom and their marriage?"

Aspen stepped away and leaned against the counter, crossing her arms. "Not much, honestly. When I'd ask about her, he'd smile and tell me I looked just like her. He'd tell me things about me that reminded him of her, though they were always the same things. I guess she was outgoing and had a lot of friends, and she was confident and knew her own mind."

"I can see that in you."

"Can you?" She shook her head. "In the past, maybe, but it doesn't seem like that these days. Anyway, he never said anything about their marriage. Today, Brent said that my mother loved me, and I realized that my father never told me that she did, never once."

Ouch. "Perhaps your father's definition of love was different from your mother's. Perhaps he just didn't understand hers."

Aspen shrugged.

"Maybe they just didn't understand each other. Maybe he didn't trust her love for you because..." He let his words trail before he finished the sentence. But Aspen knew what he was getting at.

"Because Dad didn't trust her love for him?"

"If what Brent said was true, then..."

Aspen blew out a long breath. "It's so frustrating trying to piece this together. It's like trying to complete a jigsaw puzzle with no picture and only half the pieces."

"Is there anybody else you could ask about this? Grandparents? Siblings?"

"My dad had a brother, but their family didn't live near here. They didn't know my mom well, and what they knew, they didn't like. Though they never said that to me, my cousins weren't so careful with their words. I don't know that I'd trust their impressions. And we were never close to my mother's parents."

"Are they the ones who live in Florida?"

"They're in North Carolina. They moved here when Mom was a senior in high school, but they only stayed a year before they moved away again. I guess my grandfather was in hotel management, and he got transferred a lot. My understanding is that they weren't living here when Mom and Dad got married. Dad didn't keep in touch with them. So, I guess I could ask them, but..." She shrugged.

"Maybe they wouldn't know much about the marriage either."

"And my dad's parents hated my mother. I mean, they never said that to me, but they didn't have to. So could I trust anything they told me? I don't know anybody who would be able to give me an unbiased opinion."

"Maybe you could get all their opinions and weigh them against each other."

"Or maybe I should just let it go. My father wasn't a killer. Brent Salcito can't be right about that."

"If Brent thought it, then I wonder if your father was a suspect in her disappearance."

"Huh. I hadn't thought of that."

"Can you get the police reports, or maybe talk to someone who investigated?"

"That's a good idea. And, you know, people tell me she had a lot of friends. Maybe I should figure out who they were. There have to be some who are still around, don't you think?"

"Seems likely." She could talk to Dean and Deborah, but Garrett didn't think they'd want him telling Aspen about their friendship with Jane. In fact, based on the conversation he'd had with his uncle that morning, he knew they wouldn't.

It felt deceitful, keeping that information from Aspen. But he couldn't betray his family.

He hated being in the middle, feeling like he had to choose.

"Thank you." Aspen stepped back toward him.

He hugged her. "I didn't do anything, really. Just listened." Guilt wrapped itself around him, almost as tangible as the feel of Aspen in his arms.

"You did more than that. Dad told me another way I'm like my mom. He said she had to express every thought before she knew what she was thinking. She was an external processor, and I'm the same way. Used to drive my father crazy. He'd want to sit quietly, and I'd babble about everything that happened to me all day long. He'd say almost nothing, just nod along. And by the time we were finished, I'd have some clarity." Her expression turned darker. "Is that weird or...crazy? I never thought about it, but maybe it's a sign."

Like a flash, he remembered all the times she'd used that word. Crazy.

She'd asked if it would be *crazy* to remodel the entire house.

She'd worried that buying the nicer used sofa would be a *crazy* decision.

When they'd been talking about her wearing her handgun, she'd said she felt like a *crazy* person.

Earlier that day, it'd been Garrett who'd used the word, suggesting the messy house had been a trigger that had made her...

Crazy.

And his use of the word had made her...

He wasn't going to say it.

How many times had Aspen wondered if she was like her mother? How many times did she second-guess her decisions for fear of it?

He took Aspen's upper arms and set her away so he could get a good look at her face—and she his.

"Aspen Kincaid, you are not crazy. You're one of the sanest, most rational people I know. You might be like your mother in a few ways, but you have a sound and ordered mind."

"I know." But when she blinked, a tear dripped down her cheek.

"And your mother wasn't 'crazy.' I don't know what she had, but it seems pretty clear that she suffered from a mental disorder caused by a chemical imbalance. That word... We need to stop using that word." He was going to eradicate it from his vocabulary permanently.

She said again, "I know."

"I'm not sure you do," he said. "But I assure you, whatever mental illness your mother suffered, she didn't pass it along to you." He pulled her close again, wishing he could convince her. Would she always wonder? Would others, like Uncle Dean, make it worse with their assumptions and theories?

Would Aspen always question her own sanity because of her mother's illness?

He held her close and prayed that God would help her see herself the way Garrett saw her, the way God saw her. As a beautiful, kind, generous, and determined woman.

A woman he was falling for more every moment.

CHAPTER NINETEEN

After Garrett started laying the tile in the bathroom, Aspen reapplied her makeup and headed out.

When she'd returned home from her coffee with Brent, she'd only wanted to light a fire in her fireplace, turn on an old movie, and escape for a few hours. The state of her living room had destroyed that notion, which was why she'd been so upset.

But Garrett had given her some good ideas to follow up on. She called the police department and asked to speak with Chief Cote, but he'd gone out of town for a couple of days. Frustrated, she left her name and asked that he call her when he returned.

With Brent Salcito's words fresh in her mind, she decided to see if she could track down some of her parents' old friends. If what he said was true, if there was any way her father had hurt her mother...

It couldn't be true. It couldn't.

But people changed. And sometimes otherwise good people could behave very badly. How had Garrett put it? Everybody had triggers that made them crazy. Maybe Mom had pulled one of Dad's. Maybe he had hurt her.

Aspen couldn't imagine. But she knew Dad hadn't become a

believer until after she was born. How could she know what he'd been like before he'd surrendered to Christ?

His last words echoed in her mind. *"I didn't do right by her... Do what I never had the courage to do."*

What had he done? What had he *not* done?

Aspen's fears dishonored the man who'd raised her so well. Who'd loved her so well. If there was any chance her father had killed her mother, then Aspen didn't want to know.

But Dad had asked her to come here, to uncover the truth. How could she disregard his last wishes?

She parked in front of the library for the second time that day. Though it was an older building, the inside was new and modern, brightly lit and surprisingly large for such a small town. She approached the circulation desk and spoke to a young woman with dark brown hair pulled back in a tight bun. All she needed were reading glasses to look like the quintessential fussy librarian.

"Do you have old Coventry High yearbooks?" Aspen asked.

"Of course. What year?"

Aspen gave the woman her parents' year of graduation, and they headed to a section in the back, where she saw a number of books about the history of Coventry and the surrounding area. The librarian found the year Aspen had asked for.

Aspen took the book, asking, "Any chance you have Plymouth State yearbooks as well?"

The librarian's lips shifted to one side. "Hmm, that's a good question. Let me find out."

After she walked away, Aspen slid into a chair at a table far from the other patrons and opened the thin yearbook. First, she found the senior portraits. She gazed at the one of her mother, which looked so much like the image Aspen saw in the mirror every day. Jane was younger here than she'd been in the framed wedding picture Aspen had kept at her bedside all her life.

Aspen snapped a picture with her phone, then found her dad's portrait.

Aspen's mother was a stranger to her, but her father... She traced the lines of his face, that strong jaw. He was handsome, no doubt. In his eyes was the man she'd known. Even in the photo, she saw his serious nature. But he was also good and kind. He wasn't much of a jokester, but he knew how to laugh. This photo showed none of the smile lines that would someday grace his face. It showed none of the grief the ensuing years would bring.

She snapped a picture, wishing she had an original. Maybe her grandparents did.

Turning the pages slowly, she peered at every image for more glimpses of her parents.

Dad had not only served as student body president, but he'd also played football and baseball. She saw him in multiple photos, most of them posed. There was one snapshot. He was in a crowd in what looked like a cafeteria. He wasn't the subject of the photo, just happened to be caught in the background. He was smiling at...

Jane Kincaid.

Her mother wasn't facing the camera either. She was seated at another table, looking off camera. Her father would have had a side view of her. Jane seemed to have no idea Dad was looking her way.

Aspen studied the two faces. Dad's focus on Jane. Jane's focus elsewhere.

But Brent had said Aspen's mother had a thing for him, not the other way around. So maybe Jane did know he was looking. Maybe she was pretending not to care.

Or maybe Aspen was reading way too much into a random snapshot.

She turned the page.

Though Dad was pictured in more of the organized pictures, Mom was pictured in more of the snapshots. In fact, Aspen counted no fewer than ten pictures of Jane in the thin yearbook. She was involved in zero clubs, but she seemed to know everybody.

Considering she'd only gone to the school for one year, that was impressive.

In more than one place, her mother was pictured with the same blond woman. Since the snapshots were not captioned with names, she searched the senior portraits to see if she could find the girl.

And there she was. Deborah Davis.

Aspen was just about to message Garrett—he'd probably get it, since he was connected to her Wi-Fi at the house—when a woman tapped Aspen on the shoulder.

She turned to find a much older version of that face smiling down at her. "Lana said you were looking for..." Her voice trailed, and she bent nearer to the yearbook. "What a funny coincidence. That's me."

"You're Deborah Davis?"

The woman straightened and gave Aspen her full attention. Then she blinked. "Oh, my gosh. You look just like your mother."

"She was your friend," Aspen guessed.

Deborah Davis held a pile of books in her arms. "She was my very best friend."

Aspen said, "Will you sit with me for a moment?"

Deborah set the books—oh, they were yearbooks from Plymouth State—on the table and slid into a chair. She could hardly keep her eyes off Aspen's face. "It's like seeing into the past." She reached out as if she might touch Aspen's cheek, then dropped her hand. "I'm sorry." Tears filled the older woman's eyes, and she shook her head. "Forgive me." She swiped them away with the back of her hand. "I'm a little off today. I just went with my husband to the doctor, and I'm still reeling from..."

"Everything okay?"

"It's his heart. But they say we can manage it with medication."

"Still scary, though."

Deborah sat back and took a deep breath. "Listen to me telling you our secrets as if you were your mother. Seeing you has definitely thrown me."

"Did you know I was in town?"

"Of course. Everybody knows you're in town." She patted Aspen's hand. "And here you are, looking at old photos of your mom. Is that why you wanted those?" She gestured to the college yearbooks. "Lana told me what year you wanted for Coventry High, so I guessed you'd want the next few for Plymouth."

"You guessed right. But honestly, Miss Davis—"

"Foley now. Missus. But you can call me Deborah."

"Deborah, I was trying to find old friends of my mother. I've heard so many"—she grasped for a word and settled on—"unpleasant things about her. I wanted to find somebody who knew her as a friend. I mean, I know she did a terrible thing, but..." Aspen wasn't sure how to finish the sentence. She wasn't sure how to ask the woman what she wanted to know.

"Your mother wasn't always who she became at the end. In high school, she was perfectly normal. Perfectly *sane*. She was vivacious. She had a big personality. She wasn't in school two days before everybody knew who she was. She was pretty, like you." Deborah studied Aspen a moment, then said, "Honestly, you're prettier than she was. I mean, you look like her, but her nose was a little longer, her face a little rounder. You have all her best qualities, and your father's too."

"That's very kind."

Deborah brushed off the words. "Even though your mother wasn't drop-dead gorgeous, she was incredibly attractive, in that she attracted everybody. She and I hit it off, and suddenly I became one of the most popular girls in school. Which was weird for me, let me tell you. I'd always been a wallflower. But I knew my own mind, and your mother liked that. She didn't like sycophants and fawners. And they flocked around your mother like pigeons in the park."

"What about my dad. Was he a fawner?"

"Ah-ha. You are definitely your father's daughter. Very insightful question. You knew him. What do you think?"

Aspen couldn't help the smile she felt creeping across her lips. This woman might be a librarian, but she had the temperament of a first-grade teacher.

"I suspect my father was neither sycophant nor fawner."

"You are correct. I wish I had a gold star." Deborah beamed as if her favorite student had won a prize. "He was probably the only guy in school who didn't fall over himself trying to get close to her."

"There's this picture, though." Aspen flipped through until she found the one of her parents. "It's the only one with both of them in it, and Dad's looking at Mom."

Deborah studied it, grinning. "Sure, he found her intriguing. We all did. She wasn't just new to town. She was like nobody any of us had ever met. People couldn't help but look at her. But that was as far as it went with Michael. He found her amusing like one might find a puppy amusing. He never gave any indication that he had feelings for her."

"And yet," Aspen said, "here I am."

Deborah shifted her attention to Aspen, and her grin faded. "Yes, well... Your father might not've been interested in your mother, but she was most definitely interested in him."

"Was that why? Was she the type to want what she couldn't have?"

Deborah's head tilted to one side, her eyes narrowing. "That's an interesting question, and I won't dismiss it outright. Your mother certainly wasn't accustomed to people not immediately loving her. But I think it was more than that. I think your father had something she knew she needed. Stability. Her family had moved countless times during her childhood, and she was a little wild herself. I think, deep down, she knew she needed somebody like your dad, somebody to keep her grounded."

"Dad was always like that, then. Grounded. Stable."

"Always. I knew him from kindergarten, and nothing rattled him. He was as firm as the mountains and as predictable as the changing seasons."

Aspen couldn't help the smile. "That's a very colorful description."

"I'm a closet writer." She winked. "I think all librarians are."

Aspen liked this woman.

And she liked that her mother had also liked this woman. It was a connection between them, however tenuous. "How did they get together, then? If Dad wasn't interested—"

"Oh, that's... that's a little harder to explain."

Aspen settled in her chair, trying to communicate without words that she had nowhere else to be.

Deborah sighed. "Truth is, they weren't *together*. They never dated. They weren't even really friends. In college, your mom and I got involved in the different clubs devoted to saving the environment. It was us and my boyfriend at the time, who I married after college, and another guy we went to high school with. And then, of course, a lot of other students at Plymouth. But the four of us were pretty tight.

"Your mom still had a thing for your dad. He'd pledged a

fraternity, and she went to every party they threw trying to get close to him. But he wasn't into that aspect of fraternity life."

Aspen would have guessed that.

"During our freshman year, Jane's parents moved away. She stayed with me for the summer. Your dad was back from school, too, working hard. We saw him out occasionally. At church, at The Patriot."

"The restaurant was there back then?"

"Sure. It's been in Coventry forever. And your dad went to the occasional party."

"He did?"

"He wasn't much of a drinker, but he had friends. He knew how to have fun."

That was true, though Aspen couldn't imagine him at a party with a bunch of teenagers. Of course, he'd been a teenager once too.

"Anyway, at the end of the summer, we were at one of those get-togethers, and your mother managed to get him alone. I don't know what happened. I do know that she fancied herself in love with him. A month later, she told me she was going to have his baby."

"Oh. You're saying...?" Aspen tried to imagine her father having a one-night stand. The man she'd known would never have done that, but he'd been young once, too, with hormones and desires.

Deborah patted Aspen's hand. "Your father was a good man, and your mother... Well, she was good in her own way. I loved her very much, but she could be determined. And she'd determined that she wanted your father. And when she wanted something, no power in the world could stop her, not even your dad."

So Aspen's mother had *seduced* her father?

Lovely.

And then another thought occurred to Aspen. "Did Mom get pregnant with me on purpose? Was she trying to trap him?"

Deborah lifted her shoulders and let them drop. "I never asked."

Which meant that the thought had occurred to Deborah too.

The more Aspen learned about her parents and their past, the more she wished she'd never come to Coventry.

Deborah took her hand and held on tight. "Your mother was a complicated person. By then we were starting to see signs of her mental illness. Getting pregnant with you wasn't rational. Marrying your father when the two of them had nothing in common—I mean *nothing*. That wasn't rational."

"Dad married her, though." And Aspen's father *was* rational. In a moment of weakness, he'd slept with Jane, but to marry her, after she'd seduced him and possibly gotten pregnant on purpose? That didn't make sense.

"For you, dear," Deborah said. "Your father married your mother because he knew that, if he didn't, he'd have fewer rights as a father. He admitted as much to my husband once, that he'd put up with Jane forever to protect you."

Put up with her.

"He didn't love her at all?"

"I think he did. He tried to, anyway. Once they were married, he did everything in his power to make her happy. He quit school to take care of you. He bought Jane everything she needed. He was a good, good man, and he tried his best. But to tame Jane was to tame a tornado."

Aspen gazed at the college yearbooks. She couldn't imagine learning anything in those that would rival what Deborah had told her.

"Can I ask you something else?"

"Anything."

"The other person from your high school, the man. Was it Brent Salcito?"

Deborah's eyes widened. "How did you know that?"

"He told me this morning that he and my mother were involved. That they were having an affair."

Deborah sucked her lips between her teeth and shook her head. "Brent was head-over-heels for Jane, but an affair? I don't think so. No, she'd have told me. She was a lot of things, but she loved your father. And she was fiercely loyal."

Deborah seemed so sure. But Brent...

"Why would he lie?"

"I think that most of what happened between them was in his imagination. She was kind to him, but she was kind to everyone when she was in her right mind. They spent a lot of time together. I think what he saw as romance she saw as friendship. I doubt it helped that my boyfriend and I were paired off, so when the four of us were together..." She shrugged. "But Jane didn't see it that way. I think he was just—"

"Delusional? Mentally ill, like Mom?"

"Not delusional. In love. Love can make us stupid sometimes."

Aspen didn't know if that was true. She'd never been in love and, based on what she knew about her parents, she wasn't sure she ever wanted to be.

She could maybe see it happening with Garrett. Eventually. If she were to stay in Coventry, she could imagine love growing between them. Not the kind of love her mother had for her father, though, planted and cultivated in her disturbed mind. And not the kind of love her father'd had for her mother, a love borne out of fear and obligation.

Aspen wanted no part of that kind of love.

But true love, the kind they talked about in romance novels.

The kind based on a mutual faith in Christ, on respect and honor, maybe.

Someday.

Considering everything she'd learned, the last thing she wanted was to stay in this town, where everybody judged her by her mother's reputation.

As much as Aspen liked Garrett, she needed to step away from him.

"How're the table and chairs working out? Dean said they were stable, but when I saw how beat-up they were—"

"I'm sorry. What?"

"Garrett did give them to you, didn't he? The table and chairs? Dean's been planning to strip them for years, but he'll never get around to it."

"Wait. You're Garrett's...aunt?"

"I'm sorry. How rude of me. I should have told you."

Garrett's aunt had been Jane's best friend, and Garrett hadn't thought to mention that?

Even that day, as they'd discussed people who might know about her parents' marriage, Garrett had stayed silent?

Aspen could only nod like an idiot. She set the yearbook she'd been looking at on top of the others. "You've given me so much information that I don't think I'll need these anymore."

Deborah studied her through squinted eyes. "I doubt Garrett knows your mother and I were friends. We've never talked about it."

Aspen nodded slowly. "Even with me back in town, and him working at my house?"

"Garrett and Dean have discussed that a little. But with Dean's health—"

"Oh. Right. Garrett said his uncle..." She took a deep breath. "I'm sorry. Of course you've all been distracted. And it's his heart? Have you told Garrett?"

"He's not answering his phone, which tells me he's probably up at your place."

"He is. I'll instant-message him and tell him to call you. He should get that if he's connected to my Wi-Fi."

"Thank you." Deborah stood, lifting the books. "I'll take care of these. I'd love to have you over for dinner sometime. I'm sure Garrett would like that too. Maybe later this week?"

"I'd like that."

CHAPTER TWENTY

Late Wednesday morning, Aspen followed the map on her navigation system toward a retirement community in Hooksett, just north of Manchester. She'd managed to locate the people who used to own her house and had decided to pay them a visit. Though she had donated most of the things in the attic to the thrift store, she'd held on to the photographs. Maybe they would appreciate having them back.

At the library the day before, she'd messaged Garrett about his aunt trying to reach him regarding his uncle. He'd responded with...

How do you know this?

Met your aunt at the library. She and my mother were best friends.

She'd waited while the three little dots on her screen danced. It took him a few moments to formulate his reply.

Dean told me this morning. I didn't think to ask him at the time if he'd mind if I told you. After our talk, I planned to ask, but he had that doctor's appointment.

That could be true. Probably *was* true. Garrett had no reason to lie to her.

She was still frustrated to have learned it from Deborah instead of him. It would have saved her a lot of time.

Not that the time had been wasted. Seeing her parents' yearbook, their faces as young people, happy people...

She wished Garrett had told her, but she understood his loyalty to his aunt and uncle.

A few moments later, the dots started dancing again, and it was a long time before five words came through.

I'm sorry, Aspen. Forgive me?

She stared at the screen, sighing. Garrett was on her side and had been ever since she'd arrived in Coventry. She had enough enemies. She certainly didn't need to start suspecting her friends. She'd texted, *Forgiven.*

They hadn't talked the night before—he'd gone to see Dean and Deborah before she returned home. But they'd messaged each other a few other times during the day, and all was well between them.

Now she parked outside a single-story building with white siding and green awnings over the windows. Before she got out of her car, she prayed for wisdom and insight. She wasn't sure exactly what she was looking for. These people had owned the house at the time of Aspen's mother's disappearance. The house had changed hands between then and when Dad had bought it, but maybe they'd remember him. Maybe her mother or father had had some connection to the house at the time.

Or, maybe this was a wild goose chase.

Aspen had needed to get out of Coventry, a drive to clear her head, and this had seemed the perfect excuse.

She'd sent the yearbook pictures of her parents to the drugstore to have prints made. With those and the snapshots from the attic, she trudged through the parking lot to the door. She was directed down a hallway where older folks, some in wheelchairs, others in armchairs with walkers at their sides, sat chatting.

Finally, she reached the proper door and knocked. When a man called out, "Come in," she pushed it open and stepped inside. It could have been a luxury studio apartment with the pale walls, dark and ornate crown molding, pretty curtains, and an area rug that looked both old and expensive over hardwood floors. Hospital beds ruined the effect.

"Hi. I'm Aspen Kincaid. Your wife and I spoke on the phone?"

She'd called the day before and tried to ask her questions, but the woman who answered had seemed confused. She told Aspen she didn't do well with phones and couldn't she spare a minute to come by and see them?

The man was seated on a chair beside one of the beds. His bushy gray eyebrows lifted. "Is that so?" He turned to the bed. "Polly, did you talk to someone on the phone yesterday?"

The head of the bed rose, and a woman came into view. She had white frizzy hair that was matted on one side. She peered at Aspen with brown eyes. "Do I know you?"

Aspen took a step closer. "We've never met."

The man stood and crossed the room. If Aspen had expected him to be feeble, she'd have been wrong. He seemed healthy and strong as he extended his hand. "Ron Barnett. This is Polly, my wife."

She shook the man's hand and nodded to the woman. "Thank you both for seeing me."

He ambled back to his chair, then gestured to one against the wall. "Pull that one up closer so Polly can hear you."

Aspen did. "I live in a house you used to own up in Coventry."

The man grinned. "I loved that place. Our family made memories there for, what was it, Polly? Twenty years?"

Mrs. Barnett said nothing. Her head was tilted to one side, and she wore a gentle smile.

Aspen took the snapshots she'd found out of her purse and handed them to him. "I was going through the attic and found these."

He took his time flipping through them, leaning close to his wife so she could see. They remarked on the kids, tossing out names and ages, places they'd gone and things they'd done.

The woman was alert and aware for a few moments before she seemed to slip away again, wearing that kind but vacant expression.

Mr. Barnett clutched the photos to his chest. "Thank you." He eyed his wife and shook his head. "She doesn't come back to me very often these days. Whenever she does, it's a gift."

Aspen felt her eyes tingling. This was what marriage should look like. This was the for-better-or-for-worse kind of marriage she wanted. This man, who seemed perfectly capable of taking care of himself, was here because his wife needed him, and he wanted to be at her side. Simple as that.

Would her father have loved her mother this way, if things had been different? Could her mother have loved him back?

Mr. Barnett set the photos on the other bed. "Was that why you came, to give us those photos? Or was there something else?"

"I was wondering if you remembered either of these people." She took out the pictures she'd had made and handed them over.

He peered at her father's first. "Who are they?"

"My parents. That's Michael Kincaid."

He studied the image a long time. "He doesn't look familiar." He looked up. "Should he?"

"He lived in Coventry when you did."

"It was a vacation home for us. We didn't know many of the locals."

After handing the photograph to the woman—she gave no reaction to it—he focused on the photo of her mother.

This time, Aspen caught a flicker of recognition.

It was a long moment before he spoke. "This is the woman who..." He looked up, held Aspen's gaze a long time. "This is your mother?"

She nodded.

"Do you know the story about the lumber company?"

"Yes. But, before my father died, he said something that made me think there was a connection to your house. He'd bought it, which was odd enough."

"Why would that be odd? It's a great house."

"Because we lived in Hawaii."

The man's eyebrows shot up. "Oh. Oh, I see. And he didn't tell you why?"

"No. He was hit by a car. I only had a few moments to speak to him before they intubated him. He didn't make it."

"I'm sorry to hear that." The man peered at the picture again. "The explosion happened in the spring. We'd been there that month, mostly because we needed to check in with the contractor, but he was an older guy. And that was before the explosion. And your parents would've been kids at that point, right?"

"They were twenty."

"I can't imagine how they could have been connected to us." He held the photos out to Aspen. "I wish I could help."

She took them, trying to keep disappointment from showing on her face, and stood. "I'm sorry to have intruded."

He pushed to his feet. "We love having company. You know it's bad when you eagerly anticipate a visit to the proctologist." He laughed at that, shooting a look at his wife.

She still wore that mild, empty expression.

Despite Aspen's chuckle, the man deflated a little. "Anyway, it was no bother. I hope you find what you're looking for."

Aspen made her way past the people in the hallway and out into the cold morning air.

There had to be some reason why Dad had bought that house, but Aspen was beginning to think she'd never figure out what it was.

CHAPTER TWENTY-ONE

ASPEN WASN'T ready to go back to Coventry. After she left the retirement home, she drove south to Manchester, ate a crisp salad with grilled chicken at a restaurant where not a soul stared at her, and then continued to a place Garrett had told her about, armed with all the information she needed for the countertop.

She walked rows and rows of granite slabs leaning against what must've been incredibly sturdy racks. She recalled Garrett's design for her kitchen, a design she'd instantly loved, and looked for a slab that matched it.

It was ridiculous how many shades there were. Maybe she shouldn't have been surprised. This was the Granite State, after all.

She finally settled on a creamy color with veins of light gray, taupe, and beige running through it. It would be perfect for the island, and there was enough to do the other countertops as well. She gave the clerk the specifications Garrett had printed for her, adding his phone number to the top of the paper. "If you have any questions, call him. He's in charge."

"You got it," the guy said.

She handed over her credit card, trying not to wince at the price. She'd get it back when she sold. She had a lot of problems in her life at that moment, but fortunately, money wasn't one of them.

That chore done, she headed for the mall, where she purchased a new laptop to replace the one that had been stolen. Then she headed for a department store and found a pair of flannel pajamas, some wool socks, and a knit cap, along with a few sweaters and turtlenecks. She threw in a pair of long underwear, just to be on the safe side.

One way or another, she was going to find a way to stay warm. Her furnace was doing a better job, but it still couldn't seem to raise the temperature in her upstairs to more than sixty-nine degrees, which was about five degrees colder than she wanted it.

With that in mind, she picked out a down comforter along with a microfiber duvet cover that looked cozy and warm.

With plastic bags hanging from her wrists, she headed for the door and stepped outside, shocked to see the sun already falling low in the sky. It wasn't even four o'clock. She wished she'd remembered how early it set. It would be dark by the time she got home.

Would Garrett still be there?

She hoped so. She needed somebody to talk to. Not just *somebody*, though. She needed Garrett.

She missed him.

Despite what she'd told herself the day before about not getting involved with him, she longed for him, her protective polar bear. He was a good listener who asked insightful questions and helped her think.

He was also fun to be with, kind and gentle and, despite the thing with his aunt and uncle, trustworthy.

She liked him more than she should, considering she was

leaving as soon as she figured out what happened to her mother —or gave up trying.

She made the two-hour drive back to Coventry. It was fully dark by the time she turned off the highway onto Rattlesnake Road. She'd driven home with Garrett after the burglary, but this was the first time she'd made this drive at night by herself.

Once she passed the condominium complex, it was dark. Not just nighttime dark, but zero-lights-anywhere dark. It reminded her of the highway that ran across the center of the Big Island, where the only light came from the billions of stars overhead.

Only here, the tall pines on either side of the road seemed to bend over her, blocking her view of the sky. The road twisted up the mountain. Though it hadn't snowed in days, she feared icy spots now that the temperature had dropped so low. She was going slowly, much slower than the posted speed limit of forty-five. Not that anybody would complain. She was all alone.

And then headlights appeared in her rearview mirror. The vehicle came up behind her, fast. Much faster than could be safe with all the hairpin turns. As it approached, she sped up a little, figuring the other driver was in a hurry. But she didn't dare go as fast as that driver.

She couldn't pull over because there was nowhere to stop. On the left, there were only trees. On the right, a drop-off just a few feet beyond the snowbank piled on the narrow shoulder. No, stopping wouldn't be safe.

As the car got closer, she feared it wouldn't be all that safe to stay on the road, either.

He bore down on her, and she gripped the steering wheel tightly. But the car slowed.

And then it careened into the left lane. She hit the brake, happy to let the crazy driver pass. But he didn't.

He swerved and clipped the back of her car.

She managed to keep her tires on the road, braking hard.

The other car sped ahead, braked, and veered into her again.

Her front wheels skidded off the pavement.

She tried to get back on the road, but the car was right beside her, blocking the way.

She braked. The wheels locked up. The car bumped over the snowbank and barreled toward the forest. A thick tree loomed ahead.

She yanked the wheel to avoid it, feeling sudden weight-lessness.

And then she crashed. She heard the sounds of crunching metal, felt the jarring motion. Her eyes were wide open, but everything went black.

ASPEN WAS SUSPENDED in her seat, the seatbelt the only thing keeping her from falling to the passenger door beneath her. In front of her, the airbag had deflated and hung toward the ground.

She couldn't see anything outside the car. Her headlights must've smashed against something because they were out. Or maybe...

Her dashboard lights were out as well. All the lights were out.

And the engine was off.

The world was silent.

She wiggled her toes and moved her feet in circles. Then she tested her hands, her arms. She touched her torso and felt no pain. No blood. The whole thing had happened so quickly. She'd be bruised the next day, but otherwise, she didn't think she was hurt.

Thank God she'd been going so slowly.

If she clicked off the seatbelt, what would happen? It felt like…like the car was angled downward and wanted to keep going. Something must've stopped it from rolling onto its back. She peered out the window and saw dark tree trunks against darkness beyond. Lots of darkness. Not more trees. It was open. Like…

Like she was at the top of a cliff.

Which, considering where she'd been, made perfect sense. She'd caught sight of the lake in the valley below when she'd driven this with Garrett. Of all the places to go off the road…

She angled forward to try to see how far she was from the cliff, but the car swayed, and she froze.

It was leaning on something. It had to be a tree.

Maybe a thick tree that could hold the weight no matter what she did.

Maybe a thin trunk that would bend over at any second, sending her and her small SUV hurling downward.

She had to get out.

She found the door latch and pushed, shocked when it opened easily. Rather than fight gravity by holding it open, she let it close again very gently to keep it from latching. She inched her feet beneath her, tucking the toes of her tennis shoes into the space between the center console and her seat. When she was sure she wouldn't fall, she unfastened the seatbelt and moved it out of her way, balancing on the console. Then she pushed the door open again.

The car swayed.

"Lord, just hold it steady, please."

She couldn't prop the door up while she climbed, so she wriggled into the gap between the door and the car. Its weight rested against her back and scraped as she pushed through. She ignored the pain.

The car shifted, eager to get past whatever held it in place.

She pretended it didn't matter. Pretended all was well. Managed to get her hips over the edge. She was just about to fall when she saw a flashlight beam in the woods. Somebody was coming.

Silently. And slowly.

She held onto the edge of the car and twisted out, flipping her feet toward the ground. She hung on by her fingertips, ignoring the pain of the car door resting against them. She dropped into the snow.

The car groaned and twisted.

Aspen crab-walked backward as it shifted.

Something snapped, and the car fell onto its roof and slid out of sight.

A moment later, she heard a crash.

And stared into the darkness at the empty spot where her vehicle had been moments before.

The person with the flashlight said nothing.

A rescuer would be calling for survivors. A rescuer would be running, frantic.

Whoever held that flashlight was no rescuer.

It was the person who'd run her off the road, coming to finish the job.

Aspen flipped to her hands and knees and crawled, staying low, moving toward the road above. Praying whoever was looking for her thought she had gone over with the car.

Except the trail she was leaving in the snow would prove otherwise.

It was just a matter of time before whoever that was caught up with her.

She was cold and wet and terrified. She had her handgun, but she'd much rather stay out of sight than have to use it. To be on the safe side, she paused long enough to slide it from its holster, undo the safety, and shove it in her pocket.

She reached the road and bolted toward town, keeping to the shadows on the far side. Whoever was after her would lose her tracks on the pavement.

But she couldn't remain exposed.

After what she judged had been about fifty yards, she leapt into the woods on the opposite side, trying to keep her tracks to a minimum. She climbed until she thought she was well-hidden and snatched her phone from her pocket. Thank God it was there. Thank God she hadn't tossed it on the console or left it in her purse.

She prayed for service. She'd just passed the condos, right? There could still be service here. She dialed 9-1-1 and rejoiced at the operator's voice.

She whispered, "I'm on Rattlesnake Road. Someone rammed into me and forced my car off the road. I think he's coming after me."

The woman got all the information and promised to send help.

But Aspen was ten minutes outside of town. How long would it be before the police arrived?

Would whoever held that flashlight find her before then? She needed a way out of the woods, and she needed it now.

She dialed again.

Garrett answered on the first ring. "Hey, how was your—?"

"I need help. I think someone's after me."

She told him what had happened.

"I'll be there in five minutes."

She slid her phone into her pocket. Maybe she shouldn't have called him. Had she put him in danger? But in that moment, all she wanted was off the mountain. And away from whoever was following her.

She kept low and silent and waited a few yards from the road.

Long minutes passed before the sound of an engine reached her. Headlights approached, the vehicle going very slowly. That had to be Garrett.

She bolted into the road and lifted her hands to get his attention.

He did a U-turn and stopped right beside her. The passenger door flew open. "Get in."

She'd barely closed the door when he hit the gas.

CHAPTER TWENTY-TWO

"I told you, he rammed into me. Twice."

Detective Pollard nodded at Aspen the way people do when they think you're insane but don't want to say so.

Garrett could feel fury dripping off her body like the snow from her parka.

They'd been at the police station for an hour at least. Aspen had told a uniformed officer her story no fewer than three times before this detective, a fifty-something man with a full head of curly black hair—brought them into a small conference room. The door was closed, but through the window in the door, Garrett could see a handful of officers going about their evening business.

"How long had he been following you?" Pollard asked.

"He hadn't been. He came flying up behind me."

"And then he just rammed you?"

"I thought he was trying to pass me, but then his car hit mine."

"Why didn't you just pull over?"

"Where? There's no shoulder. It's not like—"

"There's a shoulder on Rattlesnake." The man said the

words as if Aspen were crazy. Or lying.

"Not past the condos." Garrett had been trying to stay out of it. He had nothing to offer but moral support. But Pollard was seriously getting on his nerves. "The road's barely wide enough for two cars. And with the snowbank—"

As if Aspen weren't there, Pollard responded to Garrett with, "She could've pulled over onto the dirt, though."

Garrett forced his tone to stay even. "It's not dirt, it's snow, and she's not a local. She doesn't know how to drive in the—"

"All right, all right." He waved off Garrett's words and focused on Aspen. "Look, I'm not saying nobody hit you. But how can you be sure it wasn't an accident?"

"Twice, detective. He hit me *twice*."

"Even still, it could have been an accident. And it sounds like he came to help you, but you took off."

"It didn't feel like he was coming to help me."

The detective's gaze flicked to Garrett with a definite *Can you believe this woman?* look. "What would that *feel* like, exactly?"

She took a steadying breath, and when she spoke, it was with slow, even words. "He never called out to me. He never said anything."

"What should he have said?"

"I don't know," she snapped. "How about, 'Hey, you okay?' Or 'Don't worry, help is on the way.' He also wasn't running. Wouldn't you run, detective? If you saw a car go off the road, saw a car about to go over a cliff, wouldn't you pick up the pace a little?"

The man made a note on a little notepad.

A thought occurred to Garrett. "Did anybody call it in?"

The detective glanced up from his paper. "Only Miss Kincaid."

"Don't you suppose someone who was there to help would

have called 9-1-1?"

"Assuming there *was* someone, service is spotty—"

"Are you calling her a *liar*?" Garrett asked.

"Not a liar." He stretched his lips into what he must have thought passed for a smile. "Just confused."

Confused.

Oh.

"I. Am. Not. My. Mother." Aspen's words were spoken slowly and deliberately.

"Just calm down, ma'am."

Before Aspen could spout a scathing reply—not that the detective didn't deserve it—Garrett said, "Someone ran her off the road. It's been over an hour. Why hasn't anyone called it in?"

Pollard gave Garrett an indulgent smile that made his fists clench. "We'll look into it." He turned back Aspen. "So you say he rammed into you."

Garrett growled under his breath. If this guy hadn't been a cop, he'd have punched him already.

"And then what happened?"

"And then my car hit the snow and—"

"I thought you said you drove an SUV."

Aspen ground her teeth so loudly that Garrett winced at the sound. She took a breath and started again. "And then my *small SUV* hit the snowbank and went over. I remember seeing a tree and swerved to avoid it. The car must've gone up an incline because it flipped onto its side."

"How fast were you going?"

"Not very, but I didn't check the speedometer. I was too focused on the guy trying to kill me."

"People get into accidents all the time, ma'am. I'm sure he was just trying to get past you. Are you sure you didn't just run off the road accidentally? Maybe you imagined—"

"I didn't imagine it."

The detective smiled as if he found her amusing.

That did it for Garrett. He stood. "Is this *funny?*"

The man's smile faded. "You can sit down, sir, or you can leave."

"So you can ridicule her in peace? I don't think so."

The man pointed with his chin to the chair Garrett had vacated. "Your choice."

But through the glass door, he caught sight of the police chief stepping into the building. Garrett reached for Aspen. "Come on."

She took his hand. Hers was still freezing, no doubt a result of scrambling through the woods with no gloves on—and the chilly treatment she'd gotten from this incompetent jerk.

Pollard said, "If you want to give your statement, sit down."

Before Garrett could tell the guy where he could shove his notebook, Aspen said, "We'll just go talk to your boss. We'll be sure to tell him how helpful you've been."

Garrett couldn't help the smug look he gave the other man as he followed her to the door.

He hoped it was justified and the chief would take her seriously.

She'd already spotted Cote and beelined past the officers and desks to where he stood on the far side of the room. "Can we talk to you please?"

"Sure. Sorry I didn't get back to you. I was driving into town when I heard what happened." Cote led them into a glass-fronted office. His, according to the nameplate on the desk. The chief directed them to two chairs and closed the door.

"FYI," Garrett said, "Pollard's a piece of crap."

Cote sat on the far side of the desk without comment about his detective. He spoke to Aspen. "How you holding up?"

"I'll be all right."

"You gave your statement already?"

"For as much good as it'll do. Your detective seems to have gotten me confused with my mother. He thinks I'm either lying or insane."

Cote squinted the tiniest bit as he glanced beyond them and through the window into the larger room. He masked the expression quickly. "I'll take care of it. Tell me what happened."

Once more, Aspen related the events from the time she spotted the headlights in her rearview mirror to when Garrett picked her up. Cote took no notes, just listened, nodding along.

When she was finished, he turned to Garrett. "Did you see anybody?"

"Just Aspen."

"Any cars?"

"No, but I was only there for a minute."

"You were home when she called?"

"On my way there, which is how I got to her so quickly."

"Where'd you been?"

It was a strange question, considering Garrett had nothing to do with anything. Rather than question the chief, he simply answered. "After I left Aspen's—I'm her general contractor—I drove to my aunt and uncle's house."

"How long were you there?"

"They weren't home."

Now, Cote's eyebrows lifted. For the first time, he made a note on a pad on his desk. "Did you call them?"

Garrett shifted, suddenly nervous as if he'd done something wrong. "Why does it matter?"

"Just trying to get a sense of the timeline here."

The answer didn't make sense, but Cote didn't explain further.

A beat of silence passed before Garrett said, "I called, but they didn't answer."

Another note on the pad. "And after you picked Aspen up, you came straight here?"

Garrett was about to answer, but Cote's phone rang. He grabbed it, spoke a moment, then set it down. To Aspen, he said, "Your car's being pulled out. They'll tow it to Larry's."

"Where's that?"

Garrett said, "I know it. It's in town."

"Is it...?" She'd held up well so far, but now her voice cracked. "Do you know what kind of shape it's in?"

"Pretty banged up," Cote said. "You're very lucky you got out before it went over the edge. Fortunately, it didn't go all the way down, so we were able to pull it up. There are other places up there where the drop-off's much deeper. Your car only fell about twenty feet before it landed head first."

Twenty feet? Garrett hated to think what sort of shape Aspen would have been in after that, assuming she even survived. He slid closer and wrapped his arm around her shoulders. Thank God, *thank God* she'd gotten out. The very thought of what could have happened if she hadn't...

Or if that person had found her.

He couldn't stand the thought of someone hurting Aspen. Somehow, in the space of a week, she had become immensely important to him. He could see himself falling for her. Maybe he was already halfway there.

But somebody had run her off the road. And in that spot, on the edge of the mountain, right by that steep drop-off, if she'd been going the speed limit... If she hadn't been able to stop...

He had no doubt the person who hit her had planned for her to careen over the edge.

Someone had tried to kill her.

"What did you guys find?" Garrett asked. "Evidence of other cars, anybody else there?"

"There are other prints. Somebody was tromping around in

the woods. The only question is, why. Were they there to help, or harm?"

Aspen explained again why she'd believed the second, and Cote listened carefully, nodding as if he agreed.

When she was finished, he said, "Definitely suspicious. And nobody's called it in, either."

Cote was taking it seriously. Thank God.

"We're already talking to local body shops, asking them to alert us if anybody brings in a car with damage to the right side. You didn't get a plate number, make, model?"

"It was a sedan. White, maybe, or silver. I don't know. It was so dark."

He made a note of that. "And you didn't see the driver?" When she shook her head, he asked, "One person in the car? Two?"

"I don't know."

After they went over the details one more time, Aspen asked, "Can I get my things out of my car?"

"Of course. It should be in the lot soon." Cote looked from Aspen to Garrett and back. "This, coupled with the break-in at your house the other day... I wish I could offer you protection, but it doesn't work that way. You have to be prepared to protect yourself."

Garrett thought of the handgun she'd relinquished when they'd walked into the station. At least she'd been wearing it, but no handgun would protect her from a madman trying to run her off the road.

"What do you suggest I do?" she asked.

"Maybe you should find a place to stay out of town, and don't tell anybody where you're going. And, maybe"—again, his gaze flicked to Garrett—"don't stay alone."

He would stay with her. If that was what it took to keep her safe, he'd do it.

But with the attraction he felt, and considering their kiss the other night, would that be wise?

Did he care?

"Do you mind if I ask…?" Cote rested his arms on the desk and leaned toward her. "Why are you in Coventry, Miss Kincaid?"

"My father bought that house. It's mine." She spoke the words as if she felt she had to defend herself.

Cote's expression was patient, but he said nothing.

She sat up straighter. "I want to find out what happened to my mother."

"Ah." He leaned back. "You and a whole lot of other people. What makes you think you can solve that mystery?"

"I don't know that I can. But I have to try. For my father's sake. He asked me to."

"He did? He *asked* you to do that?"

"He said to do right by her. How can I do that if I don't find her?"

Cote regarded her for a long moment. Garrett had the sense that there was something he was holding back. Something he wanted to say.

But he opened his desk drawer and fished around. "I already have your number." He pulled out a business card and handed it across the desk. "Now, you have mine. If you have an emergency, call 9-1-1 first. Then call me."

Garrett stood and waited until Aspen did the same. "Pollard won't be running the investigation?" Garrett clarified.

"He works for me," Cote said. "I'll take care of what happened earlier."

That wasn't exactly an answer, but Garrett knew when he'd pushed his luck far enough.

The chief walked them to the door. "Rest assured, I'm taking this seriously. Where will you stay tonight?"

She pressed her lips together and shrugged.

"Let me know where you land—not back at your house. Until we figure out what's going on, you're not safe there. Understood?"

"Maybe they have a room at the hotel," she said.

Cote's frown reflected Garrett's feelings about that. The hotel would be the most obvious place to look for her.

No, she wouldn't be staying there. "I'll find her a place." Garrett turned to Aspen. "Someplace nobody will think to look for you. Someplace you'll be safe."

THEY LEFT THE POLICE STATION, and Garrett drove Aspen to her house. Based on the way she hurried to her front door, her gaze darting all around, he guessed she was as nervous to be there as he was. After he made sure nobody was there, she packed a bag quickly. Five minutes after they arrived, they drove away.

Nothing had happened. Nobody had been there. Still, Garrett wondered how many minutes he'd shaved off his life-span with the worry and stress of those moments.

Not that he minded. Whatever it took to keep Aspen safe.

Twenty-five minutes later, he pulled into the lot at Larry's Auto Body. He and Aspen climbed from the car when the flatbed turned in just a few moments later. It drove under the lights in the parking lot, and he got his first look at Aspen's SUV.

And swallowed hard.

Beside him, Aspen gasped.

The front-end was smashed to pieces. The hood was bent. The windshield shattered.

Garrett urged Aspen close by his side to remind himself that she was all right. She must have gotten out before most of that damage had happened. But the impact of what might have been...

She turned to him, and he wrapped her in his arms. He didn't know what to say. His emotions rose so fast, so powerfully, he was afraid to speak, afraid they'd leak out. Fury and rage at whoever had done that. Terror, thinking of what could have happened. Thinking of how he'd almost lost her.

This woman he hadn't known two weeks before suddenly meant everything. And someone had tried to take her away from him.

Someone had tried to kill her.

She sobbed against his chest, and tears stung his own eyes. He would do anything in his power to keep her safe. But what could he do?

Who would do this? This was *his* town. These were *his* people. Surely none of them would have attempted murder. But if not a local, then who? Who would want her dead? And why?

Aspen sniffed and leaned back. "It all just hit me."

"Me too." He didn't let her go, just gazed down at her. "I'm going to keep you safe. I promise. We'll find a place for you."

"I feel like I should tell you I can take care of myself. I'm not some damsel in distress."

"Of course you're not." He looked at the place where the flatbed had disappeared around the corner of the building. "If you were, he'd have gotten to you. But that doesn't mean you don't need help. There's nothing wrong with asking for help."

"Good, because I wasn't about to refuse it."

He loved that humility, that authenticity. He realized there were a whole lot of things he loved about Aspen Kincaid.

"We should probably..." She stepped out of his arms and turned, seeming to steel herself for the job.

Though the car was out of sight, the sounds of the chains

that had held her car in place being tossed aside reached them. Metal scraped against metal, the low hum of an engine roaring to life.

He took her hand. "Come on. Let's see if anything's salvageable."

Together, they rounded the building and stopped beside the wreckage.

Larry caught sight of them and yanked off his gloves as he walked their way. "Garrett. This isn't your car, is it?"

"It's mine," Aspen said.

Larry shifted to her. He was heavyset, in his thirties with longish mousy brown hair and greasy fingernails. He looked her up and down, not in a lascivious way but with surprise. "Did you push it over yourself? You've got nary a scratch."

Larry was the type of guy to use the word *nary*.

"I managed to get out before it went over."

Larry nodded like he was impressed. "God had His eye on you, my friend."

"I have no doubt that's true."

He turned to the wrecked car. "Haven't gone through it yet. Cote said you can take anything you can find, just don't touch the outside."

Aspen didn't move toward the vehicle, though. She seemed frozen in place.

"I can do it, if you want." At her nod, Garrett walked toward the mangled metal, sucking in a deep breath as he did. It was all too much to consider, and he certainly didn't want to start considering it at that moment. With Larry's help, he got a rear door open and crawled inside.

Her purse was there, zipped up tight, thank heavens, so her things weren't all over the place. He grabbed it and crawled back out. When he handed it to her, he said, "This is all that's in there."

"The rest is in the back."

Of course it was.

He anticipated trouble with the hatch, but aside from a few scrapes, it was undamaged. He opened it and slid back the cover used to hide cargo from passersby. He found a few plastic shopping bags, one from an electronics store. He peeked inside.

A new laptop.

He hefted the packages, and Larry slammed the hatch shut. "It all looks fine, even the laptop."

Aspen smiled for the first time since Garrett had picked her up on the mountain road. "Amazing."

Garrett handed Aspen the lighter bags and turned to Larry. "What do you think? Can it be repaired?"

The man chuckled. "You're kidding, right?"

He had been. There was no salvaging that mess. Garrett focused on Aspen. "Sorry, babe." Babe? Had he just called her *babe*?

But she either didn't hear or didn't mind. "It's not like we've grown attached, the car and me. I only owned it for a week. I'm just thankful it held up."

He seconded that.

With her purchases in the back of his truck, they said goodbye to Larry, and he backed out of the parking spot. But he didn't leave the lot. It was after eight, and he hadn't eaten dinner yet. "How about we pick up a pizza? There's a great place in town."

"Okay." Her voice was small, as if she were fighting emotions. Rather than question her—who wouldn't be emotional after the night she'd had?—he simply squeezed her hand before fishing his phone from his pocket. "What's your poison?"

"I like everything but green peppers and mushrooms."

When he ordered a small goat cheese and pear pizza, her

eyebrows lifted suspiciously. He winked at her, then added a traditional pie—this one with every kind of meat a person could want. They wouldn't finish them both, but he was never sorry to have leftover pizza in the fridge.

"It'll take about fifteen minutes," he said. "It's only a five-minute drive. We'll just stay here out of sight until it's ready."

She nodded, leaned back, and closed her eyes.

While they waited, he texted Dylan, told him what happened, and asked if there was any chance Aspen could stay with him and Chelsea. Because of Chelsea's position as owner and CEO of HCI—not to mention the trouble she and her family had had in the past—their house's security was top notch. Aspen would be safe there.

But Garrett got a response almost immediately. *Wish we could help. We're in NY and won't be home until Friday. If she still needs a place to stay after that, we'll be happy to have her.*

So much for that idea.

Garrett and his friends had a group chat, so he texted it, asking if anybody had any ideas.

He got responses immediately. Fitz offered his place, but hadn't Aspen told Garrett Tabby's mother was staying there? He'd only met Mrs. Eaton a few times, but she could be a lot to take.

James offered his place, as did Braden. Both of them had new babies at home, though. They were kind to offer, but there had to be a solution that didn't put anybody out.

Reid didn't text back. Garrett guessed it was Ella's bedtime because he had no doubt Reid would offer their place as well.

But it was Andrew's response Garrett was hoping for. *I just texted Grace. She'd love to have Aspen stay with her.*

That was the perfect solution. Grace didn't have a baby at home or a mother staying with her or a five-year-old. She had an extra room, which he knew was furnished, since she'd fostered a little girl for months. The girl had been returned to her family, so the room was available. And Grace lived within spitting distance of Garrett. He could see her front door from his.

That would be great, Garrett told his friend. *I'll text her myself, work out the details.*

He did, and a moment later, Grace responded. *Happy to have her, but I'm in town for an event at the youth center. I'll be home by ten. She can come here for the key, if she's in a hurry to get in.*

Aspen was leaning against the passenger door, eyes closed.

"Grace said you can stay with her. She lives near me, and Andrew lives across the lot from her. You should be safe there."

Aspen's eyes opened. "If you think it's all right."

"Safer than the hotel. I'd have you stay with me, but..." He shrugged.

She met his gaze and then looked away quickly, though he caught the small smile in the darkness. "Maybe that's not such a good idea."

He felt a twinge of pleasure to know that, apparently, her mind had gone to the same place his had. Not that either of them would let their bodies follow, but the memory of their kiss suddenly felt like a solid presence between them.

He was looking forward to having a second kiss. But definitely not moments before she tucked into his extra bedroom. He wouldn't get any sleep at all.

"Thing is, Grace won't be home until ten. She said you could come by where she is and get the key, but... not that I have any right to say, but I'd rather you not be alone. You could just stay at my condo until she's home."

"If it's no trouble."

As if he wanted her anyplace but at his side. Shifting into drive, he said, "Pizza should be ready any minute, and I'm starving."

CHAPTER TWENTY-THREE

Garrett watched closely as Aspen bit into the pear-and-goat-cheese pizza. Her eyes widened in surprise, then closed as she savored the flavors. She swallowed, then opened her eyes. "Wow."

"Told you."

They were at his small kitchen table. Good thing he kept the place tidy so he hadn't been embarrassed when she walked in. Not that it was impressive. Just a two-bed, two-bath, two-story condo, one of the smaller units in this development. The sofa was secondhand, as was the recliner. And the lamps. But they were all decent and clean. The walls were bare. He'd thought about getting artwork or something to hang, but he'd never gotten around to it. The nicest furniture in his house, a round maple table and matching chairs, had been a gift from Uncle Dean for Garrett's last birthday.

Aspen had remarked on the set as soon as she'd seen it, guessing right away that Dean had made it, then gushing about its beauty.

She swallowed a second bite of the pie. "My dad's restaurants serve flatbread pizzas. I ought to have the chef try to replicate these flavors." A moment after she said the words, she blinked, and sadness tightened her lips at the corners. "I guess I could pass along the idea."

"Did you sell them?" Garrett asked. "The restaurants? I assume, since you have no plans to go back to Hawaii..."

"Yeah. To one of the managers. He got a loan for some of the cost, and he's paying me back the rest of it monthly until it's paid off."

"It was kind of you to extend him financing."

She shrugged, sipping her soda. When she set the glass down, she said, "I wanted them to go to somebody who would love them as much as Dad did. Gene worked for Dad as long as I can remember. He'll take good care of them."

"And you didn't want to hold onto them? I mean, they were your father's, and your place of work."

"A lot of people told me I should wait a year after his death before I made any life-altering decisions, and I tried to do that. But being in his kitchens, in the places he'd built and loved...it never felt right without him. It was just too painful."

"Is that how you feel about Hawaii too? Or are you planning to go back someday?"

"I have friends there, but most of them have married and had families or moved away. I loved growing up in Kona, but this is a huge country. I'd like to see more of it, experience more of it. Maybe I'll go back after college." She didn't seem too keen on the idea, though. Which didn't bother him one bit.

"But you're going to stay in the restaurant business," he said. "That's what you want to study, right?"

She finished off her slice of pizza, then took her time wiping her fingers on her napkin. Finally, she smiled at him. "Tell you the truth, I hate it."

He snatched a slice of the loaded meat pie, but he set it on his plate without taking a bite. "Didn't you tell me you're going to get a degree in hospitality?"

"Maybe I'll like it better if I get some training."

"Why study it if you don't like it?"

"What else can I do? That's all I've ever done. It's all I know."

"But that doesn't mean..." He sat back. "You're starting over in every other aspect of your life. Why not a new career?"

"You have a knack for asking probing questions."

"So I've been told." Though often the word hadn't been *probing* but *irritating* or *nosy*. He wasn't nosy, though. He was interested. She didn't have to answer if she didn't want to.

"What if I'm not good at anything else?" she finally said.

"What if you are?"

She snatched another slice of pizza. Without looking at him, she said, "That's not the plan."

He glared at her purse on the counter behind her, knowing the ever-present notebook was inside it somewhere. If only that had been lost in the wreckage. "Sometimes, plans need to change."

She bit into the pizza.

"What is it with you and plans, anyway?"

Only after she chewed and swallowed and sipped her drink did she meet his eyes. "The Bible says that all things should be done in an orderly way."

"The Bible also says that a man makes his plans, but God directs his steps. Sometimes people's plans need to change. Sometimes we don't know what's best for us."

"You don't understand."

"Explain it to me then, your penchant for list-making. Why are you so...?"

"Obsessed?"

He'd been trying to find a kinder word.

"I didn't always want to work for my father." Pizza seem-ingly forgotten, she stared past Garrett for a long moment. "Don't get me wrong. I loved him, and I loved being with him. But the work itself... Between managing the employees and dealing with the customers—mostly tourists—it was a constant battle. I love working with children. I hate working with adults who act like children."

"One good thing about my job is that I get to choose the people I interact with on a daily basis. I choose the contractors, and if they do a lousy job, I find better ones."

"Ah, but the clients..."

He smiled at her. "I've had some rough ones, but my current client, I have to say, is my favorite."

She looked down, but not before he caught her smile. She separated a bite of pear from her slice and ate it before she spoke again. "I hired a lot of the employees myself, and they *seemed* fine. Were fine, really. But nobody ever comes to an interview and says, 'By the way, if I get a hangnail, I'll need the day off.'"

"That would get old."

"It's just... I feel like some people figure out what they were born to do. Like you and fixing up houses. You're so good at it, but it's not just that. You love it. It's fulfilling, right? Or am I making assumptions that aren't accurate?"

"Your assumptions are spot on." He loved that Aspen knew him so well.

"I wasn't born to manage restaurants," she said. "I was good at it, but not because it came naturally to me. I learned by watching my father, by doing what he did."

He guessed she was going to tell him that lists had helped her become competent at her job. But as she often did, she surprised him.

"When I was in high school," she said, "I wanted to be a

teacher. I taught in children's ministry at church for years, and I loved it."

He could picture her in front of a classroom of children, telling the story of Jonah and the whale or Moses parting the Red Sea. "I bet you were really good."

"The kids liked me. Dad told me he'd pay for college, but I didn't think we had the money. I realize now that maybe that wasn't the case, but at the time, I thought he'd have to take out a bunch of loans, and I didn't want either one of us to be saddled with debt. So I worked really hard to earn a scholarship. I joined a bunch of clubs. I ran for student body president—and won."

"Good for you."

"I figured that, the more things I was involved in, the better my chances would be for scholarships. So I did all that, and I took all the honors courses. And I volunteered at church. Of course, I still worked for Dad, even though he told me he didn't need me and I should slow down and concentrate on school. I thought I could handle it.

"I was halfway through my senior year when it all fell apart. I flunked a math test. I missed a deadline for early admission to college. And I started a fire in the kitchen at the restaurant because I was studying for a test and not paying attention. The chef got it out, no damage done, but that really shook me."

"I can imagine."

"The Saturday after that, I was retaking my ACT, hoping to improve my score, and I had a breakdown. A total emotional and mental breakdown. Right there in the classroom in front of the other students." She met his eyes and held the contact, as if trying to communicate some message he didn't understand.

"It was bad, Garrett. They pulled me out of the test and called an ambulance. I thought I was having a heart attack."

"A panic attack, I assume."

"Yeah, but I thought... You can imagine what I thought."

When he didn't guess, she explained. "I thought I was like my mother."

Oh.

"They wanted to hospitalize me, but my father absolutely refused. I remember being in the ER, listening to him on the other side of the door arguing that I needed to be at home with him. He took me home and got me in to see a counselor."

"Once again, I'm impressed by your father."

The corner of her mouth ticked up. "He was such a good man. The counselor was helpful and told me I had too much going on and that anybody would have cracked under the weight of it. I'm not sure if that's true, but..." She lifted one shoulder and let it fall. "Anyway, she gave me some tips about handling stress."

"Did you get the scholarship? Did you go to college?" He knew she hadn't finished, but maybe...

"I thought, since I couldn't handle the stress of high school, I'd never be able to manage college."

"But you managed a restaurant?"

"Eventually, and yeah, that's also stressful. Probably more so, especially considering I didn't like the work. But it felt safe. I let my fear direct me." Her lips pressed and lifted in a sort of shrug. "Anyway, the counselor got me started making lists and plans. When everything's written down, I don't have to remember it all. Life feels more manageable."

That made sense, but there had to be a limit. "Sometimes plans change. You can't know what the future holds."

"That's always been my problem. Once I write it down, it feels like it's permanent. I want it to come true. I feel like, if I start changing things, I'll veer off course."

"Maybe you've set your course in the wrong direction. Ever hear that old adage about the guy who reached the top of the ladder only to discover he'd leaned it against the wrong wall?" He'd hoped to make her smile, but he was disappointed.

She settled back against the chair, closing her eyes. "You don't understand."

"I want to, though. Explain it to me."

Seconds stretched into minutes. She sipped her soda.

He ate his pizza. Maybe Aspen was done sharing, and though he'd be disappointed, he was pleased she'd told him as much as she had.

The fact that he wanted to know more, to know everything about her...

He should change the subject, let her off the hook. And he would. In another minute. He was just about to when she spoke.

"The course I set isn't for a destination. I don't make the lists in order to climb the ladder of success or achieve my goals."

"If not to achieve goals, then what is the point?"

"I make my lists and follow my plans because it keeps me sane."

She couldn't be serious.

But nothing in her countenance told him she was kidding. She didn't even seem to realize that what she'd said didn't make sense.

"Don't you see? An ordered mind is a sane mind. As long as my mind stays orderly, I won't be like my mother."

"So you're saying that, if your mother had kept lists, she wouldn't have suffered from a mental illness?"

Aspen looked away. "Oh. Well... Not necessarily."

"Because for some people, lists are the problem, right? Aren't there people who suffer from OCD who compulsively make lists?"

"I'm not obsessive or compulsive." She leaned away from him, eyes wide. "I'm not—"

"I didn't say you were. You're as sane as any of us. I'm just saying..." He took a deep breath, prayed for wisdom, and gentled his voice. "Your mother was mentally ill. That's a brain-chemistry issue. All the lists in the world wouldn't have cured her of it."

"I know." Her voice was small. She looked away. "I know that. It's just..."

He wanted to throw his opinions at her, the few facts he knew about mental illness. He wanted to anticipate what she was thinking and tell her why she was wrong. Instead, he kept his mouth shut and waited.

"I know lists wouldn't have fixed my mother. And she had plans. To blow up a building—that took planning. It just makes me *feel* sane. I feel like, if I can just follow my path, then I won't go the way she did."

He scooted his chair closer and took Aspen's hands in his. "You are not your mother any more than I'm my father. In some ways, we take after our parents. Believe me, I don't want to be anything like my dad, and when I see his personality traits cropping up in myself, I want to hate that part of me, to destroy it. But I don't have to do that. I only have to surrender myself to my heavenly Father. As followers of Christ, we are first His children. We should strive to be like Him."

"That's so easy to say."

"It's about faith. Do you believe God has given you a sound mind? That's His promise, you know. It's right there in the Bible."

"I know that. But I think that my lists—"

"Your lists aren't keeping you sane. Your God has given you your sanity, your ability to think, your ability to reason."

"There are Christians who suffer from mental illness."

"Yes, that's true. I'm not..." He sent up a silent prayer for wisdom. "I don't have all the answers, Aspen. But, looking at you"—he leaned in, gazed into her beautiful eyes—"I see a woman with a sound mind, a beautiful heart, and a tender spirit. You are your mother's daughter. And your father's daughter. But mostly, you're God's daughter."

Feeling brave, maybe stupid, he continued. "I'm not saying you should stop making lists. I'm saying you should make all the lists you want, but remember that God's plans trump yours. It's humility to yield to Him."

"I see what you're saying."

But her face said otherwise.

"It seems to me..." He paused, very aware that he was pushing his luck. But he believed he was seeing something about her that maybe she couldn't see herself. He forged ahead. "It seems to me that you've spent a whole lot of your life trying *not* to be like your mother. You've focused a lot of time on trying to *not be* something you never were. I wonder how much time you've spent trying to figure out who you really are."

Her eyes filled with tears.

Great. He'd made her cry. *Idiot.* He grabbed a clean napkin. "I'm sorry. I didn't mean to upset you. Just ignore me."

She smiled, though tears trickled from her eyes. She took the napkin he offered to wipe her cheeks. "You haven't offended me. I never thought about how much time I've dedicated to making sure I'm not crazy."

"We're not using that word, remember?"

Her lips twitched. "Right. That's part of what this trip is about for me. I feel like...like I don't know who I am. Like maybe, if I can figure out who my mother was, maybe I can figure out who I am."

"I'm not saying that your mother had no bearing on who you are. But I suspect you've become who you are not because of her but despite her."

"Except for all the energy I've expended trying not to be her."

He conceded that with a nod. "I don't know what you're hoping to discover here," he said, "aside from the facts about who your mother was and what she did, and maybe what became of her. But you don't need to worry about your sanity or your value. And you aren't going to find your answers in your parents' history or in your plans or your lists. You're certainly not going to find them by earning a degree in something you don't want to do. God created you. He's the one who decides who you are. He's the One with the answers."

She dabbed at the tears, smiling through them. "You're right. I know you're right. In my head anyway. Especially about college. I should figure out what God wants me to do. Maybe going to Florida isn't the best idea."

"I can't speak for God, but I sure wouldn't mind if you stuck around a little while." He might as well spill it all. "Maybe I'm imagining this thing between us. We haven't known each other long, but you're...amazing. I've never felt for anybody else what I feel for you."

He watched for some reaction. She didn't nod, but she also didn't look away, just gazed at him with those big green eyes.

"I think there might be something here, with you and me."

She blinked, and was there the slightest lifting of her lips? He forged ahead.

"I'd like you to hang around. Maybe, you and I can see"—he lifted her hands and kissed her knuckles—"where God takes us. Because you weren't on my list, either. But if you're part of God's future for me, Aspen, I don't want to miss that."

Her eyes widened.

Had he gone too far, too fast?

But that slight smile grew. "When I was in the woods, when I was convinced somebody was trying to kill me..."

Her words chased his happy thoughts about the future away.

"I called 9-1-1, because that's what people do. And then I called you. I knew you'd be there. Which is to say...you're not imagining this." Squeezing his hand, she leaned closer, so close he could feel her breath on his cheek. "I'm right there with you." Her smile slipped as she sat back. "There's still the little problem of finding my mother. And the fact that somebody ran me off the road a few hours ago."

Cold fear gripped him. He'd just counseled Aspen to turn her fears and her future over to God, but that was easier to say than do. "Nobody's going to hurt you. Not if I have anything to say about it."

CHAPTER TWENTY-FOUR

THIRTY YEARS AGO.

Four days. It would all happen in four days, the Thursday night before spring break. The Planner's father had been nagging him to transfer to a different college, preferably his alma mater, and the Planner had agreed to interview with them on Friday. Since his mother and sisters would be out of town, he and his dad would make a whole weekend out of it. They'd leave for Boston Thursday night. Not until they were out of the state would he tell his father what had happened.

At that point, his father would demand he transfer, probably in exchange for establishing the Planner's alibi. He'd agree and then back out later, unless he could get the Crusader to transfer with him.

One step at a time.

They'd already moved the device into his car, so the Builder's part was finished.

The Crusader's gaze darted around the room as if evaluating threats. "I did what you asked. Michael—"

"No names," the Planner hissed.

"Sorry," she said. "He likes the place. He calls it 'our overlook.' Isn't that sweet? We've been back there a few times. He'll know where to meet me when I call him."

Squelching jealousy, the Planner slid his hand over her arm. "But you haven't told him anything?"

"Of course not. Of course not. He'd stop us."

"Okay then. Thursday night, you'll pick me up. I'll park near the new development. We'll go to a pay phone, and you'll call him and ask him to meet you at the overlook." He couldn't bring himself to call it *their* anything. "Then you and I will do it. It'll only take a few minutes. You'll drop me at my car, then go up to the overlook and meet him. He should already be there. If we do this right, he'll have left the house right away. Will he have the baby with him?"

"Maybe. Depends. Sometimes, his parents stay with us, so they might be there to watch her."

"Good. I hope they are. Then they'll say he wasn't home at the time of the bombing, lend credence to the idea that he could have done it."

She nodded along. They'd gone over the plan a hundred times already, but her mental state worried him.

"I can do this by myself," he said. "Maybe you should stay home—"

"I have to be there." She spoke with both vehemence and volume. "I have to see it happen. I have to!"

"Lower your voice."

She leaned in and whispered, "We're going to take them down. We're going to protect our home, the earth. We're going to protect the forest that gives us life for ourselves and for our children. For Aspen."

He wasn't sure he'd go *that* far, but he loved the forest too.

Mostly, he loved her. He'd do anything for her.

The Builder pushed back and stood. "You don't need me."

A glare at their mutual friend prompted a low remark. "She's going to blow the whole thing if she doesn't keep quiet."

"I've got it," the Planner said. "You and I won't talk again until after."

The Builder gripped the Crusader's shoulder and squeezed, then walked out.

It was just the two of them. He took her hands and leaned close. "I'm worried about you. I think maybe it would be best if you stayed—"

"I have to be there." She quit the fidgeting, though it seemed to take great effort. She met his eyes and bent toward him. "I'm under control. You don't have to worry about me."

That she felt she had to convince him scared him more than anything. She was self-aware enough to know she was spinning out.

But he was doing this for her. He wasn't about to rob her of the joy of seeing her dream come true.

"Meet me Thursday at nine o'clock. We'll go together from there. We can't take the back way in." The Builder had told him the device was stable, but he wasn't about to go bouncing on an old logging road with it in his arms. "We'll take the main entrance, make sure the lot is empty, then set it up where the Builder said."

The Crusader's eyes sparkled in anticipation. Her complete lack of fear was as admirable as it was terrifying.

Did she really understand what they were doing?

Of course she did. This whole thing had been her idea.

"We'll take the logging road when we leave. We should be out of the woods before it goes off. We'll go straight up to the spot. You drop me at my car and then meet him."

"It's perfect."

"You remember what to tell him after?"

"That he has to say I was with him. If he doesn't, my partner"—she kissed the Planner's cheek and giggled—"will send the evidence to the police, and he'll be implicated."

She seemed to understand. Despite the wild look in her eyes —some combination of glee and excitement—she comprehended the gravity of the situation.

He hoped.

"We won't see each other over spring break. You'll be questioned. When they come to talk to you, you only need to remember one word."

"Lawyer."

"Exactly. You have the number I gave you?"

She nodded.

"He's good. If your husband won't pay him, I will."

There were benefits to having a trust fund.

"He'll pay." Her confidence in her husband only irritated him, though it was probably merited. Despite everything, it seemed her husband loved her.

After she left, the Planner finished his beer, tipped the bartender, and made his way out. It was dark by the time he reached his car, so he didn't see the figure leaning against his driver's door until he was almost to it.

Hiding his surprise, he stopped and crossed his arms.

"I think you should call it off," the Builder said.

"Why didn't you say that inside?"

"She'd have blown a gasket and alerted the whole bar."

The Planner made a show of looking around the nearly empty lot. "It's not like anybody was there to hear."

"It wasn't empty. That bartender and a couple of the customers have been here every time we've met. When our pictures are on TV—"

"*If* they are."

"—they're going to recognize us. Her, at least. She doesn't exactly go unnoticed."

She did turn heads everywhere she went. And once she got to talking, she was impossible to forget.

"Somebody could report these meetings," the Builder said. "Even if not, you know they're going to question her. Do you really think she'll be able to keep her mouth shut? I'm not sure she has any idea what we're doing."

"She knows. She gets it."

A loud sigh filled the space between them. "You know I'd do anything for her. For you too. But I'm not ruining my life over this. They're going to know it was us."

The Planner's lips stretched into a smile. "Knowing it and proving it are two different things."

CHAPTER TWENTY-FIVE

DIM LIGHT FILTERED through the gauzy curtains. Aspen stretched on the narrow twin bed, then flinched at the pain. Her body had taken a beating the night before, and everything ached. She thanked God for the aches.

It could have been so much worse.

It'd been a strange night. Thoughts of Garrett and memories of the evening they'd shared had lulled her to sleep quickly.

He liked her, liked her enough to ask her to stay in Coventry, to suggest they see what could happen between them. At the time, she'd felt so secure in his presence, so confident that, as long as he was beside her, she could conquer anything.

Grace had texted a little before ten o'clock that she was home, and Garrett had grabbed Aspen's things from his truck and walked her to Grace's door. It wasn't a long walk—Garrett lived in the next building on the opposite side of the narrow parking area. When they reached Grace's stoop, the air between them suddenly felt charged. Thinking of awkward moments after the few dates she'd had in high school, she giggled, and he laughed.

And then his expression had shifted to something much different.

He set her packages on the porch and wrapped her in his arms, chasing off the chill of the cold night. He lowered his head. And waited.

But not for long before she closed the distance between them and pressed her lips against his. The kiss didn't start tentatively like it had a few nights before, but tenderly. The tenderness shifted as the events of the night, the memories, the fears intruded. She clung to him as if he were her only link to sanity, to safety. As if, in his arms, nothing could touch her.

He responded, backing her against the front door, shielding her body with his, diving in for more.

More. She'd wanted more.

Nobody had ever kissed her like that.

Nobody had ever stirred such desire inside her.

It felt like an instant, or an eternity, had passed when he moved his lips off hers, only to skim over her neck. He trailed kisses to her ear, and she felt his sigh.

Everything in her wanted to tell him not to stop. The cold, the wind, the fact that they were within viewing distance of no fewer than twenty windows—she didn't care.

She only wanted more of this. More of him.

A car drove by, its engine seeming too loud in the sacred moment.

Garrett's breath tickled the hair over her ear. "Do I need to apologize?"

For stopping. "Do I?"

His chuckle rumbled through her, plucking cords of desire that he'd already set to humming.

He stayed there another moment, then backed away to meet her gaze. She'd expected amusement, but his expression held none. Only desire and...and something darker.

And then she'd remembered the rest.

Because Garrett's kiss might have been the most amazing thing that had happened to her that day, some could argue even the most momentous. But it hadn't been the *only* thing.

There'd also been those headlights rushing up behind her.

That car forcing her off the road. The snow. The tree. The cliff.

"You'll come with me to your house tomorrow morning," he said. "If we stay together—"

"There are things I need to do."

"Then I'll come with you."

She would like that. She would *love* that. But...

But.

"Whoever ran me off the road... He's not going to come after me in broad daylight in the middle of town."

"You don't have a car."

"I could borrow your truck." She tossed the words out, adding a flirty tone that sounded foreign to her ears.

His grimace told her he wasn't impressed. "I can't tell you what to do, but I'm not going to help you put yourself in danger. Either I come with you, or—"

"There are deliveries coming to the house tomorrow. One of us needs to be there."

"Or both of us could be there."

Was he right? Was she foolish to keep trying to dig up information alone? Maybe.

Though the police chief hadn't said so, she'd had the feeling he wanted to tell her something. But he hadn't, and she assumed that he'd held back because Garrett had been there.

"If I leave Grace's, I'll get a ride, or I'll use a ride-sharing app. I'll always be with somebody. Okay?"

Based on the set of Garrett's lips and his narrowed eyes, it wasn't okay.

But he didn't argue. After another kiss, this one too brief, he knocked on the door behind her. Only after Grace had ushered Aspen inside did Garrett make the short, cold walk home.

She'd fallen asleep with the memory of his lips on hers.

And then she'd had nightmares about the rest.

A strange night indeed. She checked the time on her phone, not shocked to see she'd slept until after nine. She wasn't an early riser anyway, and years in the restaurant business had trained her to stay up late and sleep in.

The night before, when they'd chatted a few minutes before bed, Grace had told her she had to work this morning and would be leaving early, so Aspen wasn't surprised when she heard no noises coming from within the condo.

She showered, changed into something warm, and helped herself to coffee and breakfast, thankful that Grace had insisted she make herself at home. It wasn't hard to do. Unlike the giant house on the mountain, Grace's condo felt cozy. It was compact, nestled between other homes. She heard car doors slamming, voices, children's laughter. She wasn't alone here.

She liked it.

Beautiful as the house on the mountain was, she wasn't sure she'd ever feel comfortable living in a place like that. She needed to be part of a community, and this little condo develop-ment felt like it might be just that.

After she finished her toast, she pulled out the list she'd made the night before and started working through it, beginning with a call to the insurance company. They assured her an adjuster would be looking at the car that afternoon. She should get a call back by the following day or Monday. Next, she called the rental car company, secured a sedan, and arranged to pick it up on Friday. Grace had already offered to drive her if Garrett couldn't.

Next, she located the business card Chief Cote had given her the day before and dialed.

He answered on the second ring with, "How you holding up?" The older man's voice was somehow both gruff and comforting.

"How'd you know it was me?"

"I'm a detective, Miss Kincaid. I have years of investigative experience under my belt." There was a short pause. "Plus, you're the only person I know with a Hawaii area code." Humor filled his voice.

"You *are* good at your job," she said.

"The best. You're at Grace's?" Aspen had texted him the night before, telling him where she'd be staying.

"I am. I was hoping you could make some time for me today. I'd like to ask what you know about the lumber company bombing and my mother's involvement in it."

"That's a good idea." His tone no longer held amusement. "I have a meeting this morning that'll probably go through lunch. Could you come by the station late this afternoon?"

They set a time and ended the call.

She consulted her list, which she'd updated that morning with the to-dos that had occurred to her overnight, and moved on to the next item.

She dialed Jeff Christiansen.

After their greetings, she asked the question that had occurred to her at some point in the middle of the night, when sleep had been elusive, the fears and theories fresh.

"You told me you knew my father when he lived here."

"I did," Jeff said. "Our families had known each other for years."

"Do you remember where he worked back then? Someone told me he was in construction." And hadn't Mr. Barnett, her house's former owner, told her they'd had work done on their house that spring? Maybe that was the connection.

"I don't think it was construction," Jeff said. "I don't remember exactly, but I could swear he had to get a special license for the job."

"Like a certificate, or—?"

"No. A license to drive a truck. What do they call it? CDL. A commercial driver's license."

"He drove a truck?"

"Not an eighteen-wheeler. A construction vehicle, I guess. A dump truck or something."

"Huh. Do you have any idea what kinds of construction projects—?"

"I'm sorry. I don't. I remember he made decent money, enough that he was able to rent the house where you guys lived."

"Where was that?"

"I don't remember exactly. It was in town, a couple blocks off Main Street. Little—maybe two beds, one bath, but your dad was proud of it. I might be able to find the address here somewhere in my files."

How could he have it in his files, unless... "Did you act as Dad's attorney back then?" She couldn't imagine why her father would have needed an attorney. He hadn't owned property or a business. And then a thought occurred that had her heart beating fast. "Was he planning to divorce my mother? Was that why—?"

"I'm not a family law attorney, so even if he were—and he never shared plans to do that with me—I wouldn't have represented him. There was another matter he needed my help with."

"What matter?"

"I'm not at liberty to say."

The cliché rolled off his tongue as if he'd spoken it a thousand times in his life. And maybe he had. But it didn't seem to apply. "Jeff, my father is gone. Surely attorney-client privilege doesn't still apply."

"I'm afraid it does. Unless there's some compelling reason for me to violate that confidence, it holds."

She chewed on those words a moment. "Are you saying there's no connection between his dealings with you and what my mother did?"

Jeff cleared his throat. "I'm saying attorney-client privilege applies, regardless."

"Is it something that would help me find out what happened to my mother?"

"Aspen, I'm not playing a game with you." His tone had taken on that of a disappointed tutor. "This isn't twenty questions, and there's no way of phrasing your inquiry that will result in any information from me. This is not a wink-wink-nudge-nudge situation. Your father entrusted me with his legal needs, and I take that very seriously. I won't betray that trust, even after his death. Not with hints. Not with anything."

She quelled a rise of irritation. Jeff Christiansen had ethics, and she admired that. She just wished she could compel him to see things a little differently. "Someone tried to run me off the road yesterday."

A beat of silence was followed by, "What do you mean? You were in an accident?"

"I mean someone followed me up Rattlesnake Road and rammed into my car, twice."

The attorney gasped, but Aspen wasn't finished.

"I nearly crashed into a tree, then hit a weird incline. My SUV ended up on its side. I got out moments before it slid over a cliff."

"Were you hurt?" He sounded genuinely concerned.

"The point is, it wasn't an accident. Somebody did that to me, on purpose."

"I'm so sorry that—"

"I'm not looking for your sympathy. I'm saying… Look, I know you're trying to fulfill your obligations to my father, but could you at least consider something for me?"

After a moment, he said, "I will, if you'll consider something for me."

She hadn't expected that. "Fine. Me first. Maybe the dealings you had with my father have nothing to do with any of this. But if they do, then don't you think my father would want you to elevate my safety over your confidentiality agreement?"

"Ah. But it's not like you think it is. And now it's my turn. Do you remember when you first told me about your plan to come here?"

Back in November, the first time she'd spoken to him. She'd found his name in her father's paperwork related to the house. "I remember you tried to talk me out of it."

"Because that's what he would have wanted. What happened to you last night, that's what your father was trying to avoid. That's why he moved to Hawaii. That's why he never told you all the things you're bound and determined to dig up now."

"But he told me to come here. He told me—"

"Either you misunderstood what he was asking, or he was out of his mind."

He'd been lucid. She also knew he hadn't said everything he'd wanted to say before a coughing fit summoned the doctors.

Had she misunderstood?

"He told me to find her, to do right by her."

"I wasn't there for that conversation," Jeff said. "And it's not that I don't believe you, but I don't believe that's what your father wanted for you. For himself, perhaps. But not for you."

"You don't know what he said or what he wanted. You hadn't known him for years."

Jeff didn't argue her points. His voice was low and steady. "I believe your father wanted you to be safe above all. In fact, I know that's what he wanted. He told me more than once, and not just when you were a baby. I helped him purchase the house here a couple of years ago, if you remember. He told me then as well."

"But maybe I'll be safer if you tell me—"

"Because of that"—he spoke over her—"I will tell you nothing. Not today, not tomorrow, not ever. Your father trusted me, and I won't betray that trust. If you want my counsel, here it is: Leave town. Sell the house, get out of New Hampshire, and don't look back."

THE CONVERSATION with Jeff was still ringing in her ears an hour after she ended the call and checked that task off her list.

Could he be right? Could she have misunderstood? Dad hadn't been able to finish what he'd wanted to say, but he told her to find her mother.

Hadn't he?

She was beginning to question everything. The thing that wrecked her, the thing that broke her heart into a thousand little pieces, was that she'd never know. She'd never be able to ask him to clarify. Dad was gone. And it seemed his last task had been to send her on a journey that put her life in danger.

Which didn't make sense at all.

Aspen's father would never have risked her safety. Never.

Maybe Christiansen was right. Maybe she should leave Coventry and not look back.

But she wasn't going to do that. Because she needed to know

what happened to her mother. She needed to know what her father thought she might uncover.

And now there was Garrett.

She put in a call to the Barnetts, but the phone in their little room at the nursing home rang and rang. She tried the front desk, and though they answered and were friendly enough, they wouldn't give Aspen any idea where the Barnetts had gone or when they would be back to their room.

Frustrated, she left a message for Mr. Barnett to call her when he returned home.

She spent the rest of the morning setting up her new computer and downloading files from the cloud, thankful she'd stored almost everything there. She searched the county records for her father's name and found the record of his purchase of the Rattlesnake Road property and how much he paid.

Wow.

Seeing the sum in black and white paused her fingers on the keyboard.

He'd bought the house for over four hundred thousand—in cash.

He must have been saving for years and years. Which meant he'd been planning to buy the property for a long time. Why?

The obvious answer didn't make sense. Maybe Jane Kincaid *was* there, buried somewhere on the property. But if that were the case...

The coffee inside her gurgled and churned.

The only way Dad could have known where Jane Kincaid was buried was if he'd buried her himself.

And if he had...

No. No, her father was not a killer. He was a kind, gentle, tender man. He would never have hurt Aspen's mother. Never.

There had to be an explanation that didn't implicate her father in her mother's death.

She snapped the laptop closed.

It was after lunchtime—not that she'd had the stomach to eat—when she pulled up her ride-sharing app and called for a car. Twenty minutes later, she stepped into the library, spotting Deborah behind the circulation desk.

Aspen approached Garrett's aunt, smiling when the older woman caught sight of her.

She rounded the desk and met Aspen in the lobby. "Garrett told us what happened last night." She took Aspen's hands and squeezed. "I'm glad to see you're okay."

"I am. Thank you."

Deborah's lips pinched tightly. "You don't have any idea who it was?"

"I wish I did."

Deborah shook her head. "Probably just a couple of drugged-up teenagers. We have our share of those in town, I'm afraid."

Aspen didn't dare believe the attack had been random, but she didn't say so. "I was hoping you could answer a couple of questions for me."

"How can I help you?" she asked, leading Aspen toward a deserted area.

"I have two questions. First, do you remember where my parents lived after they had me?"

Deborah stopped at the end of a row of shelves. "Not exactly. I lived in Plymouth, so I didn't go there much. Sorry."

Aspen was disappointed, but she moved to her second question. "Do you remember where my father worked or, if not, at least what he did for a living?"

"He laid concrete."

"Oh. Jeff Christiansen said he needed to get a special

license, but I thought it was a driver's license. Why would he need that?"

"You've seen cement trucks, haven't you? I'm sure it's no picnic driving those things."

So he *had* worked in the construction industry, but he hadn't been a builder.

She'd been thinking that perhaps the construction work the Barnetts had done that winter might have brought Aspen's dad to their house, but their house had already been built. Why would they have needed concrete?

Every answer she got led to more questions. Would she never get to the bottom of this?

Deborah's hand slid over Aspen's. "I don't think I helped you very much."

"You did. I just don't understand...so many things."

"Well, I might not be able to give you the answers you need, but I can offer you a friendly dinner. How about you and Garrett come tonight?"

"Oh. I'd like that." The thought of spending time with people who'd known and loved her mother was irresistible. "If it's all right with Garrett."

"I don't know how to get in touch with him, but you were able to the other day. Why don't you check with him?"

"Sure, and as long as Garrett agrees, I'll see you tonight."

Deborah went back to the circulation desk, and Aspen followed as far as the lobby, pulling her phone from her pocket. She made a Wi-Fi call to Garrett.

"I'm glad you called," he said by way of answer. "I didn't want to wake you."

She glanced at the time. "It's two o'clock."

"I know. I just thought maybe you had a rough night's sleep."

She had, but she didn't say so. "I'm at the library. Your aunt invited us to dinner."

"Oh, good. That's great. Will you still be there, or—?"

"I'm going to the police station at four to meet with Chief Cote. Maybe you could pick me up there when you're finished. I'm happy to hang around until it's convenient for you to come get me."

They made a plan, and she hung up, then found Deborah to confirm their evening plans and offer to bring dessert. Deborah seemed delighted at the prospect.

That task finished, Aspen returned to the computer and searched for a list of concrete companies in town. There were a number of construction companies that did foundation and other concrete work.

Dad could have worked for any one of them. Or one that no longer existed. Or one that didn't have a website.

Even if she found where he used to work, would they tell her the jobs they'd worked on thirty years earlier? Would they even have records going back that far?

Probably not.

Giving up on that, she tried the Barnetts' number again. Still no answer.

With nothing else to do before her appointment, and with last night's conversation with Garrett fresh on her mind, she searched local schools to find where she might earn a teaching degree.

There was Plymouth State, her parents' alma mater, just thirty minutes or so from Coventry. There were also a whole host of online options. She'd initially discarded that idea, believing she'd need in-person classes, not for the learning but to meet people. But if she stayed in Coventry, she already knew people. Maybe she could earn her degree from one of the online universities.

Did she want to be a teacher? She'd loved working with the kids at the church, but was that something she'd want to do forty hours a week—or more, if what she heard about teachers held true?

Really, what she loved was teaching kids about God. She loved volunteering for the church.

Maybe... She did another internet search and discovered there were degrees in church ministry. Maybe she could go that direction. The thought of running a children or student ministry program at a church made her heart thump with excitement.

Did Garrett's church need somebody in that position?

Whoa, she was getting ahead of herself.

But the way her whole being sizzled with the idea... Maybe she was finally figuring out God's plan, which would use not only her skills but her passions as well.

She researched possibilities until it was almost time to meet the chief, new ideas pinging in her mind. She didn't have to settle for a job she hated in a place where she didn't know a soul. Coventry might be cold, but she already had friends here. Her parents had been from here. Maybe she could handle the winters if the other seasons were as lovely as Garrett claimed.

She realized as she waved goodbye to Deborah that she really wanted to find out.

Aspen stepped out the front doors into the chilly late after-noon. The clouds hung low and heavy. The forecast had promised more snow—a dusting, the weatherman had said. Just three inches. She'd never seen *dust* that thick.

Living here would take some getting used to. And good snow tires.

The library was situated in the center of town, next door to the town offices and two doors down from the police station. Though she'd promised Garrett she wouldn't go anywhere by herself, she felt confident she could manage the fifty-yard walk without incident, especially with so many people out and about. People walked from shop to shop as if it weren't freezing cold. As if it were a lovely afternoon for a stroll.

New Hampshireites were made of sturdy stuff.

Maybe if she stayed, she'd become as accustomed to the weather as all these folks were. Assuming, that was, that the locals quit shooting her dirty looks. And whispering behind hands as she walked by.

And trying to kill her.

Having survived the short walk with zero attempts on her life, Aspen pushed into the police station and asked for Chief Cote. A moment later, he ushered her back to his office.

"I'm glad you came by." He rounded his desk and settled on the far side. "How you holding up?"

She was in very good spirits, buoyed by the prospects of staying in Coventry, going to college to study a subject she'd actually love to learn, and Garrett. "I'm good," she said. "I'd be better if I knew who ran me off the road yesterday." She slid into the chair she'd occupied the night before.

"Our search didn't turn up any useful information. We saw where we think Garrett turned around and where you went over, but that was it. There were no signs of another car parking along the shoulder."

"Someone was following me." Irritation and fear rose so fast, it was a struggle to keep her voice level. "Someone with a flash-light was looking—"

"I believe you." He added a smile to accompany the words. "We found the footprints, just not any sign of what they were driving. I'm guessing they parked in the street, out of the snow."

He didn't think she was lying, or crazy. She took a breath to recenter herself. "Did the footprints turn up anything?"

He slipped on reading glasses and consulted a notebook. "Snow boot, man's size ten or thereabouts, my guys tell me."

"Let me guess—that's a pretty common shoe size for a man?"

"Unfortunately. We've asked the body shops in the area to alert us if anybody brings in a car with right-side damage. Patrol guys are on the lookout for the same."

"Feels like a needle-in-the-haystack situation."

"Coventry's a small haystack, but if the driver has any brains at all, he won't take his car to a body shop anywhere near here. We've expanded the search as far south as Concord. I'm hopeful."

"Do you have any guesses about who it might've been? Any suspects?"

He slipped the readers lower on his nose and looked at her for a long time. She wasn't sure what he was hoping to find there, or what he saw. After a moment, he leaned back. "Can I trust you to keep what I say between us?"

The thought of not telling Garrett what she learned didn't sit well, but she said, "Yes."

"I interviewed five people. I've got detectives looking into their alibis and checking their vehicles as we speak. I won't be surprised if one of them was driving that car."

"Who are they?"

"I spoke to both Bart Bradley, the father-in-law of—"

"Rachel, the woman who died," she said. "And?"

"He was home alone, which isn't unusual for Bart at night. He never leaves his house after dark. His car had no damage. Same was true for Rhonda Patterson."

"Rachel's sister."

His eyebrows lifted, and she got the sense he was impressed.

"She sort of introduced herself to me the other day," Aspen said.

"Knowing Rhonda, it wasn't a friendly introduction."

She pictured the woman at the coffee shop, the fury and hatred in her expression. "Not so much."

"She was home with her family. They ordered pizza, and the delivery guy confirmed seeing her and her husband at her house. Didn't figure she'd done it—she wouldn't wear a man's boot, but her husband... Anyway, wasn't him."

"Okay, then. You said you interviewed five people. Who were the other three?"

"I'll tell you, Aspen. But this really does need to stay between us. You and Garrett McCarthy have gotten close, but this isn't something he needs to get involved in. Or to know about."

The mention of Garrett's name sent a flash of worry through her. Surely Chief Cote didn't think he'd had anything to do with this? He couldn't have. He was the one who'd rescued her. "I'll keep it to myself."

"I was a rookie detective at the time of the lumber company bombing, but seeing as how we only had two detectives on the force back then, I worked the case."

She mentally shifted gears. "Okay."

"How much do you want to know?"

It was a fair question, considering her mother was the number-one suspect. "I need to know everything. Even if it's hard to hear."

"Why don't you tell me what you already know?"

"I know when it happened and where. And I know my mother was the only suspect, and that she disappeared after, though I don't know when exactly. I know she was mentally unstable and believed the company was harming the environment."

"Your source?"

"Old newspapers, mostly."

"You haven't talked to anybody in town about it?"

"Marion Eaton, Tabby's mother. She's the one who told me about the bombing. Brent Salcito and I talked a little about it. Deborah Finley told me about Mom and what she was like back then, but we didn't discuss the bombing."

Aspen watched the detective closely as she said the names, but his expression gave nothing away. His chair creaked under his weight as he leaned forward. "What you've heard and read in the papers is true. But it's not the whole truth. There were a number of details we kept from the public." He paused as if waiting for her to speak.

She wasn't sure what to say. She certainly didn't want to say anything that might stop him from sharing. "Is it okay if I ask why?"

"A number of reasons. We had our suspicions, but we didn't have proof. We didn't want to scare anybody off or warn them we were onto them."

"I thought everybody knew my mother did it."

He nodded slowly. His words were measured when he said, "Despite what the papers say, your mother can't have acted alone."

Aspen sat back. "What? I thought... Why do you think that?"

"First and most obvious, she didn't know how to build a bomb."

"She could have learned."

"Bomb-making is not like mixing up cupcake batter. And we uncovered zero evidence that she'd bought the supplies or books on how to do it. And there's the fact that she wasn't entirely in her right mind back then. She might have, in her state, *attempted* to build a bomb. But to have successfully accomplished it?" His skepticism was evident in his shrug. "We didn't buy it."

"Who do you...? Wait, first, what other reason? You said, 'first and obvious.' Which makes me think there's a second and—"

"Less obvious but no less true," he said. "Your mother was in the midst of what your father called an *episode*. We don't know what she suffered from—maybe schizophrenia, maybe something else—but it was debilitating. Your mother's friends were starting to come to grips with her issues, but your father seemed to understand better. He knew the terminology even then, which meant he'd done his homework. He'd been trying to get her to see a psychiatrist for some time, but she'd refused repeatedly. He even tried to have her committed against her will, claiming he feared she was a danger to herself. According to the records, authorities talked to her friends—this was months before the bombing, mind you—who contradicted his claims. One of her friends claimed your dad was bitter because... Are you sure you want to hear this?"

"I'm sure."

"She wasn't exactly the model wife and mother."

Which went along with what Brent had told her. Mom hadn't spent a whole lot of time at home with her family, whether she was romantically involved with Brent or not.

All this information, and the chief wasn't even consulting a notebook. "You must have an exceptional memory."

He smiled, crinkling his wrinkles. "It was a big case, the first murder I worked as a detective. I took it very seriously. But also, I pulled up all the old reports last night after you left." Smile fading, he continued. "I know your next question already. You want to know who our other suspects were. We looked at everybody in the college's environmental club, but our focus narrowed very quickly to four people, the four people closest to her."

He seemed to be waiting for Aspen to say something, perhaps to guess, but how could she know. She only knew...

Oh.

"You aren't saying..." She leaned forward. "I only know about a few of my mom's old friends. I've met Deborah Finley, and I know her husband, Dean, knew Mom back then. And Brent Salcito, the mayor. You can't mean them. They're still in town. They were never charged with anything, were they? I didn't see any of their names in the papers."

"Remember, we kept a lot of stuff back from the press."

"Why?"

"A number of reasons, not the least of which was the fact that they were kids. I mean, they were all *technically* adults, but they were twenty. Their parents lived in this town and had for generations."

"You questioned them this morning?"

"Last night."

At his nod, she let the truth settle. She'd seen Deborah at the library that afternoon. She'd already known about the incident on the mountain, but she'd claimed she heard it from Garrett.

Not so. She'd heard from Cote when she'd been questioned. Unless she'd already known. Unless she'd been the driver of the car.

Aspen was almost afraid to ask her next question. "You think one of my mother's old friends ran me off the road? Why, though? What would they have to gain by hurting me?"

Another shrug. "If we knew the motive, it'd be a lot easier to nail down a suspect. I'm guessing somebody doesn't want you poking the bear, as it were. The people who conspired with your mother to blow up that building have escaped judgment for a long time. They want it to stay that way. Maybe you won't expose them—maybe you can't. But you can start everybody asking questions about it again."

"But you wouldn't be involved at all if not for the fact that somebody broke into my house and then tried to kill me. Their actions are stirring the story up more than mine are."

"I love irony."

She wasn't a fan at the moment.

She couldn't imagine Deborah trying to hurt her. The woman seemed so kind and open. Maybe Garrett's uncle, though. Or Brent, the man who'd bought her coffee and pastries a few days earlier.

Cote was patient as she processed everything he'd told her. She was ready to hear the rest. "Go on."

Instead, he said, "I could use a cup of coffee. It was a late night. Are you up for a walk, or is it too cold for a Hawaii girl outside?"

Getting out of that small, stuffy room sounded good to her. "I've got my coat and gloves. I'll be fine."

Aspen zipped her jacket and was pulling on her gloves by the time Cote opened the back door of the police station for her. They stepped outside into a parking lot. The air was chilly, and the sun had already disappeared behind the tall trees all around them. It would be dark by the time they walked back, but she felt safe with the police chief at her side.

He led her across the lot, then up a narrow alley away from the main road.

"Let's go back to what we know." Cote's pace was quick despite his girth. "My partner and I looked at the closest people to your mother. Deborah Davis—now Finley—was her best friend and involved with the environmental club on campus. The night of the bombing, she was at work. Seven people corroborated her alibi."

"And Dean?"

"He was in his dorm room that night. His roommate can put him there."

"So he wasn't involved."

Cote's lips quirked at the corner. "Assuming his roommate can be believed, he wasn't present when the bomb went off."

Which wasn't exactly the same thing. "Do you not believe the roommate?"

Cote shrugged. "Sometimes people lie. Not saying he did, but..." He walked a few steps before continuing. "Brent Salcito, who was, by all accounts, your mother's..." His words faded, and he glanced her way. "Your mother was, uh..."

"Brent believed they were in love," Aspen said. "Deborah said they weren't even dating."

Cote seemed relieved that Aspen already knew that. "I suspect the truth is somewhere in the middle of those two extremes. Brent was in love with your mother. How your mother felt about him—that I don't know. But, based on all the information we got, they were together. Dating." He seemed to cringe at the word. "Sorry. I'm sure that's—"

"Finding out my mother wasn't faithful to my father ranks lower on the worst-news-ever scale than finding out she was a killer." Aspen tried to keep her tone light even if the words twisted in her heart. "Keep going."

"Brent was with his father in Boston. Or so they claim."

"You don't sound convinced."

"The Salcitos had an apartment in the city, and they say they drove down Thursday afternoon. Nobody saw them in the city that night, so we only have Brent's word and his father's. They did have an appointment at Boston College the next day, though, which they'd made weeks before. Brent transferred to BC the next semester. Martin, Brent's father, claimed he and Brent planned the father-son weekend because his wife and daughters were at some cheerleading competition in Massachusetts."

"Do you believe them?"

He shrugged. "Good police work is ninety percent guessing." He smiled to show he was kidding. "Martin Salcito's a good man who loves his kids. He'd never been in any scrapes with the law, and neither had Brent. We had no good reason not to believe him."

"But you don't," she guessed.

"We couldn't prove they were lying. We couldn't put Brent with your mother at the lumber company or anywhere else in Coventry or in Plymouth the night of the bombing. And, honestly, nobody thought the kid was a killer."

"Maybe everybody was wrong about him."

He shrugged. "Maybe."

"My mother *was* a killer?"

"Your mother was mentally ill and, by all accounts, not thinking straight. I'd like to believe that, if she'd been thinking straight, she would have seen the car in the parking lot that night and decided not to detonate that bomb."

They reached the end of the alley, and he turned right. They passed an attorney's office and an insurance agency. Beyond those was the coffee shop she'd been to twice already. It must be a local favorite.

"Somebody died," Aspen said. "I know you think Mom did it, but you also think somebody else was involved. It seems to me it might've been worth the effort to dig a little deeper into their alibis. Maybe put a little more pressure on them."

"You're not wrong. The lead detective was a local. He knew

all the families. He was happy to be able to strike those kids off the list of suspects."

"Even if they were guilty?"

Cote didn't respond to that.

"If you'd been in charge...?"

"I might have done things differently, but I wasn't in charge. Truth is, they were good kids. They were A-students. Smart and hard-working. They'd never gotten into any trouble. They obeyed their fathers and kissed their mothers and went to church. They weren't bad kids."

"But my mom was, I guess. Her family was new to town, so that detective didn't have any problem pinning the whole thing on her."

"Your mother wasn't in her right mind, Aspen. Witnesses saw her car—she drove a red hatchback—turning off the road that led to the lumber company. They saw a woman driving. Her car was found abandoned up on Rattlesnake Road."

"Rattlesnake? My road?"

How had she not known that?

"Ayuh. At the top, though, a mile or so past your place. There're houses up there now, but back then they were just starting to clear the land. Your mother's involvement was never in question." Cote continued in a gentle tone. "Your mother needed to be hospitalized. Your father was right about that. Unfortunately, until she did something to harm herself or others, nobody could force it."

They entered the coffee shop. Cote ordered a drink and offered to get hers as well.

"I need more than just coffee. You go ahead." After he paid, she ordered a caramel macchiato from Josie, the woman who'd been there before. "I need to bring dessert to dinner tonight."

The thought of sitting at a table with Dean and Deborah after hearing all of this made Aspen's heart race, but she wanted to meet Dean. She wanted to get to know him and Deborah better, to form her own opinions. They were Garrett's family, the people who'd taken him in and raised him. How could she suspect them of anything?

But Cote obviously did.

"How many will there be?" Josie asked.

"Four. What do you recommend?"

"The fruit tarts are good for dessert. And everybody loves the chocolate tortes." Aspen asked her to box up two of each and paid for them. She joined Cote in the room where she'd sat with Brent a few days earlier. Cote had chosen a small table by the window. A fire had flickered when she and Brent were there. Now the little warmth that came from the fireplace emanated from a few burning coals.

Aspen set her box down, slipped off her jacket, and sat. "So maybe Mom acted alone, or maybe—"

"She didn't act alone. We covered that."

"But I mean, the night of the bombing."

"Maybe."

"Are you saying...? Do you think Deborah, Dean, and Brent were in on it, even if they weren't there? Or one of them? Or a couple of them?"

"Do you want to hear what I *know*, or what I *believe*?"

"Both."

"You know what I know. Your mother, Dean, Deborah, and Brent were good friends who were all involved in the same club on campus. We suspected one or more of them helped her with the bombing, but they all have alibis. Your mother wasn't capable of building a bomb. From here on out, I'm speculating, and I could be wrong. If I'm right, then the people who worked with your mother are accomplices in a murder, not to mention destruction of property and a whole host of other crimes.

They're terrorists, and they need to be brought to justice. So what I'm telling you needs to stay between us. Okay?"

She nodded.

He leaned across the small table and lowered his voice. "You read about the witnesses who saw your mother driving away from the bombing that night. What we didn't release..."

His voice trailed, and a moment later the brunette set their coffees on the table between them. "You need anything else?"

"We're good, Josie," Cote said. "Thanks." He waited until she walked away. "What we didn't release to the papers is that somebody saw the car headed up *to* the lumber company as well. To get to the headquarters, you had to drive through a neighborhood on the edge of town. One of the residents was having a party that night. It turns out that, when your mother passed, a woman had just arrived. She looked inside the car thinking it was a friend pulling up and saw two people. The witness thought it was a man and a woman."

Oh. "So one of them was there. Brent or Dean. But you said you had no evidence."

"We believe there was a man with your mother. Witnesses have been known to get things wrong. It could have been a woman with short hair or hair pulled back. But definitely two people went in."

"But Deborah and Dean were back at the college, and Brent was in Boston."

"Deborah's alibi is rock solid. *Maybe* Dean was at the college. Maybe his roommate was mistaken or lied. The roommate was also involved in the club, so it's possible."

"A woman was dead. Surely the roommate would have told the truth."

"You'd be surprised what people will do."

She really didn't want Garrett's uncle to have been an

accomplice. "It could have been Brent, right? You said nobody could corroborate the story that he was in Boston that night."

"It's possible."

"Or...could it have been somebody else from the club? Or do you have another suspect?"

Cote's expression turned tender, as if he hated what he had to say. "I told you earlier we looked at the *four* closest people to your mother. We've talked about three. The other is..."

The answer was obvious, and ridiculous. "My *father*?" She'd said the word too loud and forced a quieter volume. "You think my father helped her? That's crazy."

"I agree."

"He wouldn't... You do?"

"I don't think your father had anything to do with the bombing. I'm just telling you where we looked. If it wasn't Brent or Dean, your father was the next most likely suspect."

"Who do you think it was?"

"Remember, we're talking about what I believe, not what I can prove." At her nod, he continued. "I believe Brent went with her that night. I believe he planned the whole thing. By all accounts, he'd have done anything for your mother. He was logical where your mother, according to what everybody told us, wasn't thinking clearly. Brent would have been able to plan the whole thing and cover their tracks. Do I think Brent wanted to blow up that building? Not necessarily. Do I think he would have done it for your mother?" Cote shrugged.

But if Brent was with her at the bombing, then he would have been with her afterward as well. "Do you think he killed her? Or maybe helped her get away or something?"

"He loved her, Aspen. I have no reason to believe he would have hurt her. Hidden her? Maybe, but we kept a close eye on him. I can't imagine how he could have pulled it off. Not as a twenty-year-old, not without help. And for how long could he have hidden her? How would he have done it with your mother in that mental state?" He shook his head. "No, I never bought that."

She remembered something else she'd learned. "The witness said only one person drove away."

"Multiple witnesses at that point. Everybody in about a five-mile radius heard that bomb explode. The people at that party went outside to see what had happened. They were watching the flames through the trees when they saw your mother's car. And yes, only one person could be seen inside."

"Maybe he was crouched down in the backseat."

"Maybe."

Or maybe... "Is it possible Brent had a wig or something? Maybe he killed my mother *in* the bombing."

Cote smiled. "You could be a detective, Miss Kincaid. Very thoughtful question."

"And?"

His smile faded. "We only uncovered one body, and it belonged to the victim. The property and the forest surrounding it were thoroughly searched."

"But he could have buried her or—"

"They drove up at nine twenty and drove back out at nine thirty-two. The bomb went off at nine twenty-eight. There was no time for him to bury her. We think either your mother left Brent at the lumber company for some reason—maybe they fought. Though I can't figure out how he would have gotten out of there and home without being seen. More likely, he was crouched down in the passenger seat or the back. He was smart enough to know people would be outside looking, so that's my theory."

"You think Brent was her accomplice."

"One of them. Thing is, Brent didn't know how to build bombs either. And he was smart enough not to try."

"Somebody else was involved? Who among them could have built a bomb? I mean, they were twenty, like you said. They didn't have the Internet. They weren't exactly criminal master..."

But something Garrett had said, words tossed out as if they didn't matter at all, floated to Aspen's memory. "Dean was a chemistry major."

Cote's eyebrows lifted. "You ever decide to go into law enforcement, give me a call."

She tried to smile at his remark, but the expression felt wrong. "That I'm suspecting the uncle of my..." She didn't know what to call Garrett. He was more than her contractor, but did "boyfriend" fit the bill?

It wouldn't for long, not if he learned what she was thinking. What she'd just said.

But Cote didn't look surprised. Of course he'd already known Dean's major.

Just to be sure, she said, "You think Dean built the bomb."

"I'm sure of it. But being sure of it and being able to prove it are two very different things."

"He was never charged?"

"Nope. If he did it, he bought all the supplies with cash and not anywhere local. I have no idea where he put it together or where they stored it. I could never get to the bottom of any of that."

"Maybe that's the connection to the house," Aspen said.

"Huh." He sat back. "What is your father's link to the place?"

"I haven't figured that out."

Cote stared past her a long moment, then shook his head. "If they used the house back then, your dad could only have known about it if he was involved."

"Maybe Mom told him?"

"Maybe. But all the evidence must have been cleaned up long ago. When did he buy the house?"

"Two years ago." So that theory didn't hold water. "Where do you think my mother went?"

Cote leaned forward and rested his weight on his forearms. "You know as much as I do now. What do *you* think?"

"Dad said she disappeared. Nobody seems to think she's still alive. You must have a theory."

"Nothing I could back up with facts. Unlike my theories about the bombing, all I have regarding your mother is educated guesses. I can't imagine Brent having hurt her, not as much as he loved her. He claimed your father did it. He made a big stink about how they used to fight, how your father was jealous."

"Dad would never do that." The very thought of it was abhorrent. "And anyway, he was home with me, right?"

"He wasn't, actually. His parents—your grandparents—were there. They stayed with you sometimes. They said your dad got a call from your mom and left about nine o'clock."

That was suspicious. Even still... "You don't think my dad had anything to do with the bombing or with my mother's disappearance." She said the words with confidence, praying she was right.

"The bombing, no."

She sat back. "You don't mean... You don't think my father hurt her."

"Your father said Jane called him and asked him to meet her up on Rattlesnake. I guess they'd gone up there a couple of times. He said he went, but when he arrived, she wasn't there. Then he heard the explosion and went home to make sure you were all right."

"My grandparents were able to confirm that, right?"

"I'm afraid there's a pretty decent chunk of time missing."

Aspen didn't want to hear the chief's theories. She wanted

to cover her ears to keep any more of his words from entering her mind, to keep the doubts at bay. But she'd come here for answers.

"What do you think happened?"

He started to speak, then closed his mouth. After a moment, he said, "Since you came back, an idea's been forming...about that house."

She swallowed but kept quiet.

"You're an intelligent woman. I'm sure it's occurred to you as well. Maybe your father bought that house because your mother is buried somewhere on the property. But if that's the case—"

"My father didn't kill my mother."

"If he found out about the bombing, if he found out about her affair with Salcito? Extreme circumstances can make people do extreme things." The tone was placating. "Would you be willing to let me get ground-penetrating radar out there? If she's buried on the property, don't you want to know?"

Aspen had come to Coventry to find her mother.

But if Jane Kincaid was buried near the house Dad bought, then Dad had known all those years. And if he'd known where she was buried...

He'd killed her.

Was it even possible? Was Cote right?

She couldn't believe it. She wouldn't.

Cote watched while she wrestled with her thoughts. Wrestled, but there was really only one answer. Because Dad had sent her there to find her mother. To do right by her. And she couldn't do that until she found her. She had to keep going, no matter how much it hurt.

She swallowed again. "Do it."

Cote pushed back in his chair. "We'd better head back. I'll

get it set up, but it'll probably take a couple of weeks to schedule it."

As she grabbed her box of desserts, she thought of one more question. "I assume you checked on Brent, Deborah, and Dean's whereabouts last night."

Cote led the way out of the coffee shop and back to the sidewalk. "The mayor is at a retreat in Maine. We called the hotel, and they confirmed he checked in a couple of days ago. His car's in the parking lot as well—undamaged. He's not our guy."

"And Garrett's aunt and uncle?"

"They say they were at dinner, but if they were, they paid in cash. The servers who were on last night aren't on today, so it's taking some time to confirm their alibi." He glanced her way, an unreadable—but concerning—expression on his face. "I can tell you that Deborah's car wasn't at the house when I went to question them. They tell me it's in the shop for engine work. I'm waiting to hear back from the mechanic about that."

"But you think it could have been them?"

"At this point, they're my only suspects."

CHAPTER TWENTY-SIX

GARRETT HAD BEEN WAITING thirty minutes by the time Aspen met him in the lobby of the police station. She was already wearing her coat and gloves, and her cheeks were pink. She carried a vaguely familiar pale blue box.

Her lips stretched into a smile, but there was no heart behind it.

He stood. "You all right?"

She nodded but continued through the room and out the door. He grabbed it before it closed and then held it open for a woman going in. By the time he caught up with Aspen, she was standing by his pickup.

He opened her door, and she climbed inside, keeping the box level.

He had so many questions about what she'd learned, but she seemed...off, somehow. So after he climbed in, he went with, "What's in the box?"

"Dessert for tonight."

"Oh." Then it hit him. "It's from Josie's."

She nodded.

He maneuvered into traffic. "Did you learn anything?"

She said nothing, so he risked a glance her way to find she was nodding.

"Something disturbing, I guess."

"The chief asked me not to talk about what he told me. Sorry."

"Oh." He wished she'd make an exception for him. It wasn't as if he'd tell anybody. But Aspen didn't seem to think an exception was in order. "Are you okay?"

"I'm processing."

Garrett stopped at one of the few stoplights in town and faced her. "Can I do anything?"

"I think I should just go back to Grace's. I'm not sure I'm up for company tonight."

"Are you sick?"

"No. Just...out of sorts."

"You need to eat, and I happen to know Dean fixed a delicious meal, one of my favorites. We don't have to stay long."

The light turned green, and he continued driving toward his aunt and uncle's house. He wanted Aspen to meet the two most important people in his life. More than that, he didn't want to miss out on an evening with her. Once they got there, she'd perk up.

But how presumptuous to think he knew what was best for her. "We can cancel, if you'd rather."

"I do want to meet your uncle," she said.

"We can leave right after dessert. Or...anytime you want. Just say the word."

Aspen's side of the cab was silent. Not being able to talk about what she'd learned was probably making whatever she'd heard feel even worse.

She needed a distraction. Dean and Deborah would be able to provide that, if nothing else.

They rode in silence until he parked in the driveway. "You ready?"

She nodded and pushed open her door.

He ran around to help her from the truck. "Uncle tells me a gentleman always helps a lady in and out of vehicles."

He'd expected at least a smile.

"Can I carry that for you?"

She handed him the box, which he shifted to his other hand before sticking out his elbow. "They have some drainage issues, so the driveway stays wet for a while. It might be a little slick."

She slid her hand into the crook of his elbow and held on tight.

He loved the feel of her leaning on him, trusting him. Later, after dinner, after he took her back to Grace's, he'd coax what she'd learned from Cote out of her. He could be trusted with it, and she needed to share it.

He was glad she'd decided to come. Once Dean spent an evening with Aspen, he'd understand why Garrett was enamored with her. He'd realize she was nothing like her mother. The grudge he held against her would have dissipated by the time they dug into Josie's desserts, of that Garrett had no doubt.

As usual, they hadn't reached the front door before Deborah pushed it open. "Welcome! Hurry, hurry. It's cold out here."

He chuckled. "Auntie, if you'd leave it shut until we got there—"

"Oh, shush. Can I help it if I'm eager?"

They walked up the concrete steps, and Deborah pulled Aspen into a quick hug. "I'm so glad you came." At the sight of the box in Garrett's hands, her eyebrows lifted. "And what is that?"

"I picked them up at that coffee shop," Aspen said.

"Josie is a master." She took the box from Garrett and stepped back. "Dean's in the kitchen."

Garrett helped Aspen with her coat and hung it on the hooks right inside the door before shrugging out of his own. They walked up the half flight to the main floor, Deborah right behind.

With a hand on Aspen's back, Garrett urged her toward the kitchen, where his uncle was facing the stove. "Uncle Dean, this is Aspen Kincaid."

He turned to them. Though he wore a smile, Garrett saw wariness behind it and hoped he only recognized it because he knew the man so well.

Aspen stepped forward, hand outstretched. "It's a pleasure to meet you. Garrett's told me a lot about you."

Dean shook her hand. "Glad you're here."

"Thank you for the table and chairs."

"They were just taking up space."

Garrett peeked beyond him. "I'm starved."

"Chicken scampi," Dean said to Aspen. "I was gonna do shrimp, but I didn't know if you ate shellfish."

"I do, but I like chicken," she said. The scents of garlic and spices filled the air. "It smells delicious."

"You guys sit. It'll be ready in a minute."

Behind them, Deborah said, "What can I get you to drink? I opened a pinot grigio to go with the meal."

"Just water for me," Aspen said.

"I'll have the same." Garrett occasionally sipped a glass of wine with dinner, but if Aspen didn't want any, he'd skip it too. She seemed uncomfortable enough already, and the last thing he wanted to do was make that worse.

Maybe she was nervous because this was akin to meeting his parents? If that was the case, he didn't mind knowing she cared enough about him to want to make a good impression.

Deborah got them both glasses of water, poured some wine

for herself and Dean, and then sliced a loaf of Italian bread Dean had been warming in the oven.

By the time it was steaming from a basket in the center of the table, Dean had carried over the bowl of pasta and a green salad.

"Looks delicious," Garrett said.

"It does." Aspen had her hands in her lap, but he could see they were clasped together.

"Garrett," Deborah said, "since you brought the guest of honor, will you pray for us?" Deborah's hands went to Dean on one side and Garrett on the other at the round table.

Garrett took it and reached for Aspen's.

She took his hand, then settled her other into Dean's with a tight smile.

Garrett thanked God for the food and for Aspen's presence at their table. He asked for God's blessing on the meal and the conversation. Silently, he added a prayer that Aspen would relax and feel comfortable.

After the chorus of amens, they dug into the feast.

Dean's gaze kept slipping to Aspen at his side. When she turned his way and caught him looking, he said, "I'm sorry. It's just so strange."

"Uncanny." Deborah added, smiling. "How much you look like your mother."

Aspen seemed to take the remark as an invitation. She said to Dean, "You knew her too."

"Not as well as Deb. But yeah." Though Dean seemed to think he'd lobbed the conversation ball back into her court, Aspen said nothing. After an awkward moment, he added, "She was...unique. I've never known anybody with her passion."

"Brent Salcito said the same."

Dean's hands stilled over his meal. "You talked to Salcito?"

"We had coffee on Tuesday. He said she was the female Bill Clinton."

The moniker was amusing, and Garrett chuckled.

Dean only nodded. He'd always been on the quiet side, but his behavior tonight bordered on rude.

"Are you still close with Brent?" Aspen asked.

"No." He twirled a forkful of angel hair pasta and popped it in his mouth.

Deborah's laugh felt forced. "We went our separate ways after...college."

Garrett heard the hesitation and wasn't surprised when Aspen called her on it. "After college? Or after the bombing."

Deborah's skin paled a little. She set her fork down, keeping her gaze on Aspen. "We were all questioned about it, you know. Us and Brent, and the rest of the club. But they mostly focused on us because we were closest to your mother. It's not that big a school. Everybody knew what happened, and a lot of people knew we were friends with your mother. It became...awkward."

"Maybe this isn't the time to talk about all that." Garrett tried to think of a segue to a lighter topic.

Dean shoved another forkful of food into his mouth as if, by keeping it full, he would be spared having to speak.

"I'm sorry." Aspen attempted a smile. "It's been a really long day, and my mind is..." She took a deep breath. "I'm sorry to bring that up over dinner."

"We understand, hon," Deborah said. "It must be hard, what you're going through."

"Being run off the road?" Aspen said. "Barely escaping death? Sort of hard, yeah." Aspen watched her a long moment before cutting her pasta into small pieces and taking a bite.

Deborah said nothing.

Garrett felt like there were two conversations going on at the table, and he was only hearing one of them.

Aspen set down her fork and sipped her water. "So, did you stay at Plymouth?" She directed the question to Deborah.

"I transferred to New Hampshire College in Manchester."

Aspen turned to Dean. "This meal is delicious. Thank you so much for making it."

He looked up from his plate and smiled. It almost looked genuine. "It's my pleasure."

"You like to cook?"

"I love it."

"And he's really good," Garrett said, grateful for the subject change. "Did you know Aspen's father owned restaurants?"

"Is that so?" Dean asked. "How many?"

"Four. There were two on the Big Island—Kona and Waikoloa. One in Waikiki and one on Maui."

"Touristy places?" Dean asked.

"The first one was in Kona, and it started out as a local favorite. Dad expanded to a second restaurant when I was little. When it was featured on one of those Food Network shows, it exploded, and he opened the other ones."

"Good for him," Dean said. "He always was a hard worker. I didn't know he liked to cook, though. Do you?"

"It's funny," she said. "I can cook, but it's not something we did together very much. We were at the restaurant most nights. We ate there, but Dad wasn't the chef at that point. Even though he loved to create amazing dishes, he handed over the recipes to the cooks. When we didn't have to be at the restaurant, we usually did something fun together. Surfing or hiking, if there wasn't some school activity I needed to attend. I haven't done a lot of cooking in my life."

"What a unique experience, practically growing up in a restaurant." Dean nodded across the table to Garrett. "This one's a great cook, mostly because I made him learn."

Garrett chuckled. "I didn't complain too much." Those

were some of his favorite memories from when he'd first come to live with them. Deborah had worked more nights back then, but Dean was always home.

"Only because I let you sample the food." Dean winked at Aspen. "The kid was un-fillable. Never seen somebody eat so much."

"I was a growing boy."

Dean eyed the giant portion of pasta on Garrett's plate. "What's your excuse now?"

"It was a busy day," he said, spearing a piece of chicken. "I need to keep my strength up. Even if it means forcing down this roadkill."

"Oh, you two." But the affection in Deborah's voice was obvious. To Aspen, she said, "Ignore them. That's what I do."

Aspen smiled and turned back to Dean. "I can see why you like to cook—mixing all those ingredients to see what you can create. It's different, but a little like what you studied in school, right? Did you finish your chemistry degree?"

Dean's playful expression dissipated, and his skin turned red. He glared at Garrett, the look so fast Garrett might have imagined it. "No." He stabbed a bite of the meal and ate it.

Either Aspen didn't notice Dean's discomfort or didn't care. If Garrett had to guess, despite how well he knew her—and liked her—he'd guess the second. "Did you change majors, or colleges, or both?"

Dean swallowed the food. "After your mother blew up that building and murdered—"

"Dean," Deborah said.

"...that woman... After I was questioned about my involvement—"

"That's enough," Deborah said.

But Dean ignored her. "After everybody and his cousin thought I was involved, I quit school. I never went back."

Garrett expected Aspen to apologize for dredging up old, painful memories. But she didn't.

Garrett said, "I'm sure she didn't mean anything by it."

Dean glared at Aspen another moment, then grabbed his slice of bread.

"Having you here," Deborah said, "it's a little disconcerting for us."

"I understand," Aspen said. "The thing is, I came to Coventry to figure out what happened to my mother. What do you think happened?"

Deborah and Dean shared a look.

Dean answered. "She blew up that building, and then she took off. No idea where she went. To tell you the truth, I always figured she realized she killed somebody and lost it. I wouldn't be surprised to find out she's been alive all this time, one of the millions of nutcase homeless people wandering around."

"Uncle!" Garrett's gut twisted at the unkind words. What was happening here?

"You think she's alive?" Aspen asked.

"Not necessarily." He shrugged as if the whereabouts of Aspen's mother didn't matter at all. "There was no body. What did your father think?"

"He thought she was dead." Aspen's attitude was just as puzzling. She didn't seem hurt or shocked by Dean's words. It was as if she'd come prepared for a confrontation. "He said that she wouldn't have been able to survive and stay hidden in her state of mind."

Dean nodded. "Wherever she is, she's not here. So if you're looking for her, you're looking in the wrong place. You probably ought to move along."

"There's no need to be rude." This meal had not gone the way Garrett hoped. He wasn't sure who he blamed more for that. Aspen had started it, but Dean was doing his best to finish it with a win.

Aspen turned to Garrett with that same forced smile he'd seen more than once that night. "It's okay, Garrett. It's good to know where I stand." Her tone was light, but he heard the undercurrent of anger.

"Let's change the subject," Deborah said. "How's the house coming along?"

It wasn't easy, but Garrett shifted gears. They managed to get through the rest of dinner and dessert without talking about Jane Kincaid or the bombing or anything else unpleasant. Even Dean engaged in the conversation, giving Garrett hope that maybe his uncle could accept their relationship.

When the last bite of pastry was finished, Deborah started clearing the table. Aspen stood to help, and Garrett did the same.

Dean pushed his chair back. "Son, I could use your help with something in the shop."

"Okay." He looked at Aspen. "I'll be back in a few minutes." Only at her nod did he follow his uncle down the stairs.

GARRETT STEPPED into the workshop behind his uncle. He'd been polite long enough. Now, he needed answers. "What was that about?"

It was clear when Dean turned to face him that he hadn't asked Garrett to follow him because he needed help.

"You told her about me? That I studied chemistry?"

"What difference—?"

"You don't understand anything." Dean's skin was red and mottled. His hands were clenched at his sides.

Garrett flashed back to the episode Dean had had the week

before—the shortness of breath, the weakness. He reached toward him. "Why don't you sit—?"

"I'm fine." He yanked his arm away. "I don't trust her. You were supposed to keep an eye on her, let me know what she's been up to. And now I find out you've been telling her about *me*, about *us*. Where's your loyalty?"

Garrett stepped back, shocked. "I've always been loyal to you. I didn't know your college major was a state secret."

"It's none of her business." Garrett had never heard his uncle speak with such venom. "She's bad news. I'm telling you, she's here to ruin lives, and if you aren't careful, yours will be the first." Dean took a deep breath and blew it out. "I know you like her, or you think you do. But she's not who you think she is. Sane or not, she's not the woman for you. She's here to stir up trouble, and she's pulling you right in with her."

"You don't know anything about her."

"I know enough. I only want the best for you, son."

"I'm not your son." The words slipped out, words he'd never said to this man. He'd always wished he was.

Dean straightened his shoulders, eyes wide.

Garrett couldn't unsay that. And he wasn't about to back down because he'd hurt Dean's feelings. "I love you, Uncle. I do. But Aspen means something to me. I won't let you poison me against her because you didn't like her mother. She has every right to ask questions about what happened back then. She's lost both her parents. It's logical she wants to know what happened."

Dean crossed his arms across his broad chest. "So you're not going to keep your distance from her?"

"No. I'm not."

Dean nodded slowly. Silence stretched between them until Garrett feared something was about to snap.

And then it did. "If that's your choice, I guess you'll be keeping your distance from me."

If Dean had struck him, it couldn't have hurt Garrett more. He could think of nothing to say.

So he turned and walked out.

He climbed the steps to the landing and stood there a long time, staring down at the tile beneath his feet. The tile he and Uncle Dean had laid together. Garrett had been an angry fourteen-year-old, fresh from his parents' house. Dean had taught Garrett how to spread the mortar, how to set the tiles, even how to use the wet saw. Garrett had broken more tiles than he'd laid, but Dean had never once shouted at him. He'd never shown a hint of disappointment.

In that gentle way of his, he'd come alongside and taught Garrett how to lay tile. Then how to grout it. How to build things. How to design things.

He'd taught Garrett what it meant to be a treasured child. He'd taught him how to be a man.

Was their relationship so fragile that it could crumble the first time Garrett defied him?

Maybe his uncle had never loved him at all.

He trudged up to the second floor, only then realizing he was hearing no happy chatter between Deborah and Aspen. As horribly as Dean had behaved, Deborah had been nothing but kind. Why wasn't she making conversation?

He found her at the sink, washing dishes. He looked around, but Deborah was alone. "Where's Aspen?"

Deborah turned to him. "She's not with you? She went to the powder room right after you two walked out. I figured she went to see the workshop."

"She didn't come down."

But even as he said the words, fear churned in his gut.

Had she gone down?

If so, what had she heard?

He peered down the hallway, but the bathroom door was wide open, the light off. He walked that direction, just in case, but Aspen wasn't there.

He took the half flight back to the coat tree, knowing what he was going to find.

Her coat was gone.

CHAPTER TWENTY-SEVEN

Aspen could hardly see. It was dark. Ridiculously dark. What kind of desolate world was this? No streetlights, no cars. The houses were set so far off the road that the lights from their windows were like pinpricks in the blackness.

She tripped over a chunk of ice, and it skidded into the snowbank. She swiped angry tears, which weren't helping. It was her own fault. Her own stupid fault for going to Dean and Deborah Finley's house in the first place.

She'd known when Dean called Garrett away that he'd wanted to talk to his nephew alone, and Aspen had needed to know why.

So, she'd excused herself to the bathroom, and when Deborah wasn't looking, she'd tiptoed down the stairs. She didn't know what she'd thought she'd learn. Even if Dean had been the one to force her off the road the previous night, he surely wouldn't confess that to Garrett. But she'd felt compelled to find out what she could.

She wished she hadn't.

Which was foolish and stupid, but what else was new? Wasn't it foolish and stupid to be in Coventry, in the town that hated her mother and hated Aspen by extension? What was she doing here?

She'd thought she could figure out what happened to her mother. As if she had any insights the police didn't already have.

She'd hoped to learn more about the woman who'd borne her. And she had.

To her detriment.

But she'd believed that, if nothing else, there was Garrett. He'd come to mean something to her. For the first time in her life, she'd thought maybe she was falling in love.

Stupid, stupid, stupid.

She'd taken out her heart and handed it over to him, and he'd been lying to her all along.

You were supposed to keep an eye on her, let me know what she's been up to.

Dean's words told Aspen they'd agreed on this plan long before tonight. Garrett hadn't disputed what he said. Hadn't clarified.

Garrett had been Dean's *spy*.

Which meant he knew his uncle was involved. In the bombing? Maybe. In the attempt on her life?

From the moment she'd looked into Dean's eyes, she'd known exactly what he was.

The enemy.

And now she knew Garrett was too.

She reached the corner of the residential street and peered to the right and the left. She hadn't been paying enough attention during the drive and had no idea which way to turn to head back to town.

As if she could walk the entire way. She needed a plan.

Headlights came on at the house across the street from where she stood. She was tempted to hide, but why? She wasn't doing anything wrong. And it wasn't Dean's house.

What were the chances that a random person would want to hurt her?

In Coventry? Even money.

The car drove out of the driveway, its beams crossing over Aspen. It turned the opposite direction, then stopped and backed up, stopping again when it was even with her.

Aspen considered pulling the handgun from her holster but waited as the stranger's window came down.

"You all right?" It was a woman's voice, and vaguely familiar.

"Yeah, just..." Just what? Trying to walk back to town without a map on a freezing cold night?

The woman said, "Caramel macchiato, right?" When Aspen didn't respond, she smiled. "I take it by the fact that you're out here on the street that the desserts didn't go over well."

Aspen felt herself smile. "You have a good memory. It's Josie, right?"

"Yup. And you're...?"

"Aspen."

"Great name. You need a ride, Aspen?"

"Oh. Um..."

Josie didn't press, just waited while Aspen contemplated the question. She did need a ride. But could she trust Josie? She should have called Grace already. If she'd been thinking straight, she would have. But it would take Grace some time to get here, time that Garrett could use to find her.

If not Garrett, Dean. The thought brought a healthy spike of fear.

But was Josie safe?

"Can I ask you a question?" Aspen said.

"Sure."

"How long have you lived in Coventry?"

"Three years."

"Is your family from here? Do you know a lot about the history of the town?"

In the light of the moon, Aspen saw the woman's eyes narrow. "Uh, no."

"Do you know anything about me?"

"Aside from your penchant for asking weird questions?" She infused humor into her voice. "Let's see... You've had coffee with the mayor and the chief of police this week." The humor faded. "One of my customers reamed you out for something that, from what I could tell, had nothing to do with you. And, I admit, I've noticed a couple of people trying to get a good look at you. I've heard whispers. But I have no idea what any of it's about."

"My mother was a murderer." Aspen said the words to garner a reaction, but Josie barely flinched.

"That doesn't make you one. Or does it? Am I risking my life here?"

"I've never hurt anyone."

"Judging by the look I caught on your face when I first saw you, I'm guessing you're thinking about it."

Aspen laughed, the sound strange in the quiet night. "Maybe. Where are you headed?"

"Back to town. Come on."

It was a risk, but standing on the street felt like more of one. And it wasn't as if this woman was a total stranger. Aspen climbed into the passenger seat.

"Where to?" Josie asked.

"I can have my friend meet me wherever you're headed."

Josie seemed about to argue but instead said, "I'm going back to the shop."

"Is it still open?"

"Yeah, but I'm not working tonight." She shot a smile Aspen's way. "I live there. I have an apartment upstairs."

"Oh. Nice commute." Aspen texted Grace where she was headed and asked if she'd mind picking her up.

Grace responded almost immediately. *On my way.* She didn't ask Aspen what had happened or why she needed a ride. Aspen appreciated that.

Josie made a few turns and got them back to what looked more like a main road. It was wider, anyway, even if there were still no streetlights.

"You want to talk about it?" she asked after a few minutes.

"I thought I had someone I could trust," Aspen said. "Turns out, I was wrong."

Josie nodded. "Sorry about that." Another few beats of quiet passed. "You're new to town, right?"

"Just passing through. I inherited a house here. I was thinking about hanging around, but now... Any chance you want to buy a house?"

Josie smiled. "Thanks anyway." She sneaked a glance at Aspen. "I think this is a great town, but it seems like you have history here."

"My parents did."

"Will you go back to... Where'd you move here from?"

"Hawaii. I hadn't planned on going back..." But why not? Her plan to see the States, to broaden her horizons, was based on nothing but a flimsy dream. She should go back to what worked. Kona worked. Kona was home. The people there were warm and friendly, unlike this cold, horrible place.

Maybe she was romanticizing Hawaii and demonizing New Hampshire. Under the circumstances, her bias felt fair.

"I came to Coventry to get a fresh start," Josie said. "And it's been good for me. But if I had history here? If people whispered behind my back? Sorry, but who needs that? Maybe you should go someplace where nobody's ever heard of you or your mother."

"Why'd you need a fresh start?"

Josie's open expression shuttered as if she'd pulled a cord. "No particular reason."

A lie, but Aspen didn't call her on it. She could hardly handle her own problems.

Problems that would be solved if she'd give up this foolish investigation. Her mother was dead and gone. So was her father. Christiansen was right that Dad would never have sent her into danger, which meant Aspen had misunderstood what Dad wanted from her.

She didn't need to be in Coventry. She didn't need to know what had happened to her mother.

She wished she hadn't learned what she had. Did she really think the rest of the story would bring closure? Or peace? No chance.

There was no peace to be had in Coventry, New Hampshire. Not for Aspen, anyway.

It wasn't even nine o'clock, but Aspen slipped into her new flannel pajamas as soon as she got back to Grace's house. She padded down the stairs in her socks and found Grace in the kitchen.

"I'm making some tea," Grace said. "I thought it might warm you up."

"Sounds good." Aspen still hadn't gotten warm after her stroll in the freezing cold weather. Grace's car had been idling in front of the coffee shop when Josie parked. After thanking her new friend for the ride, Aspen had slipped into the passenger seat.

Though she must have had a lot of questions, Grace hadn't asked any of them on the ride. Instead, she'd made small talk as if it were perfectly normal that Aspen's date with Garrett had turned into a ride from a stranger.

She'd let Aspen slip upstairs the second they walked into the condo.

Now, she leaned against her kitchen counter, nibbling a granola bar. Still not asking questions.

Aspen answered the unspoken one anyway. "Garrett lied to me."

Grace nodded.

"He pretended to care about me, but he was only spying on me for his uncle."

That garnered a reaction. "Why would his uncle want him to spy on you?"

"That's a good question." Aspen sighed, the sound loud in the quiet place. "There's a reason, but Chief Cote asked me to keep it quiet." Aspen had given Grace the bullet points about what she was doing in town, so Grace knew about her mother and the bombing.

The kettle whistled, and Grace poured steaming water over teabags in two mugs. "I don't know Garrett that well, but I think he's trustworthy. He's got a good heart."

As if Grace could tell that just by looking at a person.

Grace seemed to read her thoughts because she added, "I've been told I'm insightful."

"People can surprise you."

Grace smiled but didn't agree or disagree. "Sugar? Milk?"

Aspen blew across the hot liquid. "This is fine. What kind is it?"

"Chamomile. It helps me sleep. I thought you might appreciate that."

She sipped, and the liquid filled her middle, warming her immediately. "Thank you."

Grace's phone dinged. She glanced at it. "It's Andrew wanting to know if you're here. I assume Garrett asked him. Do you mind if I tell him, just to put their minds at ease?"

Aspen shrugged. She didn't care what Garrett knew or didn't know about her, not anymore.

Grace tapped on her phone's screen and set it down. "There, that should—"

It dinged again.

She glanced at it, then typed quickly. She didn't look pleased.

A moment later, the doorbell rang.

Grace sighed. She tapped her phone screen once more, then turned it so Aspen could see. It was a camera view.

Garrett was standing on the stoop. Andrew was behind him, saying something. Andrew grabbed Garrett's arm, but Garrett shrugged him off.

The bell rang again.

"I'll get rid of him," Grace said.

"No. It's all right." She was going to have to do this eventually. She walked across the living room to the front door and swung it open.

"Thank God you're all right." Garrett seemed genuinely relieved to see her.

Aspen had nothing to say to that.

"Look, I don't know what you heard."

Andrew was standing behind him, looking from him to her and back. "You want me to stay, Aspen?"

"He won't be here long." She turned back to Garrett. "I've already heard enough."

Andrew stepped closer, gripped Garrett's arm in some sort of guy-solidarity, then slid past Aspen into Grace's house.

Aspen shoved her feet into the boots she'd left by the door and stepped out onto the concrete.

Grace handed out Aspen's jacket. "Holler if you need us."

Then, she left Aspen and Garrett alone.

Garrett said, "Listen, it's not—"

Aspen slipped on her coat. "You've been spying on me for your uncle, feeding him information about me."

"He asked me to." Garrett's tone was pleading. "But I didn't do it. I didn't tell him anything about you except that you didn't know where your mother was. I thought that was all he wanted to know. I thought if I told him you didn't have any idea what happened to her, that he'd let it go. When he pressed the issue, I told him I wouldn't betray your trust. I would never—"

"But you did. You did pass along information about me."

Garrett's mouth opened. Then closed. A hard look filled his eyes. "I told him one thing, one thing only to get him off your back."

"So you did it *for me*? Is that what you're trying to tell me?"

"Yes. That's exactly what—"

"Funny how your uncle still feels *on my back*."

"You'd never even met him until tonight. Or am I wrong about that? Because you two seemed at odds from the moment you walked into their house."

"I've never met him. But he thinks he knows me because he knew my mother."

"I've been trying to tell him—"

"And it never crossed your mind that he knew more than you realized? That maybe he was involved."

Garrett leaned back, his eyes wide. "What are you talking about? Involved with what?"

"The bombing, Garrett. He was a suspect."

He looked genuinely shocked. "My uncle had nothing to do with that."

"You really believe that he asked you to spy on me for no reason? Come on, Garrett. You're smarter than that."

He licked his lips, looked around, shook his head. His volume was lower when he spoke. "Why do you think that?"

"Why *don't* you?"

"Why would I?"

"He asked you to spy on me."

"He said...he said there were people in town who wanted to know what happened to your mother. People who had a right to know, who wanted justice. I thought he was asking on their behalf. My uncle is a good man. He would never have been involved in something like that."

Garrett was either stupid or lying.

No.

He trusted his uncle. He trusted his uncle enough to betray her.

She should let it go. She should go inside and close the door and pretend she'd never met Garrett McCarthy.

But fury and fear and frustration bubbled up inside her. She couldn't quell those feelings. Even though she'd promised she wouldn't tell anybody, she couldn't stop the words that were dying for release.

"Did your uncle tell you he and Deborah were questioned last night? That the police are checking their alibis?"

"What?"

"Dean is a prime suspect. Cote thinks he's the one who tried to kill me."

Garrett stepped backward, down one step, then another. "You're lying." But his face had lost all its color. His voice sounded not confident but fearful.

She'd lobbed a grenade, and it'd hit hard.

Might as well make it a twofer.

"I can't work with someone I don't trust." She held out her hand. "I'll take my key."

He found his keyring, slipped the key off with hands that trembled, then held it out.

She took it, but before she could pull her hand away, he wrapped his around it, stepping back to the stoop with her.

His nearness sent a whole new batch of emotions flying. She remembered all the sweet things he'd said to her. She remembered all the kind things he'd done for her. She remembered how she'd felt when he'd come to her rescue on the mountain the night before.

She remembered the kiss they'd shared in that very spot.

All those memories made this so much harder.

"I don't know what's going on," Garrett said. "I didn't know he'd been a suspect back then. I had no idea... My uncle would never try to hurt you. I'm sure, when the police finish their investigation, they'll find the real culprit."

And there it was. He might care for her. Maybe. But his loyalty rested with Dean, and it always would.

She tried to yank her hand away, but Garrett held on.

"I know you're angry. I need you to hear me. I didn't spy on you. What my uncle did or didn't do... What happened back then with your mom and him and...all of it. It's not you and me. I'm not my uncle any more than you're your mother. We can't let them do this to us."

"Who is *them*?"

"Dean and...I don't know. Whoever else is involved. Whoever actually ran you off the road. I care about you. I don't want to lose you."

It didn't matter. It didn't matter what Garrett said. Because he would always side with Dean and Deborah and Brent and Coventry. It would always be them against her.

Always.

She yanked her hand again, and this time, he let her go.

"Aspen, I care about you. I'm falling in love with you."

She'd dreamed of the first time she'd hear those words from a man.

The reality was nothing like the fantasy.

"I wasn't supposed to tell you that your aunt and uncle were questioned, so don't tell anybody. Can I trust you to do that?"

"Of course, you can trust—"

"Tell your uncle I'm selling the house and leaving town. Tell him tonight. I'm done digging. I'm letting it go. I'll be gone by tomorrow. Maybe that'll make him back off."

"Don't do that. Please. Just...just wait."

Wait. Until someone actually succeeded in killing her? Maybe she'd end up in a grave right beside her mother.

That would be one way to find her.

There was nothing to wait for. There was nothing else for her in Coventry. And there was nothing between her and this man. She took a step back. There were so many things she wanted to say, feelings she wanted to share. Truth was, none of them mattered. She settled for one final remark so there'd be no misunderstanding. "You're fired."

CHAPTER TWENTY-EIGHT

Hoping Aspen would come back out, would change her mind, Garrett stared at Grace's front door a long time. Then it opened again, and his hope soared.

To crash and burn when Andrew appeared with a pitying look.

Garrett stormed away.

Andrew caught up and walked beside him back to Garrett's condo.

He opened his door, tempted to step inside and slam it in Andrew's face. He didn't turn when he said, "I don't want to talk about it."

"We don't have to talk."

Much as Garrett wanted to be alone, he stepped in and left the door open.

Andrew followed and closed the door behind himself. "I would like to point out, though, that when Grace and I broke up, you peppered me with questions until I wanted to slug you."

That was different.

"Insightful questions," Andrew said. "Really personal, probing questions. I thought I'd return the favor."

"I thought you said we didn't have to talk."

"That was just to get in the door."

Garrett walked through the living room and breakfast nook into the kitchen, not needing food or drink but just to move. He marched back out to face his friend. "She thinks my uncle is out to get her."

Andrew's eyebrows rose. "Is he?"

"Of course not. Dean would never..."

But the hatred Garrett had seen in his uncle's eyes that night, the loathing, the fear.

What was Dean afraid of?

Garrett didn't want to consider it, but he'd gone to Dean and Deborah's the night before, just stopped by to talk to them about Dean's diagnosis. They hadn't been home.

When he'd called that morning, he'd told them what happened to Aspen. He'd completely forgotten to ask them where they'd been.

Where *had* they been?

Andrew settled on the arm of the club chair. "Why does she think that?"

Garrett had to think back to figure out what Andrew was asking about. Why did Aspen think Dean had run her off the road? Because Cote had questioned him. Cote was checking Dean's alibi.

Garrett had been running on adrenaline and fear since he'd discovered Aspen missing. He'd called her cell repeatedly. He'd driven around his aunt and uncle's neighborhood, but there'd been no sign of her. He'd called Chief Cote, who'd told him they'd keep an eye out. He'd texted and called Grace, but she hadn't responded. He'd finally resorted to getting Andrew involved.

The adrenaline was ebbing away.

He collapsed in the sofa. "I don't think she was supposed to tell me."

"I'm not going to post it on Instagram."

"Someone ran her off the road last night between here and her house. Right by that drop-off."

Andrew slid into the chair. "On purpose?"

He dipped his head and lifted it again. "She was nervous driving on that winding road at night. If she'd been going faster, she might've gone over."

"Wow. I thought you were exaggerating when you said... But someone literally tried to kill her?"

Garrett nodded again.

"And she thinks it was your uncle? Cote told her that?"

"Apparently. I took her to Dean and Deborah's for dinner tonight. Deborah had met her at the library and invited her. I wanted Aspen to meet Dean, and him to meet her. He's been... against her since she came to town."

"In what way?"

Garrett shrugged. "It's hard to explain."

Andrew settled deeper into the chair. "It's sort of fun turning the tables on you."

Garrett glared at him, but Andrew grinned.

"When she first got to town," Garrett said, "he asked me to keep an eye on her, let him know what she was up to."

Andrew's amusement faded. "Jeez, Garrett. Why would you—?"

"I didn't. I mean at first..." He hadn't told Dean much of anything, anyway. Certainly nothing confidential. Nothing Aspen should be upset about. "I'd do anything for my uncle. He saved my life. I barely knew her. I said I'd keep my eyes open. I told him one little thing, one little thing that I thought would put his mind at ease about her. And then I got to know her, and..."

There was no excuse for any of it. He'd known the minute Dean had asked him to spy on her that it was wrong. He should have refused. He should never have led his uncle to believe...

"Why'd you do it?" Andrew asked.

Garrett's phone rang.

Aspen? Maybe she'd changed her mind.

He slid it from his pocket, and his heart fell when he saw Deborah's name. He was tempted to reject the call, but his aunt hadn't done anything wrong. He answered with, "Hey."

"I just want you to know," Deborah said, "Dean doesn't speak for me. I love you, and you will always have a place in my life. And whatever happened between you and your uncle, you'll work it out. It's going to be all right."

"No. It's not."

"Garrett, sweetheart, he's just—"

"I'm not angry with you. You and I are good. Can I speak to him please?"

"He's not really up for conversation."

"Fine. Then go to where he is and put me on speakerphone." Aspen had asked him to pass a message along. Maybe it would be the last thing he could do for her before she disappeared from his life forever.

"Hold on." A few seconds passed before Deborah spoke again, her voice distant. "We're both here."

"Dean?"

His uncle grunted.

"You're getting what you asked for. Aspen is leaving town."

No response from Dean, but Deborah said, "Oh, sweetheart, I'm so sorry. I really—"

"I have to go." As an afterthought, he added, "Love you... both." He ended the call without waiting for a response and tossed his phone onto the coffee table.

He dropped his head into his hands.

"She's leaving town?" Andrew asked.

"Yup."

Andrew's previous question still hung between them. Garrett hated the answer. Hated facing the fear that drove him. "I agreed to pass along information to Dean at first because... Because I didn't want to disappoint him. I didn't want to risk..."

He hadn't wanted to risk exactly what had happened. Rejection. Losing his uncle's affection. "The thing that kills me..." Garrett looked up to see Andrew's sympathy written on his face and had to squash the irritation that rose. "My uncle gave me an ultimatum tonight. Him or Aspen. I chose Aspen. So I lost him. And now I've lost her. And, in case that wasn't enough, I've lost my job too. She fired me. So all the plans you and I made..."

Andrew had helped Garrett put together a business plan. The work that had gone into landing one big job, one that would provide him with lots of before-and-after pictures for his website, along with a glowing review—that had been Andrew's brain child.

"I've lost everything."

Andrew leaned forward. "Let's not be melodramatic. You haven't lost *everything*. You still have friends. You still have your church. You still have your skills. You're not alone, and you never will be because you still have God."

Small comfort in that moment, but Andrew was right.

"Of those three things you feel like you *have* lost, your uncle, Aspen, and your job, which is the most important?"

The obvious answer was his uncle. His family. But Dean had asked him to make an impossible choice. Garrett had chosen wrong, according to Dean, and lost what he'd thought was the strongest relationship in his life.

It hadn't been as rock solid as he'd believed.

The job mattered. If he ever wanted to be anything more

than a glorified handyman, he needed someone to trust him with a big job. But there'd be another opportunity. If there wasn't, he could live with that too.

He'd trade both the job and his uncle and a whole lot more to have one more shot with Aspen. Because, deep in his heart, from the first lunch they'd spent together, he'd known she mattered. It wasn't that he'd cared for her from the start. It wasn't that she was vulnerable and needed a friend. Those were both true, but that wasn't driving him.

He'd known almost from the beginning that God had brought Aspen into his life for a reason.

Aspen was supposed to be part of Garrett's life. As difficult as his past had been, with the broken relationship with his father, and now the broken relationship with his uncle, he was intended to have a solid relationship in the future. With Aspen.

Across the room, Andrew's gaze never wavered from Garrett's face. He smiled. "It's the girl, I guess?"

"It's Aspen. She's the one I'm not willing to lose." He glared at his friend. "And you can keep your cracks about romance novels and...whatever else...to yourself."

Andrew's smile widened. "Far be it from me to razz you about it, all things considered."

A good point. Andrew had risked everything for Grace.

"Aspen is the woman God has for me." Garrett spoke the words, more confident in their truth by the second. "I'm going to marry her, assuming I can get her to speak to me again."

"If you're right," Andrew said, "then nothing will stop His plans."

Garrett let that thought settle, and for the first time since his argument with Dean, he felt hope.

CHAPTER TWENTY-NINE

THIRTY YEARS AGO.

Tonight was the night.

So far, everything had gone according to plan. The Planner and the Crusader had met and driven to a pay phone, where the Crusader had called her husband and asked him to meet her at their overlook. She'd had to get emotional, even managed to conjure some tears, but ultimately, he'd agreed.

His parents were at the house because the baby was sick, so he wouldn't have the kid in tow. It was all working out perfectly.

He and Jane took the main road to the side street that led to the lumber company. He'd traveled this route more than once during the planning stage, but he'd never seen so many cars parked along the road. Somebody was having a party.

He averted his gaze from the cars parked there. Hopefully, they were all empty, but one could never be too sure. Jane didn't seem worried. She chatted about what a difference they were going to make, about how they were changing the world.

He wasn't sure about that. This would be a blip, an inconvenience for one company. If they managed to close this one down, another would come in and buy up their land and their equipment. They were only making a statement, nothing more. But it would make Jane happy. For that, he was willing to risk his freedom.

After this, she'd be his. He was sure of it.

They reached the parking lot and were about to drive past to the loading zone in the back, where they'd leave the device, when he caught sight of a car in the lot.

A car.

"Stop."

She slammed on the brakes, and he pointed. "Someone's here."

Jane's eyes were wide and excited. "Bad luck for them, I guess."

She eased her foot off the brake and continued on.

"We can't do it. We're not trying to hurt anybody."

But she didn't hear him or didn't care.

She giggled and kept going.

He planted his hand on hers on the gear shift. "You have to turn around. We're not doing this tonight."

She ignored him, parking exactly where they'd decided. Out of the view of the cameras. Dressed in all black, he'd planned to keep his head down and run across the lot. He'd set the timer for five minutes, and they'd be out of there before it detonated.

But he wasn't going to do any of that, not now.

He turned to her and took her hand. "Jane, there's somebody inside. We're trying to save the forests, but it's not worth killing for."

Her head bobbed. He'd gotten through to her.

"Okay, okay." Her gaze flicked from him to the building and back. "Why don't you go see what you can see. Maybe the car is just broken down or something. Go see if there are any lights on inside."

Rather than argue, he said, "Don't get out of the car. Promise?"

Again, she nodded. "I won't move."

He climbed from her little hatchback and crept across the lot, keeping low. No need to take the device with him. There was no way he'd be setting it up and starting that timer, lights on inside or not. That was a line he was not willing to cross.

He reached the building, then crept around the side and out of sight. He stopped beside a grouping of windows and checked his watch. He'd wait sixty seconds, then go back to the car. He'd tell Jane he'd seen a light on and get them out of there.

While the second hand made its slow circuit, he picked up a sound. Was that...? Yes, inside, somebody was crying. A woman, by the sound of it.

Crouching again, he jogged back across the lot to Jane's car, parked on the far edge. He slid into the passenger seat.

The driver's seat was empty.

He climbed back out, looked around. "Jane!" It was a whispered shout that sounded too loud in the silent night.

There was no answer.

He checked the backseat, dread filling his middle.

The device was gone.

No.

He stood in time to see Jane bolting across the lot. "Get in, get in!"

"Tell me you didn't—"

"We have three minutes. Go, go!"

"There's someone inside!"

She stopped abruptly, eyes wide. Shook her head. "It's empty. It's empty. You said it would be empty!"

"There's a car."

"Nope. It's empty. Nobody's here." She climbed into the driver's seat.

What should he do? He could run to the building, bang on the window, try to get the woman out.

She wouldn't hear. Even if she did, she wouldn't know what he was saying. She wouldn't get out in time.

He could try to stop the device, but he'd have to find it. The area where they'd planned to leave it was large enough, it would take time in the darkness.

Either way, it would go off. He'd die too. Or survive and be charged with murder.

"We have to go!" she shouted. The car started moving.

It was too late to save the stranger. He could only save himself and the woman he loved.

He yanked open the back door and dove, barely getting it shut before she floored it.

He was still trying to sit up when he felt her pick up speed. He peered out the front. "You're going the wrong way! You're supposed to take the…"

The explosion shook the ground beneath them, nearly sending them off the road.

Somehow, Jane kept the car on the narrow drive.

He was screaming, screaming at her to turn around. Everybody would see. They'd be caught.

But the Jane he saw in the rearview mirror wasn't the woman he'd fallen in love with. Her eyes were wild. Her hands were clenched on the wheel as she raced down the hill from the burning remains of the lumber company. She was talking, but her words made no sense. Or maybe he just couldn't comprehend them in light of what she'd just done.

What *they'd* just done.

When they reached the bottom of the hill, he ducked while she took the corner too fast. All those cars. All those people would have heard the explosion. They would have come outside. They'd see Jane's car.

It was over. It was over, and they were going to prison.
For murder.

CHAPTER THIRTY

It wasn't even nine a.m. when Aspen drove through Coventry the following morning. Grace had taken her before work to pick up the rental car.

Clouds hung low over the mountains with the promise of snow, but it hadn't started yet. With any luck at all, Aspen could be packed up and out of town before the first flakes fell.

Her phone rang. She'd neglected to connect it to the rental's Bluetooth, so she pulled over in the middle of town—right in view of anybody who cared to look. She didn't care. They could glare at her and gossip about her all they wanted. If Dean happened by, he wouldn't dare try to hurt her with the whole town as witnesses. Besides, if Garrett had reported back to his uncle that she was leaving town—and she felt confident he had, considering he'd been reporting back to his uncle all along—then Dean had no reason to hurt her now.

She yanked her phone from her pocket and saw Jaslynn's name. She hadn't spoken to her best friend since the night she'd pulled into town.

She connected the call, but emotion gathered in her throat and cut off her words.

After a few seconds of silence, Jaslynn asked, "Are you there?"

Aspen cleared her throat. "Yeah. I'm here. Your timing is...timely."

"Your redundancy is...redundant."

Aspen smiled. "I miss you." Her voice pitched high, revealing the despair she'd hoped to hide. The truth, like the emotions, had risen from deep in her heart. She missed her best friend. She missed her father. She missed feeling loved and cherished. She'd thought, maybe, with Garrett... But what they'd had was an illusion.

"Oh, honey," Jaslynn said. "I miss you too. What happened?"

"I'm going home. I can't stay here anymore."

"Because of the guy who ran you off the road?"

Aspen had texted her friend a little bit about that night and asked her to pray. She hadn't told her she believed the driver had been trying to kill her, though. No sense worrying her. By the tone of Jazz's voice, she was worried enough without all the information.

Aspen said, "That and I found out... It seems Garrett's been passing information about me to his uncle."

"Garrett, the hunky contractor?"

"I never called him hunky."

"I read between the lines. Are you sure?"

"I overheard them talking. He denied it, but, really, what's he supposed to say? He's not going to admit to getting close to me just to spy on me, to kissing me—"

"He *kissed* you?"

"It didn't mean anything."

Not to him, anyway.

"What a jerk. He was just using you to get information?"

"Yup."

Garrett had known she'd be at Tabby's Monday night. For all Aspen knew, he'd told Dean, and Dean had broken into her house.

It all made sense now. Of course it'd been Dean. Garrett had told him Aspen wouldn't be home.

The realization felt like a fresh betrayal.

"Why did he do it?" Jaslynn asked. "I thought you two were hitting it off."

"I guess that was all an act." But it had felt so real.

"Are you going straight to Florida, then? Have you talked to your grandparents?"

"No. I'm just going home. Last night, I called the landlord at our old building, and he has a one-bedroom available." There was something to be said for a five-hour time difference. It'd been late in New Hampshire, but it'd still been business hours in Kona.

"Don't do that," Jazz said. "Don't give up everything because this one thing didn't work out. I'm sure your grandparents would love having you nearby."

"Why are you sure of that?" Aspen hadn't intended the sharp tone. She tempered it when she spoke again. "They hated my mother. People who hated my mother don't like me. It's that simple."

"That's not true. They're your grandparents."

"You know how many times they came to visit when I was a kid? Three. Three times they made the trip."

"It's not exactly cheap to fly to—"

"I haven't talked to them since the funeral."

"Have you called them?"

She hadn't. She should have, but...

"It doesn't matter. I don't have family left, at least not any that want me around."

Outside the rented sedan, people hurried by. On the opposite side of the street, a woman chatted with a man in a suit. A mom ushered three little kids up the steps into the library. Outside the door to The Patriot, two groups of people met each other and stood and hugged and talked.

The world went on around Aspen, these people, this town that hated her. Good people who saw ugliness in her. And why not? Her mother had murdered an innocent woman. If Aspen's guess was correct and they found her mother's body buried near the house, then her father had killed her.

No. She couldn't believe that. She wouldn't. Even if it was true.

"You have me," Jaslynn said. "We might not be sisters by blood, but we're sisters in every other way."

"I thank God for you." If not for Jazz, Aspen would have nobody.

"What will you do?"

Aspen shrugged, not that her friend could see. "I texted Gene."

"The guy who bought the restaurants?"

"I'm hoping he'll have a job for me."

"But you hated working there, even more after your dad passed."

But it was familiar. Easy. Nobody would reject her or hate her at the restaurant. She might not like the job, but she was competent and respected. The longtime servers would be friendly to her.

Maybe that was the most she could ask for out of life.

"I'll take online classes." Though at the moment, the thought of it exhausted her. "I'll figure something out. Right now, I just want to get out of New Hampshire." And never look back.

"I wish I could be there with you."

Aspen wished that too. She wished so many things that

could never be. She needed a friend. She liked Grace and Tabby and the other women she'd met in Coventry, but they were Garrett's friends first. They'd choose him.

Aspen didn't have a soul in the world who would always choose her.

~

BEFORE ASPEN PULLED AWAY from the curb, a text came in. It was from Garrett.

I'm outside Grace's condo, and I'm not leaving until you talk to me.

She responded, *I hope you're dressed warmly.*

We need to talk. I wasn't spying on you. I didn't tell my uncle anything.

He'd already admitted to having passed on information about her, so that was a lie.

She'd shifted into drive when another text came in.

I care about you. Please can we talk?

She ignored him, flipping on her blinker to pull away from the curb. But a line of traffic was coming through the light behind her.

Her phone dinged again. *I can wait here all day. You have to come out sometime.*

She sighed. She was angry with him, but she didn't want him to waste his time or freeze his toes off. *Go home, Garrett. I'm not there. I'll leave your handgun and a key to the house with Grace before I leave so you can get your tools.*

Come on, traffic. Where were all these cars coming from? Probably people hurrying to get their errands done before the snow started. Would they worry in New Hampshire, though? Maybe a snowstorm was just another day at the office for these weird people.

Where are you? Garrett texted.

It was none of his business where she was or what she was doing.

Finally, she merged into traffic and continued to Rattlesnake Road.

She was just passing the condominium complex when her phone rang. Probably Garrett. She glanced at the number. It was Mr. Barnett calling her back from the nursing home.

She doubted he'd have any helpful information, but she'd still like to talk to him to confirm. Somehow, Dad had known about the house. Maybe he'd chosen it randomly. Maybe he'd known work was being done there.

A fresh thought occurred to her. Maybe the Barnetts had been having landscaping work done. Freshly turned dirt wouldn't be out of place if that were the case. Was Jane Kincaid buried under one of the many trees in the yard?

The thought made Aspen ill.

In any event, when Cote got the ground-penetrating radar, if Aspen's mother was buried there, he'd find her.

Aspen let the call go to voicemail. This high up the mountain, it would drop anyway.

She made the long, winding drive up to her house, growing more unsettled the higher she climbed. Those clouds overhead looked ominous. She needed to get her things and get off the mountain before snow started falling. She considered all the items she'd purchased to make the house livable. Should she try to box everything up and have it shipped?

Right. The cost to get it all to Hawaii would be higher than the value. Instead, she'd contact Trudy at the thrift store, ask her to coordinate with Garrett to pick up everything Aspen left behind and donate it to the poor. She could trust Trudy with that job, and the woman's son had that truck.

There might be a few things she'd like to take with her.

She'd go through everything, toss what she wanted to keep in the rental car, and box it up when she got to Manchester. That was her destination tonight. She'd find a hotel. Tomorrow, she'd get a flight home.

The house was quiet when she walked inside. Everything was in order, nothing out of place. Nobody'd been there. Maybe she would have been safe staying there the previous two nights. She didn't mind that she hadn't, though. She'd felt more comfortable in Grace's little extra bedroom after fifteen minutes than she'd felt in this giant, secluded place after a week.

She started to head up the stairs, then remembered the call she'd gotten and veered toward the kitchen, where the cordless phone was charging on its cradle. Reading the number from her cell, she dialed the Barnetts' room at the nursing home.

Mr. Barnett answered.

"It's Aspen Kincaid," she said. After asking after him and his wife—they'd been gone the day before because of a doctor's appointment—she got to the point. "I wanted to ask you a question about the remodeling work you had done on your house thirty years ago."

"What do you want to know?"

"Did you have any landscaping done?"

"In March? Heck, no. They get freezes that far north well into April."

So much for that theory. "You didn't have any concrete poured, did you?"

"Well, now, as a matter of fact, we did. That was the year we had the detached garage built. We had a boat, and we were sick of paying to store it elsewhere in the winter."

Aspen's heart sank to her knees. She pulled a chair close and sat.

They'd had concrete poured.

Dad had worked for a concrete contractor.

And he'd met Jane right up the street the night of the bombing.

It confirmed her greatest fears. She'd thought she was prepared for it, but...

But how did anybody prepare to learn that her father'd murdered her mother?

The man she'd loved more than anybody in the world. The man who'd loved her, who'd taught her to ride a bike and tie her shoes, who'd taught her about Jesus.

A murderer.

"Does that help you?" Mr. Barnett asked.

She cleared her throat of the emotion trying to clog it. "Yes. Very much. Thank you." She hung up before he could ask anything else. She couldn't be polite now. She couldn't be anything but heartbroken.

The whole world shifted with the truth of it. Who was Aspen? The daughter of a murderer. The daughter of *two* murderers.

Thank God He didn't make children pay for their parents' sins. But there were still consequences, and those consequences had most certainly made their way into Aspen's life. Of course she was alone. Considering who her parents had been, did she deserve better?

In her bedroom, Aspen packed her things. What she'd purchased at the mall a few days before was in the trunk of her car. Maybe they'd fit in the suitcase, except why would she need flannel pajamas in Kona? Wool socks? The knit cap?

She wouldn't. She'd bring those things inside to leave for Trudy. Aspen didn't want any reminders of New Hampshire once she was gone. She wished she'd never come to this godforsaken place.

Except it wasn't that. Most of the people Aspen had met were believers. God was very much here.

Maybe He'd just forsaken her.

No. She couldn't think that way. If she walked away from God, she'd have nobody. She couldn't face that kind of life.

It was strange the way everything fit into the suitcase she'd brought from Hawaii. All she'd picked up in New Hampshire—not the stuff but the information, the people, the experiences... They didn't take up any space in the bag.

Too much space in her heart.

She dragged the luggage behind her down the stairs, letting the heavy bag bounce on every step. What did she care about the contents? About the floors? None of it mattered.

In the living room, she added one of the throw blankets she'd purchased to her suitcase. She shoved in as many of the kitchen utensils as would fit. She'd sold almost everything she and Dad had owned, so she'd be starting from scratch when she got to Hawaii. Going back had never been her plan.

When she was finished, she dragged the suitcase out the door and along the walkway, remembering the first moment she'd seen this place. Garrett had been shoveling the walk so she wouldn't have to trudge through the snow to her front door.

He'd seemed so kind.

Had it really all been a lie?

Maybe. Maybe not, if his texts were any indication. But even if he had grown to care for her, how could anything come of it when his uncle hated her enough to try to kill her? When her very presence threatened the man's freedom. Garrett's feelings for her, if they existed at all, didn't matter.

Her feelings for Garrett didn't matter either.

Jane and Michael Kincaid's decisions thirty years before had ended two lives. They had shifted the lives of a lot of people. Their decisions were still affecting people now. And there was nothing Aspen could do about that.

She understood why Dad had relocated as far away from here as possible. She wished she'd never come.

After hefting her suitcase into the trunk, she dug through the shopping bags she'd tossed in earlier and pulled out the socks and pajamas and hat. She opened the suitcase one more time to shove in the things she wanted to keep, leaving those destined for the thrift store in the shopping bag. It was a small trunk and not easy to maneuver, and she was so intent on the task and the thoughts bombarding her that she didn't hear the sound of an engine until it was right behind her.

She turned in time to see a pickup truck park. Not Garrett's.

Dean Finley climbed out.

ASPEN BOLTED for the front door, expecting to hear footsteps right behind her.

She didn't, though.

"Wait!"

She heard his voice, but it was farther away than she would have expected. He wasn't following her. He wasn't chasing her.

Still, she didn't stop until she'd climbed the three steps of her front stoop and opened the storm door. She turned, keeping the glass door propped open so she could step in the house and slam the door.

Dean had moved to the walkway but stopped where it intersected with the drive. He lifted both hands in the universal sign of surrender.

She pulled the handgun from the holster at her waist, disengaging the safety as she did.

She didn't aim it, but she held onto it, just in case. He needed to know she wasn't helpless.

"I'm not here to hurt you," Dean said.

"Why are you here?"

His hands lowered a little. "Do you mind if I just...?" He dropped them to his sides. "If I keep them like this...?"

"It's fine." The initial burst of adrenaline and fear were already draining. Nothing about the man looked threatening. Even the anger he'd aimed her way the night before seemed to have dissipated. But Aspen wasn't stupid. Somebody had tried to kill her. "Just...stay there, and we'll be good."

He leaned against the front of her car. "Garrett tells me you're leaving town."

"Which is what you wanted, right?"

"Do you know why?"

"Because you built the bomb. Because you're afraid the truth will come out." She threw the words out there in full confidence. It *seemed* true. Cote thought it was true. She expected Dean to respond with shock and outrage, or even amusement at her foolishness.

Instead, he seemed to sag, shoulders hunching, head dropping forward.

"It's true, right?"

Very slowly, he looked up. And nodded.

That he didn't deny it both thrilled and terrified her. She was getting to the bottom of the mystery—that one, anyway. But why would he tell her the truth? After so many years, why confide in Aspen?

She felt the heaviness of the gun in her hand. She wasn't defenseless. If he came after her...

Please, God. I don't want to hurt anybody. And I don't want to get hurt.

But she couldn't figure out how this could end without one or both of those happening.

"My presence here stirred everything up," Aspen said. "Cote started looking at the case again. People started talking

about the bombing again. It probably took a long time for everybody to forget your part in it."

"Most never knew." Dean looked past Aspen, then up into
the darkening clouds. A long moment passed before he faced
her again. "They knew your mom and I were friends, but they
blamed her for the bombing. Everybody blamed her and her
alone. Cote and his partner knew, of course. But they couldn't
prove it. I never understood why they didn't go public with that
information. At least about me."

"Why would he go public about you and not Brent?"

"Brent was the rich kid. Aside from the Hamiltons, Brent's
family was the richest in town. Still are. Brent's mother was the
county prosecutor back then. His father was a successful
lawyer. He'd been the mayor a few years before. He wielded a
lot of power in Coventry. I could understand why the cops
didn't want to name him without proof."

She'd known the Salcitos were wealthy. How else could
they have afforded to keep an apartment in Boston? But she
hadn't realized they were that influential.

"My family'd been in town a long time," Dean said, "but my
folks didn't have any connections. Both my parents worked at
Hamilton. And anyway, if they'd known, they'd have turned
me in."

She heard the house phone ringing. Not very many people
had that number—Garrett, Jaslynn, Cote. Whoever it was,
hopefully they'd call back. "My understanding is that Cote's
partner was happy to cross you off the list of suspects. He
thought you were a good kid."

Dean's smile was sad. "I had been, before."

She felt sorry for him. She felt sorry for everybody who
suffered because of her mother's scheme.

"I'd never even told Deborah," Dean said. "All these years,
she never knew."

What a secret to keep from the woman you loved. How had he managed it?

How had Dad managed to keep his secrets for so long?

"The three of us planned it—Jane, Brent, and me. I built the bomb. I was on campus that night. I knew when Jane and Brent were gonna set it off. But we had all decided that, if the building wasn't empty, we'd come back another time."

"So what happened?" Aspen asked. "The woman's car was in the lot, so what—?"

"I don't know." The words were filled with defeat.

"How do you not know? You were in on it. What did Brent tell you?"

"We never talked about it, not once after it happened. At first, it was because we didn't want people to suspect us. We just stayed apart, hoping everybody would forget. I was afraid his part in the bombing would be discovered. I assume he was afraid mine would be. Weeks went by. Months. I never went back to college. He finished the semester and transferred."

"But it's been years. You live in the same town. Have you really never—?"

"Brent was my closest friend. We'd been friends since preschool. But we haven't had a single conversation, in public or in private, since that bomb exploded. So I don't know what happened. I have no idea, and I never wanted to know. I just wanted to forget I'd ever met your mother." He sucked in a breath, then blew it out and sucked in another.

"Are you all right?"

He pressed his hands against his chest, seemed to struggle to breathe.

He was having one of the episodes Garrett had told her about. She shoved the gun back in its holster and rushed down the walk to where he stood. "What can I do?"

But he couldn't seem to catch his breath, or to talk.

"Come on." She wrapped her arm around his back. Together, they made it up the steps and into her house.

Maybe this was all an act. Maybe he would turn on her as soon as they got inside. She was armed, but could she kill this man, Garrett's uncle?

Was she enough like her parents to take a life?

She didn't think so. But had they considered themselves capable of murder before they'd done it?

It was a risk she'd take—her life and Dean's felt like they hung on some invisible scale. She was younger. She was innocent of murder. But her life wasn't more valuable than his, and she wasn't about to leave him outside in the freezing cold to have a heart attack and die alone.

She helped him to the sectional, and he collapsed into it, still struggling. She crouched in front of him. "Do you have medicine? What can I do?"

"It'll pass. Just..." He sucked in air, blew it out. Did it again. After a few minutes, he seemed to calm, though his face was beet red and his hand shook.

It hadn't been an act. This man was very sick. "Can I get you anything?"

"I'm okay. Just..." He rested against the back of the sofa and closed his eyes.

She sat on the other section of the sofa and waited. After a few moments had passed, after his color returned to normal, he opened his eyes and met her gaze.

"Sorry about that. They come on suddenly, when I get upset. I should really take the medication they gave me."

"I'm sure Deborah and Garrett would appreciate that."

His lips turned up at the corners as if he wanted to smile but couldn't quite make it happen. "There are a couple of things I want to tell you."

"Aside from your confession?"

"Yeah. Aside from that." His almost-smile faded. He tried to sit up higher on the sofa but couldn't seem to make it happen.

Should she help him? Now that the episode had passed, she didn't want to get that close.

He finally settled again. "I was really selfish. Asking Garrett to spy for me—that was unconscionable. He feels like he owes me. He doesn't. He's brought us so much joy. Deborah wasn't able to have children, and I was against adopting. I didn't figure I deserved to have kids. More than that, I didn't want anybody looking into my past. When my sister, Garrett's mom, asked if we'd take him in, I agreed because I felt like maybe I could earn forgiveness. Maybe if I did some good, it might counteract some of the bad. I knew the Lord, but it took me a long time to understand that God had saved me by grace, that there was nothing I could do to make up for the bad or be good enough for Him.

"But I fell in love with Garrett. Deb and I both did. He doesn't owe us anything. Anything. He's been..." Dean's eyes reddened around the edges, and he lowered his gaze.

Aspen looked away to give him a moment to pull himself together.

"He didn't want to do it," Dean said. "Spy on you. At first, he said he would. But then he came back after this place was broken into. He all but accused me of doing it."

"Did you?" she asked.

He met her eyes and held them. "No. I didn't break in, and I didn't try to run you off the road the other night."

He'd confessed to building a bomb that killed a woman. Why would he lie about that?

But if it wasn't Dean, then who?

Before she could vocalize the question, Dean continued. "Garrett told me you didn't know where your mother was, that you were in town looking for answers. And he never told me anything else about you. Not a word. Except that he was coming to care for you."

She closed her eyes against the emotion building there. Garrett did care for her. It hadn't all been an act. It hadn't been a ploy to get information.

Garrett had told her the truth.

It didn't change anything. She still had to leave. Knowing what she believed her father had done, how could she stay? But it helped to know.

"Last night," Dean said, "I realized... Deborah helped me realize how selfish I was being by giving Garrett that ultimatum."

"What ultimatum?"

"He didn't tell you?"

"I overheard that you'd asked him to spy on me, and I left. After that, I didn't give him the opportunity."

Dean leaned forward. "I told him I would cut him out of my life if he kept spending time with you. It was unbelievably selfish. I was letting my fear rule me. I just wanted you gone from our lives, gone from Coventry."

Aspen couldn't think of a response, though the honesty that roughened his voice clawed at her heart. Everybody wanted her gone.

But Dean wasn't finished. "Garrett chose you. When I told Deborah, she was furious. Sleeping on a crappy sofa in my workshop last night, I realized... Here I've gotten away with murder for thirty years, and I was going to ruin my son's life just to keep getting away with it."

Garrett wasn't his son by blood any more than Jaslynn was Aspen's sister by blood, but the relationships were just as strong.

"So that's why I'm here," Dean said. "To tell you the truth, to apologize. To tell you I was wrong about you. You're not your mother. You look like her, you're kind like her, but you're not her. And if you have half the feelings for my nephew that he has for you, then you have my blessing."

His blessing? What was she supposed to do with that? "You've just confessed murder to me, Dean. Am I supposed to forget?"

"I told Deborah this morning. My dad passed a couple years ago, but I'll have to tell my mom. It'll break her heart, but... I'm gonna tell Cote right after I leave here. It's time I pay for my sins. I'm sick, and I feel about a million years old. Who knows? Maybe they'll go easy on me. I figure I'll end up in prison. But I've had thirty years of a life I wasn't entitled to. Thirty years with the woman I love, twenty raising a young man whose respect I earned but never deserved. I've had a good life. If it ends in prison?" He shrugged. "Maybe I can do some good there."

"What about Brent?"

His expression darkened. "He's gonna have to pay for his crimes too. He'll hate me. He'd probably try to stop me if he knew what I was up to. But it's time we both face what we did."

She scooted closer to Dean and took his hand. "I'm sorry that woman died. I know it wasn't your plan."

His eyes filled with tears, but this time he didn't turn away or try to hide them. "I knew her. Everybody knew everybody in town back then. She was a sweet lady who'd been dealt a hard hand when she married that husband of hers. She was kind and..." His words were choked off by a sob. "I never meant for anybody to get hurt."

Aspen squeezed his hand. "I know that. I know."

"And your mother." He squeezed Aspen's hand. "I cared for her. I wish I knew what happened to her. I'm sure it's torture not knowing."

"I'm pretty sure I know where she is. I'll probably never really know what happened, but at least I can lay her to rest. I need to talk to Cote. I think he'll be able to confirm it. I'm just glad to know that you didn't hurt her."

"I never would have." He sniffed the tears away. The sniff turned into a cough, which turned into a coughing fit.

"I'll get you some water." She hurried through the door and around the corner into her kitchen and filled a glass with ice from the dispenser, all the information Dean had given her clamoring for attention in her mind. He'd confessed. He'd tell Cote everything,

Poor Garrett would be heartbroken.

But his feelings for Aspen were real.

Another thought urged its way forward. If Dean hadn't tried to kill her, then who had?

Brent Salcito. He was the only other option, except he'd been out of town. They'd confirmed his alibi. But who else could it have been?

Filling the glass with water, she considered her next move. Once Dean told Cote, both Dean and Brent would be arrested. And then she'd be safe.

Maybe she wouldn't have to leave Coventry. Maybe she wouldn't have to leave Garrett.

The thought had her smiling for the first time all day. She was turning to take the water to the living room when a shadow crossed over her.

She barely registered the form of a man before something smashed into the back of her head.

The water slipped from her grip. The glass fell and shattered on the floor.

She reached for the counter to keep from falling but missed. She collapsed in a pool of water and ice and glass.

The man was on top of her. She would have screamed if she could've found her voice, but it must have shattered with the glass.

A hand groped her midsection. She tried to push him away, but she felt weak and disoriented. She could hardly see through the pain in her head.

The man stepped away almost as fast as he'd come. Only then did she realize what he'd been doing.

He'd taken the gun.

She was unarmed and injured.

She scrambled on hands and knees across the kitchen floor, but once she bumped into the cabinets, there was nowhere to go. She turned and looked up at the man who'd attacked her.

Brent Salcito aimed the pistol at her chest.

CHAPTER THIRTY-ONE

GARRETT PACED in his living room, pausing to check the cars in front of Grace's condo every time he reached his front window.

How was he supposed to win Aspen's trust if she wouldn't even talk to him?

Once she left town, he'd lose her. But he wasn't exactly versed in the fine art of stalking. She didn't want to see him. It was one thing to stand outside a condo in a crowded complex. It was an entirely different thing to follow her up to a secluded house in the woods when he knew he wasn't welcome.

She must've picked up the rental car. During their text conversation, she'd said she'd leave her gun at Grace's, which meant she had to return before she left town.

Garrett would wait until he saw her park. Now that he'd been fired, it wasn't as if he had anything else to do.

He glanced out the window as he'd done every thirty seconds for an hour. No movement at Grace's place. No new cars parked out front.

But one was pulling up. Not Aspen's rental, based on the markings on the side. Garrett watched the police cruiser pass, Chief Cote in the driver's seat.

He yanked open his front door and walked toward Grace's condo just as the chief parked. Despite his girth, Cote climbed from the car quickly.

"Is everything okay?" Garrett asked.

"Been trying to reach Miss Kincaid, but she's not answering. Thought I'd take a chance and stop by."

"She's not here." Garrett felt confident that Aspen hadn't lied about that. Though, angry as she'd been, maybe his confidence was unwarranted. "I don't think, anyway. Maybe you should knock."

Cote was already on his way. He pulled open the glass door and banged on the wood.

After a few moments, he banged again, calling her through the door. There was no answer.

"Worries me she's not answering her phone," Cote said.

Garrett was standing at the bottom of the stoop. "If she's at the house, she doesn't have cell service."

"I tried the house phone too." Cote's lips pressed together. "I don't like not being able to reach her."

At least it wasn't only Garrett she was ignoring.

"Why are you here?" Garrett asked.

"Got some information I thought she'd want." He huffed down the steps and regarded Garrett a long moment. "You might want it too. Not sure how much she told you."

"She said you wanted her to keep what she learned to herself."

"I did, but you two seemed pretty chummy."

"She told me Dean's a suspect." Maybe he shouldn't have shared that, but he wanted whatever information Cote had uncovered. "I don't think she meant to. We were fighting, and..." Rather than explain the whole horrible moment, he just shrugged.

"*Was* a suspect. You'd told me yourself your aunt and uncle weren't home at the time she was being run off the road. When I questioned them, your aunt's car wasn't at their house. Dean claimed they'd taken it to the shop for some engine work and then gone to dinner."

"Was he telling the truth?"

"Ayuh. The mechanic wasn't in his shop yesterday, but he called this morning. Deborah's sedan needed a new timing belt. There's not a scratch on it. We also got in touch with the waiter who was on duty at the restaurant where they said they went, and he confirmed he'd served them."

"So he didn't run Aspen off the road." Garrett blew out a relieved breath, ashamed that he'd ever suspected Dean in the first place. "But if it wasn't Dean, then who do you think did it?"

"I have my suspicions. That's what I wanted to talk to Aspen about. I was hoping maybe she remembered something or..." He shrugged. "I need more than my suspicions to make an arrest. And it bothers me that she's not answering her phone." He started back to his cruiser.

"Where you going?"

"To check the house."

Maybe once Aspen learned that Dean hadn't been the one to run her off the road, she'd listen to Garrett. Maybe they could get past this after all.

Garrett fished his keys from his pocket. "I'll follow you."

CHAPTER THIRTY-TWO

Aspen's head felt like it might split open as Brent yanked her from the floor and manhandled her out of the kitchen. He didn't speak, not that she could have processed anything he had to say, not with the world spinning like it was. With his gloved hand, he held her arm in a tight grip and pushed her through the door and into the living room.

She hadn't given a thought to Dean in the moments since Brent had hit her. Didn't know what he'd hit her with, though it hadn't been his fist. Something hard and cold. She remembered that much. She felt a trickle down the back of her head but couldn't summon the strength to touch the spot. She could barely process putting one foot in front of the other. The gun pressed to her back kept her moving.

A knife, dripping with crimson, lay on her white sofa.

Her gaze flicked to Dean. His head had fallen forward. Blood seeped from a wound on his upper back.

She froze, gasped for breath as if someone had punched her. "You...you killed him."

"He's not dead yet, but he will be soon enough." Brent

pushed her forward and then yanked her to a stop. "Pick it up, Aspen."

She didn't know what he wanted her to do. She couldn't take her eyes off the man she'd just spoken to. Dean had been coughing. She'd gone for water. How long had she been in the kitchen? Thirty seconds? A minute. How had this happened?

"Pick up the knife, Aspen." His words were cold and calculating.

She understood, then.

Dean would be dead. Aspen would be framed for his murder. The police would find her fingerprints on the murder weapon.

The cold, hard butt of the gun pressed into her back. "Now, please."

Please. As if it were a request.

It was a regular kitchen knife. A butcher knife like what her father would use to slice thin strips of filet for the steakhouse flatbread. She could picture him in his restaurant kitchen as he'd demonstrated the technique for a cook. He'd carefully arranged the pieces of meat on the crust, then added sliced cherry tomatoes and a spattering of bleu cheese. There'd been spinach, she thought. A balsamic glaze, both sweet and tangy.

She could picture Dad lifting his eyes to the cook's but catching sight of her. He smiled, his love as evident and consistent as the waves crashing against the shore just outside the windows. *It's all right, sweetheart. It's going to be all right.*

She heard the words in her heart and wanted to believe them. But her father was gone.

She reached over the sofa.

"Use your right hand," Brent said. "You're not a leftie."

She shifted, took the hilt of the knife in her right hand as if she might cut into a roast.

"Turn it around," he said. "Like you're about to stab some-one. Hold it like you mean it."

She did as he asked, her stomach turning at the warm, sticky blood that had dripped onto the handle and now clung to her palm.

Salcito had armed her. Could she shift, use it against him?

He pressed the gun into her back again. "Drop it now."

She didn't think he'd shoot her, not there. That would ruin his whole plan.

But she was weak, unsteady, her head pounding. Even if he didn't shoot her, he could subdue her. Maybe she could mortally wound him. But she wasn't willing to bet her life on it.

She dropped the knife back onto the sofa.

"Where are your keys?"

She patted her pockets. "Here."

"Get them."

She wiped her hand on her jeans to remove as much of the blood as she could, then pulled out the keys.

He snatched them and pushed her forward. Across the room, out the door, down the steps, and up the walkway. Dean's truck was parked behind hers. But Salcito didn't seem concerned about that. Her car beeped, and the trunk popped open.

He pushed her toward it. She knew what he planned. The thought of allowing herself to be confined in the small trunk of her compact rental had nausea churning her stomach. Though perhaps at least some of that came from the concussion that blurred everything except what was right in front of her eyes.

He yanked out her suitcase. "You can either climb in, or I'll put you in. If we go with option two, it's going to hurt."

She had no doubt it would, and he was still armed.

With Garrett's handgun.

She prayed that wouldn't be the cause of her death. She didn't want Garrett to have to live with that.

She climbed into the small space, pulling her feet in behind her.

She lay on the hard floor while Salcito studied the trunk door. He found a red handle—the thing used to open the trunk from within, she assumed. He stepped out of her line of sight for a moment, then came back with an open pocketknife. It only took a few seconds for him to sever the cable holding the handle in place. Then he slammed the lid, leaving her in total darkness.

The darkness felt good.

She hadn't realized how much the light was making her head pound until it was snuffed out.

She heard Brent moving. Heard a car engine start, then rumble. He was moving Dean's car, though not far by the sound of it. A moment later, her car door opened. She felt the car shift as Salcito climbed in. The engine roared to life.

And then, they were on the road, not driving down toward town but up toward...what? What was higher up on the mountain?

Garrett had told her once. Houses owned by tourists. Summer homes.

The homes that had been under construction the night her mother had gone missing.

Brent would kill her and dispose of her body probably somewhere it would never be found.

People would believe Aspen had committed murder and then vanished.

Just like her mother.

CHAPTER THIRTY-THREE

Garrett parked behind his uncle's truck in the driveway.

Dean was here? There were no other cars in sight. Would Aspen have parked in the detached garage? Only if she planned to stay.

But Garrett doubted she'd gone to the trouble.

Maybe Dean was waiting for her too? But his pickup was empty.

Had they gone somewhere together?

That didn't make sense, but Garrett couldn't come up with another explanation.

Cote'd already climbed from the cruiser and was halfway up the walk, his gun unholstered and at the ready, by the time Garrett caught up with him.

He turned and leveled a hard stare at Garrett. "Get back in your truck. I'll let you know when it's safe."

Garrett turned that way as if he'd comply.

As soon as Cote disappeared inside, he crept that direction. If Aspen was in danger, he wasn't about to sit in his pickup and hope Cote could handle it. Stupid, maybe. But two people he loved were involved in this. He needed to know what was going on.

He heard Cote's voice but couldn't make out the quiet words through the storm door. Then Cote yelled, "McCarthy, get in here."

Garrett bounded up the steps and into the house. He froze at the threshold.

Uncle Dean was seated on the sectional.

But he wasn't seated. He was slumped forward, his shirt stained red.

Cote said something, but Garrett couldn't make out the words over the roaring in his ears.

"Jesus." He felt unable to formulate more of a prayer than that as he rounded the sectional and crouched down beside his uncle. He touched his neck and felt a pulse.

"He's alive. Help me!"

"Ambulance is on the way. Lay him flat and try to stanch the bleeding." Cote moved up the stairs, gun still out, and disappeared from sight.

Garrett got Dean on his stomach, then snatched one of Aspen's throw blankets from the back of the sofa and pressed it to the wound on Dean's back. "I'm here, Uncle. You're going to be okay."

He'd literally been stabbed in the back. Sounds came from his mouth, but nothing Garrett could make out.

"Don't talk. Try to open your eyes."

Based on the stains on the white sofa, he'd lost a lot of blood. A *lot* of blood.

The blanket, a cheap fleece number, soaked it up. "Uncle, are you with me? Don't give up."

Dean spoke again, his words so quiet Garrett couldn't hear.

"Save your energy."

But he was trying to say something. Keeping pressure on the wound, Garrett angled his ear toward his uncle's mouth.

"Wasn't her."

Wasn't who? And then he realized... "Aspen? Of course not." Why would he say that? Aspen wouldn't... But this was her house, and her car was gone.

"Wasn't her."

"Who did this?" Garrett asked.

But Uncle Dean didn't say anything more.

"You have to fight." Garrett's words were loud in the silence. "Deborah needs you. *I* need you. Please, don't die." Garrett leaned down and felt faint breath against his cheek.

Please, Jesus, please, Jesus, please, Jesus.

He couldn't lose Dean. He couldn't.

"I'm sorry," Garrett said. "I'm sorry I couldn't do what you asked me to. I love you."

Cote hurried back down the stairs. "She's not here. Place is empty. What is she driving?"

"Aspen didn't do it. Dean just said—"

"What was she driving!"

"I don't know! A rental, I think."

Cote spoke into his radio, but Garrett couldn't focus on the words. His uncle's life was slipping away, and there was nothing he could do about it.

Sirens sounded, and a moment later, paramedics streamed into the room.

A hand gripped Garrett and pulled him out of the way.

"It's okay." The voice was familiar. Garrett focused on the man's face. Thomas. His friend. A volunteer fireman. And paramedic. "We got this."

Thomas all but pushed Garrett to the other side of the room, then hurried back to Dean's side.

Garrett couldn't move, just stared as people surrounded his

uncle. Furniture was moved. A gurney brought in. Dean transferred. They were in the ambulance and screaming out of the driveway within minutes.

Garrett headed for his truck, but Cote stopped him with a hand on his arm. He tried to yank away, but Cote didn't let up his grip. For an old, out-of-shape man, he was surprisingly strong.

"You don't know what Aspen was driving? You're sure. She didn't give you any idea—?"

"We haven't talked since last night. She was getting the rental this morning, but I haven't talked to her since then." He took a breath, let the question fully enter his brain. "Grace probably took her to get the car. Maybe she knows. She'd know where—"

"What's her number?"

Garrett pulled out his phone, navigated to Grace's contact information, and held it out for Cote.

He lifted his own cell, then swore. "Where's the house phone?"

"Kitchen."

Cote started that direction.

"Dean just told me she didn't do it."

Cote reached the door that led to the kitchen but glanced back. "What did he say exactly?"

"He said, 'Wasn't her.'"

Cote nodded. "You're sure? Because—"

"He said it twice. 'Wasn't her.'"

The police chief looked around at the cops who'd streamed into the place. He seemed to be considering that. "Okay." He leveled his gaze at Garrett again. "If that's the case, then somebody else was here. Somebody was here. And she's not. Which means—"

"She's in danger."

"Either she's a murderer, or she's in the hands of one." He stepped into the kitchen. A uniformed officer followed, and Garrett did a moment later.

A lamp, one Aspen had bought at Trudy's the week before, lay on the floor. The uniformed officer crouched beside it. "That's blood," he said.

Blood.

Aspen's blood?

Another uniformed police officer came in through the back door. "No sign anybody's been out there. Garage is empty."

Garrett stayed out of the way, hoping to hear something that would give him hope.

Cote had Aspen's house phone pressed to his ear as he crouched down. He was talking to Grace, but Garrett didn't pay attention to his words.

Pieces of ice and glass littered the floor, all resting in water. Someone had dropped a glass of water and made no effort to clean it up.

Two sets of wet footprints led from the kitchen and through the breakfast room. Two sets. Aspen's and someone else's. Garrett followed them into the living area and to the front door.

A uniformed cop had already seen the footprints. Garrett watched him as he stood from where he'd bent over the faintest ones on the stoop, then walked down the three steps to the walkway, gazing at the driveway.

The snow had started as flurries when they'd been headed up the mountain, but it had picked up. This storm was predicted to be a doozie, dropping a foot or more across the state before it was finished. The flakes were already sticking to the cold asphalt. Any tracks that might've been there would be covered up in minutes.

Aspen was out there, somewhere.

He swiveled when he overheard Cote speaking into his radio, ordering an APB on a car, presumably Aspen's.

Did he really think she'd done this?

When Garrett had followed Cote up the mountain, he hadn't passed any cars headed down. If Dean had only been stabbed minutes before, then that meant Aspen and her captor must have gone the other direction.

Cote could have cops all over the state looking for Aspen's car, but they weren't going to find it. Because her car wasn't heading *toward* civilization but away.

He pushed out the front door and down the three steps, where he spoke to the uniformed cop who still stood there. "They had to have gone up the mountain."

The man nodded. "We'll find her. Wasn't that your uncle?"

Garrett recognized the cop as someone he'd gone to school with. He nodded.

"We've already notified your aunt. Why don't you head to the hospital? Give me your number, and I'll call you when we find the person who did this."

That made sense. Deborah would need him. If the worst happened, if Dean didn't pull through, Deborah would need him all the more.

Garrett pulled a business card from his wallet and handed it to the cop, Gladstone, according to the name tag on his uniform. Gladstone gripped the card, but Garrett didn't let go.

"Aspen Kincaid, the woman who lives here"—he leveled his gaze at the man—"she didn't do it. My uncle said it wasn't her."

"We'll get to the bottom of this."

Maybe, but when? When would they start looking for her? At the moment, they seemed more intent on figuring out what had happened than they were on finding whoever had attacked Aspen and Dean. "She didn't do it. She's not a danger to anybody. She's *in* danger."

"I understand."

Did he? Or was he placating him?

The cop tugged the card. "Go on to the hospital, Garrett. We'll be in touch."

Sure they would. But to tell him what?

Garrett let go of his business card and jogged to his pickup.

He should be with Deborah. She needed him.

But Aspen.

Police cars had blocked him in. He engaged the four-wheel drive, yanked his wheel to the side, and drove across the snow-covered yard.

While he bounced over the terrain, he debated. Left to town and the hospital? Or right to Aspen?

As soon as his wheels hit pavement, he yanked the wheel to the right.

Dean had paramedics and EMTs and nurses and doctors and Deborah.

Aspen had nobody. Nobody who cared enough to find her. Nobody who believed in her. Nobody but Garrett.

And You, Lord. Protect her. Lead me to her.

CHAPTER THIRTY-FOUR

ASPEN HAD BEEN WHISPERING a constant stream of prayers ever since she'd been locked in the trunk. The first couple of verses of the ninety-first Psalm filled her mind and her heart as she begged God for help. *I dwell in the secret place of the Most High. I abide in Your shadow. You're my refuge. I trust in You.*

She couldn't remember the rest of the words, only that the Psalm promised protection. *Protect me, Father.*

Save me.

Only He could save her now. She was defenseless.

Utterly defenseless.

The car hadn't traveled far when it slowed down and took a sharp turn. It stopped, and she heard a mechanical hum, which lasted only a few seconds before it stopped. The car moved forward slowly.

Salcito had pulled into a garage. Were they at his house? Garrett had said there were only summer homes higher up the mountain. Maybe Salcito owned one. But why would he own a summer home in the town where he lived?

She didn't understand.

Not that it mattered.

They were here, wherever *here* was, and Salcito was going to kill her.

Even so, she would trust in God.

The only person who cared whether she lived or died was thousands of miles away, spreading the gospel in Kathmandu. Aspen had never really had her mother's love. Her father had adored her, but he was gone.

There was Garrett. If Dean was telling the truth, he cared for her. He'd be sorry if she didn't survive.

The thought of him brought a sob. She'd treated him so poorly. She should have trusted him. She should have at least let him explain. If she could go back and undo one thing, that would be it.

If she'd believed in him, then he would have been at the house with her. She wouldn't be where she was. None of this would be happening.

She'd been stupid.

Maybe Garrett wouldn't forgive her, even if she were given the chance to apologize. But Aspen wasn't defined by the people who loved her or didn't love her. Her worth wasn't wrapped up in other people's opinions.

Her future wasn't defined by her past. It certainly wasn't defined by her parents' past.

Maybe she was the daughter of a murderer. Maybe she was the daughter of *two* murderers. But before either her mother or her father had existed, God had known Aspen. He'd loved her. He'd chosen her. He'd *died* for her.

She was her father's daughter. Her mother's daughter. But mostly, she was God's daughter. He got to decide who she was. He decided her worth.

And God thought Aspen was priceless.

A car door opened and closed. Then there was nothing but

silence that stretched for minutes that felt like hours. She kept praying. It was all she could do.

Her head pounded, but it was better than it had been. The blood on the back of her head didn't seem to be flowing anymore. The low ache of nausea that had plagued her since the blow at the house, even more so in the trunk of a moving car, faded.

She'd suffered a concussion, no doubt. That wouldn't be what killed her.

She figured a gunshot would do that job.

Please, Father. Please save me.

Suddenly, the trunk lid opened, and light filled her vision, sending shard-like pain into her head. She closed her eyes against it, then opened them slowly, shielding them with her hand until they adjusted.

Brent grabbed her arm and yanked her up. "Let's go." He helped her step out of the trunk and onto the concrete floor of a garage. Two cars were already parked there, including a silver sedan with a dented front fender and a long scratch along its right side.

The car that had forced her off the road two nights before. Which reminded her. "You're supposed to be in Maine."

"I was. I stole a friend's keys and drove his car back here, then switched it with the car my friends leave here year-round. I'll have their dent fixed by the time they come up this summer."

"Nobody'll miss you at the retreat?"

"I'll show up for the dinner tonight. My car's been there all along. The whole point of the retreat is to spend time alone with God, so yes, nobody'll miss me."

Clever. Diabolical.

"How'd you get to my house?"

"I walked. It's less than a mile, all downhill. Glad I didn't have to walk back up."

Past the car, a door led into the house, but with a firm grip on her, Salcito pulled her the other direction to the driveway. After they stepped outside, he tapped a keypad on the threshold, and the garage door lowered.

The snow was coming fast, covering everything in a veneer of white. It would hide whatever tracks they'd leave.

Cold wind had her shuddering as Salcito led her around the garage and onto a walkway that had been recently shoveled. They took it to the back and rounded the house toward a deck covered with inches of snow. When they reached the stairs leading up to it, he said, "Sit here."

She did. Melting snow seeped through her jeans seconds after she sat. Her knees were already wet from crawling through ice water on her kitchen floor. She wore no coat, no gloves, no hat.

He could simply tie her to the railing and leave her there, and she'd freeze to death. She looked past him at an amazing vista. The trees dropped off, giving her a beautiful view of the lake and the mountains on the far side of town.

At least it was a pretty place to die.

He looked down at her. "I'm sorry it had to come to this."

Her teeth chattered. "You would much rather have k-k-killed me two nights ago on the road, I g-g-guess."

"It would have been easier," he admitted. "Easier still if you'd just recorded what you'd learned in your laptop. I hacked into it, but I didn't find anything about what you'd figured out."

So he'd been the one to break into her house. "You should have stolen my n-n-notebook." He might as well have, for all the good it'd done her. All her careful planning, and here she was, about to die.

If she got out of this, she was going to burn her notebook. She'd rather follow God's plans for her life than her own, anyway. Like Garrett had said, the notebook didn't keep her sane. If anything, her compulsive need to follow her carefully laid-out blueprint had thrown her off course.

Nope. From now on, she'd trust God with her future. If she had one.

Unlike her, the mayor was properly dressed in a puffy parka, a black skull cap, and black gloves. "I was really trying to avoid the conversation you and I have to have now."

She crossed her arms against the chill and tucked her fingers beneath her armpits. It didn't help much. "C-c-c-conversation?"

"You know where your mother is. I need to know."

"I don't understand." She paused through a chill. "You didn't kill her, so why do you c-c-care?"

His eyes narrowed. "Why do you say that?"

Which part? She'd ask the question, but she was pretty sure her jaw was freezing shut.

Her toes were already numb. Her fingers stung.

How long would it take to die of hypothermia? Surely longer than she'd been outside, but she was so cold. She'd never been so cold in her life.

"Why don't you think I killed her," Brent asked.

"If you d-d-d-did"—she shivered violently—"you'd know where she is."

He leaned against the railing beside her. "That's a logical conclusion." He blew out a long breath. "You're nothing like her. You look like her, no question. Your voice is so similar, it's eerie. But you're so...rational."

Aspen didn't know what to say to that.

"If Jane were in your position, she'd be panicking or making baseless threats. She'd be screaming, thrashing, trying to get away."

"What would be the p-p-point? Nobody's going to hear m-m-m..." She couldn't finish the sentence for trembling that took over.

His smile was sad. "See what I mean? Rational. If Jane had only been a little more rational..." He didn't finish his sentence, either, though not, she guessed, because of the cold.

"Tell me where Jane is."

"So you can k-k-k-kill me f-f-faster?"

"At least you'll be out of your misery."

"Your concern for my well-being is t-t-t-touching."

He crouched down until his face was inches from hers. "Tell me where she is."

"D-don't know."

"I was outside when Dean was at your house. I heard you tell him you knew where she was. And that you hadn't yet told Cote."

He'd listened to their entire conversation? No wonder he'd killed Dean. But Dean had confessed everything to Deborah, and Deborah would tell Cote. Did Deborah know that Salcito had worked with Aspen's mother?

If so, then even if Dean died, Salcito was going down.

"D-d-deborah knows. She'll t-t-t-tell."

"I heard all the lies Dean spun," he said. "One thing I've learned in my years as a lawyer and a politician is that, when an unexpected situation crops up, you work the problem in front of you. I'll deal with Deborah later. First I need to find your mother. Where is she?"

Aspen shuddered, both from the cold and from his words. How would he deal with Deborah?

Would he have another murder on his conscience?

Assuming he *had* a conscience?

"Not until you"—she paused through another shudder—"tell me what happened."

"If I do, you'll tell me where she is?"

"So you can let me f-f-freeze to d-d-d-death?"

He shrugged out of his jacket and slipped it over her shoulders. His lingering body heat enveloped her as she pushed her hands into his sleeves. He zipped it up, his closeness sending a whole different kind of quaking through her body. But he backed away quickly. "Better?"

She nodded, hating herself for loving the warmth he'd given her. She took a few breaths and forced herself to calm. She was still cold, but it was tolerable with the jacket on. "I came to find out what happened to her. At least give me that."

He sat beside her on the stoop. The narrow staircase had him too close, but she wasn't going to complain if it meant she'd get to breathe for a few more minutes. "Everything went according to plan until we got there that night. The building was dark. But there was a car in the parking lot. We'd decided that if we thought anybody was there, we'd leave. But Jane..." He shook his head slowly. "When she decided to do something, nothing could stop her."

CHAPTER THIRTY-FIVE

THIRTY YEARS AGO.

It was a miracle Jane hadn't been pulled over after the explosion.

Maybe not a miracle, though. Every police officer, fireman, and paramedic in town—probably within a few towns—was headed to the sight of the explosion. Nobody was looking for a red hatchback, not yet.

And the overlook was only a ten-minute drive from the lumber company, along back roads that wound through the forest and past summer houses that were mostly abandoned in March.

Though Jane drove, she seemed to have lost her grip on reality.

Brent feared that something in her mind had snapped. He directed her, afraid she'd forget her destination. She did what he told her to do, but when he caught her eyes in the rearview mirror, it was obvious that she wasn't all there.

They drove up Rattlesnake Road, past the condo development that was under construction and the one house on the road.

"Slow down," he said. "I'm parked right..."

But she zoomed past his car.

"Jane, you need to drop me off."

"It was empty. The building was empty."

"Fine. It was empty. Turn around and take me to my car."

But she kept going, all the way to the top. Then she slammed on the brakes, and they screeched to a halt. She jumped out before slipping it into park, and he had to reach into the front seat and jam the gear shift forward to keep it from driving into the woods.

She'd lost it. She'd completely lost it.

He didn't know what to do.

All his planning, his careful plotting, and she'd blown it. She'd broken the first rule. The one rule they'd all agreed on.

And murdered a woman.

It could only have been a woman. He'd heard her voice in her sobbing. A sad woman, alone in the building.

Please, let her have been alone.

Jane was running toward the overlook, going too fast.

He followed her. He didn't know if she was trying to kill herself or if she was just too far gone to understand what she was doing. A tiny part of him thought maybe it would be better if she flew over the edge.

But he pictured her body at the bottom, broken and bloodied.

No matter what she'd done, he loved her.

He was faster and caught up with her before she careened over the edge. He grabbed her wrist and yanked her back. "What are you doing? You're going to kill yourself."

Her eyes were wild, insane. She yanked something from her pocket, lifted it and brought it down toward his head.

He managed to deflect her hand, catching the glint of metal an instant before pain registered in his palm. A knife?

She'd sliced his palm with a knife.

He didn't know where it'd come from, only that if he hadn't seen it coming, she'd have stabbed him in the chest.

"What are you doing?" he asked. "Stop it. Sweetheart. You need to pull it together."

But she was out of control. She reared away, took a few steps back, closer to the edge of the cliff. It wasn't far down, maybe twenty or thirty feet, but she probably wouldn't survive a fall.

"Please, Jane." He kept his distance, afraid that if he stepped closer, she'd back away. Another two or three steps and she'd go over. "Listen to me. It's going to be okay." It had to be. They could still fix this. "We just have to follow the plan. You remember the plan?"

But Jane wasn't listening. She wasn't *there*.

She let out a visceral scream and came at him again. He managed to grab her wrist and turn the knife to the side an instant before her body crashed into his.

He lost his balance, and they both tumbled. She landed on him. He wrapped his arm around her and turned her over so he was on top. He needed to get her under control. He needed to pull her back from...from wherever she'd gone. He needed to reason with her.

He pinned her wrists to the ground and levered himself up over her. "You need to listen to..."

His words faded as he took in the sight.

He'd angled the knife outward. Out, toward air. Hadn't he?

But there it was.

Protruding from Jane's neck.

Blood spurting from the wound, painting the ground crimson.

"Jane. Oh, my gosh. Oh, my gosh." He pulled out the knife and pressed his hand to the wound as if stopping the blood flow might save her life.

But in the moonlight, he knew the truth.

Her eyes were no longer wild.

They were empty. Empty of the woman he loved.

She was gone.

Only a few seconds passed before he heard the sound that must have been there all along.

Someone was there. Breathing heavily.

He stood and came face-to-face with Michael.

Jane's husband.

Brent didn't know what to say. There were no words to fill the silence between them. The silence hovering over the body of the woman they both loved.

Michael spoke first. "It was you, wasn't it? The explosion?"

He'd heard it? In town? Or had he already been up at the overlook?

Would it have been so loud?

Brent didn't know. He should have known how far away it could be heard. He hadn't considered that in his planning.

Michael crouched down beside Jane. He reached out as if he might touch her, then pulled back.

Fury rose within Brent. "You never loved her. Not like I do. You stole her from me, but you never loved her!"

Michael gently closed Jane's eyes.

"How can you be so calm?" Brent screamed. "She's dead. She's—"

"Calm?" Michael sat back on his heels, and his shoulders heaved. Moments passed. Finally, he looked up. In the moonlight, Brent saw the wetness on the man's face. "You just killed my wife."

"It was self-defense. I didn't mean for it to happen. She came at—"

"I saw what happened." He stood, shook his head. "I'll tell them. You won't go to prison...for that, anyway."

He started across the dirt toward the road.

When Brent looked that direction, he saw what he'd missed before. The black minivan he'd always sneeringly thought of as Michael's "dad car" was parked farther up the road, nearly hidden in the darkness beside a thick bush.

He was going to get in it. Drive to his house, or maybe the closest pay phone, and call the police.

And then Brent would go to prison.

"You'll be implicated." He didn't yell the words. He didn't have to.

Michael stopped in the middle of the asphalt and turned. "What are you talking about?"

"In the bombing. Jane set it up to frame you."

The other man's gaze flicked from Brent to where they'd left her. "In her state of mind? I'll take my chances."

"She couldn't have done it by herself. You're right about that."

Michael's eyes narrowed. "What does that mean?"

"The person who made the bomb did it with your tools, wearing your clothes. We kept all that stuff, along with hair Jane collected for us. All that evidence will be sent to the police station tomorrow."

Again, he studied the body that lay behind Brent. "Why?" He sounded perplexed, hurt. "Why would she do that?"

"She needed an alibi. She was going to ask you to tell the police she was with you tonight."

Michael closed the distance between them so fast that Brent barely had time to step back. "It was your idea, wasn't it?"

"I was trying to keep her out of prison."

"Nice going. If only you'd tried as hard to keep her out of the grave."

The words hit their mark.

Brent stumbled back. His legs suddenly felt like jelly, and

he barely kept himself from falling backward. Over the cliff and to his own death. He went to his knees, then leaned onto his hands and vomited.

His body was beginning to understand what had happened.

It would take his mind and heart some time to catch up.

When he sat back on his heels, Michael was still standing there, glaring down at him. "So, you and my wife—and Dean, I guess—decided to blow up... Was it the lumber company?"

Brent said nothing, but Michael had put it together.

"Her plan was for me to meet her here, then go home with her as if we'd been together the whole night. She was going to blackmail me into telling the police she'd been with me. Do I have that right?"

Brent just nodded.

"And then, what? We'd go on with our lives?" He scoffed, shook his head. "No. You knew I wouldn't be able to live with it. I'd leave her, and you'd step in. You did all this"—he gestured as if he could encompass all the horrible events in the sweep of his arm—"as one big elaborate scheme to steal my wife."

Brent crawled away from the vomit and forced himself to stand on shaky legs.

"And now she's gone," Michael said.

Brent couldn't stand the condemnation he saw on the other man's face. He averted his gaze, then caught sight of the glow in the forest below.

A fire.

Caused by the explosion.

Caused by the *bomb*.

Had they found the woman's body yet?

There were no secrets between them now. Michael needed to know it all. Then, hopefully, he'd do the right thing.

Do right by Brent, anyway.

"The building wasn't empty."

Michael's eyes widened.

"We'd agreed not to do it if there was anybody there, but Jane..." He closed his eyes against the memory of her face when she'd run from the building. The pure unadulterated joy he'd seen. "She decided to do it anyway."

"You should have stopped her."

He didn't bother to explain what had happened. It didn't matter now.

"Your wife murdered a woman. And you're going to be implicated. You can tell them I was with her, but nobody will be able to prove that. It'll be your word against mine. Maybe they'll believe you. Maybe they won't.

"My partner will mail the evidence to the police station tomorrow. The police will follow up on that. Jane will be dead, and you'll be implicated in what happened here as well. Maybe none of the charges will stick. But maybe they will. Maybe you'll get sent to prison. Maybe your little girl will grow up knowing her mother murdered an innocent woman, and her father murdered her mother."

Michael cringed as if the idea caused him physical pain.

"Or," Brent said, "we hide her body. Everybody's going to believe she set that bomb off, and she did. The blame will fall exactly where it should. They'll come after me and my partner, but we'll both have alibis. Nobody will be able to prove anything. Jane will disappear. Just...be gone. The world will think she realized what she did and ran away to avoid facing charges."

He wasn't sure what he expected Michael to do. Yell at him, maybe come after him. Maybe collapse. But the man stood his ground and said nothing.

Brent added for good measure, "You'll get to raise your little girl."

"And you'll get off scot-free." His words were cold.

"I didn't kill her. You know that. You know it was self-defense."

"You set off the bomb. You—"

"I didn't set it off. I tried to stop her. I failed. I see now that I should never have... She was losing it. I thought I could keep her under control."

"If you'd backed me up when I tried to have her committed..." Michael's words trailed, and he blew out a short, humorless laugh. "I knew she was a danger to herself. *You* knew she was a danger to others. But you kept that tidbit to yourself."

He had. It was stupid, and he'd never forgive himself.

None of that mattered now. "If you take me out, then I'll take you out. You and I will both lose. But you know who'll lose even more?"

Michael didn't answer. He didn't have to. The truth was written across his face.

Aspen meant more to him than justice. His daughter meant more to him than anything.

He'd loved Jane out of obligation.

He loved Aspen from a place of pure adoration.

The details were spinning and setting themselves in place in Brent's mind. "It's very simple. You take Jane—and the knife. You bury them somewhere. The knife has my blood on it." He lifted his hand to show where he'd been cut, registering only then the blood dripping down his arm. "You can take my jacket too." He shifted so Michael could see where Jane's blood drenched the arm of his canvas coat.

"And then?" Michael asked.

"You have evidence against me. I have evidence against you. We both leave here tonight and say nothing about what happened. We claim we don't know what happened to her. We haven't heard from her. We keep our mouths shut, and we go on with our lives."

"Just like that?"

Brent lifted his shoulders, let them drop. "I'll never forgive myself for what happened tonight."

Michael stared at him a long moment. "Not exactly a fitting punishment."

Brent couldn't hold his eye contact. He slipped off his jacket and dropped it on the road. Then he walked away. When he was well past Michael, he broke into a jog until he reached his car a few hundred yards down the mountain.

He went home, bandaged his hand, changed his clothes, and left with his father for the city.

Hoping Michael would keep his mouth shut.

CHAPTER THIRTY-SIX

"You just left her there?" Aspen's words seemed too loud in the silent, snowy world.

Brent stared ahead at the beautiful vista. The gun rested on his lap, but he never let up his grip.

He gestured with his chin. "It was probably right around there."

She followed his gaze to a break in the trees. Boulders had been positioned between the land and the drop-off, but they were spaced far enough apart that anybody could get past them. Assuming they'd even been there back then.

"This was their overlook?" Aspen asked.

"My dad had a friend in the city looking for a summer home. He bought this property not long after Jane died. I've been coming up here for cookouts for years. My son takes care of the place when they're not around. That's why I have the garage door code. I've never once been here that I didn't think of her."

"Sure. You obviously loved her so much, what with how you blackmailed my father so you wouldn't have to face what you did."

"You think I'm proud of that?"

"I think you're a coward."

He let those words settle. "So was your father, I guess."

"My father did what he did to protect me. Not himself."

Poor Dad. Aspen's heart broke for him. He'd faced an impossible choice.

He would have known it wouldn't be easy to take on the town's richest family. It would have been him, a widower and single parent who poured cement for a living, against the son of the county prosecutor and the former mayor.

Maybe he'd have been cleared. Maybe he wouldn't have.

Daddy had agreed to Brent's crazy scheme to protect her.

Of that, she had no doubt.

And she knew something else too. Whatever he'd meant to say before he'd been intubated a year before, she'd misunderstood. He never would have sent her back here to face all of this. He never would have put her in this danger.

He'd wanted to do himself what he hadn't before had the courage to do.

He certainly hadn't meant for Aspen to do it.

If only she'd realized that. But she'd needed to know what happened to her mother. Or she'd thought she had, anyway.

Now she knew. How would her life be better for the knowledge?

Brent shifted beside her, reminding her that her life wouldn't be all that affected by what she knew because it wasn't going to last that much longer.

"Now you know the story," he said. "Where is she?"

"Your plan is to dig her up, I guess. Destroy the evidence linking her to you?"

"My plan is irrelevant to you. Where is she?"

"It's not going to work. Even if I tell you where she is, you won't be able to get to her."

"You let me deal with that. Wherever she is, I can get her."

Not if Mom was buried under cement. "I don't know for sure. It's just a guess. Even if I don't tell Cote, he's going to find her. The plan has already been set in motion."

"What plan?"

She wasn't going to tell him about the ground-penetrating radar Cote had arranged. That kind of radar could see through cement. He knew what Dad had done for a living. He'd figure it out.

"When they find her body," Aspen said, "and they will, you can tell them what happened, that you acted in self-defense and then panicked and buried her. Maybe they'll believe you. But if you kill me"—she turned and leveled her gaze at him—"that'll be the crime you burn for."

He swallowed hard. "They'll have to prove it. But you're going to disappear."

"They'll know."

"Like they knew I was involved with the bombing. Yet, here I am." He lifted both hands and let them drop. "Because it's not about what they *know*, it's about what they can *prove*. And without a body, without a murder weapon, they won't be able to prove a thing."

"You're a monster, you know that?"

"I'm just a man, a man who made a stupid decision a long time ago. A man who got away with it and intends to keep getting away with it." He pushed to his feet and looked down at her. "Where is she?"

Aspen shook her head. "I'm not going to tell you."

He lifted the gun and pressed the barrel against her head. "Where. Is. She?"

The feel of that cold, hard barrel...

The knowledge that he could take her life with the squeeze of a finger.

Terror overcame her.

A scream crawled up from her belly, but she clamped her lips shut and pressed her eyes closed. And breathed. In and out. In and out. She focused her thoughts elsewhere, on the sting of the cold air. The feel of downy flakes landing on her nose and cheeks. The sound of the wind whispering through the trees.

Whether at the top of a mountain in New Hampshire or at the edge of the world on a Hawaiian beach, God had created a planet filled with beautiful people. People like her best friend and her father, who'd loved her so well. People like Garrett, who'd tried to protect her.

Garrett, whose heart would break. Would he live the rest of his life not knowing what had become of her? Would he believe she'd killed his uncle and then escaped?

No. Garrett would never think the worst of her, not the way she'd thought the worst of him.

Forgive me.

God did, and Garrett would. In time.

Protect him, Father. Let him have a good life.

She had. Maybe not as good a life as some, but certainly not as bad as others. At least she didn't have to live with what Brent Salcito had lived with for thirty years. At least she didn't have to spend her life dragging around a weight of regret.

Her God had freed her of all of that.

If this was the end for her, so be it.

The gun pressed harder against her skull, jabbing into her skin and making the ache from her concussion throb.

She was done with it. She was done with all of it.

She wasn't going to just sit there and let him threaten her.

Whipping her hand up, she whacked the gun away.

And then opened her eyes.

What had she done?

Salcito was off-balance.

She'd surprised him. She pushed up and rammed into him, sending him sprawling, and darted around the house, expecting to hear the roar of a gunshot, feel the sting of a bullet.

But he didn't pull the trigger.

She darted into the trees between this house and the one beside it. These houses were too close together to offer very much in the way of forest between them.

Salcito crashed through the woods behind her, uttering obscenities under his breath. Why didn't he just shoot her?

Because he wanted to know where her mother was.

As she reached the neighboring house, she took a deep breath and screamed. She screamed as loudly as she could, praying the sound would carry. To whom, she had no idea.

Maybe one of these houses was occupied.

Salcito was gaining on her.

She had to find something to defend herself with. But there was nothing. Nothing.

She ran toward the trees on the other side of the house. Managed to get out of the yard and into the woods again.

But Salcito was close.

Too close.

She snatched up a fallen branch covered in snow.

She turned, took a swing.

But the branch was longer than she'd realized. It whacked a tree trunk nearby, vibrated with the impact, and fell from her frozen fingers.

Salcito dove and tackled her.

She landed in the snow. She inhaled to scream, but his hand clamped over her mouth.

He glared down at her. "You're going to wish you hadn't done that."

CHAPTER THIRTY-SEVEN

THERE WAS nothing on this road. Nothing but tracks, which were already being covered by the quickly falling snow. Garrett had been slowly following those tracks on the narrow road in the thick forest, keeping his window open, hoping to hear something, maybe see something.

Aside from the low hum of his engine, the world was silent.

Until he heard a scream.

He pressed the gas harder and went higher up the hill, past houses, until the road ended in a cul-de-sac.

The tracks led to a house.

He parked, jogged up the driveway. Somebody had driven into the garage, but footprints led around the back.

He crept that way, staying as quiet as he could.

In the distance, he heard a low *thwack*. But he couldn't see anybody. Where was she?

CHAPTER THIRTY-EIGHT

Aspen stared up into the furious face of Brent Salcito. The man she'd met at church the previous Sunday, the man who'd bought her pastries at Cuppa Josie's...that man was gone.

This man didn't wear a mask of kindness.

His eyes were bulging. His lips drawn back in a sneer. He straddled her, holding her arms over her head in a tight grip. She struggled to wiggle away, but he outweighed her and overpowered her. His other hand clamped down on her neck.

He squeezed.

"You're right," he said. "I can explain away the knife and the jacket. It'll be clear I hadn't been the one to kill her and bury her, or I wouldn't have hidden those things with her body."

Aspen gasped for breath, the world darkening around her as Salcito's fingers pressed against the arteries in her neck. She tried to wiggle out of his grip, but he was too strong.

She was utterly powerless.

"I'll come up with a story about how your father found us together," Brent said. "How, in a fit of jealousy, he attacked me and killed his wife. How I didn't tell the truth because I was afraid I'd be implicated in the bombing. You're right, Aspen. If they find your mother, I'll figure a way out of it. I always do."

He bent lower, low enough to whisper in her ear. "I always hated you. I know it's wrong to hate a baby, but I loathed you. You were the reason she married Michael. You were the only thing keeping Jane from me. I know it's too late to get Jane back, but I'm not one bit sorry to kill you." His fingers tightened, clamping over Aspen's windpipe. "In fact, I think I'll enjoy it."

Blackness crept from the edges of her vision until all she could see was the face of the man who would end her life.

So she closed her eyes. *Father, expose all this man's evil deeds.*

Protect Jaslynn. She'll grieve for me. Wrap her in Your arms and comfort her.

Protect Garrett. Please, let him know I would never hurt his uncle. Bless him. Give him a good life.

If only she could have known his love. If only she could have experienced life with him. Slept beside him. Seen the faces of their children. Held his hand and walked with him into old age.

If only everything could have been different.

Suddenly, she felt free.

Free of pain.

Free of the weight of her murderer.

It was over.

She gasped in a deep, full breath and opened her eyes.

CHAPTER THIRTY-NINE

G ARRETT CREPT in the direction of the sound. It had come from a neighboring property.

It took precious seconds to pick his way through the forest between the houses. Aspen wasn't in the yard next door. Garrett hurried past, then into the woods again.

Where he saw a man on the ground, propped up on two arms. One hand was pressed into the ground.

The other was pressed into the neck of the woman Garrett loved.

He charged. Tackled the stranger.

Rolled him over and onto the ground, but he kept their momentum going until Garrett was on top. He landed a punch to the man's face, only then getting a good look.

The mayor?

Brent Salcito, the man who'd claimed to love Jane Kincaid, had tried to kill her daughter.

Garrett punched him again.

Salcito was big enough to overpower a woman, but he had nothing on Garrett. Salcito landed a few blows against Garrett's side, but Garrett hardly felt them as he punched the man a third time, then a fourth.

Salcito quit fighting and moved his hands to protect his head.

It took considerable effort not to punch him again.

But...Aspen.

He pushed up from the ground. Salcito had quit fighting. His eyes were closed.

He turned to find Aspen still lying on the ground. Eyes open. In a flash of panic, he feared she was dead. But he could see the vapor rising from her mouth as she exhaled.

He wanted to go to her, to pull her into his arms. He wasn't going to leave Salcito alone, though. He stood. "Aspen? Are you injured?"

She shifted to look at him. And smiled. "I thought..." The words came out raspy, and she cleared her throat. "Are you really here?"

He wasn't sure what she meant by that. "Can you walk?"

"Um..." She pushed herself up to sitting and must've seen Salcito at his feet. Her eyes widened, and she looked around on the ground. "Where is it?"

"What?"

"This." Salcito's voice was cold, angry.

Garrett dove, registering the moment his body hit the snow what Aspen had been looking for. Thank God his instincts had pushed him to act before his mind managed to catch up.

The gunshot was deafening in the silence.

Garrett rolled, didn't pause to check if he'd been hit.

Salcito scrambled to his feet.

Garrett barreled into him a second time. This time, they crashed into the trunk of a tree.

Salcito's head bounced off the hard wood, and he pitched sideways.

Garrett took advantage of the blow to the older man's head. He yanked his opposite arm and twisted his body.

The mayor landed face down in the snow.

Garrett snatched the gun from his limp hand, stuck it in his pocket, and rested one knee on the man's back.

He fought to catch his breath.

The shifting of bracken, the snap of a twig, told him Aspen was moving.

"Are you all right?" she asked

"I'm fine." He hoped he was, anyway. He didn't feel any pain, but he knew enough to know adrenaline could mask it.

He didn't *think* he'd been hit.

He looked her way quickly, but he wasn't going to be dumb enough to take his focus off Salcito again. "Are you?"

"Yeah. A little dizzy, but—"

"Can you drive?"

"I think so."

"My truck is parked in the cul-de-sac. Go to your house and tell Cote—"

"Cote's at my house?"

"Yeah. In fact..." He pulled the gun out of his pocket and aimed straight up. He squeezed the trigger, then squeezed it again.

The gunshots echoed through the forest.

"Maybe they heard that," he said. "Maybe not. Either way, head for the road. If the police don't come, drive down."

"Are you sure you're okay?"

He glared down at the man beneath his knee. "The mayor and I will be just fine." If the man made any attempt to escape, Garrett would shoot him.

He sort of hoped Salcito would try.

<h1 style="text-align:center">CHAPTER FORTY</h1>

As Aspen emerged from the forest, she heard the growl of an approaching engine. She stepped onto the road, and a police cruiser stopped beside her.

Chief Cote stepped out. The way he took in her appearance, his eyes wide and filled with worry, she wondered what she must look like.

"Where are you hurt?"

It was all starting to register.

She'd been hit hard. Abducted. Nearly killed. Rescued.

Cote gripped her arm, maybe to keep her from falling. His face was inches from hers as he studied her. "What happened?"

"Garrett saved me. They're in there." She pointed into the trees behind her.

Other police cars came. Uniformed officers streamed that direction.

How had they all gotten there so quickly?

Someone wrapped a blanket around Aspen's shoulders and told her to sit in Cote's police car. She did, staring toward where she'd left Garrett.

A moment later, he emerged from the woods.

Aspen stood to get a better look at him.

He closed the distance between them and wrapped her in his arms. "Thank God you're all right."

She pressed her cheek into his soft sweatshirt. How was it this man never wore a coat?

She still wore Brent Salcito's. The man had tried to kill her, had blackmailed her father after watching her mother die. But his coat was warm, at least. "How did you know?" Aspen felt as confused as she was relieved when she looked up into Garrett's face. He was really there. Part of her still worried it was all a hallucination brought on by lack of oxygen and insanity. "How did you find us?"

"We were at your house. I saw the tracks in the snow that led up here and followed."

"Oh." She remembered Dean, and her stomach dropped to the snowy pavement. "Dean. We have to call an—"

"He's already on his way to the hospital."

"He's alive?"

"He was." Garrett looked over her head. "I pray he still is."

Aspen stepped back. "They're going to find my fingerprints on the knife, but I didn't do it. I would never—"

"I know, sweetheart. I know." He set her at arms' length and studied her. "What hurts?"

She considered his question and did a little survey. "My head. He hit me with... I'm not sure what. Something hard." She touched the spot. Her fingers didn't come away with fresh blood. She had some aches and pains, but they were nothing compared to what could have happened. "Thank you, Garrett. For coming after me. For believing me. I'm so sorry I didn't trust you."

He pulled her against his chest again. "It's all right. It's over now."

She leaned back to face him. "Why didn't you go to the hospital with Dean?"

He squinted in confusion. "I had to find you."

"Salcito meant for everybody to believe I'd stabbed your uncle and then taken off."

"Even if we hadn't shown up when we did. Even if we'd never found you, I would never have believed that. Never."

"Truly?"

He kissed her forehead and held her against his chest again. "You could never hurt anybody. I know that. One of these days, you're going to figure out how much you mean to me. One of these days, you're going to see yourself as I see you."

He'd believed in her, even after everything. She didn't remove her cheek from the soft fabric of his sweatshirt but needed to ask the question. "How do you see me?"

He held her a little tighter. "As the woman I love."

CHAPTER FORTY-ONE

Aspen had been checked out at the hospital and released. She'd given Cote a statement—though not a complete statement. The time would come for that later.

Brent Salcito had been taken to a different hospital. According to Cote, he was refusing to talk. The only word he'd uttered since his arrest had been "Lawyer."

She wasn't a bit surprised.

Now, she sat beside Garrett in the hospital waiting room. Deborah sat on his other side.

Dean had been in surgery by the time they'd arrived there. An hour later, he was still in surgery. Deborah said the doctors hadn't given her much hope but promised to do everything they could.

Others had arrived while they waited. Older folks Aspen had never met, along with a crowd of people her own age. Andrew and Grace, James and Cassidy, Braden and Carly and their baby girl. Tabby was there, though Fitz was on duty. He'd be by when he got off work. Jacqui and Reid had come, sans Ella, Reid's little girl, who they explained was with her mother.

The way Reid explained that told Aspen he wasn't happy to

share his daughter. There was a story there. Maybe a story she'd be around long enough to hear.

Even Dylan and Chelsea had come. They'd returned from wherever they'd been that week.

Each new person walked in, hugged Garrett, and then hugged her. The group had prayed together more than once. None of them had asked for details about what happened. Maybe they realized Garrett's mind was on his uncle, and Aspen... Aspen was still trying to come to grips with the whole thing.

A white-coated doctor stepped into the room and assessed the crowd. She was probably in her forties, shorter than Aspen, and couldn't have weighed a hundred pounds. She had dark brown curly hair and hazel eyes. She caught Deborah's gaze and made her way toward her. Aspen was close enough to hear, though the doctor lowered her voice. "Do you want to step away, someplace private? Or do you mind—?"

"Just tell us," Deborah said. "Is he all right?"

The room quieted, and everybody turned to the surgeon, who spoke to Deborah but raised her voice loudly enough for everyone to hear. "Your husband came through the surgery."

Murmurs of *thank God* and *Praise Jesus* rumbled through the small room.

Deborah leaned against Garrett, who steadied her.

"The knife missed his heart by a hair. It did plenty of damage, though. We've stitched everything up, and we're monitoring him closely. His heart rate is lower than we'd like it. We're struggling to get it up. We've already done one transfusion, and we might need to do another before the night is over." Her gaze lifted to all the friends. "If anybody'd be willing to give blood—"

"Absolutely," Andrew said. "Where do we go?"

The woman smiled. "I'll send someone in to show you." She

spoke to Deborah again. "He's not out of the woods yet, but I have hope."

Garrett's arm slipped around his aunt's shoulders. He pulled her close and kissed the top of her head. "There's always hope."

"He's in recovery if you two want to see him."

Garrett squeezed Aspen's hand and followed Deborah and the surgeon out of the room.

While they were gone, Aspen settled on a chair and prayed for Dean's full recovery.

She prayed for Garrett's heart as he struggled to understand what had happened thirty years before.

And she prayed for wisdom. She was going to need it. Because Garrett had expressed his love for her, and though her feelings might not have been quite as deep as his, she was falling hard for the man who'd rescued her.

Who'd walked with her through the most difficult weeks of her life.

She just hoped he'd forgive her for what she had to do now.

CHAPTER FORTY-TWO

Garrett was seated at Dean's bedside when the doctor stepped in Monday morning. She might have been the height and weight of a middle-school girl, but she was competent, considering three days had passed since Dean had been stabbed, and he was still alive.

But the surgeon's every visit so far had come with caution as she'd listed all the things that could still go wrong. She'd told them Friday night, then Saturday, then again on Sunday, that Dean was still in grave danger.

Garrett hated that expression. *Grave* danger. It brought to mind headstones and caskets and death.

He couldn't lose Dean, not now. Not yet. He muttered his millionth prayer, asking once again for God to heal his uncle as he joined Deborah at the end of Dean's bed. Together, they watched while the doctor checked on the patient.

"Has he been awake much today?" she asked.

Garrett waited for Deborah to answer, but she was quiet. She'd been unnaturally quiet throughout this whole affair. His aunt, who was usually bubbling over with joy and laughter and stories, had hardly spoken for days.

Garrett was almost as worried about her as he was about Dean.

"Not today." Garrett squeezed Deborah's hand. "He woke up for a few minutes last night around ten o'clock."

Garrett had insisted Deborah go home and sleep. There was no reason for both of them to stay all night, and she needed rest. She claimed she'd gotten some, but the dark smudges beneath her eyes told a different story.

"Was he lucid?" the surgeon asked.

"He didn't say anything."

Dean had looked afraid when his eyes first opened, but Garrett had reminded him that he was in a hospital. At that point, he'd relaxed but still hadn't spoken. Garrett had assured him that Deborah was well and at home resting, and that Aspen was also alive and well. Then he'd talked about the Bruins game, which he'd just finished watching, and told his uncle how the Celtics were doing. He'd babbled about nothing until Dean fell back asleep. "Why doesn't he talk?"

Garrett wasn't accustomed to so much silence from his aunt and uncle. Thank God for Aspen, who'd braved the snow-covered roads and spent the better part of every day at the hospital with them. She kept them company with her chatter. She brought food and insisted they both eat. She brought magazines and books and had even purchased a deck of cards and challenged them to gin rummy. Deborah had passed, but Garrett had taken her up on the offer. They'd played for hours.

With every tick of the clock, he'd been more convinced that Aspen was the woman for him. He'd fallen more in love with her every time she'd walked through those doors.

"It's the medication," the surgeon said. "The painkillers are helping him rest, which is the best thing for him." She smiled. "I'm going to be honest. I didn't think he'd make it this long."

The words ticked up Garrett's blood pressure, but he focused on the happiness in the doctor's expression.

"His heart rate is right where we want it. He's healing well. We're going to start weaning him off the medication today and see how he does."

Garrett said, "Are you saying—?"

"Is he going to be all right?" Deborah's voice held hope for the first time in days.

The surgeon stepped closer and gripped her arm. "I don't make promises, but if I had to guess, I'd say he's going to make a full recovery."

Deborah collapsed against Garrett's chest and sobbed. Deep, heart-wrenching sobs. It seemed all the fear she'd been afraid to voice for three days was coming out now, soaking his sweatshirt.

He held her close and looked over her head at the surgeon. "Thank you."

She nodded and stepped out.

A moment later, Aspen stepped in. "I didn't want to interrupt." Her gaze flicked from Deborah, still in his arms, to the bed, where Dean lay still. Her eyes widened. "Is everything okay?"

"It's good news," Garrett said.

Aspen closed the distance, and he held out a hand to her. She squeezed it, then stepped near the bed and gazed down at Dean. "You hear that? You're going to be all right."

Deborah moved to the other side of the bed.

Garrett's eyes tingled at the sight of the woman he loved with the aunt and uncle he adored. His family.

But when Aspen looked at Deborah, Garrett caught something unsettled in her gaze. Deborah returned the look.

He once again had the feeling that there was a conversation going on beneath the surface, a conversation he couldn't hear.

CHAPTER FORTY-THREE

DEAN HAD AWAKENED for a little while Monday afternoon, but he'd still been confused. Aspen was certain that, when he'd looked at her, he hadn't known who she was. Or maybe he'd thought she was Jane.

She'd stayed out of the way and kept her head down. She wanted to be there for Garrett, but she didn't want to cause Dean distress.

Tuesday morning, Aspen wasn't sure what she'd find when she knocked and then stepped into Dean's room. She definitely hadn't expected the beaming smiles sent her way from all three in the room.

Garrett rushed around Dean's bed and met her in the doorway with a hug. "He's awake and aware."

"I'm so glad," she said. "Is it okay that I'm here?"

"Of course." Garrett took her hand and pulled her to the bed. She guessed that Dean hadn't confessed to his nephew what he'd confessed to her. "Dean, Aspen's been to visit every day."

Dean's gaze caught hers. He remembered.

His confession. His promise to tell Cote everything.

"I'm glad you're all right," Dean said.

"You're the one in the hospital bed." She walked to his side, happy to see he was recovering. Ever since they'd arrived at the hospital Friday night, she'd been remembering those last few days with her father. Sitting at his bedside, praying he'd wake up.

Watching as he'd slipped away.

She was so thankful Garrett would be spared that pain, anyway. "How you feeling?"

He glanced at Deborah, who stood on the other side, before answering the question. "Good. Strong. Ready to face the future."

Which meant she had to do the same.

It was hours before Dean fell asleep again. When he finally did, she said, "I'm going to stretch my legs."

Garrett stood. "I'll join you."

"Actually..." Aspen turned to Deborah. "I was hoping you and I could talk."

Garrett's gaze flicked from his aunt to Aspen. Neither of them looked at him.

Deborah pushed to her feet. "That would be lovely." She squeezed Garrett's hand. "You keep Dean company." She led the way out of the room.

They walked in silence to the waiting room on the floor. It was empty at the moment, a small favor.

Deborah walked inside and sat against the wall.

Aspen took the chair at her side and angled to face her. "Dean told me he was the one who built the bomb."

Deborah's eyes widened in surprise. The look lent more credence to what Aspen had realized Friday night during Brent's explanation of the events thirty years prior.

The older woman said nothing.

Aspen had options.

She could keep what Dean had told her to herself and let Dean and Deborah continue to live their lives as if nothing had happened.

She could tell Cote what Dean had told her and let Dean face the consequences of the damage the bomb had done.

Or she could tell the truth.

"But it wasn't Dean, was it? It was you."

Deborah swallowed and looked away.

"Brent didn't tell me any names. But he overheard what Dean told me—and said he'd lied. And he told me that the bomb builder's alibi was work. But Dean wasn't at work the night of the bombing. He was in his dorm. You were the one at work."

Deborah said nothing, just stared across the space.

"Dean was trying to get me out of town because he wanted to protect you." Again, Deborah said nothing. "Friday night, he told me he was going to tell Cote everything. Earlier, he made that clear once again."

"He said he's ready to face the future." Deborah's words were flat. "I wondered what that meant."

She waited for Deborah to say something else, maybe to beg her to keep quiet, but she didn't speak.

"Why did you do it?" Aspen asked.

Deborah inhaled a breath and blew it out. "Your mother was such a force, Aspen. She changed my life. I'd gone from living this dull, drab existence to being pulled into something that mattered, something much bigger than myself. I just...I wanted to make a difference. I wanted to be a part." A small smile graced her lips, and she shook her head and met Aspen's eyes. "Truth is, I worshipped your mother. I'd have done anything for her."

"Were you studying chemistry?"

"No. They asked Dean to build it, and he flat out refused. But he and I talked about it privately. He told me how it could be done. I think he wanted me to know he hadn't refused because he was incapable. He was always trying to impress me."

"So you took that information and...?" Aspen was confused. "Did he really give you a step-by-step?"

"He told me enough to know what kind of bomb would be best. There are all different kinds. He'd given me a hint about what materials he would have used. He had books in his dorm. And there were books in the library where I worked. I had access to them but didn't have to check them out, so there was no record of my having read them. I made copies of what I needed."

"You drove across state lines to get the materials?"

"It wasn't hard. I went to Vermont once. I went to Massachusetts twice. I paid cash."

"Did Dean know?"

"He had no idea. But when it was done..." She sighed and stared beyond Aspen for a long moment. "He never asked me directly if I'd done it. We pretended it didn't happen. We got married and lived our lives."

"And then I came back, and you were so kind to me."

"None of what happened was your fault. I've been riddled with guilt for thirty years. Seeing you again... It brought it all back, no question. I figured if I treated you well, you'd never suspect me."

"I didn't, not until Friday."

They were quiet a long moment. Aspen hated what she had to do. She took the older woman's hand. "I can't keep this secret for you."

Deborah didn't look her way. "Okay."

"I've seen the damage secrets can do to a family, to a community. Bart Bradley deserves justice." He was a horrible man, but maybe part of that was the result of what had happened, of how he'd lost his daughter-in-law, his son, and his grandchildren. "Rhonda Patterson deserves justice."

Whether the news would give them peace wasn't the point. Aspen had a responsibility to expose all of it.

And though she felt guilty, she knew those feelings were displaced. She hadn't built that bomb. She hadn't conspired to destroy a building. She hadn't killed an innocent woman.

"More than that," Aspen said, "I'm not willing to keep this secret from Garrett. I won't let what happened thirty years ago come between us."

Of course, telling Cote the truth might do just that. Would Garrett forgive her for what would happen next? Would he be angry at her for exposing his beloved aunt?

Aspen prayed her honesty wouldn't change his feelings for her. She couldn't be sure, though. Despite all the worries swirling in her middle, she would do the right thing, the rational thing. That was who she was.

She would do her best and trust God with the rest.

Deborah said. "I've spent the weekend fearing that Brent would tell. He hasn't yet, but…"

If Brent thought it would get him a reduced sentence, he'd turn on Deborah.

"We should tell Garrett first," Aspen said. "Then figure out where to go from there."

Deborah looked into Aspen's eyes. She ran a hand down Aspen's hair, then rested her palm against her cheek. "I'm sure your father was very proud of you."

Tears filled Aspen's eyes. "I think so."

"Your mother would have been, too, I think. I wish I'd known… There are so many things I wish I'd done differently. I shouldn't have let your mother talk me into the scheme. I should have worked with your father to get her help instead of ignoring all the signs. I'm ashamed of my behavior."

Aspen rested her palm on the woman's hand on her cheek, then shifted them both to her lap. "I don't understand most of what happened back then. What I do know is that you, my mother's best friend, have been nothing but kind to me. As hard as this is going to be, I want you to know that you have my friendship. I know that doesn't mean much—"

"It means everything."

When Deborah pulled Aspen into her arms, for the first time since she'd stood at her father's bedside in Kona, she felt at peace.

CHAPTER FORTY-FOUR

THREE MONTHS LATER.

Aspen parked her new Jeep in the driveway and stared at the house. She'd only been back once since that terrifying day in January. Even then, she hadn't gone inside.

That day, she'd followed Chief Cote to the detached garage, where ground-penetrating radar had revealed her mother's grave. She'd stopped at the edge of the broken concrete and gazed into the dirt below. They'd removed her mother's remains, but Aspen had wanted to see where she'd been buried.

They'd found Jane Kincaid lovingly wrapped in a red-and-white checkered picnic blanket, Brent's jacket and a knife with his blood on it next to her.

Aspen had contacted her grandparents, who'd claimed her body and taken her to be laid to rest in their home state of North Carolina.

One of these days, she'd visit them and see her mother's grave. They'd made her promise.

Her father's parents had traveled from Florida to New Hampshire to hear the whole story, or so she'd thought. Turned out, they'd mostly come to visit Aspen. They, too, had secured her promise to visit soon.

Aspen *did* have family who loved her. She wished they'd all been better about showing it over the years, but she wouldn't complain.

When the news broke that Brent Salcito had been arrested, Jeff Christiansen contacted Aspen and the local police. It seemed Dad had written a letter explaining everything and had given it to his lawyer before he left town with instructions to make it public if Brent was ever arrested or if Dad were murdered. She guessed that one of the reasons he'd left New Hampshire was because he'd feared Brent might not be content with their arrangement.

Dad's letter, along with Aspen's statement, had been enough to put Brent away for the rest of his life.

The local newspaper—and a few farther away—had followed the story. Suddenly, Aspen wasn't a villain in everybody's eyes anymore. For a while, people had still craned to look at her, but at that point most no longer saw her as the daughter of a murderer but as a hero for solving a thirty-year-old mystery.

Enough time had passed that recently most people didn't give her a second glance. They were accustomed to her, and she was accustomed to them.

She was content.

The snow had melted. Today, the house was completely different than what it'd been the first time she'd seen it.

It was almost eerie how similar it looked to the images Garrett had shown her back in January. She hadn't believed at the time it could ever look this beautiful. Of course, she also hadn't believed this cold, wintery world would ever thaw.

Bright green grass thrived on the newly leveled front yard, and birds chirped in the treetops surrounding the property. It was still chilly, though people kept telling her it was unseasonably warm for April.

She'd get used to the temperatures. Coventry was a different world from where she'd grown up. Different but beautiful. She was coming to love the tree-covered mountains, the sparkling lake, the charming downtown. Even the cold felt cozy.

She closed her car door and headed toward the new walkway, which was lined with bushes Garrett had planted. They were small, but they'd grow over time. Already, a few boasted pink blooms.

He'd refreshed the cedar siding, which looked brand new in the sunlight, and painted the front door dark blue to match the new shutters.

It was beautiful.

He stepped out onto the porch wearing a thin T-shirt and a wide smile. "Well?"

"I'm stunned."

Garrett had been stunned himself at the news that his aunt had built the bomb that killed a woman thirty years before. At first, he'd wanted to keep the information quiet, wanting to protect his uncle from the terrible news. But Deborah explained that, though they'd not talked about it, Dean had always suspected her.

He'd finally confronted her after Garrett had stormed out of their house that Thursday night, and Deborah had confessed.

Aspen had told Chief Cote almost everything, but she hadn't told him about Dean's false confession to her at the house that day. If she had, it might have implicated him, made him an accomplice after the fact.

That he'd known for about twelve hours should not have landed him in prison.

Garrett had come around, mostly because Deborah didn't want to keep the secret anymore. Once Brent was arrested, it was only a matter of time before her part in the bombing would be revealed.

It'd been hard, but Garrett had stuck by his aunt and uncle —and never wavered in his affection for Aspen.

Now, he grinned. "You haven't seen anything yet." He jogged down the steps and kissed Aspen's cheek. "Is it hard being back here?"

"As long as you're with me, it's fine."

He stepped back. "Well then, you'll always be fine, because I'll always be with you."

"Promise."

"You know I do." He lifted her left hand, which was devoid of rings. "If you'd just say yes—"

"Soon."

He dropped their joined hands. "I can be patient."

It was funny how Aspen grieved for a woman she had no memories of. All her life, she'd believed her mother was dead, but there'd been a spark of hope somewhere deep inside, hope that had been crushed that terrible night in January.

And maybe Aspen was still grieving for her father too.

Garrett had spent a lot of time with his uncle after Deborah's confession. She was in prison and probably wouldn't be released until she'd served seven years of her ten-year sentence. The plea bargain her lawyer had secured for her had made Bart Bradley furious, but Aspen thought it was fair.

Deborah had never meant for anybody to die.

Dean had recovered from the stab wound and was back to work building furniture. He visited his wife in the penitentiary whenever he could.

Brent Salcito was also serving time. The town had reeled from the news of their mayor. But within a few weeks, a new mayor had been appointed by the town council, and everybody had moved on.

Soon enough, she and Garrett would move on as well. Together.

He took her hand and led her through the front door. It was amazing, her house's transformation. Garrett had created a masterpiece some family would be blessed to call home someday.

Not her, though. As beautiful as it was, she'd be putting it on the market within the week.

Aspen had rented a condo in the development where Garrett lived. She was taking online classes and working part time in children's ministry at the church. One day, she hoped to get a full-time church position. God would open that door when she was ready to walk through it.

For now, she had all she needed.

Grandparents who loved her.

A home surrounded by friends and neighbors who cared about her.

And a man who would someday pledge his life to her.

He showed off his handiwork, pointing out tiles she'd chosen from samples and crown molding she wouldn't have noticed. She was glad he'd finally gotten the place done. Word had already spread about the amazing job he was doing on the old place, and his schedule was booked for months. The way he'd poured himself into this renovation—so similar to the way he poured himself into their relationship—had her heart expanding.

He opened one of the lower kitchen cabinets and pulled out a sliding shelf. "To make it easier to get pots and pans." He looked at her, waiting for a reaction.

"It's nice."

"Nice?" Apparently, that wasn't the reaction he was looking for, but she felt too overwhelmed by everything to think about the house.

She took his hand, then took his other.

His eyes scrunched. "You don't like it?"

"I like it," she said. "It's perfect. *You're* perfect."

"Ha. Hardly."

"Perfect for me," she said.

He squinted as he studied her. "I keep telling you that."

"I love you, Garrett McCarthy."

A smile spread across his face. "I love you, Aspen Kincaid."

"And I just wanted to say... Yes."

"Yes?" Confusion crossed his features, and then his eyes lit up. "Yes? Yes, as in—?"

"Not soon. Maybe in the fall, which everybody keeps telling me is beautiful. After I've had a little more time—"

Her words were cut off by his kiss, just the first of the kisses she'd get to enjoy every day for the rest of her life.

He lifted her and spun her around the new kitchen. "I told you I'd wear you down."

She was laughing by the time he set her on her feet. She gazed up into the face she adored. "I never doubted you for a minute."

THE END

I hope you enjoyed unraveling the mystery along with Aspen and Garrett. If you were surprised to discover whodunit, you're in good company. I was a little surprised myself, to tell you the truth.

If you liked *Inheritance of Secrets*, I think you'll love *Lineage of Corruption*, the next novel in the Coventry Saga, which tells the story of Josie and Thomas. Turn the page to learn more about *Lineage of Corruption*.

Lineage of Corruption

In the world of big money and big politics, nobody walks away unscathed.

The people of Coventry never suspect that Josie Smith, owner of the local coffee shop, is the daughter of a powerful senator. She went to Washington to serve constituents, but her desire to do good morphed into a desire to win at all costs. When one of those costs grew too heavy to bear, she changed her name and left DC, vowing to never get involved in politics again. But when her father becomes his party's lone voice standing against corrupt policies, his enemies will do whatever it takes to get his vote, and Josie finds herself caught in a familiar web of dirty tricks.

Thomas Windham never planned to run for office, but when Coventry's disgraced mayor is replaced by a dishonest appointee, he feels he has no choice but to throw his hat in the ring. He doesn't have a chance against the well-known politician, that is until he meets Josie, who knows more about running for office than a typical café owner would.

When Josie finds herself in danger, they form an alliance—his protection for her wisdom. The election becomes secondary as Josie's adversaries close in. But can Josie and Thomas come out victorious against enemies determined to get what they want at any cost?

ACKNOWLEDGMENTS

It takes a crowd of talented people to get a book from an idea to what you hold in your hands.

Many thanks to my brainstorming partners, Misty Beller, Hallee Bridgeman, Sharon Srock, and Lacy Williams. I come up with the seeds. You water them with ideas and suggestions. Together, we build a story worth reading

I am so grateful for my critique partners. There are many, but I'm especially grateful for Candice Patterson, Sharon Srock, Pegg Thomas, and Terri Weldon, who all contributed.

I'm grateful for my early readers, who find and alert me to typos and other mistakes and then leave me generous reviews. I appreciate you more than I can say.

A big thanks to my editor, Ray Rhamey, my copyeditor, Lesley McDaniel, and my cover designer, Lynnette Bonner. You make me look better than I deserve.

Thank you to my husband, Eddie, who has supported me in this dream since the first paragraph of my first book. I couldn't do this without you!

To God be the glory!
Robin

Amanda Series

Chasing Amanda

Finding Amanda

Standalone Novellas

A Package Deal

One Christmas Eve

Faith House

Robin Patchen is a *USA Today* bestselling and award-winning author of Christian romantic suspense. She grew up in a small town in New Hampshire, the setting of her Nutfield Saga books, and then headed to Boston to earn a journalism degree. After college, working in marketing and public relations, she discovered how much she loathed the nine-to-five ball and chain. After relocating to the Southwest, she started writing her first novel while she homeschooled her three children. The novel was dreadful, but her passion for storytelling didn't wane. Thankfully, as her children grew, so did her writing ability. Now that her kids are adults, she has more time to play with the lives of fictional heroes and heroines, wreaking havoc and working magic to give her characters happy endings. When she's not writing, she's editing or reading, proving that most of her life revolves around the twenty-six letters of the alphabet. Visit robinpatchen.com/subscribe to receive a free book and stay informed about Robin's latest projects.